Secrets of Ravenshire:
Romance and Revenge

Noëlle de Beaufort

Musée de Merbeau Press

Secrets of Ravenshire: Romance and Revenge is a work of fiction. Names, characters, places, and incidents are the product of the author's imagination or are used fictitiously. Any resemblance to actual persons, living or dead, events or locales is entirely coincidental.

Musée de Merbeau Press

Published in the United States of America

ISBN-10: 1-7328827-0-3

ISBN-13: 978-1-7328827-0-6

DEDICATION

To my parents, Barbara and Curt Buford, who read to me as a child, instilling in me an enduring love of books, libraries and history.

ACKNOWLEDGMENTS

Originally conceived as a single novel, the story and characters in *Secrets of Ravenshire* demanded a trilogy as the first segment in a planned epic series spanning centuries.

Present at the inception was Anne Gettman, my then-office mate, who read my initial daily efforts and encouraged me to keep writing. Bobbi Eve and Ruth Zehnder, my sisters, and Barbara Buford, my mother, eagerly read the work-in-progress and provided pointed and thoughtful critiques. My mother, the daughter of a teacher, expected perfection in spelling and grammar from her husband and six children—and from everyone she ever met.

The late Robert Cawley's writing classes were invaluable. The critique group I joined in 2004—John Long, Troy Criz, Eiko Ceremony, Ginger and Phil Edwards, Jo Anne Plog, and the late Phyllis Skalak—offered me constructive and insightful feedback. Carrying forward from that group to the present day are Inge-Lise Goss, Ernie Walwyn, and Debbie Prince, who continue to challenge and inspire me.

Beta readers Bobbi Eve, Lin Hellman, Jo Anne Plog, Linda Flanagan, and Richard Kram provided helpful comments to improve the story flow.

Any remaining mistakes are, of course, my own.

PREFACE

After my grandfather Wyndward James Martin died in 1960, we inherited Wyndy's large rambling Victorian beach house on Long Island. I had loved hearing his stories when I was younger. At eleven, I was acutely aware of the void in my life created by his passing. I wandered around the gardens he kept so lovingly after my grandmother's death – his tribute to her memory. I sat on the beach, watching the waves that kept on coming no matter what occurred in the mere lives of the planet's human inhabitants, feeling insignificant, wondering if life would ever hold joy again.

I explored the old house, found secret passageways that I didn't tell my brothers and sisters about, wanting my own special secret in our noisy brood of six know-it-alls. One rainy day, while my siblings were watching old movies on TV, playing the board game of the moment, I decided to overcome my fear of spiders and rodents. Taking a deep breath, I pulled down the ladder from the top story's ceiling and climbed into the dusty attic, untouched for decades. Wiping away the cobwebs, enduring a couple of scares as black and brown mites scurried away, I tentatively stepped forward, hoping the floor would hold and that termites had not eaten away the boards beneath me. I found an old dress form, and trunks of old-fashioned clothing. I thought how much fun it would be to dress up with my sisters. One Halloween we went out as suffragettes in the moth-eaten dresses. No one knew what suffragettes were in our neighborhood.

But I digress (a bad habit). As I got to the back of the attic, I found paintings of my ancestors, wrapped in old sheets, and marked with the names on the back. One was my great-great-great grandmother, Gabriella Wyndward-James. Her red hair looked just like mine! But my eyes were a bluish gray, not like her green ones. And then I found her husband's portrait. Eyes the color of mine stared back at me from the depiction in oils of Edward James. I was hooked. As if finding these treasures wasn't enough, old valises, hatboxes, and trunks beckoned.

It rained for three days straight. Each successive day, I followed the same pattern, sneaking away and going through the hoard of carefully wrapped old china, silver and knickknacks. Then, in the last trunk (it sounds melodramatic, but it's true), I found worn leather diaries, old letters and manuscripts detailing the family history back to the earliest ancestor, Lucius Titus Ventus, in ancient Rome.

I talked my father into bringing back the big trunk for my room in the city. I didn't tell him what was inside, although it was very heavy. I took the key and kept it on a gold chain around my neck, hidden, so no one could open it. My parents thought it was merely an old, heavy trunk that their eccentric daughter wanted as a memento from her grandfather's house. My father and brothers hauled the massive trunk down several flights of stairs, spewing what mild cusses were permitted in the presence of my father, while extracting from me promises of future obligations to them, until my treasure was settled into the family station wagon.

Digging through the old diaries, I found a sealed letter addressed in a hand reminiscent of Thomas Jefferson: *To the Wyndward descendants.* Every nerve in my skin vibrated with anticipation. Did I dare open it?

You know I did. It was from Philip Laurence, Gabriella's tutor and archivist of the Wyndward family legacy. For decades, I've studied these materials, and searched out more diaries and letters held in the Ravenshire libraries in England that are still in our extended family's hands. I combed through the archives of Wyndward Trading, and interviewed all living relatives. There will not be a day for the rest of my life that I don't find something interesting or new about my ancestors.

I've decided to publish the story of Gabriella now, and as I work through all the material, more will follow. By reading about her life, I found out that I'm not the only non-conformist in my family tree. I hope that you enjoy reading about her as much as I did.

—Noëlle de Beaufort, December 2017

CHAPTER ONE

Friday, March 8, 1811 – Lord Ravenshire's Carriage
Bri

The Marriage Season in London set a treacherous course for the unmarried of the upper class. Fashionable Society, known as *le beau monde*, offered a regimented game of manners designed to win a suitable mate while simultaneously seducing the unwary: any misstep would be exploited by the gossip rags. If the Season were analogous to the popular gentlemen's card game, Whist, and the four suits were instead four attributes – beauty, wit, honor and wealth – then wealth trumped all no matter what card was dealt.

Into this dense jungle of Regency etiquette ventured Lady Gabriella Wyndward. Unable to resist the command of her father, Henry, the 11th Earl of Ravenshire, she braced herself for the ordeal that lay before her. Inside the elegant coach bearing the Wyndward family's ancient crest featuring a raven, sail and sword, the chill between father and daughter rivaled that of the brisk spring air.

Trekking through the obstacles of *le haut ton* or *le bon ton*, abbreviated as the *ton*, the young woman, known as Bri to her family, clutched the cushioned leather bench seat across from the earl as the carriage rocked and bounced over uneven cobblestones, and leaned forward. "Why? Why must I attend another tea party at Aunt Gwyneth's with mindless women whose idea of enlightened conversation is to rank the eligible men of the *ton* by their titles, the size of their fortunes and the cut of their clothes? I find it enormously irritating. Instead, I should be accompanying you to review the estate and trading company accounts with our bankers."

Haunted by the tragedy of his wife dying in childbirth, Lord Ravenshire had never been able to withstand his daughter's entreaties. Until now. "Bri, I have indulged you to a fault. Our social order may strike you as unnatural, but it is the social order under which we live. Occasionally you must make an appearance at functions you deem dull. You must attend with grace, not pique. And you know perfectly well why you cannot accompany me to the bank. Your analytical acumen is remarkable, but it is hardly within the acceptable confines of Society for a woman to openly manage an estate's or a trading company's commercial interests. Why do you suppose such an individual is called a 'man-of-affairs?' "

"But—"

"Until the point when I decide to include you in outside financial meetings, if ever, you will abide by my decisions regarding the conduct of *my* business affairs."

Bri leaned back and crossed her arms in frustration.

"Do not pout. As your grandmother would say, 'It's unattractive, unbecoming and uncalled for.' I shall speak to Sir John about our arrangement."

With a sigh of resignation, Bri uncrossed her arms and reached for her father's hand. "I know Aunt Gwyneth is trying to make it easier for me. It's just that I haven't seen these women except occasionally at Christmas gatherings or Ravenshire Summerfests. They went off to boarding schools like Aunt Gwyneth, or lived abroad like Clarissa, while I was tutored at Ravenshire."

"Tutored by Philip Laurence, as was I. You had the same education as any scion of the finest families in England. I saw to that. Don't embarrass your aunt or me."

Bri surrendered. "I shall try not to tarnish the family honor. And you must promise to tell me all about your meeting with Sir John."

"As if you would let me forget." Feeling the carriage slow its pace, Henry looked out the window. "We've arrived. Off with you, my darling, and make the best of it."

Bri kissed her father on the cheek. After the footman extended the folding carriage steps, she held out her hand to Jean-Louis Chevalier, her father's driver, bodyguard, confidant and her protector *extraordinaire*. His grip steadied her on the steps. The French former trapper glanced at the earl, then Bri. A silent observer who missed nothing, he inclined his head toward her aunt's townhouse on Berkeley Crescent. "Beware. A den of gossip is as deadly as a viper's nest."

Henry laughed. "To Jean-Louis, we are all prey."

Raising an eyebrow, Jean-Louis shrugged. He escorted Bri up the steps to the four-story white-washed stone townhouse. The earl had brought back the ornate mahogany double doors, carved hundreds of years earlier, from one of his sojourns to the Far East. The entry had been re-constructed to accommodate their massive size.

As Jean-Louis trotted down the stairs to retake his driver's perch, Bri turned and waved to her father.

***

Henry

Henry returned his daughter's wave from the window of the carriage. *Brilliant but naïve. Was I wrong to shield her?*

As Jean-Louis guided the earl's stately Arabian team into the London traffic, Henry's thoughts turned to Duff Blackburn, whom Bri, as a child, had affectionately nicknamed Blackie. As the earl's most trusted associate at Wyndward Trading, Blackie directed operations with complete discretion during Henry's months-long travels. Except in the earliest years of Blackie's tenure, they never traveled together. The earl's protégé had an undeniable aptitude for commercial transactions, oft demonstrated over the past twenty years. Diligent and clever, Blackie consistently developed creative solutions to new challenges.

Blackburn had recently told Henry that he now felt secure enough in his financial and social position to attend the Marriage Season to find a bride. Over the years, Henry had observed Blackburn's interactions with Bri. Their spirited debates were always good natured and they appeared to genuinely respect each other. Henry felt close to his protégé, and he harbored no objection to Blackie as a potential son-in-law. Although he was much older than Bri, it was not unusual for men to wait to marry. The real test would be if Blackie could accept Bri in her new role as the earl's secret man-of-affairs, one who dealt with the arcane techniques of managing accounts as well as directing his investments.

Lately, however, Henry had been troubled over an instance of questionable leadership on Blackie's part. A report of public verbal abuse and possible misrepresentation of facts had been brought to his attention by Alan Mason, a former employee whose tenure exceeded Blackie's.

Dismissed by Blackie while Henry was out of the country, Mason told a compelling story. Henry had arranged for the former associate to receive his full pension while he watched for any sign of inappropriate behavior from Blackie. Ambition was no sin to the earl, and the employee might have been jealous of Blackie's place of trust, but Henry wondered if his protégé's brilliant operational insights and negotiating skills masked a darker side.

This nagging seed of doubt formed part of the basis for his decision to make Bri his financial agent. Most gentlemen in Society were "too busy" to attend to their investments, although the truth was they were bored with the stewardship of their wealth. They liked to spend it, they liked the power it provided, but they thoroughly disliked the details of its creation and maintenance. The pedigree of one's tailor counted for more than the results achieved by one's man-of-affairs. Not that anyone discussed such topics openly. It was the height of bad taste to discuss one's wealth in public. In private, only the closest of associates dared broach such a subject.

If Blackie could accept Bri as his equal, then he would be up to the challenge of leading the trading company after Henry died, with Bri as the owner. If he could not accept Bri's role, then the two of them would be locked in a constant battle for control. *As clever as Blackie might be, in a duel of wits with Bri, the best Blackie could hope for would be a draw.*

The carriage stopped at the entrance to James & Co., the earl's bankers.

***

Friday, March 8, 1811 – Atelier Maximilian
Gio

A dwarf, erratic strands of white hair spreading in all directions, stood at a table mixing oil paints. His smock, stained with splotches of pigment, suggested an unfinished piece of art. A partially completed life-sized portrait on canvas perched on a wooden easel, tilted to allow the ideal angle as soft, fading afternoon light flowed into the studio. The diminutive artist intended to capture a mood of warmth by matching the pinkish tinge the rays threw on the canvas.

Gio heard his son's voice from the front gallery. "This way, Mr. Blackburn."

There was no response from the subject of the portrait.

When they reached the studio area, a sunroom bathed in northern light, the dwarf turned to greet them.

Blackburn straightened his stance. "Lord Ostwold, I did not expect to see you today."

The artist shrugged. "Atelier Maximilian takes commissions for portraits done by my son, Maximilian. I paint only when moved by my muse. For the final depiction of the eyes and skin color for special clients such as you, Mr. Blackburn, my son allows me to dabble a bit."

"Your 'dabbling' is another man's masterpiece." Blackburn inclined his head in a slight bow. "I am honored."

***

Blackburn

Multiple canvases in various stages of completion circled the area. Spying his half-finished portrait, Blackburn squinted to evaluate whether the canvas captured his likeness. The promise of the final result pleased him. Maximilian had depicted the perfect facial structure and stance as his image stood at a window, regarding the harbor from the offices of Wyndward Trading. It conveyed a position of commanding strength. *This is a convincing portrayal of a worthy successor to Henry Wyndward. Someday.*

The voice of Maximilian interrupted his thoughts as it echoed through the atrium-like studio. "My father has a few thoughts before we finalize your portrait."

"Mr. Blackburn, I make it my business to know our *special* clients." The wrinkled little man bowed.

Is he mocking me? With a hint of a preening swagger, Blackburn stepped forward to inspect the brushstrokes more closely. He knew that Lord Ostwold, known for years simply as "Gio" before his rightful title was restored, had survived a turbulent social world of changing loyalties, and was widely considered to be the premier portraitist of the aristocracy. If not for the recommendation of Lord Ravenshire, Blackburn would never have been considered by Atelier Maximilian.

Gio walked over to Blackburn's portrait-in-process and switched his gaze methodically between the portrait and its subject. He nodded his head toward Maximilian while locking his gaze on Blackburn. "As I said, occasionally I make a small contribution to my son's work. The eyes are the soul of any portrait." Gio stared intently at Blackburn. "Yours are an unusual color, somewhere between turquoise and aqua. Interesting." He shrugged. "But, as I was saying, I wait until the painting is in its final stages before taking up a brush." Gio was silent for a few moments while he examined the portrait. "Mr. Blackburn, your portrait shows you gazing over the Wyndward fleet. Some might call it over-arching ambition at this stage of your life, with the earl in his prime. Has he approved this depiction?"

Blackburn flinched. He felt the flexing muscles in his cheek betray him. *Damn. The dwarf is renowned as a master of observation. I must not underestimate him.*

The painter shrugged. "Not that the earl's approval of your portrait is necessary. Unless, of course, the trading offices are paying our bill. Maximilian?"

Is he playing me? Blackburn ended the game. "On second thought, Lord Ostwold, your insight is invaluable. Perhaps you are correct. The earl might find the scene a tad arrogant. I mean him no disrespect. What would you suggest?"

The dwarf tilted his head, as if searching his mind. "If memory serves, it was your suggestion that Wyndward Trading import exotic Brazilian timber, no?"

"Yes. But how would you know that?"

"The earl spoke approvingly of your recommendation and years of work on that project. We dine often, you know. I've known him and Lady Gwyneth since their youth. By the way, she's a talented watercolorist."

He knows the earl and his family better than I do after twenty years. I never knew Lady Gwyneth painted.

As if inspired, the dwarf snapped his fingers. "That's it! You should be overlooking the vast rainforests of the Amazon." Distracted, he looked around the studio. "Somewhere I have woodcuts of the forests of Brazil." After a fruitless search, he abandoned the effort. "Such a scene acknowledges your actual contribution, the transaction that sealed your position as heir apparent, without appearing to take more credit than the considerable amount that is your due."

Although chastised, Blackburn was secretly pleased. "Excellent suggestion, Lord Ostwold. I defer to your judgment." He had learned a valuable piece of information. *Never again will I underestimate this wizened dwarf.*

***

Friday, March 8, 1811 – James & Co., Bankers
Henry

To Henry, the bank's quintessential old world building embodied the history of the realm. Passing through white marble columns into an interior foyer paneled with oak, he walked on dark green marble floors imported from Italy. The James family took pride in the huge oil paintings of the long line of ceremonially dressed patriarchs of the James & Co. banking family that covered the walls of the reception area.

The earl's favorite touch of decor was a pair of Grecian urns, dating from antiquity, blossoming with fresh-cut flowers. The contrast of the cold marble, the static wood and the doomed, though still vibrant flowers, struck Henry as oddly perfect. The petals offered an impression of life once nurtured by the sun, now surrounded by inanimate objects, resting inside a repository of capital, the breath of trade.

Approaching footfalls announced seriousness of purpose as well as seriousness of self. Bald and wearing round spectacles, the diminutive Mr. Duncan approached the bank's most important client. He spoke a bit too rapidly, betraying his nervousness. "Welcome back to James & Co., Lord Ravenshire. Sir John is awaiting you in his private office."

As they made their way down the long, somber hallway, Henry

admired the outstanding etchings of England's major castles lining the walls. He wondered how Sir John's health fared these days. The last time the earl had seen his oldest friend, the banker's frailty had shocked him.

Duncan knocked lightly and opened the door. Sir John looked up from his work, smiled broadly, and rose to greet the earl.

Lord Ravenshire noted the momentary pressure of the banker's hand upon his abdomen and heard his deep intake of breath. *His pain persists.*

"Ravenshire, you old fox!"

"Jamesey, you old hunting dog!"

After they shook hands, Sir John again placed his hand over his abdomen.

They took their seats at the table under a window that overlooked the bustling activity of the city.

"How are you feeling?"

Sir John dismissed the question with a wave of his hand. "One learns to live with these things."

Henry leaned forward. "I hate to see you suffer. I again ask you to accept my offer of the services of Nashmir. He kept Wolcott alive for longer than anyone expected, with long periods of lucidity, after finding our old friend near death in the high mountains of Tibet. He is an expert in herbal remedies. I have personally seen him cure illnesses at sea or in remote regions where there was no hope for survival. His knowledge of plants is unparalleled. Come for tea tomorrow afternoon and discuss your symptoms with him. Perhaps he can discern a treatment protocol among the herbs he has cultivated in the small greenhouse we established in my townhouse courtyard. We have a larger assortment at Ravenshire, should those prove insufficient."

Sir John looked down at the floor for a few moments.

In deference, Henry refrained from speaking.

The banker raised his eyes to gaze at the man he had known since he was a boy. "Ravenshire, I have discounted your views on eastern medicine in the past. Lately, however, no amount of medicine can tame the pain. Some days I force myself to make an appearance at the bank. As you know, my eldest son, Edward, led an early life rather like yours. An adventurer, he was more intent on 'experiencing the world' than taking up his position here. But he returned six months ago. Sterling, Annabelle's husband, is doing well developing new business for us in the Jewish community. My other son, Andrew, remains estranged. In short, Ravenshire, I am less concerned about the leadership of James & Co. now than I was one year ago when these pains first started. I am finally at the point where I will surrender to you and your Tibetan healer."

"Excellent, Jamesey. Come for tea tomorrow at five o'clock."

"Agreed. Of course, we must never mention this to Lady James. She believes in physicians and is ready to start the bloodletting. Now, would you have a cigar? Some port?"

"Ah, no cigar for me, Jamesey. Given them up. But a little port is good for us all."

Sir John rang for Duncan.

The private secretary silently retrieved the port and glasses from the concealed bar across the room.

After Duncan left, the earl broached the subject on his mind. "You may recall that I employed my old tutor, Philip Laurence, to educate Bri."

"Of course. By the way, Lady Gabriella looked lovely at the last Ravenshire Summerfest."

"Has it been that long?" Henry shook his head. "Her beauty equals her intelligence. Bri perceived no barrier to learning. In some respects, she quite outdoes us all."

Sir John raised an eyebrow. "She did strike me as being remarkably clever and well read."

"The reason I bring this up is that over the last two years, Bri has taken over more and more of the financial management of my accounts. Blackburn manages the operations of the trading business, but, unbeknownst to him, all financial decisions are made by Bri. Though it may shock you, Jamesey, Bri will be acting as my man-of-affairs. Naturally, this must be kept secret between us. I assume that you will assign the handling of my accounts to your son, who, no doubt, will handle this matter with the utmost discretion. Bri will communicate with him in writing and meet with him only at my townhouse to maintain this secret. What do you say?"

Waiting a moment to speak, Sir John mused aloud. "Well, I must agree that we certainly cannot have the *ton* aware that Lady Gabriella is acting as your agent or estate steward. That might tarnish the occupation as women's work." The banker guffawed at the improbability of that outcome. "Irregular, to be sure, but not beyond the capabilities of James & Co. But what if she were to marry?"

"That is a subject for another day."

"No one ever called you predictable, Ravenshire. At least you have Blackburn to handle operations. He's a dependable sort. Shall I ask my son, Edward, to join us?"

Henry nodded.

Sir John rang a small silver bell, summoning Duncan. "Please ask the young Mr. James to join us, Duncan."

"Yes, sir. Immediately, sir."

While waiting, Henry raised his glass of port. "To our children."

"To our children."

Two men appeared at the door. Both had jet black hair.

The brown-eyed man spoke first. "Lord Ravenshire, I heard you were here and wanted to stop by and greet you before your meeting with Sir John and Mr. James began."

Henry stood and extended his hand. "It's a pleasure to see you again, Mr. Sterling." Sir John's son-in-law's family had changed their surname generations earlier to Sterling from Silverberg. The marriage of Annabelle James to Eli Sterling had been quite a scandal at the time, but for the most part, the prevailing prejudices against Jews were kept under wraps out of respect for Sir John. He turned to Sir John's son. "Young James, if I may call you that, you look well after your long absence." The son's black hair came from his mother, Henry assumed, and his gray eyes from his father. Edward's strong, firm jaw gave Henry confidence. Well-cut clothes imbued the young banker with an air of authority. He exhibited the physique and bearing of a military man.

"An honor, Lord Ravenshire. I've studied the wide range of your investments and trading activities since my return from the Far East. It's unusual to find an adventurer who is an astute manager of his legacy."

Mr. Sterling smiled. "I'll leave you gentlemen to your business."

Henry nodded adieu.

Sterling closed the door as he left.

Henry and the banker's son sat facing Sir John behind his desk. "Young James, your father and I have been discussing my plan to implement a rather unusual set of instructions for managing my accounts. Sir John?" *This will be the test. Can he explain it without revealing disapproval?*

Sir John did an adequate job of setting out the details while Henry studied Edward's reaction. The young banker's face maintained an inscrutable expression, and Henry wondered if Sir John's son had undergone a deeper instruction in the ways of the Far East, perhaps the Asian fighting arts. It would be a point to discover later. *Could the young James be another potential mate for Bri? Could he spar with her intellect and accept her independent spirit?*

***

Edward

Edward controlled his facial muscles to hide his shock. Thoroughly appalled, he betrayed no sign of it. "Highly irregular," as his father described the proposed arrangement that Lady Gabriella act as Lord Ravenshire's man-of-affairs, was an understatement. While Edward had encountered strong women in his travels, none had any financial training, and he looked upon the unavoidable meeting with Lady Gabriella, the adolescent he'd last seen six years earlier, determined to beat him at Whist. The fact that she had succeeded still rankled him. *By now, she is no doubt an arrogant, self-satisfied creature of Fashionable Society.* The thought of meeting her invoked in him only one emotion—dread.

CHAPTER TWO

Friday, March 8, 1811 – Lady Gwyneth's Townhouse
Bri

Nambotha, a tall, well-muscled man, impeccably outfitted, with a shaved head and skin the color of polished ebony, exuded an air of calm in the midst of turmoil. He had acted as a guide for the late Comte de Merbeau and the comtesse on a safari in East Africa years earlier. After their return to Nairobi, he accepted a position as their butler in London. As the comtesse had no children, he had lavished attention on Lady Gabriella since their first encounter.

In a hushed tone, Bri said, "I hope I am the last to arrive."

Unable to repress a smile, Nambotha took her cloak and bonnet. "Your aunt has been making apologies for your tardiness for the last ten minutes, Miss Bri." No one else referred to her that way, and Nambotha did it only in private.

Bri grimaced. "I am in difficulty now." She followed Nambotha through the foyer to the parlor.

"Lady Gabriella has arrived, Madame la Comtesse."

Rising to greet her niece, Gwyneth took Bri's arm and led her through introductions to the other guests. "Lady Gabriella has finally arrived. You remember Lady Melanie Thornton, daughter of the Earl of Stonefell?"

"Of course, Lady Melanie, delightful to see you again." Bri struggled to remember the protocol of introductions. She greeted

Lady Marianna Mayfield, daughter of the late Earl of Aynsley, then Lady Patricia Roswell, daughter of the Earl of Wexington, and, finally, and Lady Penelope Firth, daughter of the Duke of Somervale.

The last person standing was not unfamilar to her. Excitement rose within Bri as she embraced Lady Clarissa von Dusterberg, daughter of Count von Dusterberg of Berlin, with whom she and her father had spent a summer in South Africa, where he had been posted as ambassador from Prussia. "I'm so happy to see you again."

Lady Clarissa whispered in Bri's ear, "We'll talk after everyone else leaves."

Bri nodded and took her seat as tea was poured. Looking around at the other women, she wondered how the buxom, full-bodied Lady Penelope would fare during the Season. By reputation, the Marriage Market could be cruel and unforgiving. As the daughter of a duke, she would face a bevy of fortune hunters. Bri hoped that the young woman's obvious warmth and dark-haired beauty would overcome resistance to her unfashionable physique. Her violet eyes would captivate most men.

"I'm so excited for the Season to start, Lady Gabriella." Lady Penelope's exuberance was contagious and the others giggled.

As if paralyzed, Bri froze. *They giggle? How will I navigate through a Season of simpering drivel?*

***

Friday, March 8, 1811 – James & Co., Bankers
Edward

Since returning from his sojourn of self-discovery throughout the Far East, Edward had been stunned to learn the secrets bankers kept about their clients' peccadilloes. The hypocrisy that pervaded their public and private lives disgusted him. While the stunning news that the earl's daughter would act as his man-of-affairs fell into a different category of secret, he feared it would sorely try his patience.

His admiration for Lord Ravenshire and duty to his father forced him to overcome his initial revulsion at the terms demanded by the earl. "I reviewed my schedule just before our meeting, Father. Next Friday at ten o'clock might be a good time for me to call on Lady

Gabriella to begin our discussion of these accounts. Would that time be agreeable, Lord Ravenshire?"

Sir John cleared his throat. "Edward, next Friday is the morning after the first ball of the Season. You have responded that you will attend. Most of the *ton* will be asleep at that hour in general, let alone after a ball that does not end until past midnight."

Edward held up a hand to stop his father's argument. "I concede that I committed to make an appearance at Lady Elisabeth's ball in deference to our family connections as well as accede to your wish that I participate in the Season. I assure you both, however, that I will not end up at my club, gambling into the wee hours as many of my old schoolmates no doubt will do. But perhaps Lady Gabriella would prefer a later hour."

"Not necessary, Young James. Lady Gabriella is being dragged to the ball by her aunt much against her wishes. She would rather add up accounts than dance." Henry laughed.

That is even worse. She must be quite a drone and unattractive in the extreme. I remember her wild red hair and green eyes, and an unmistakable stubborn streak during the occasional gatherings years ago. She gloated when she beat me at Whist. Today, she's probably the kind who steps all over her dance partner's shoes. Edward vowed to make a *very* brief appearance at Lady Elisabeth's ball, to avoid the clear intention of these two fathers to see their children affianced. *Perhaps I should marry someone to put a stop to the incessant plots of self-appointed matchmakers. I suppose I could send my selection to the country and we could lead separate lives, maintaining the fiction of marriage to take our place in Society. My money and position might attract someone who had her own interests, perhaps even a young widow.* Abruptly, he returned from his reverie to the voice of the earl when he heard his name mentioned and realized he had missed the relevant comment.

"I like to see that in a young man. But don't make your life all work, Young James. It leaves a void." Detecting a tone of wistfulness, Edward attributed it to the fact that the earl's wife had died during the birth of their daughter.

Lord Ravenshire rose to his feet. "I must stop at the trading company, and then dinner at my sister's home awaits me. Thank you both for accommodating my request. I look forward to seeing you for tea tomorrow, Jamesey, and you, Young James, at Lady Elisabeth's."

Edward was puzzled about the tea comment, but ignored it. "Of course, Lord Ravenshire. Delighted to see you again after so many years. I look forward to renewing my acquaintance of your daughter a week from Friday."

"Excellent."

Sir John laughed. "In school, Edward, Lord Ravenshire's favorite comment was 'Excellent.' To annoy him, we called him 'Your Excellency' or 'Young Viscount' because it was so contrary to social convention."

The earl chimed in. "To think that such trifles counted for rebellion before the wars that followed our university days."

As if a practitioner of mental telepathy, Duncan materialized to escort the earl to his carriage.

Once they were out of hearing range, Edward turned to his father.

"Tea?"

"Yes, son. Henry's Tibetan valet has some experience with the healing arts of the Far East, and has prevailed upon me to try them."

Edward hesitated momentarily. "Father, I am familiar with the healing skills of some Tibetans from my travels. My previous entreaties to you to try these remedies have been rebuffed. But rather than being annoyed that you ignored my advice, I shall set my feelings aside and encourage you to have faith in these curatives, which are thousands of years old. Convinced of our superiority, we are often too parochial to see their value." Putting his hand on his father's shoulder, Edward silently conveyed his deep love for his father.

Months earlier, after receiving a brief note from his mother imploring his presence as his father's illness accelerated, Edward immediately departed the Far East. Through some method he did not understand, the earl had expedited delivery of his mother's plea. Still, travel was difficult, and in the months it took him to reach London, Edward feared he would be too late. Luckily for them all, his father's constitution was robust enough to fight the unknown disease, which all feared was cancer. Sir John had outlived his physician's estimates for nearly a year, though his pain had intensified in severity over the last few weeks.

Looking at his pocket watch, Sir John declared, "Your mother is waiting for us."

***

Friday, March 8, 1811 – Lady Gwyneth's Townhouse
Bri

Bri sipped her tea. "This has an unfamiliar bouquet."

Her aunt smiled. "Jasmine, from the shipment Henry received from the Orient last week."

Lady Clarissa leaned forward. "I traveled to the Orient with my father a few years ago, and found its fragrances and flowers intoxicating."

"Intoxicated by foreign lands?" Lady Patricia scoffed. "Perhaps the spices went to your head. I have no desire to leave these shores."

Glaring at Lady Patricia, Bri said, "Perhaps we are not all so provincial. Shouldn't we have open minds?" She directed her attention back to Lady Clarissa. "What is the most exotic place you have visited?"

"Madagascar, undoubtedly. It is a mix of so many cultures: Arab traders, French and Portuguese colonists, African tribes, and Asian trading companies, all vying for a portion of the lucrative spice trade. Scents of spices blowing in the island air are indescribable. We were the guests of Sultan Sarduba, who is a most gracious host, although he is a major proponent of the slave trade. His personal slaves were abducted from many diverse cultures before being sold to him. Especially memorable was the palace healer, a woman of Polynesian origin. Her beautiful voice and skill on the lyre created haunting musical sounds that floated over the gardens of the Sultan's estate in the evenings. It was as if we were surrounded by a mist of music...the chords invoked notes of spiritual transcendence. But, sadly, she was not free to leave."

The Comtesse de Merbeau cut off Lady Clarissa just as Bri was bursting with more questions. "That is a lovely story, Lady Clarissa. But as you are all going to the first ball of the Season at Lady Elisabeth's mansion next week, we must discuss the real reasons I brought you young ladies together. One's first entrée into Society can be somewhat fraught with fear of missteps as well as excitement. With that in mind, I thought it would be nice for you to meet in advance, so that you could be acquainted outside the stiff confines of a ball. It was wonderful for me to have your mothers as confidantes during my Season, as we all attended the same boarding school in Switzerland. Since the wars of Napoleon made it impossible for you to go to our school, most of you each attended small boarding schools in London, and Lady Clarissa in the Cape Colony, while Gabriella studied with a tutor. As a result, you have not had the same opportunities to form friendships in Society as your mothers and I did."

Lady Melanie took a deep breath. "My mother told me that the first ball of the Season is trial by gown and dance step."

"The gown *is* important." Lady Gwyneth put down her teacup and leaned forward. "I was wondering if any of you young ladies knew which dressmakers are *au courant* this Season?"

Bri practically choked on her tea. This was descending into the prattle that she detested, although she recognized that her Aunt Gwyneth had her best interests at heart. She took a deep breath and watched for reactions in the other young ladies.

"My preference is Miss Cortland's on Knightsbridge." Lady Marianna had a distinctly breathy, child-like voice that irritated Bri immediately. "She disdains those Continental styles that reveal too much bosom." Turning toward Bri, she sat up straighter. "I may be a bit old fashioned, but I would prefer to attract a husband who is looking for solid virtues rather than an ample bosom." She took a sip of tea to punctuate her point.

"I agree with you, Lady Marianna, and I ordered one gown from Miss Cortland's, but most of my ball gowns have been ordered from Mrs. Watson's Shoppe." Lady Melanie brushed a stray wisp of blonde hair from her forehead. "She has such exquisitely restrained taste, designing classic styles that are appropriate for unmarried young women such as us to wear in Society. My brother assures me that men don't like women who are too forward. By the way, he is attending the season also, now relieved from military duty due to an injury."

Lady Penelope leaned forward. "How tragic. What kind of injury?"

"He lost the sight in one eye. His eye patch is rather rakish, actually."

"So he'll look like a pirate. How dashing." Lady Patricia's voice had the air of a woman of experience.

The comtesse looked to the buxom Lady Penelope. "And which dressmaker do you favor?"

"I like both Miss Cortland's and Mrs. Watson's taste, and I also like the elegant designs of Mme. Mottier, who I believe is your own *couturière*, Madame la Comtesse. I find her quite attuned to the preferences of young women. I think we can be a bit daring, as long as the gown is elegant."

"How wonderful!" The comtesse looked visibly relieved. "We can see her tomorrow and prevail upon my long patronage to make Gabriella a ball gown on short notice." Internally, she cringed to burden her dressmaker with their timing *faux pas*, but she knew that Mme. Mottier would meet any of her demands.

Lady Patricia chimed in. "Mrs. Watson is the one I prefer."

"Which dressmakers do you favor, Lady Clarissa?" Bri hoped that Lady Clarissa would have a dressmaker more youthful than the one who dressed her aunt. Although the comtesse's taste was impeccable and she always looked elegant, her attire was not that of a young woman.

"Well, I know this may sound a bit scandalous to you, but since my father is from the Continent I do tend to favor styles that you may consider somewhat *avant garde*." Lady Clarissa hesitated. "I found the most magnificent colors and designs at Mlle. Bellerobe's. She used to dress Josephine, you know." Everyone in the *ton* had heard that Mlle. Bellerobe used the obvious pseudonym meaning *beautiful dress* in French to conceal her true identity. Since gossip was the life's blood of Society, word of Mlle. Bellerobe's reputation as a courtesan rapidly circulated. It was whispered that she had been banished by Josephine because of a rumored affair with Napoleon. Widened eyes and a noticeable lack of breathing, followed by quick sips of tea, even if their cups were empty, constituted the muted signs of shock from well-bred young ladies of the *ton*.

Except for Lady Gabriella Wyndward. "Oh, how intriguing…tell us more."

Gwyneth blanched.

"Well, if truth be told," said Lady Clarissa, "it is quite an adventure and a maze of a shop. Fabrics hang from the ceiling, almost like makeshift walls, a library of color. Her creations are simply beautiful. One of a kind, not merely a ribbon here or a tuck there to set you apart from seven others in the same dress, year after year, if you know what I mean. And well, at the risk of sounding daft, her gowns make me feel rather like a fairy princess, floating on a cloud."

"I suppose if we have to parade ourselves around to attract the right husband at these dreadful functions in the *ton*, then at least we might as well pretend it is a fairy tale," conceded Bri, somewhat surprised at her own reaction. *I want to see Mlle. Bellerobe's shop.* "When are you going again? I'd like to accompany you."

"Tomorrow at two o'clock."

"Perfect. I have some things to attend to in the morning, but the afternoon is clear. I'm really looking forward to this! It will be quite daring. Would anyone else like to come along?"

Bri's bright tone elicited no response. She realized her stumble when there were unanimous declines from the other young ladies. Her aunt's disapproving look brought her up short.

The comtesse eased the discomfort by changing the subject. "Who are the most sought after young men this Season? Do any of you fancy a certain one?"

Adopting a confidential tone, Marianna said, "I hear that the Elliott, Viscount Hanforth has recently returned from Africa, where he shot lion, elephant and rhinoceros. He's supposed to cut quite a dashing figure. He always wears safari gear in the manner of the hunter, and has acquired significant land holdings in Africa. I hear he wears his blond hair quite long and has arresting blue eyes. He sounds *quite* divine, and *quite* wealthy."

"He is my first cousin." Lady Clarissa took a sip of tea.

Marianna paled at her *faux pas*.

Oblivious, Lady Melanie chimed in. "The viscount is a friend of my brother Donald. Apparently, Lord Hanforth has put off marriage too long and promised his family that he will take a wife this Season. My brother is available too, and, as the only son, he will inherit all my father's estates."

Bri thought she detected a note of envy or anger in Melanie's tone.

"Do you resent that?"

"Oh, for heaven's sake, Gabriella." Gwyneth's voice conveyed utter frustration with her impulsive niece. "You cannot make the world an equal place for men and women. Women simply cannot inherit except in unusual cases where no male relatives exist to make a claim on the estate. And in most of those cases, a decision is at the discretion of the king."

"I must admit that it is a bit disconcerting to hear oneself talked about as a commodity to be auctioned off at a Society ball." Lady Melanie looked around for someone who might agree with her.

A couple of the other young ladies softly murmured in agreement.

"Hold on." Lady Patricia leaned forward. "Let me go back to your earlier comment. Why would your brother go into the army if he was first in line to inherit? That's madness!"

Lady Melanie downcast her eyes. "It was not always so. My two older brothers died in hunting accidents."

Bri knew it was illegal dueling that had killed them, but it would be ill-mannered to reveal that fact. Lady Melanie either did not know the truth or preferred to bury it beneath a lie. Lady Patricia had a penchant for gossip. *Best that she never know the truth.*

Condolences were offered by the other women.

"We are seeking suitable, wealthy husbands as much as they are seeking suitable, wealthy wives." Lady Penelope spoke with a frankness that made them all laugh. "But some of us have been tainted with the fever of romance. Too much of Lord Byron's poetry, I suppose, but it seems to me that making a good match is secondary to being truly in love."

"Is there someone special for you, Penelope?" More than curious, Lady Clarissa sounded somewhat envious.

"Well, I have not met him, but I saw him when my cousin Peter Firth was leaving his club. I was in the carriage waiting for Peter when I caught a glimpse of him. He was of ordinary height, but with light blond hair and dark brown eyes that captured my heart. I pressed my cousin for his name." Her voice became shy as she made her disclosure. "It's Baron Beauchamp."

Bri sat back in her chair. "Baron Beauchamp went to university with my father. He must be over fifty!"

Lady Penelope's face reddened. "I don't think age matters in love."

Trying to recover, Bri smiled. "The baron *is* a charming gentleman."

"Indeed. You may have quite a bit of competition." Lady Patricia's cool tone inserted a dose of reality into the conversation.

The comtesse intervened. "Now, ladies, don't get carried away by these notions of romance. Society has its rules and duties. Romance can fade. Wastrels and scoundrels may be attractive and romantic at first, but they rarely make good husbands."

Bri looked perplexed. "Why must attractive and romantic men be scoundrels?" She paused, and then brightened. "We need to persuade good men to be more romantic. We should declare that love and love alone shall rule our choices this Season." Bri leaned forward to push her daring suggestion. "We could change the rules of Society by refusing to accept proposals from those we consider unromantic."

Lady Clarissa echoed Bri's puzzlement. "I cannot imagine accepting a proposal simply because a man is suitable from my father's point of view. We cannot be forced to marry." Her defiant tone brought forth mumblings of agreement from most of the others.

The comtesse de Merbeau would have none of it. "Listen to me, young ladies, and listen well. Changing the world we live in is not an easy task, nor is living the life of a spinster. Not all of you have the advantage of Gabriella's inheritance, and she is unfair to encourage you in rebellion. If she decides *not* to marry," acknowledging the gasps of shock from her rapt audience, "as she has often threatened, she will not want for material goods or estates. Those of you with brothers know a different course awaits you. You would have to live on the charity of your eldest brother, and his wife may not be pleasant. Mark my words, you need to marry and establish your own home and family. That is where a woman's power rests, not in these foolish notions of romantic love. You learn to love a man with time, not in a moment of passing fancy."

Admonished, the young ladies cast down their eyes and looked at one another to see who would break the silence first.

Bri could not restrain herself. "Please understand, Aunt Gwyneth. I don't mean to destroy the position of women in Society. I am simply talking about alternatives that seem more fair and equitable."

Lady Clarissa added, "We are all quite nervous at the prospect of the upcoming balls. None of us has had any experience of the *ton* and Society. It is a bit daunting. Must we accept it all without question?"

"No, my dears, but you'd best consider the consequences before you get caught up in a cause that will not feed you, clothe you or house you." The comtesse added more gently, "It is getting late, and we should not leave on this note of acrimony. Let us have more tea and talk of the upcoming ball." The maid appeared as if by silent command with another pot of tea and poured more for each in turn.

Lady Penelope cleared her throat. "Madame la Comtesse, what is the protocol of the first ball? What is expected of us?"

The comtesse's voice warmed. "There will be a receiving line, of course, and at the end, each guest may receive a dance card. It is a new Austrian custom that many hostesses are using. It will be printed with five lines. The gentlemen will approach you and ask to sign your dance card. You cannot refuse, but if they sign more than one line, or you dance with a man more than once, it is tantamount to announcing your engagement. Eyes follow all that you do. There are ample breaks between series of dances to sample the *hors d'oeuvres,* sip Champagne and chat with the gentlemen. Sip, ladies. It is not seemly to drink overmuch or too gaily. A mention in the gossip rags is not to be desired."

The clock chimes rang seven times, and the group looked up, startled.

Lady Marianna stood. "Thank you for a most instructive tea party, Madame la Comtesse."

As the others rose from the chairs and settees to thank the comtesse, Nambotha brought their cloaks.

All the ladies left except Lady Clarissa, who stayed behind, talking with Bri about their impending visit to Mlle. Bellerobe's.

Overhearing this exchange, the comtesse made a suggestion. "Shall we see Mme. Mottier in the morning?"

"That sounds fine, Aunt Gwyneth." Bri quickly glanced at Clarissa to confirm their afternoon foray. "Perhaps we can all three have lunch before we visit Mlle. Bellerobe's salon."

Aunt Gwyneth nodded her ascent. "An excellent idea. Are you familiar with *Chez Michel,* Lady Clarissa?"

"Yes! It's a lovely spot. My father has put a rented carriage at my disposal to do 'feminine' things, as he terms them. I'd say that lunch and shopping fall into that category."

"Then let's plan to meet at half after twelve tomorrow. I'll send a footman with notes for Mme. Mottier, Michel and Mlle. Bellerobe tomorrow morning so we can efficiently accomplish our tasks. Would you like to join us for dinner tonight?"

"I'd be delighted, Madame la Comtesse. My father is in Scotland, so I would have been dining alone."

"Come into the study while I write the notes, and then we wait in the Music Room for my brother to arrive for dinner."

Bri followed her aunt and new friend into the hallway. "It is so wonderful to see you again. I was afraid all the young women here would be cold and distant like Lady Marianna."

Clarissa nodded. "And Lady Penelope is quite taken with her hoped-for paramour, but his age is rather shocking. I hope she gets to dance with him. Lady Melanie seemed pleasant but a bit shy, maybe prudish."

"And Lady Patricia certainly holds strong opinions." Bri shrugged. "I admire her candor, but I can see where it would put off some people."

"Now girls, remember your breeding." The comtesse opened the door to the study, walked over to the roll-top desk and set out paper, pen and ink to write her notes to the dressmakers and Michel.

The study was formal but welcoming. The walls were covered with a pale green silk. An oriental rug with a deep green background and delicate designs of flowers and vases covered the wood floor. Two burnt orange leather chairs were placed in front of the fireplace, with a small table between them. The writing desk was on one side of the fireplace, under a window that framed a maple tree in its panes. On the other side of the fireplace was a small chest in the Chinese style with various artifacts on the top, including a set of three porcelain vases that appeared to be antiques.

Over the fireplace, an oil portrait of Lady Gwyneth and a distinguished gentleman caught Clarissa's eye. "What a wonderful portrait!"

Gwyneth smiled. "My late husband and I posed for that. Gio really captured us."

"Gio? As in Giovanni? Lord Ostwold? He's famous throughout Europe."

"Gio would be offended to hear that. He believes he is famous throughout the world, even on continents that he has never seen."

Bri laughed. "Gio taught my aunt to paint when she was a child. She is a master with watercolors."

Clarissa scanned the room and saw a grouping of watercolors of flowers. "Are those yours, Lady Gwyneth?"

The comtesse nodded.

"They're delicate and vibrant."

"I haven't painted for a long time. Maybe I'll start again once we get through this Marriage Season. It's not just a trial for you two. I have to chaperone these affairs."

"Bri—may I still call you that now that we are older?"

"Of course. The name 'Gabriella' was a mouthful for a child learning to talk, so it's always been Bri to my family. And you are family to me now."

Bri linked arms with Clarissa and escorted her to the Music Room. *Today I met new friends and tomorrow I'll see a scandalous couturière. If I can manage my way around the expectations of my aunt and father, I might enjoy the Season on my own terms.*

And what Lady Gabriella Wyndward set her mind to, she had never failed to accomplish.

CHAPTER THREE

March 8, 1811 – Inverness, Scotland
Mirela

Catherine opened the sealed letter from her grandson and unfolded it. Written in code to avoid discovery of their plot in the event their communications were intercepted, Catherine was ever alert to the dangers she faced as she developed her plot to exact revenge on the Wyndward family. In letters, her vengeance was called "finding the right home."

She knew her grandson's rightful home. It was Ravenshire. Her daughter's death at the hands of the man she called "the depraved 10th Earl" obsessed her, drove her and compelled her to act, even while her grandson argued for strategic patience.

> Dearest Grandmother,
> I trust this letter finds you well. Finding the right
> home for you here is an involved process, and I
> appreciate your patience.
>
> Please know that progress is being made. I believe
> that making an offer to the owner's daughter will be
> more effective than dealing directly with the owner
> on the most recent property we discussed.
>
> Such an approach preserves our best long term

interest in this property. I shall have an update for you in a few months with my recommendation to move forward.

Your loving grandson,
D

Mirela, a Gypsy and Catherine's only friend and companion of many years, looked up from her Tarot cards. As always, the fortune teller knew the contents of the letter before Catherine opened it. "More delays."

"I should know by now that I don't need to read any letter when you are around." Catherine crumpled the letter in her hand and threw it into the fire. "He knows I will not rest until the progeny of the man who killed my daughter are as dead as she is." Grim-faced, she stared off into the distance. "Fate extracts its price."

The Gypsy had known the woman behind the plot under her birth name of Galda. An earlier name change to Sorcha and now Catherine as well as the transformation of her physical appearance had enabled Galda to maintain the secrecy of her origin.

Mirela understood that her friend's lust for revenge would never be satisfied with half-measures. She turned over another Tarot card. "The cards do not lie. Death breeds death."

***

Friday, March 8, 1811 – Wyndward Trading Offices
Henry

Arriving at the Wyndward Trading offices after his meeting with Sir John, Henry set his mind to the restructuring of operations that he would have to institute if Blackburn could not be trusted. While he believed in his protégé, his nature was to plan for all potential outcomes. Walking through the wide foyer, he nodded to his workers, and went directly up the two flights of stairs to the executive offices. All private offices had windows overlooking the harbor.

Approaching Blackburn's office, he heard the voice of Avery Sheldon, who headed African operations. "That's the key conduit to all sub-Saharan trade. How can you be sure we can send cargo through Egypt while Napoleon remains in control of the Mediterranean?"

Blackburn's response echoed through the hall. "I'll handle Egypt."

"But we lost over a third of the shipment the last time we traversed Egypt."

Henry's deputy raised his voice. "Others lose more than half. I've made arrangements with a secretive figure known as The Pharaoh for protection, but there is a fee. As I said, I'll handle Egypt. Prepare the shipment manifests for my review."

Henry frowned, but brought his facial muscles under control by the time he reached Blackburn's office and walked in unannounced. "What's the controversy?"

Sheldon glanced at Blackburn before answering. "Lord R., I am concerned about losses in shipments through Egypt. That country's terrain is full of bandits awaiting cargo-laden caravans. I want to circumvent pervasive pilfering."

Blackburn sighed. "All shipments through Africa are pilfered to some extent. I have established a relationship with an intermediary there who says they can protect our shipments for a fee of fifteen percent of the cargo value. It saves time and reduces the threat of Red Sea and Mediterranean piracy, which would result in a hundred percent loss. Moving goods through Africa without middlemen is impossible. And middlemen get their *baksheesh*, their commission, one way or another. This way we cap it and they guarantee the cargo will reach its destination."

"Bribe, you mean, not commission."

"You run Africa, Sheldon." Blackburn scoffed. "Do you mean to tell me you've never paid a bribe to get a shipment through?"

"A small commission, not a bribe. And fifteen percent is not a third."

"That loss occurred before my arrangement with The Pharaoh."

Henry decided to test Blackburn. "Sheldon, let's try it Blackburn's way for a few shipments, then review our options going forward. In the meantime, are shipments coming up Africa's west coast reaching England, evading the French Navy?"

"So far."

"Cautious to a fault." Blackburn's needling of Sheldon clearly irritated the African specialist. "I'll expect those manifests on my desk tomorrow."

"Agreed." Sheldon nodded to Henry and left the office.

Taking a seat and directing his gaze at Blackburn, Henry probed. "Have you met with this intermediary?"

"Yes. I go to Egypt once every year or so, and The Pharaoh is well-connected."

"I assume you're following our standard procedures to evade Napoleon's barricade of English ships?"

"*Je ne voyage pas sur nos navires.* I don't travel on ships that can be identified as ours. Nor would you without the proper papers."

I taught him the intricacies of forged travel papers. A French passport comes as no surprise. "You are a resourceful man, Blackie. Just don't get caught."

Blackburn sat back in his chair and smiled. "Wouldn't you pay my ransom?"

"Money doesn't always work. I assume we continue to disguise our ships as Portuguese or North African, with linguistically capable captains and crew. Tell me about the intermediary."

"The man known as The Pharaoh has connections throughout Africa as well as China with traders whose ancestors have been importing and exporting over the Silk Road since antiquity. I heard of him through the son of one of our Chinese suppliers. As you know, Asian plans relating to commerce stretch a hundred years into the future. We need to adopt their thinking."

Henry tilted his head. "Can you have your hundred year plan on my desk tomorrow?" Seeing Blackburn's mouth drop open, he laughed. "Work on it." The earl leaned back in his chair and clenched his fingers behind his head. "I haven't been to Egypt for five years. Avoiding detection by Napoleon's confederates keeps one on edge. 'Tis a fascinating place. I trust your judgment, Blackie, but don't tweak Sheldon's nose too much. Make him feel part of the process. We need him. I learned long ago that one man can't do everything."

"You're right. You arrived to overhear our third or fourth discussion of the same topic, so that's why it sounded a bit heated. I'll work it out with Sheldon."

"How are Gonzales and Fong coming along with their areas?"

"Standard obstacles. All being handled well." The clock chimed six times. Blackburn reached for his jacket. "I have a meeting with my tailor. Can we meet tomorrow morning to go over pending items?"

"I'll be here at ten." Henry headed toward his office, first stopping to see Sheldon.

As he entered Sheldon's office, Henry saw his Africa specialist standing at the window, twirling a quill in his hand. He did not appear aware that flicks of India ink were spraying over his breeches.

"Sheldon, ink is flying through the air."

"Damnation!" He stood and pulled out a handkerchief to blot it, making it worse. He threw the pen on the desk where it skidded to a stop. "That man makes me lose my temper. Forgive me, Lord R."

"No forgiveness needed." Henry moved to close the door. "I need your honest and absolutely confidential opinion, Sheldon. You've been with me since the beginning. Do you trust Blackburn?"

The man in charge of Africa, a former safari leader with contacts all over the continent, was ten years older than Henry. He took a deep breath before speaking. "Until the last couple of years, I would have said, 'Yes.' But something has changed. I can't put my finger on it, it's just that gnawing feeling that he's off. I have no basis to say this, but I wonder if he arranged for the last shipment to be pilfered so he could be the 'savior' with an intermediary to 'protect' our cargo."

Sheldon put his hands on his forehead and ran them back through his gray hair. "Maybe it's my old age, maybe I'm jealous of his ingenuity. He's a clever one, I'll give him that. But I've always been a hunter, both a stalker of prey and alert to a predator nearby who might be stalking me. That's how I feel around him now: Blackburn is a predator. It's as if he's circling me, penning me in, readying me for the kill. I tell you, Lord R., there's just something off about him I didn't sense before."

Henry took a seat and motioned to Sheldon to do the same.

"I, too, feel unease. In the early years, I must confess, I felt camaraderie with him, some connection beyond commerce. The nature of trading is trust. I have been lucky up to now, because my instincts, and yours, have been on target. Remember the Albanian who offered us the forty percent discount on commodities from Africa and Asia? Neither of us trusted him. We later learned he offered us the discount on goods he never sold for full price, and that the forty percent discount was merely his starting point. Our guts served us well, then, Sheldon. You're thinking your doubts are based on old age and envy. I'm thinking my doubts are based on old age and concern about how my daughter will fare in the Marriage Season."

"Did you talk to Mason?"

"Yes. I have no basis to judge whether his claims are justified or not, but I paid out his pension to avoid any ill will. He worked with me, as you have, since the earliest days of the trading company. His turning on Blackburn might have been jealousy, but now I'm on notice with your discomfort." The earl stood. "Maybe our judgments aren't clouded. Maybe our instincts are correct. If he is corrupted, we must tread carefully, build our case and give him no clue. So continue to argue with him. Don't change your approach. That might alert him to your suspicions. You and I will talk when he is not around. Have Gonzales or Fong mentioned any doubts?"

"No."

"Then keep this between us. Is there—"

"What?"

"I hesitate to even voice this thought." Henry remained silent for a few moments. "Could he have recruited accomplices in our offices?"

Sheldon tilted his head, and then rotated it toward the ceiling, searching his memory. "I don't think it extends beyond the standard flattery of sycophants. He doesn't strike me as one who would put himself at risk of exposure." His face clouded.

Henry noticed Sheldon's discomfort. "Something else?"

"I just remembered that young clerk he'd groomed who had the unfortunate riding accident. And a few years earlier, there was the associate who jumped off Blackfriars Bridge." He sat up straighter and leaned forward. "You don't think—"

"Until this moment, no, I didn't. We've worked alongside him for twenty years. Is he capable of murder?"

Sheldon shrugged. "In Africa, there is a saying: 'Sometimes you are the hunter. Sometimes you are the hunted.' In the bush, I killed marauders to save myself and my hunting party. All men are capable of killing. You might kill in self-defense, to save a loved one, to save your country. If you convince yourself that your survival depends on another's death, is it inconceivable that Blackburn would kill to protect some secret?"

Henry tilted his head and sighed. "I too, in my travels, have been set upon by brigands, pirates and would-be assassins. I killed when necessary in self-defense and I would kill for my family. But for money? Am I naïve because I've always had wealth?"

Sheldon shrugged. "Probably. Look at it this way. I've a couple of friends who have had many mistresses. Killing, I think, is like having a mistress. With the first one, you're always looking over your shoulder. You lie. You sweat. You think you will be unmasked. Some are. But many are not. The second time is easier. The third is easier still. And so it goes."

"You've given me a lot to think about, Sheldon. Be vigilant. Give Blackburn no hint of suspicion. His instincts are sharp."

"As sharp as a knife that guts a lion."

"I take your analogy. But the lion might lunge when least expected and the gutter be gutted."

***

Friday, March 8, 1811 – Interior of Blackburn's Carriage
Blackburn

On the way to his tailor's shop, Blackburn mulled over his relationship with Lord R., a man of noble birth who had always treated him as an equal. Confident there was no one the earl trusted more with his commercial empire, despite Sheldon's whiny protestations, Blackburn felt secure.

When Lord R. traveled, Blackburn brought funding requests to James & Co. Never once had the earl questioned a decision of his, even when he had been wrong in the early days of his tenure. Lord R. had been patient, waiting for Blackburn to see the folly of his hubris, and then allowed him to remedy his errors. Blackburn wondered, often, what would have happened to him if he had not gone to the earl to reveal his mistakes? He might have survived one, even two, but then it would have been over. The plot would have been defeated before the seeds had been planted.

Acting against his grandmother's demands, his own instincts had been correct. *To win trust, I had to be honest and self-effacing. At least in the beginning.* His new plan required the proper clothing, a step up from his current attire. If he was to attend the Marriage Season and win the heart of Lady Gabriella Wyndward, marry her and secure his future, he would have to look the part.

***

Friday, March 8, 1811 – Lady Gwyneth's Townhouse
Clarissa

Clarissa gazed at the magnificent mahogany bookcases that reached to the ceiling on three sides of the room, framing a bay window on the fourth. Speechless, she walked slowly around the room, noting that the titles in the bookcases included original works in many languages, most of them worn from use.

The bay window overlooked the elegant Berkeley Crescent. A small pink rose plant in a hand-painted Chinese pot sat to one side of the windowsill, bare-branched but green buds were visible. The park-like crescent center had an array of flowers, just beginning to bloom. The late afternoon light fell in diffused rays on what dominated the room—two perfectly matched mahogany grand pianofortes, placed end to end. A massive oriental rug with deep, rich royal blue and burnt orange background featuring delicate details covered the polished marble floors.

During her sojourns to the continent as a child, before Napoleon's wars had made her a permanent exile from her country, Clarissa had seen several private libraries and music rooms, but none this magnificent. The ones she had seen were ceremonial, installed to impress visitors. In contrast, the owner of these volumes clearly cherished them for their content. "I can see why you call this the Music Room."

Bri smiled. "I love this room. I find in it enormous comfort. Do you play, Clarissa?"

"Yes, do you?"

"Yes, tutored at the incessantly demanding hand of M. Beauvais." Bri tilted her head and brightened. "Shall we try a duet?" Talking as she rustled through sheets of music, Bri found what she was looking for. "There are several duets here. Yes! Mozart's *The Magic Flute*. Why don't we play the aria where Papageno and Papagena are echoing each other's notes?"

"Perfect!" Clarissa took her place at one of the benches upholstered in burnt orange velvet that sat in front of each of the pianofortes, while Bri took the other. The notes filled the first floor.

CHAPTER FOUR

Friday, March 8, 1811 – Lady Gwyneth's Townhouse
Gwyneth

A s the young ladies began their duet, Gwyneth came into the room, taking a seat on the orange-and-white silk hand-painted window cushion and adjusted her sketchbook to a comfortable position. Tilting her head to one side as she viewed her niece and friend at the pianofortes, she set aside her previous work, a whimsical portrait of a cat dressed as a harlequin bowing to what appeared to be a cat princess, and began to sketch the scene in front of her. Soon, almost imperceptibly, a male Siamese came prowling into the Music Room, jumped up next to Gwyneth, and looked out the window. Soon a fluffier, gray-and-white cat appeared. A triangle of white fur on her chin and chest contrasted with unevenly mottled white paws. She pranced as she held her tail high. Lying at Gwyneth's feet, the cat looked up, her perfect feline head cocked to one side. *Da Vinci was right: "The smallest feline is a masterpiece."*

The comtesse loved her cats and often created fanciful needlepoint as well as painted designs with images of her pets. The Siamese turned and jumped up on the piano edge where Bri was playing and stared into its interior. As they finished their piece, he tentatively reached a paw toward the strings.

"No jumping into the piano, Mozart." Bri scolded with a note of amusement in her voice.

"What a clever name for a cat." Clarissa smiled. "What is the gray-

and-white one called?"

Bri smiled as the gray-and-white cat rubbed against her leg. "Misty. She's a bit sad and somewhat shy. We thought the name fit."

"You each play well." The comtesse looked up from her sketch. "I enjoyed that interlude."

"Clarissa is much more accomplished than I. I could barely keep up with her!" Turning to her new friend, she asked, "What training have you had?"

"My father insisted that I be taught by a Prussian because he felt the English were too indulgent with their students. Don't misunderstand, he indulges me quite a bit, but in the realm of tutoring, he is extremely strict. I was quite fearful of Herr Kramer until he confided in me that he was afraid of my father. After that, we worked quite well together, although it was often exhausting. He had an extraordinary range of musical interests, and a secret that I found out only after knowing him for years."

Intrigued, Bri pressed for details. "What kind of secret?"

"It amazed me at the time, and I still find it surprising. My father paid Herr Kramer more than the prevailing rate for music lessons, but my instructor felt compelled to pursue his love of music outside his engagement as my tutor. He began to compose operettas and to occasionally accompany performances in the musical theater."

The comtesse raised her eyebrows. "Did your father terminate him when he learned of this sideline?"

"He never knew until much later. In fact, when Father was traveling, I sometimes went with Herr Kramer to the musical theater to turn the pages of sheet music for him. In any case, by the time Herr Kramer's operetta, *The Princess*, was produced in Berlin, Father supported his efforts. The production was a success. It will open in London next month and my father is the financial sponsor."

"Take care, Clarissa. An operetta borders on musical theatre, but without the cachet of opera. Speak not of frequenting such venues outside our family. Proper young ladies simply do not patronize the theater unless it is a performance of Shakespeare or the opera or something equally acceptable. Musical theater is considered bawdy, crass, tawdry and risqué. And don't get any ideas, Bri. I recognize that look in your eyes."

"Don't worry, Aunt Gwyneth, I will not tarnish the family honor by singing and dancing in public. I should get laughed off the stage, anyway."

At that, the door opened and her father walked in. "What's this about the stage?"

"Oh, Henry, we didn't hear you arrive. Bri's just teasing me again. Dinner should be almost ready. Where is Nambotha?"

"Here, milady. I shall alert Dominique of the earl's arrival." The butler left the room.

"Henry, you remember Lady Clarissa von Dusterberg. She and Bri have renewed their acquaintance today. She will be dining with us this evening."

Lord Ravenshire bowed his head. "Delighted to see you again, Lady Clarissa. We thoroughly enjoyed our sojourn at your compound in South Africa. I trust I will see Ambassador von Dusterberg at Lady Elisabeth's ball?"

"Yes, Lord Ravenshire. He's coming reluctantly, but looking forward to seeing you now that we are living in London. He always says, 'War is unavoidable in Europe, but the diplomatic corps endures a series of battles of its own.' After Napoleon's invasion, as you know, we spent a great deal of time in exile in Africa, stranded and unable to return to Berlin."

"Wars try men's souls. May I escort you into the dining room, Lady Clarissa?"

"Of course, Lord Ravenshire."

The pinkish orange glow of the spring sunset filtered into the Music Room, encircling them with an aura of light. They made their way past the staircase, down a wide hallway lined with oil paintings of the de Merbeau ancestors, their visages made more mysterious by the flickering of the candlelight from the wall sconces.

The hallway opened into a large dining room in the back of the house. When they arrived, Nambotha was lighting the candles on the table. Through the windows, the gaslights of London glittered above the black silhouette of the garden. In daylight, the dazzling flowers of the garden were a source of pride to the comtesse and the gardener, adjusted for all seasons and grown in a small greenhouse.

Clarissa noted the long monk's table. "Is there a history to your acquisition of this unusual table?"

The comtesse ran her hands over the wood. "This is from the monastery near my late husband's estates in France. We don't know how old it is. The monks said it dates from the 12th century, yet it is as solid as the day it was hewn. The chairs were especially made by current local artisans to match it."

Crisp white linen placemats embroidered with "C de M" on the lower left corner with matching napkins were set in four places. A low candelabra in the center of the table was surrounded by a circular glass vase filled with water, and spring blossoms floated in it.

Once all were seated, Nambotha and Felix, the footman, entered the room with Dominique's first course, a vichyssoise from the secret recipe of the de Merbeau family.

"Lady Clarissa, my late husband, Luc, said that this recipe from his chateau was over 100 years old. He fussed over its proper preparation with our cook, Dominique, until she got it right, so it is with a great deal of pride that she offers it to us tonight. I do hope you enjoy it." The comtesse lifted her soup spoon and nodded to the others to begin.

After trying the soup, Clarissa agreed. "It's the best I have ever tasted."

Bri sipped a spoonful. "It's my absolute favorite. Dominique always makes it when I'm here for dinner."

"Tell me, Gwyneth, what were the topics of this afternoon's tea party that my daughter so dreaded attending?"

"Well, Henry, I attempted to persuade Bri that she needed to know some other young ladies in the *ton*, and to find out about the latest dress styles so that she can make a satisfactory entrée into the Marriage Season at Lady Elisabeth's ball. We were not altogether unsuccessful, although it may be that some of the other young ladies in attendance this afternoon will be inviting neither Bri nor Lady Clarissa to any reciprocal events."

The earl frowned and glanced at his daughter. "Bri, what happened? And Lady Clarissa, I'd like to hear your views, as well."

"Father, one was very cold and unfriendly, and you know Lady Patricia's penchant for gossip. The others seemed refined, sweet but insipid, exactly as I had dreaded young women of the *ton* to be. It is going to be utterly boring to be around such shallow, self-absorbed people."

Clarissa hesitated. "I must confess, Lord Ravenshire, that I made several comments deliberately designed to offend the others because their conceited mannerisms annoyed me."

Everyone was so absorbed in the conversation that they were a bit startled when Felix, the server, removed the soup tureens. Nambotha brought in a platter with four pheasants surrounded by roasted potatoes. Once served, he poured a dry white wine to accompany the meal.

Noticing the label from the de Merbeau Vineyard, Clarissa looked puzzled. "The blockade with France has been in effect for over a decade. How do you get wine shipments through?"

Henry shrugged. "We have a fleet of ships of all sizes. Blockade running is a bit of a sport among our more adventurous captains. As Jean-Louis would say, 'There are ways.' "

Gwyneth resumed her point when the servants left the room "No one said you had to be close personal friends with these young women, but they may influence what parties you may be either invited *to* or excluded *from*. I daresay I shall have to impose upon my long acquaintance with their mothers, to make sure that you are invited to the best balls of the Season. And if you think I will enjoy making amends for your foolish behavior, you are wrong. If you had just behaved properly for a short time, it would have saved us all quite a bit of trouble."

"I must agree with my sister." Henry's voice was stern. "And pardon me, Lady Clarissa, but I believe that your father would agree with me. I speak to you both in your individual best interests. You can avoid private meetings with those you dislike and vent your frustrations after the teas or balls you *must* attend, but part of reaching maturity and taking one's position in the *ton,* as well as maintaining the honor of the Wyndward and von Dusterberg names, is to be polite to others without regard to one's personal view. From what I have heard, you two young ladies made a most unfortunate impression. Gossip will precede you at the balls of the Season and may result in your exclusion from some important events. It reflects poorly not only upon you, but upon your families as well. I'm profoundly disappointed in your entirely selfish behavior."

Stunned, Bri appeared to realize that what she had considered a harmless parlor game was really quite rude.

Regret wrinkled Clarissa's brow. "Lord Ravenshire, I see now how utterly stupid we were. We shall have to try to repair this damage. And you're quite correct about my father. He would be furious, and I fear that word of our thoughtless behavior will reach him soon. I must tell him myself to avoid making the situation even worse."

As they ate in silence, Gwyneth exchanged a sly glance with Henry. *Perhaps she'll behave better the next time.*

The group abruptly straightened when Nambotha and Felix entered to clear the dinner plates. The butler poured chamomile tea.

Gwyneth deduced that Dominique had overheard their conversation and brewed chamomile to ease everyone's digestion. *A clever retainer.*

When Felix returned from delivering the dinner plates to the kitchen, he placed dessert cups in front of everyone, while Nambotha scooped up fresh vanilla pudding from a crystal bowl. After Nambotha and the footman left, the conversation resumed.

Bri's tone became plaintive. "I know you wish only the best for me, and that you arranged this Season for my benefit. And I have acted impetuously. However shall we fix this disaster?"

"That, my dear girls, is up to you." Lord Ravenshire directed his gaze at each young woman in turn. "In the future, be polite. Meanwhile, Gwyneth and I, and," speaking directly to Lady Clarissa, "no doubt, your father, will work behind the scenes to try to repair the threads that have unraveled." Looking at the two distraught young ladies, he softened somewhat. "Come, come now. It is not as if you've committed murder. We can pull through this quite well, together."

Henry pushed his chair away from the table and stood. "And now, ladies, I've had a long day, as have you. Thank you, Gwyneth for a lovely meal. The vichyssoise and pheasant were delicious as always."

The others rose.

"Thank you for inviting me, and I appreciate your willingness to speak so frankly to me, Lord Ravenshire. Madame la Comtesse, I shall never forget your kindness, and hope to prove myself a truly worthy friend to your niece." Clarissa sighed. "And the pudding was a special treat, for it reminded me of the marvelous vanilla flavors of Madagascar. I spent a truly delightful fortnight there with my father as guests of his friend, Sultan Sarduba. Dishes flavored with delicate spices were expertly prepared. I prevailed upon their chef to teach me a few recipes, which our cook has mastered. Perhaps you would all be so good as to join my father and me for dinner soon, so that we both can repay your hospitality."

"We would be delighted, my dear." The comtesse leaned forward. "I've heard so much about your illustrious father and his collection of military and heraldic artifacts from the curator of the Military Museum." Reacting to the surprise of the young ladies, she laughed, "Oh, yes, I know something about military history, as the late comte was a student of it, and I took his place on that museum's Board of Trustees after his untimely death."

Lord Ravenshire kissed his sister on the cheek. "I shall see to the carriages while Nambotha helps you young ladies with your coats." He strode outside to signal Jean-Louis and Lady Clarissa's driver to pull up to the steps.

"Do you still want to visit Mlle. Bellerobe's tomorrow, Bri?" Clarissa's voice sounded as if she half-expected a rejection.

"Oh, yes. I'm sure we can find something suitable. Perhaps the design will be classic in a new and fabulous fabric." Bri's faux cheer fooled no one.

Hugging her aunt, Bri looked more like a chastened child than the self-assured woman she usually portrayed in public and private.

The comtesse also embraced Clarissa, saying, "You are always welcome here, Lady Clarissa, and we look forward to dining with you and your father soon."

"I will confirm his schedule and we can compare it with yours to select a date."

"Then we'll see you tomorrow, at *Chez Michel*, at half past noon." The comtesse accompanied them to the door.

The two young ladies proceeded down the steps, and Henry assisted Lady Clarissa into her carriage.

"Good night, Lady Clarissa."

"Good night to you, Lord Ravenshire. And thank you for speaking to me with such honesty."

Henry nodded an acknowledgment. "This is all new for both of you."

The earl's footman opened the door to his carriage, helping Bri climb inside. Her father followed after waving goodbye to Gwyneth.

Gwyneth stood in the doorway, watching as they drove off. "Well, Nambotha?"

"Our Bri will triumph, milady. Fear not."

"Headstrong and opinionated. Have we spoiled her?"

"No, milady. She is stronger than any obstacle she might confront."

***

Henry

Bri took her father's hand, remaining uncharacteristically quiet on the ride home. She put her head on his shoulder and fell asleep to the steady cadence of the horse's steps along the cobblestones. Henry looked down at the child whom he loved so dearly, and hoped that he had not been too harsh. *Better to end these arrogant displays of pique at the ways of Society before the Season officially begins.* The pressures would surely build as it got fully underway.

Not that he wanted Bri to conform. He wanted to protect her and give her the strength to maneuver her way through Society while nurturing her independent spirit in private. If she never married, it would not matter to him, for he wished only for her happiness. But he and Gwyneth had agreed they should give Bri an introduction to Society this Season, believing that his daughter should choose independence only after giving herself the chance to meet the eligible men of the *ton*, though none, he was sure, would be likely to meet her standards. As an heiress, she had already rejected more than a few hapless suitors. The country estate where she grew up presented a different way of life, but she so loved the commerce of the city that he hoped she would find a man of like mind here.

As they drew up to their door, Henry sighed deeply and nudged Bri to awaken. "We're home, my dear," he whispered. The footman opened the door, and helped Gabriella exit the carriage. Jean-Louis turned around in his perch and saluted her, their private joke.

The butler, Thompson, and Nashmir, the earl's high-bunned Buddhist master gardener and valet, greeted them at the imposing doorway to Henry's townhouse. "Good evening, milord. Good evening, Lady Gabriella."

"Good evening, Thompson." He nodded to the Tibetan, "Nashmir."

"I alerted Jane Anne when I heard the carriage arrive. She is laying out Lady Gabriella's bedclothes at this moment." Thompson, always efficient, ran the earl's households with an expert hand.

Bri kissed her father goodnight.

Henry embraced his daughter. "Sleep well." Signaling to Nashmir, the earl walked to his study.

***

Bri

Bri climbed the staircase and entered her suite of rooms on one wing of the third floor.

Her maid, Jane Anne, looked up and said, "Oh, milady. I've poured fresh water and set out your bedclothes. Let me untie your dress." As was her habit, the maid hung her mistress's dress over a standing screen in the corner of the bedroom. There, it would air overnight, and then it would be folded and put into the armoire.

"Will you be needing anything else, milady?" The young girl had just turned nineteen.

"No. I'm quite exhausted. Please tell Nashmir to alert my father that I would like to breakfast with him about eight o'clock tomorrow, as I have to meet Aunt Gwyneth at ten o'clock at Mme. Mottier's dress salon."

"Very well, milady. Will you be getting lots of ball gowns? It all sounds so exciting!"

Laughing in spite of her fatigue, Gabriella nodded. "I expect so. Aunt Gwyneth wants me to look presentable and I have not had much use for ball gowns in the country. Only at Christmas and the occasional country dance."

"Good night, milady." Jane Anne closed the door.

Bri moved the bedclothes aside and fell onto her feather-filled bed in her underclothes and immediately fell asleep.

CHAPTER FIVE

Saturday, March 9, 1811 – Lord Ravenshire's Townhouse
Bri

J ane Anne spoke softly as she stood shyly next to the bed. "Please
wake up, Lady Gabriella."

Bri began to stir slightly and opened her eyes.

"Milady, you fell asleep in your underclothes last night and your
father is expecting you for breakfast in less than one hour's time.
I've begun to draw your bath. We've not a moment to spare!"

"*Zut!* I'm embarrassed to have fallen asleep in this condition. I
must get my wits together!"

"Yes, milady." The maid walked toward the adjoining bath area to
make sure the tub did not overflow. "Is there a dress you favor
today?"

"As I shall be shopping, I would like to wear something easy to
take off. I've never shopped for multiple ball gowns such as are
expected for the Society balls during the Season." Bri opened the
armoire holding her day dresses. "I'm afraid that what I considered
flattering in the country might seem passé here." Looking through
the small selection of well-tailored dresses, she selected a periwinkle
wool dress trimmed with navy braid on the edges of the short, puffed
sleeves as well as around the sides and hem. In addition, it had a
narrow, ruffled navy edge around the bodice, cut in the fashion of
the day. The neckline featured a depth that revealed just enough of
her bosom to remain respectable.

"A lovely choice, milady. The periwinkle color will set off your auburn hair. Did anyone ever tell you that your eyes are the color of Ireland's fields?"

"No, that's an original comparison!"

The dress chosen, Bri proceeded to remove her underclothes as she entered her large bath. She thought of the sunny room as both luxurious and functional. When she visited friends, she was often shocked that they had not installed the latest in water closet and bath pumps and pipes to deliver hot and cold water, although she recognized that her father was a man of unusual wealth and eager to implement new ideas. His keen foresight had led him to support the inventing activities of people he met, inspiring Bri to look for talent around her.

Henry had arranged for installation of water pipes and other devices in his London townhouse as well as in his country estates in an effort to lead his friends by example. Not many had followed at first, as the expense was high. The improvement in hygiene, however, was undeniable. Water closets became standard on ships before being fully accepted in the homes of the wealthy, and the Wyndward fleet had been fully outfitted early on.

In addition to water closets, Henry had arranged for the installation of pumps to bring hot water for the baths and even attached a spray-like device to the water faucet, which was very efficient as an aid in washing Bri's long hair. Ordinarily, Bri relished a bath as a luxurious time of meditation and relaxation, but today her head was full of remorse for her behavior the previous day. Pushing away intruding thoughts, she directed her focus to the upcoming breakfast meeting with her father, where she intended to outline the current state of his business affairs and to suggest some investment and new venture ideas she had been nurturing.

An undercurrent of excitement cut through all the mental activity, as she was looking forward to shopping for the necessary ball gowns despite her frequent dismissal of shopping as the shallow activity of vapid Society women.

Jane Anne came in with a thick robe and helped Bri out of the deep tub. "Are you ready for your dressing gown?"

"Yes. Is there time for you to put up my hair?"

Bri moved to the vanity table so that Jane Anne could style her hair.

"You're quite talented at this, Jane Anne, and so quick," said Bri. "I always get compliments on my hair when you style it. I can't quite get the same effect myself."

"Thank you, milady. I must confess that I enjoy it very much. It was the only good thing to come out of my indentured servitude to the wicked master wig maker who brought me here from Ireland at the age of eight."

Bri frowned. "What do you mean by wicked?"

"Although he instructed his children's tutor to teach me to read, his kindnesses ended as I aged beyond childhood. He took a bit too much interest in me, if you know what I mean. I shudder to think what might have happened had I not run away from that cursed, evil man late that cold night in November. I just ran and ran. When I stumbled in the street and fell into the path of your father's carriage, I thought I would be run over by the horses. But Jean-Louis miraculously stopped them in time. Lord Ravenshire was so kind to listen to my story. I don't know how he could even understand me, as I was crying hysterically. Then, to buy out my contract and give me a position as a maid in his home! I can never repay that kindness."

"Nonsense, Jane Anne. Neither Father nor I believe in slavery of any sort. Indentured servitude is most certainly slavery."

Jane Anne skillfully pulled Bri's hair into a lovely knot at the back of her head with delicate long curls on the sides, trailing down to her neck. "I've heard there is an academy of hairdressing in Paris and that they have salons devoted just to hairdressing. Can you imagine, milady? Sometimes I daydream about having a little salon of my own, but of course that is impossible. Please don't think me ungrateful, Lady Gabriella," she said, making eye contact in the mirror, "but I do think about it sometimes. I'll probably never get the chance, for where would someone of my station get the money to set myself up in business? An inheritance?" She laughed, adding, "My family sold me into servitude because they were so desperately poor. In leaving Ireland, I happily relinquished *that* inheritance!"

"Jane Anne," said Bri with a slight adjustment in her chair, "I think I saw a book about hairdressing at Aunt Gwyneth's house. I'll find it and bring it to you. It's in French, but I can translate it for you."

"Oh, milady, you're so busy. Would you really have time for that?"

"Don't be silly. It would be fun. Let's think about your abilities and interests logically. Maybe you could start on your day off, doing hair for one or two of my friends. If you took Thursday as your day off this week, you could style their hair before the ball. We could ask Jean-Louis to take you to their homes. Could you take Thursday off?"

Stunned, Jane Anne involuntarily backed away, as if a little afraid of her dream becoming real, even for a day. "But milady, I wouldn't know where to begin or how to arrange it, or anything."

"Well, it seems to me that if you agreed to do their hair for no charge as a way of promoting your skill, you might be able to set a fair price when they see your results. I'll see that you're paid your normal wages for the day from my funds. What is the going rate at the salons in the *ton*?"

"I couldn't say," admitted Jane Anne.

"All right, I shall find out today when I'm out with Aunt Gwyneth. Then I shall line up one or two young ladies during the day."

"Oh, milady, do you think that the ladies of Society would really agree?"

"As I have told you, Jane Anne, I always get compliments on my hair. The upsweep you accomplish with the discreet curls is wonderful," she said, turning her head from side to side to approve Jane Anne's handiwork. "If I encourage my acquaintances, I think we can arrange at least two appointments for you now, and probably more for next week." Adopting a conspiratorial tone, she added, "Besides, I have to make up for a bit of rudeness to some Society types yesterday. You'll be doing me a favor. But make sure you leave enough time for me!" Bri stood and moved toward her armoire. "Now, I must get dressed and gather my papers for my breakfast discussion. Help me with the overdress so I don't muss up my hair."

Still in a kind of trance, Jane Anne held the pale periwinkle chemise until Bri had stepped into it, and then she tied the drawstrings in the back. She slipped the overdress over one shoulder while Bri took the other, fastening the dress between her breasts with a rare chalcedony brooch that her father had brought her from one of his trips to the Far East. From her jewelry box, Bri selected matching chalcedony cabochon earrings, an oval ring, and a perfectly round carved bracelet.

Using the bedpost for support, Bri slipped on a pair of navy silk shoes and picking up her navy silk reticule, Bri turned to her eager maid, and said, "I shall work on lining up your other clients today."

"Oh, thank you, thank you, milady. You're so kind, I don't know what to say or how to act."

"Just be yourself and do the best job you can. Women must support each other's dreams in this man's world."

Bri swept out of her rooms and down the wide staircase to breakfast.

The earl's dining room was larger than Aunt Gwyneth's, but similarly situated in the back of his townhouse. The bay window that overlooked a Japanese rock and flower garden led to a small greenhouse. Inside what Nashmir referred to as his conservatory, he nurtured herbs and orchids as well as creating medicinal concoctions.

The 10th Earl originally bought a small townhouse on the block. Over the years, Henry had purchased several more, renovating and connecting half the block into what could pass for a small palace, but retaining the feel of a family home.

"Good morning."

The often silent Thompson nodded an acknowledgment and exited.

Looking up from his newspaper, her father smiled. "Good morning to you. What time do you need to leave for your meeting at Gwyneth's dressmaker?"

"About thirty minutes past nine."

Thompson returned with eggs and toast. While at Ravenshire with guests, the earl observed the nobility's custom of serving themselves breakfast from a buffet, but in London meals were prepared individually to order.

Looking at his pocket watch, Henry announced, "We have about an hour to go over your ideas. Let's get started as we eat. First of all, as you know, yesterday I met with Sir John and his son, Edward, who will be administering my, or should I say our, accounts. They have accepted my decision to have you act as my man-of-affairs. I could see they had some reservations, but they kept silent."

Thompson poured the breakfast tea.

"Edward James? I remember him as an arrogant sort. Bragged he could beat me at Whist because it wasn't a game for girls."

"And you taught him a lesson, as I recall."

Bri couldn't help a smug smile. Thinking about her father's last comment, her face clouded. "I assume you appealed to Sir John's natural tendency toward client secrecy to refrain from discussing this arrangement in Society?"

Amused, Henry smiled a wry grin. "Don't fret. Sir John is well aware of the novelty of our arrangement. I have full confidence that he and his son will honor our bid for privacy. By the way, Sir John will be here this afternoon for tea and to partake of some of Nashmir's herbal remedies." Changing to a more serious tone, he confided, "My old friend is very ill. I hope that Nashmir's herbs and unique knowledge will spare him some pain, if not his life. We're the same age, you know," he observed, looking through the wide, paned window into the tranquil Japanese rock garden.

"It is quite humbling to think I might be facing a limited future. At one-and-fifty years, I have already lived longer than many of my other old schoolmates. Wolcott died in Nashmir's arms. Others died in war. Vincent...well, a tragic early death. AJ is rumored to be unwell in Italy. Father is gone. We lost Rychard and Luc before their time. My age is one of the reasons I want you to take a more active role in managing my financial affairs. The more important reason, of course, is that you're so unusually competent at it."

"Father, you are healthy as a horse, and I must ask you not to talk of untimely death." Softly, she added, "I've had enough of it."

"I'm sorry, Bri. It is Sir John I am really concerned about, but you must face the possibility of being on your own. That is why Gwyneth and I wanted you to have this Season. You say you will not fall in love with a Society man, but there may be someone that will surprise you. Most romantic love is the stuff of novels and the ridiculous Lord Byron. Grown-ups adhere to more lasting precepts such as duty, although having thrice been romantically smitten, I do rather hope that you will find that same warmth."

Bri said, "Thrice? My mother, of course, and the baroness. Who is the third? You've never spoken of this before. Who was this other romantic love of yours? Where is she now?"

Henry winced. "Our romantic interlude ended because she died. It was in a foreign land in another lifetime, it seems, many years ago. But I see her face occasionally in my dreams. Truth be told, had she lived, I might never have returned to England and the company would have muddled along at a slow pace. So I really should not lecture you on duty, should I?" Henry took her hand in his, comforting them both from the sorrow of their losses. "And Charlotte has brought me happiness and companionship. It is not fair to her to chase the ghosts of your mother and another."

Bri wanted to hear more about her father's tragic romance, but her pragmatic nature told her that he had confided his limit of secrets for breakfast, and furthermore, she needed to go over her analysis of the overall financial condition of his businesses as well as her plans for future investments and new ventures.

As they finished eating, Bri asked Thompson to bring a new pot of tea into her father's study.

They adjourned to the study. It housed a small library with a floor-to-ceiling wall of books. An ancient oak desk served as the focal point of the room. Its ebony black leather writing surface, an ornamentation added in the last century, was set into an oak border carved with intricate Celtic designs.

It was an absurd example of the folly of wealth to a true historian. No Druid would have destroyed or defiled an oak to make furniture. The early Christian monks in Britain and Wales misunderstood the Druids, thinking that they worshiped oak trees. By destroying the oak groves, the monks intended to destroy the power of the religion. But the acorns blew to new ground. The fact the monks missed was simple—the Druids worshiped *among* the oak trees in a natural setting of earthly might. No human force could supplant that mysterious energy. To use Celtic ornamentation on such a desk reflected historical ignorance.

Not that her father was ignorant—to the contrary, he appreciated the irony of the design and explained the anomaly to every visitor. His study was full of philosophical works from his travels, not a duplicate of Aunt Gwyneth's, although, to be sure, there were some volumes in common. Rather, it was a doubling of knowledge and an almost limitless source of new ideas for Bri. She always felt a surge of creative energy in both her father's study and her aunt's Music Room.

Under the window, a long table displayed artifacts from the earl's travels. Its centerpiece was a magnificent globe whose hand-colored cartography had been painstakingly applied to the spherical form. A rare Ming vase, jade carvings of a tiger and a panda, and an ancient Chinese compass always sparked comments from visitors.

Taking their places across from each other, Bri and her father delayed beginning their conversation until Thompson had finished pouring the tea. He closed the door discreetly as he left.

"I took the liberty of preparing an agenda, Father." Bri handed him a neatly penned page from the papers on her side of the desk. "Shall we begin with an anomaly I've discovered in the trading company books?"

CHAPTER SIX

Saturday, March 9, 1811 – Edward's Gentleman's Club
Vaux

Viscount Vaux arrived at the club and scanned the room for his friend. Spotting Edward James, he nodded and made his way to the table. Falling into his chair with a sigh of exhaustion, Vaux grimaced. "I've had not a wink of sleep."

Edward put down his newspaper. "Gaming hells again?"

"You know I don't wager overmuch. But Rogers dragged Hanforth and me with him. I need the strongest tea they can brew here."

"Maybe coffee would work quicker."

"You're right." He ordered a simple breakfast of coffee and toast. "Don't want to wretch it out all over the table, James."

Raising an eyebrow, James nodded. "Thoughtful of you."

"You are one of the few friends I have with an actual vocation. I busy myself with changing the décor of my family's various homes, but I just received a request from Lady Haley to redecorate her townhouse. I am a bit nonplussed. She asked me for my fee, and I said I would review her needs and develop a budget. I am flailing around trying to determine a budget. I've always just spent whatever I wanted for my own homes. I need your advice."

Taking a sip of tea after a bite of toast, Edward sat back in his chair. "Vaux, the world is changing faster than many will be able to adjust. Machines are being developed that will be as transformative as a war or revolution. You are wise to consider a vocation, or avocation. Income from your property holdings requires constant reinvestment to maintain a competitive edge. Many don't see it yet, but foreign money is pouring in. New emporiums, restaurants and furnishings are proliferating. London is not the small, exclusive enclave it was when we were children. Those who scoff at trade and industry may weep in the years to come."

"Your philosophical turn is not soothing my aching head. To make things worse, my father insists that I attend the Marriage Season."

"You are not alone. Now that I am back from my travels, I am being forced—call that 'requested' with a strong voice—to attend as well. At least the first ball is at my godmother's. And my father and largest client seem to have picked out my fiancée for me."

"Who might that be?"

"Lady Gabriella Wyndward."

Vaux laughed. "You will have a lively debate with Lady Gabriella."

"You know her?"

"You've been gone for six years, James. I met Lady Gabriella at one of Lord Ostwold's art soirées. She's a delightful conversationalist, as long as you agree with her. You two will be an interesting couple to watch spar."

"She beat me at Whist once."

"Oh, this will be rich! Imagining how you survive your upcoming trial of wits has neutralized the lightning bolts shooting through my temple. I find her beautiful and fascinating, but she is my friend. Take my advice on Lady Gabriella, as I will take yours on financial matters—get to know her as a friend first. Don't try to control her. She will resist that as a squirming cat resists a hug."

"So she's become even more opinionated since I last saw her, if that's possible. Maybe I should just find a nice, quiet woman and be done with it."

"After you meet Lady Gabriella, no other woman will capture your attention. Of that I have no doubt." He fell into a fit of laughter and had to cough to catch his breath. His flushed cheeks puffed out until he regained his composure. "Oh, yes, James. Watching your romance with Lady Gabriella bloom or burst will be the highlight of the Season."

"Marriage is not about romance. It is a careful, deliberative process to select an appropriate life companion."

"You are so deluded. Have you not read Lord Byron's poem, 'Maid of Athens, Ere We Part?' Lady Gabriella will steal your heart forever. You will have to beg her to give you back your heart."

"Are you daft, Vaux? You sound like a silly schoolgirl. Lord Byron, indeed. Now, as to your fee. Since you have not overseen interior renovations before, it would be best to set a percentage commission over the actual cost of the furnishings and décor, to include your time and your expertise. Remember, as your expertise grows, the less time it will take you to execute your plan. What this means is that in the future, what you can do in less time should command a higher fee. Please," he implored his impulsive friend, "save some of that in a special account. The future is uncertain. We can go over this in my office when your head is healed."

"Right now, all I can consider is how to make it through the day without a nap."

***

Saturday, March 9, 1811 – Lord Ravenshire's Study
Bri

Henry removed his reading spectacles from his vest pocket and adjusted them comfortably on the bridge of his nose. "What anomaly?"

"As you know, I have spent the last few weeks going over your personal copies of all the books. On the surface, last year's results look excellent. Overall revenues were up due to our introduction of new products and commodities as well as the implementation of selective price increases for shipping."

Henry nodded his agreement that her summary matched his evaluation.

Bri continued, "Our direct cost of goods increased due to new tariffs on imported goods and the continued blockade of Europe by Napoleon, although many of our ships slip through on a regular basis. Even after averaging the increases and spreading the impact across all of our main markets in England, Africa and the Americas, these tariffs and high costs to evade blockades were not fully covered by price increases. While at first glance new prices appear to cover the tariff increases, the reality is that we were not able to re-price all goods before the new tariffs went into effect."

Henry raised his left eyebrow. "There's always a lag time, but the war increases our challenges."

"In addition," Bri continued, "general expenses for marketing, insurance, staff, etc., increased in line with repositioning and expanding our international sources for new products, but more than I would have expected. The net impact is that our revenues and profits are up in absolute terms, but our margins are down. Let me illustrate."

Bri took Henry through the numbers, and he acknowledged, "I've only looked at the bottom line. Now that you point it out, I see that our margins have eroded since last year. How do they compare with the last few years?"

Ready with the detailed figures, Bri summarized, "Steady declines over the last five years, although small, less than one percentage point per year, on average. Not bad with Napoleon on the march. But over a decade, that is nearly ten percent. You've built this business over the last thirty-odd years. There are always wars. When the trading company was founded, you knew the suppliers personally, because you conducted all your business transactions yourself. You selected the merchandise and inspected it upon arrival. Now you must rely on others, and frankly, only by careful analysis of the numbers and constant monitoring of contracts can you verify results. Your directors do some of this, but they don't investigate for potential fraud."

"Fraud? Exactly what are you suggesting?" Henry's tone made it clear that he would permit no backing down from her accusation.

Taking a deep breath, Bri launched into her explanation: "I noticed that nearly twenty-five percent of the losing products over the last few years result from contracts with new trading partners. It's not a large amount in dollars. All operate out of Egypt and North Africa. While forming only a small part of the trading operations, and easily overlooked, these new partners are having a negative cumulative impact on our margins and we should take action now before the problem grows any larger."

Henry sat in stunned silence as Bri continued. "For instance, Phu-Sak, Ltd. in Siam, and Madras Trading, Ltd. in India operate branches in Cairo and Alexandria, respectively. These new partners are small, which fits our strategy of exotic, luxurious, one-of-a-kind products and suppliers with limited output, so that we can control the market and it's too small for the larger trading companies to care about. In some cases, these new contracts are in conflict with our existing contracts with long-term partners. More investigation is in order."

"Perhaps it is just misjudgment in operations, trying to add new suppliers to meet customer demand, and so on." Henry's tone was tentative.

"That is quite possible," said Bri, "but these contracts violate our long-standing policy of asking new companies to supply us on a test basis. Instead, we have been entering into long-term contracts with them from the first shipment."

"Standard policy is to enter into one-year contracts and only renew or extend the term after satisfactory delivery and market acceptance of the products or commodities." Henry drummed his fingers on the desk. "I wouldn't be surprised to see some skimming. That happens and is tolerable within a certain range. But this might constitute a detailed strategy to subvert the trading company's policies and objectives."

Bri directed his attention to the pages of notes in the addendum to the financial statements she had prepared that listed the contracts and their term.

"It is all here," he admitted, "but I have not bothered to read this information carefully for years. Blackie is in charge of day-to-day operations, but he sees the overarching strategy and does not have much of an eye for accounting details. If he had your keen financial eye, I'm sure he would have brought these irregularities to my attention."

"In retrospect, I am relieved that we were so discreet in our examination of these files. No clerk at the office knows about my efforts, so no suspicions have been aroused. Father, I'd like your permission to do some research on these new companies."

"Precisely what do you intend to do? If embezzlement is afoot, it might be dangerous to uncover."

"I would like to meet with your solicitor to request that he contact his counterparts in each of the countries where the largest discrepancies have occurred. They can investigate the ultimate ownership of our new trading partners. It may be that competitors have targeted you, starting with small amounts and increasing your vulnerability to them until they break you completely."

The earl frowned. "That might take too long. Jean-Louis can send birds faster to his trusted associates."

"Shouldn't we do both? We may benefit from legal advice. Sir Paul is discreet. His firm can review all the existing contracts under some arcane legal request without raising suspicion."

"I shall accompany you to visit Sir Paul. Do not forget that you cannot go about acting like a gentleman."

Irritated, Bri knew that he was right. It would take time before she could really run the business for her father, and as yet, she could not pose as his agent. She sighed in resignation. "Yes, you're right. Even being introduced to people in commerce as your agent would likely scandalize the *ton* and end my entrée into Society before it has begun."

"Quite. Neither of us will mention this potential fraud to anyone except Sir Paul, Sir John and Young James, each of whom I trust implicitly. All will be as shocked as I."

Bri readily agreed. "Shall we turn to the estate accounts?"

"Let's postpone that until after dinner this evening. I cannot concentrate on it now that you have raised these issues. I was planning to spend all day at the office, so I shall gather some files myself and bring them home tonight. Blackie is in Wales today, arranging coal shipments. I can investigate things without alerting him to these potential issues. 'Tis a dilemma," he sighed, shaking his head. "I must admit that I have had a feeling of discomfort eating away at me for some time about certain aspects of the trading operations, but I never suspected anything like this."

"Well, then, I shall see you this evening, Father." Bri rose from the table. "I am truly sorry to bring you this unfortunate news. I would like to ease your mind in one way, however: the estate accounts are doing quite well."

"Ah, that is good news, at least. Except that I have nothing to do with them—their success is all due to you. It is the focus of my efforts that have come up short." He picked up the pages of accounts that Bri had prepared, and was immediately absorbed in the details he had delegated to others for so many years.

Walking into the hallway, Bri looked for Thompson. When she saw him, she said she was going out and he retrieved her capelet.

He held it for her to slip over her shoulders. She tied the sash at the neck, picked up her umbrella from the stand near the doors and applied a hat pin to her hair to attach a small navy hat with one navy feather curved around the back.

She turned. "I shall return about five o'clock."

"Yes, Lady Gabriella. Enjoy your shopping trip. Jean-Louis has the carriage ready for you."

Bri nearly flew down the steps to where Jean-Louis waited.

"Eager to shop? That's not like you."

The footman held the door.

"Let's be off."

The driver tipped his hat in mock obedience. "To the Comtesse de Merbeau? Or Mme. Mottier's atelier?"

"Directly to the atelier of Mme. Mottier, Jean-Louis. Aunt Gwyneth's driver, Guy, will take us to lunch at *Chez Michel.* After lunch, my friend Clarissa and I will take a Hackney to our afternoon appointment, and I shall be home about five o'clock."

"So, what is the afternoon appointment you don't want me to know about?"

"Oh, it is nothing scandalous, Jean-Louis. It is another dress shop appointment, and I don't want you to be bored."

"Just the same, Bri, your father pays me quite well to look after you, and I will have time after I pick him up at his office to return here to prepare for tea with Sir John. I will collect you at a little past four. Where shall I meet you?"

Realizing that she had lost the battle, Bri acquiesced. "Mlle. Bellerobe's shop on Portobello Road—"

Jean-Louis' response stopped her abruptly in the middle of her directions.

"*Foutre!* That is not the part of town you should be in alone. I shall arrange for your father to return home another way. I shall not let you out of my sight today."

Bri blinked in a rare moment of submission, struck dumb as he closed the carriage door.

Jean-Louis bounded up the outside steps of the townhouse and, in a few brief words,

Bri assumed he instructed Thompson to make other arrangements for the earl's transportation for the day.

CHAPTER SEVEN

Saturday, March 9, 1811 – James & Co., Bankers
Nashmir

Elegantly attired as usual, Nashmir nodded to the attendant standing at the huge imposing doors to James & Co. Not quite sure what to do, the attendant hesitated, and then opened the door for the unfamiliar visitor. Nashmir entered the impressive entry foyer with a determined step. Reaching the lone desk at the center of the foyer, he informed the serious-looking gentleman seated at the desk of his purpose: "I have an urgent message for Mr. Edward James."

Extending his hand to take the message, the clerk said, "I will see that he gets it immediately."

"I have been instructed to await his reply."

"Very well. I will summon Mr. Duncan." The clerk motioned to a sitting area to the right of the desk. "You may wait over there."

"No, thank you. I prefer to stand."

The gentleman in the reception area rang a bell three times, and a man Nashmir assumed to be Mr. Duncan emerged, somewhat irritated. Glancing at Nashmir for a moment, he directed his gaze toward the clerk. "What is it?" His tone bordered on petulance.

"Mr. Duncan, this…gentleman has an urgent message for Mr. Edward James and has been instructed to wait for a reply." The clerk handed the note to Duncan. Without comment, Duncan turned on his heel and headed down the long hallway. In less than a minute,

Edward appeared in the hallway, his long stride forcing Duncan to scamper breathlessly behind him to catch up, calling out, "But when will you return, sir? What shall I do about your other appointments?"

"First, I do not know, and second, cancel and reschedule them." Edward spoke in a calm, matter-of-fact manner. He extended his hand. "I am Edward James, Mr.—?"

"Nashmir, Mr. James. Very kind of you to respond so quickly. Shall we be on our way?"

Gesturing for Nashmir to lead, Edward followed him out of the bank and into the Ravenshire-crested carriage.

Inside, Edward tilted his head toward the high-bunned stranger. "You must be the specialist in herbal treatments that Lord Ravenshire mentioned. It is my father whom you will be seeing this afternoon."

"Correct. It has been my privilege to study among many master herbalists in Asia. I continue to study and correspond with my teachers and others I have met through the years. The mind must be in harmony with the body. You have traveled widely, I understand."

"Yes, I believe travel is essential to one's education and maturity. Nashmir, I have been unsuccessful in persuading my father to seek alternatives to the medical treatments offered by doctors in the *ton*. I am greatly relieved that he is taking the suggestion of his old friend, Lord Ravenshire, to avail himself of your healing arts. In general, my father makes a show of listening to advice, but rarely takes it. I believe that his newfound attitude of receptivity is due to two factors: his respect for Lord Ravenshire's opinion and his own despair at the rapidly deteriorating state of his health. I pray it is not too late. I should hate to lose him." Edward leveled his gaze at the Tibetan.

"No doubt." The eastern healer was aware of the veiled threat in Edward's voice. "Nature can heal, Mr. James. I believe that all illness can be cured by nature and meditation, but part of the cure is in believing. Most cannot accept their own responsibility for curing their ills. Your father's stomach pain could be caused by several factors. I am not a medical doctor, nor do I pretend to act in such a capacity. However, I have been a participant in some extraordinary cases of healing, and I hope that I will be able to help your father. I cannot assure you that I can help your father cure himself, but if nothing else," he added softly, "I *can* assure you that I can alleviate his pain without decreasing his mental acuity."

"The physicians in the *ton* have brought him nothing but false hope as the pain increases."

They ended their dialogue just as the carriage pulled in front of the building housing the offices of Gyfford & Wexford, Solicitors. Edward bid Nashmir farewell.

***

Edward

Entering the gray stone building, Edward proceeded directly to Sir Paul's office. He noted that the stone walls were decorated with ancient tapestries. *It is probably no coincidence that the decor suggests a castle of old. A sense of history and solid grounding instills confidence in clients.* He walked to the receiving desk and announced himself. "Edward James to see Sir Paul."

"Yes, sir, we've been expecting you." The clerk behind the desk motioned to a young man of military bearing standing to his left. "Show Mr. James to Sir Paul's office."

"Please follow me, sir."

Edward ascended the staircase close on the heels of the young man. At the top of the stairs, a seating area was flanked by doors on each side. His guide opened the door on the right.

The outer office was paneled in walnut, with deep burgundy carpeting and matching burgundy leather chairs in the waiting area. Multi-paned windows overlooked a courtyard below, where flowering trees were in bud. This scene was a striking contrast to the bustling commercial street on which the building was located.

A wiry and unusually florid gentleman sat at a large desk. He raised his eyes from his careful recording work and rose to his feet. "Mr. James, I presume?"

Edward nodded.

The clerk knocked on the door to the inner office and opened the door. "Mr. James has arrived."

Looking up from their papers, Lord Ravenshire and Sir Paul stood, acknowledging Edward with a nod.

"Thank you," said Sir Paul to the functionary as he closed the door quietly. The three of them were now alone.

***

Saturday, March 9, 1811 – Lord Ravenshire's Carriages
Bri

Jean-Louis signaled the young footman that he would help Bri into the carriage and waved him to jump on the back riding rail. The Frenchman held the door for Bri and leaned in before he closed it. "Are you certain there is a traitor at the trading company?"

"Listening outside the study door again?" Bri knew nothing was ever hidden from Jean-Louis. "No, I am not certain. That is why more research needs to be completed. My instincts tell me something is wrong."

"So now you are the huntress. Instinct drives survival. Keep your prey in your sights, but at a distance." The Frenchman slammed the door, causing her to jump. "You never know what is waiting around the corner."

"You are a most exasperating man." As Bri's carriage pulled away from their townhouse in Mayfair, Bri trusted that her father would take her recommendations seriously.

The potential fraud did not threaten the survival of the trading company. The Ravenshire estates were vast, productive and self-sufficient. The lands would remain intact in the event of war or political turmoil. Only Ravenshire Forest was technically given under grant of the crown, which could be revoked. All other lands and Ravenshire Castle were owned outright. The trading company would not be bankrupted even by major theft because Lloyd's of London had issued a commercial policy protecting Wyndward Trading against all hazards, including internal fraud. But the estates had been passed on to her father from generations of ancestors, while the trading company was his own creation, a marriage of adventure with commerce.

In the beginning, she'd been told, many sneered at her father, then a viscount, for engaging in commerce. As his enterprise grew, however, they became jealous but eventually, respectful. Few of his peers had done much but live off their family fortunes, or, she thought wryly, their wives' fortunes. *I should hate to marry a hanger-on. I would rather live alone.*

She had often imagined her ideal man. Growing up, her friends laughed at her list of requirements. The perfect man did not necessarily have to be handsome, just attractive in his own way. An intellectual who could keep up with her love of literature and ideas, but also a man of adventure, like her father, who was not as parochial as most of the foppish men of the *ton,* ridiculing other cultures and ways of life as inferior and barbaric. He should have a sense of humor and see a woman as his equal partner, not his possession. Knowledge of the arts and music would be expected. He should love children and treat everyone with kindness and respect. And it would be divine if he could waltz. It was still quite daring to waltz in Society, but to Bri it looked like such a glorious swirl. She hoped that at Lady Elisabeth's ball a waltz or two might be played. Analyzing her thoughts, she was stunned to realize that she was looking forward to the opening ball of the Season on Thursday, and the Masquerade Ball at her grandmother's palace mid-way through the Season. *Am I being seduced by the glamour of it all?*

The carriage stopped suddenly, and Bri was jolted from her reverie. Surprised, she looked through the window to see what had happened. Jean-Louis was lifting what appeared to be an injured dog off the street.

"Jean-Louis, what happened?" She opened the door, horrified that their carriage might have been responsible for hurting the dog.

The Frenchman brought the suffering animal to lie on the bench next to Bri. "Sorry for the jolt. I had to pull up hard on the reins when I saw him lying there. He's been hit by another carriage. I think his leg is broken."

Bri's heart was torn by the dog's plaintive cries. He was an unidentifiable mixed terrier breed with a black and white spotted coat. Even in pain, he seemed loving and altogether too friendly to be living on the cold streets of London. *He will have a home now. I will see to it.*

"Where can we get his leg attended to?"

Jean-Louis tilted his head down the street. "Dr. St. Cloud is just around the corner. He's made a specialty of caring for small pets and he is much sought after by Society. In his case, however, it is not because he fawns over the rich. It is that his competence is unquestioned."

"Then we must deliver this poor creature into his care immediately."

The Frenchman closed the door and climbed back up into the driver's seat.

"You'll be all right, little friend."

The dog's brown eyes looked at her with what she believed was understanding.

Jean-Louis pulled up in front of a small shop: *Dr. St. Cloud, Veterinary Care for Small Pets.* After opening the door for Bri, the former trapper gently lifted the injured dog and carried him into Dr. St. Cloud's shop. Amid various shelves of pet collars and other ancillary items, Bri noticed special types of food were marked "Made Especially for Dogs and Cats." *I must learn more about this innovative veterinarian.*

The doctor looked up from behind the counter, examining a kitten. "Put him on the counter."

"We think this dog has a broken leg."

Holding the kitten in his hands, the doctor turned toward Bri, "Would you mind holding this kitten? She is not sick, just a stray who's recently lost her mother."

Bri held out her hands to accept the tiny gray, black and orange calico.

Dr. St. Cloud carefully examined the dog and confirmed the Frenchman's suspicion. "Broken leg. I must set this, immobilize it and let him rest a few hours here. Can you pick your dog up later this afternoon?"

Bri leaned forward. "He's not mine. He ran in front of our carriage. I will take him home with me. And this little kitten? May we offer her a home also?"

"I've been thinking of starting a little adoption service for stray animals. You can be my first success."

Giving him her calling card, Bri agreed to pick up both animals later. Reading her name from the calling card, Dr. St. Cloud said, "Good day, Lady Gabriella Wyndward."

"And to you, Dr. St. Cloud."

Before she climbed back into the carriage, Bri turned to Jean-Louis. "How did you know of this place?"

"I know everything. I thought you knew that by now. Do I not drive the streets of London every day?" He shut the door with a thud.

Bri frowned with regret and remained silent. *I've offended him.*

Within a few minutes, they pulled up in front of Mme. Mottier's salon, and Bri could see Aunt Gwyneth through the front window, examining some fabric. "We'll be here about two hours, and then we're going to *Chez Michel* for lunch, where Lady Clarissa von Dusterberg will be meeting us."

Jean-Louis helped her exit the carriage. "Very well, Lady Gabriella. I shall await your command." He bowed from the waist and gestured toward the salon's elegant windowed doors.

Bri rolled her eyes at him. "Behave." *When he calls me Lady Gabriella instead of Bri, it means he's annoyed with me.*

Entering the shop, Bri was contrite. "Aunt Gwyneth, I'm sorry I'm a bit late, but we found an injured dog in the street and had to take him to a veterinarian on the way here." Bri hugged her aunt.

"Will the dog recover?"

"Yes, but he needs to stay at the doctor's for a few hours while his leg is set and the doctor can observe him. We'll have a new friend at home, or two, because I also agreed to adopt a little kitten that the doctor found on his doorstep."

"Good. I've always believed that Henry needed another canine companion after he lost Homer." A wistful look came over her face. "That retriever so loved the sea." Gwyneth turned to the patient dressmaker. "Mme. Mottier, please let me introduce you to my niece, Lady Gabriella Wyndward. As I just mentioned, she is most urgently in need of a gown for Lady Elisabeth's ball. Further, she must have several others for the balance of the Season."

"But Lady Elisabeth's ball is Thursday! Less than a week? *C'est impossible!*"

"But we simply must have something for my niece to wear." Aunt Gwyneth scanned the room. "Have not you something that is already made?"

Sniffing in disdain, Mme. Mottier retorted, "We are not a *salon de prêt-à-porter.* All of our creations are made to order, and it takes at least two weeks to finish a garment properly." Mme. Mottier took her new client's arm. "Come. I have been experimenting with a few new styles as samples, and I think they might be the right size. Let's go into my workroom."

The dressmaker Mottier led Bri, followed by Gwyneth, through the front room of the atelier to the spacious back rooms where a large sewing and draping studio was in operation. Several seamstresses were at work on various creations. *Too late for Lady Elisabeth's ball.* There were many balls throughout the Season, so multiple gowns were needed. Bri regretted being so disdainful of the need to be properly clothed, and started to fear it was too late and that she would embarrass Aunt Gwyneth and her father by having to decline the invitation to the ball at the last minute.

They approached one seamstress who was diligently applying seed pearls by hand, outlining a pale green moiré bodice with the tiny pearls and also ornamenting the edges of the puffed sleeves that looked as though they might fall slightly off-shoulder. It was a lovely dress, and more daring than Bri thought Mme. Mottier would create. Bri was very attracted to the gown. A small ruffle around the neckline and at the bottom of the sleeves gave it a feminine flair. The train could be pinned up for dancing.

The couturière lifted the moiré to inspect the beadwork. "This gown was ordered by a new client, but she has not paid the required deposit, and it has been a month since I have heard from her. My policy is to hold garments for regular customers, but she is not one." Mme. Mottier petted Lady Gwyneth's arm. "But your aunt has been one of my favorite customers for so many years, that I think we can fit it to you. This garment will perfectly complement your auburn hair, green eyes and unblemished fair complexion."

This woman flatters overmuch, but I like the dress.

"Wonderful!" Gwyneth sighed, visibly relieved that Bri would be suitably garbed at the Lady Elisabeth's ball. "Do you think this dress is a trifle too revealing?"

The dressmaker appeared indignant. "It is in fashion, Madame la Comtesse."

Gwyneth smiled. "It will look stunning on you, Bri."

"I even went so far as to put the moiré fabric on some matching slippers. Would you care to try them?"

"I feel like Cinderella," laughed Bri. *Maybe I will enjoy this ball.*

"Micheline," said Mme. Mottier, "*la jeune fille desire essayer cette robe.*"

"*Oui, Madame la Ccomtesse,*" said Micheline, and tied off the last stitch, handing the dress to her employer.

"Lady Gabriella, you may go behind the screen in the corner to try on the dress, and we will then make adjustments to fit.

Bri dutifully followed the dressmaker's instructions, and removed her periwinkle outfit carefully, which the *couturière* gently hung over the screen. She examined it and nodded approvingly of its workmanship. Micheline held the moiré dress over Bri's head while she slipped it on.

"Come out now," ordered the dressmaker, "so that I can check the fit."

Gesturing to Bri to stand in front of a mirror, the still handsome Mme. Mottier, *d'un certain age,* as they said in France, walked slowly around her new client. She pulled here, pinched there. "I think that we can adjust everything with the ribbon in the back." The gown was a perfect fit, and even the seamstresses, who were used to seeing beautiful Society women and lovely fabrics, murmured that Bri looked exquisite.

Bri was not sure she recognized herself in the mirror. Although enamored of color and style, her transformation stunned her.

"You look glorious, Bri."

"I don't recognize myself."

Her aunt brought her hand to her heart. "If only your mother could be here to see you in your first ball gown."

Mme. Mottier appeared with the shoes, and Micheline held them while Bri slid her feet into the slippers. Closing the sale, the *couturière* said, "We can create a matching green velvet reticule and perhaps a ribbon and feathers for your hair, with some of the petite pearls, eh, Micheline?"

"Ah, oui Madame. C'est bien."

"And do you have long white gloves, my dear? We have some in the front of the shop."

"Yes, I do need those. Probably a few pair for the Season. Are there special undergarments I should purchase?"

"Indeed, there are. Silk is best under these delicate fabrics," indicating the most expensive alternative. Both Bri and Gwyneth were quite prepared to take the bait.

"There will be many balls this Season, Lady Gabriella. Perhaps we should look at fabrics for some other evenings. Now that I know you fit my sample measurements, we can work quickly." She gestured to her newest client to return to the front of the salon, where they ascended the staircase to the private viewing room. They entered a chamber with comfortable chairs and mirrors, and Micheline brought in a selection of elegant fabrics. Bri and Gwyneth selected two that were quite striking against Bri's hair. One was an aqua raw silk overdress with a white silk chemise. Another style was presented, a single dress of pale blue brocade with a fleurs-de-lis pattern.

Suddenly realizing the timing of the weekend balls, she asked, "When can these be ready? I will need another gown for next week and more for the following weeks." *I have come under the spell of the Season.* The ways of the *ton* loomed large at this moment. *I do not want to look out of place at the balls.*

Mme. Mottier rang for Micheline, and said, "I just thought of another I can provide. It was originally made for a customer who changed her mind. You must accept it as is, however, as there is no time to change it."

Micheline retrieved the gown, which was a burnt orange silk that nearly matched her hair color. Bri slipped it on and it fit almost perfectly.

While the seamstress pinned a couple of small changes, the dressmaker said, "This will do very well."

Bri smiled in agreement.

"We will deliver the green gown on Wednesday and this one the following week. The others can be delivered to you in two weeks."

Relieved, Bri thanked the couturier. "Madame, I can no longer think clearly. I must have slippers as well." She sighed as she sank down into the cushions of the large sofa.

"May I also suggest a velvet cloak for these ball gowns? A midnight blue would complement all the colors you have selected today, and since it is such a simple cut, we can have it ready by Wednesday as well. We will also send along matching shoes, reticules and hair ornaments."

"Oh, yes, that would be ideal," said Bri. "Would you be so kind as to send a bill with the delivery?"

"But of course."

Gwyneth leaned forward. "Do you see why I was insisting on this visit for weeks?"

"Please don't scold me. I see how wrong I was." Bri turned to Mme. Mottier. "I truly appreciate your willingness to meet our schedule, Madame."

"We serve at your pleasure. It was a delight to meet you, my dear." The dressmaker tilted her head toward Gwyneth. "I trust your gowns were all to your liking?"

"Yes, Madame. You were so clever to maintain my measurements along with a book on my past gowns so that you could accommodate my requirements so efficiently."

"*De rien.*" Mme. Mottier bowed her head in acknowledgment of the compliment.

"I can breathe much easier now, knowing that my Bri will be the belle of the ball."

As they rose from the divan, assistants materialized with their cloaks, and they headed down the staircase toward the front door.

Lady Penelope arrived just as they reached the foyer.

Bri warmed to her new friend. "Lady Penelope, I was going to send you a note later. My maid is also an excellent hairdresser. May I send her to your home to help with your hair for the ball next Thursday as an apology for being a bit full of myself at tea yesterday? I'm afraid I was quite dreadful."

"You were not at all rude, Lady Gabriella, and I do so admire your hair. After all, it is the first ball of the Season and it is one's first impression that is so important. So, yes, I would welcome her assistance. Here is my calling card. You may tell her to arrive at two o'clock."

"Perfect. Her name is Jane Anne Kelly."

Lady Penelope raised an eyebrow. "Irish?" She shrugged as if it mattered not. "And don't worry about the tea. When we get to know each other better, we can laugh about it. I watched my older sister go through her Season, so I had some advance training. If I hadn't seen Baron Beauchamp, I would be thinking in exactly the same way." Sighing, she added, "Now, I must contrive to get him to sign my dance card!"

Momentarily betraying her fears about the ball, that no one would want to sign her dance card, Bri looked stricken, but she quickly regained her composure. "Good day, Lady Penelope!"

"Thank you, and good day to you both!" Penelope continued into the salon.

Gwyneth told Guy, her driver, to meet her at Michel's. Then she climbed into Bri's carriage.

"I hope my gesture toward Lady Penelope creates some good will to make up for the my rudeness."

"It seems to have worked. She will be the easiest to placate."

She gripped the door handle to steady herself. *How will I get through this minefield of manners?*

CHAPTER EIGHT

Saturday, March 9, 1811 – *Chez Michel*
Bri

Chez Michel was located in the oldest part of the city, and attracted both the educated men of commerce, such as bankers, solicitors and trading titans whose offices were nearby, as well as wealthy ladies of leisure. Its magnificent decor evoked a French drawing room of the previous century. Windows reached to a height of twenty feet, draped in elegant brocades in muted tones of pale blue, complementing the faux marble finish on the walls. Oil portraits of frequent patrons in period garb decorated the walls.

The proprietor, Michel d'Anjou, knew the precise mix of antiques and flattery to engage his Society clientele. The room was circled with booths, the preferred seating, while various-sized tables in the center of the room would host those who had neglected to book a table in advance. As a result, the booths held mostly women, whose leisure permitted advance booking, while the center tables seated male habitués, whose schedules were not as predictable as those of the ladies of Society.

As Henry, Sir Paul and Edward James entered, Michel motioned toward Gwyneth, Bri and Clarissa, who were absorbed in their menus at the booth directly under a likeness of Henry's as a courtier of Louis XIV. Before being shown to their table, Henry led the others through the room to make introductions.

"Don't try to memorize the menu, Lady Clarissa. Michel changes it weekly." Henry smiled as he caught the ladies by surprise.

"Henry, what are you doing here? Will you join us?"

"No, Gwyneth, we will not intrude on your lunch. We would bore you."

"Father, please join us." Bri smiled and nodded to the other two gentlemen. She knew Sir Paul, and the other man looked vaguely familiar. He was older than she, but closer to her age than her father's. *Who is this man?* Slightly taller than her father's height of just under six feet, the young man had black hair. His light gray eyes regarded her with an intensity that she had never previously experienced. She felt strange physical sensations down to her fingertips. *Perhaps he is dangerous, and my instincts are warning me to be careful.*

"First let me introduce you." Henry swept his arm around the group. "Gentlemen, please greet my sister Gwyneth, Comtesse de Merbeau, my daughter, Gabriella and her friend, Lady Clarissa von Dusterberg, daughter of the count and former ambassador. Sir Paul, my solicitor, and Edward James, Sir John's son."

Edward glanced at the wall and back at the seated ladies. "I see that you dine beneath a very distinguished courtier who bears a striking resemblance to Lord Ravenshire."

"My brother cuts quite the dashing figure in lace and satin."

"The wig is my favorite part." *Bri continued to stare at Edward.*

Henry laughed. "Gio painted my face and stance, and added the clothes later. I was rather unprepared for the result, but it amuses my sister and daughter, so I abide it with a stiff upper lip."

Sir Paul cleared his throat. "As one cannot risk discussing business in Michel's, we should probably be a boring lot at a table by ourselves. Why don't we join the ladies, Lord Ravenshire?"

Edward seconded the proposition. "A splendid idea, Sir Paul."

The earl nodded. "The decision is made. We shall join you."

The ladies adjusted their seating slightly to let the gentlemen join them in the large booth. Bri sat between Gwyneth and Clarissa, and Edward was flanked by Sir Paul and Henry. The waiter brought additional silverware and glasses for the gentlemen, pouring each a glass of the wine Clarissa had suggested.

"It is a Riesling, and may be too sweet for you gentlemen, I'm afraid."

"Nonsense, Lady Clarissa. It's delightful." Henry suggested a toast. "To the lovely ladies!"

The others echoed his words.

Bri took a sip of wine. "What are you gentlemen meeting about?"

"Now, Lady Gabriella, why worry your pretty little head about men's business meetings?"

Sir Paul's dismissive tone evoked an immediate reaction in Bri. Her cheeks slowly turned a deep crimson, revealing anger and envy that she had been excluded.

Henry recognized the signs and cautioned Sir Paul. "My daughter is conversant with the responsibilities of her inheritance and keen to delve into all aspects of our activities."

Dumbfounded, Sir Paul could only stammer his apology to Bri, adding, "It's just that you're so attractive, I didn't think that you would be interested in such things."

"I trust you will adjust your thinking in the future, Sir Paul." Bri's tone was icy.

She glared at her father.

"I will review the details of our discussions with you later, Bri, *in private*."

Furious, Bri fumed and picked up her menu to hide her expression.

"We will handle everything in your best interest, Lady Gabriella," said Edward.

She put down the menu. "Oh, will you, Mr. James? I do not believe I recall asking you to *handle* anything for me."

The tension was broken by the waiter, who announced, "Good day, ladies and gentlemen. Our *soupe du jour* is cream of asparagus, and our featured entrée is warm goat cheese and roast chicken over spinach. Have you made your selections?"

Bri spoke first. "I shall have the special." She realized too late that her anger had caused her to violate protocol by ordering before her aunt.

Gwyneth ignored her niece's *faux pas*. "I'd like the consommé and the fillet of sole, please."

Clarissa concurred. "That sounds lovely to me, too."

Sir Paul requested the pork loin with vegetable soup.

Edward ordered next. "I would like to try your special entrée, but with vichyssoise."

Henry nodded his head toward Edward. "You must try the late comte's vichyssoise some evening for dinner. It is simply the best recipe on earth." Turning to the waiter, he said, "The special for me."

Bri changed the subject. "Has anyone heard about the new operetta, *The Princess?* It will open at the Theatre Royal Haymarket in two weeks. It's been reworked for English audiences after a successful run in Germany several years ago."

Henry wrinkled his brow. "I believe I heard about it at my club last week. Someone's trying to raise funds to extend the run. Apparently the costs were not accurately forecast."

Edward picked up on the subject, "Yes, we have clients who have been approached to invest. Naturally, we have advised them to safeguard their funds. Charity donations should not be dressed up as business opportunities."

Bri's annoyance simmered into a challenge. "Why would you say that, Mr. James? At the price of seats these days, the theatre may not be such a bad investment. In fact, the number of visitors to London is increasing each year, and it is my understanding that going to the theatre is a primary reason for visiting. An enjoyable play can bring entertainment as well as education, for we see others handling problems in dramatic focus. Since the play was successful in Germany, it stands to reason that it would be successful here. In fact, I think it quite short-sighted of you to dismiss such an investment. I would have expected more from an astute banker, though perhaps you are as yet too inexperienced to evaluate investment opportunities. Isn't it true you've been long absent from London and only recently assumed your duties at the bank?"

Edward's face initially flushed with anger, but his cheeks returned to their normal appearance within a matter of seconds. "Perhaps I deal in reality instead of fantasy."

"Bri," scolded Henry, "don't deliberately provoke Edward. Our advisors should not always agree with us, as they would not then be advisors, but parrots."

This exchange was interrupted by the delivery of the soup. Even Bri was grateful for the diversion and sipped in silence for a few minutes before Henry nodded toward Clarissa. "Are you familiar with this operetta, Lady Clarissa? What is the libretto?"

Clarissa's tone calmed tempers. "The libretto is based on an old

German fairy tale about a princess and a prince who fall in love, but fate intervenes. She believes her beloved prince has been killed, only to find out he's been enchanted and lives, waiting for the spell to be broken, which, of course, it is. They live happily ever after."

"Romantic rubbish." Sir Paul shook his head. "Now that *is* fantasy as opposed to reality. Keep things in perspective, I say. On the other hand," he added, "this type of story could be very appealing to young ladies, and therefore to young men who want to please young ladies. Perhaps the *ton* will be flocking to see this musical play as part of the courting process."

"Precisely." Bri brightened. "I think we should go to see it for ourselves, Father, when it opens."

"You've trapped me, Bri. Very well. Lady Clarissa, will you be able to join us at the opening?"

"I would be delighted, Lord Ravenshire. If you are truly interested, there is a rehearsal and some auditions Monday night. You'll have the best and only seats in the house! My former music teacher has composed the score. I was able to give him a melody myself, based on a song I heard in Madagascar. It is quite exotic and lovely."

"So, you clearly have an interest in this play, Lady Clarissa," Edward said. "I must apologize for speaking in haste earlier. If I may, Lord Ravenshire, I would like to accompany you and arrange for dinner following the play as a measure of my regret for being too outspoken. Will you permit me this gesture?"

"Of course." Henry quashed Bri's unvoiced objection. "Can you join us, Sir Paul?"

"Alas, no. I have a previous engagement."

Henry took a sip of wine. "Perhaps you can see the official performance. What time does the rehearsal begin?"

"Seven o'clock."

"Very good, then we shall meet at the theatre at quarter to seven. Do you need us to give you a ride, Lady Clarissa?"

"No, Lord Ravenshire, I shall arrive earlier to meet with the composer on the final scoring. Since this is just a rehearsal, he has not yet hired the full cast and orchestra, so he will be accompanying on the pianoforte."

Edward leaned forward. "So you are not just an operetta admirer, you are a patron."

The waiter arrived with their entrées, and the group once again fell into silence as they ate.

"The patron, right now, Mr. James. Or more precisely, my father is the only patron. Herr Kramer, the composer, is my music instructor."

Before Edward could respond, Gwyneth waved the chef over to their booth. "Michel, you never disappoint us."

"Ah, Madame la Comtesse, you are too kind." The chef beamed, clearly addicted to basking in the praise of his guests. "May I offer you our magnificent light dessert of spun sugar? We have just perfected it, and it is incomparable." He put his fingers to his lips and kissed them. "We have chocolate and cherry. What is your preference?" Meeting undecided gazes, he announced, "Well, then, I will bring three of each and you will share the tastes." Michel turned with a flourish and headed toward the kitchen

Gwyneth glanced at Clarissa. "This theatre excursion will be exciting. I have always loved the opera. My late husband was a composer of some note. The other night you startled me with the descriptions of your clandestine visits to the theatre district. I was concerned for your safety as a young girl alone, although it may have sounded as if I were negative on the theatre itself."

"I understand, Lady Gwyneth. I appreciate your concern."

Bri noticed that the gentlemen exchanged eye contact, but made no comment. *Wise.*

While they were finishing Michel's *chef d'oeuvre* of spun sugar, Aunt Gwyneth kept the conversation on a non-confrontational level.

Pulling out his pocket watch, Henry announced that it was quarter to two o'clock. Bri knew that it was time to leave for their visit to Mlle. Bellerobe's, but she was intensely curious as to what her father and the others would be doing after lunch. She could not bear the thought of their discussing her father's accounts outside of her presence.

"I shall attend to Nashmir and his preparations for your father's visit this afternoon, Young James," said Henry. "I trust that you and Sir Paul will carry out my instructions."

Edward nodded. "Of course, Lord Ravenshire."

"Absolutely, Lord Ravenshire," echoed Sir Paul. "We should have an answer within a few months."

"The sooner the better." Henry and the other gentlemen slid out of the booth. Henry offered his hand to his sister as she maneuvered her way to the edge of the booth. Sir Paul extended his hand to Clarissa.

Taking the offered hand of Mr. James, Bri tried to maintain her composure. She was still angry at him and offended in the extreme that he would express views that contradicted her own. Stubborn and spoiled as only children tended to be, she was used to getting her way in most situations. Bri felt her hand tremble when Mr. James touched it and silently cursed herself for betraying any weakness toward him. In truth, she felt almost dizzy being so close to him and wondered if he would catch her if she fainted. As they left *Chez Michel*, the cool spring air brought her back to her senses.

Jean-Louis was waiting with Guy, speaking their native language. Everyone understood French, so it was not considered rude.

"Gwyneth, might your driver take me home after you, as I have promised Jean-Louis to Bri? That is to say," he added in an amused tone, "Jean-Louis has appointed himself her guardian for the day."

"Why do you need a guardian, Lady Gabriella? I thought you were totally self-sufficient." Edward's face feigned innocence.

Bri dismissed his concern. "My appointments are none of your concern."

Lady Clarissa softened her friend's answer. "We're shopping for ball gowns."

Henry added, "Near Portobello Road."

"What?" Edward nearly shouted. "That is not a safe area. You are foolhardy and may need more protection than a mere driver."

"Jean-Louis is no 'mere driver' as you describe him, Mr. James. He is one of the fiercest warriors I have ever come across in my travels. He killed a polar bear in French Canadian territory with naught but a dagger. I first met him when I was setting up the fur trade. He is invaluable to me and has saved my life on more than one occasion. Bri is safe with Jean-Louis."

"Forgive me, Lord Ravenshire. Once again I spoke in haste. I must apologize for my temper."

Bri directed her gaze at the banker. "Indeed. You must have to do it often."

Henry's eyes darted between Bri and Edward. "Nothing to apologize for, Young James. I appreciate your sense of duty and obligation toward women. Your concern for their safety is to be expected. And it is true that most drivers would not be up to the challenge, but Jean-Louis is a unique individual."

"It has been a most instructive day." Turning toward the comtesse, Edward bowed his head slightly. "It was a pleasure to meet you, Madame la Comtesse." Bowing his head toward Bri, he added, "And you, Lady Gabriella. I've enjoyed seeing you again. I regret my shortcomings as a luncheon companion and hope to redeem myself in your eyes in the future."

Disgusted, Bri said, "You may try, Mr. James."

"I've become a better Whist player. Do you remember that you beat me the last time we saw each other?"

"Did I? I don't remember. I beat everyone at Whist." *He is just as arrogant as he was that day I beat him.*

Jean-Louis appeared, and held the door for Bri and Clarissa. Waving to the men, Clarissa said, "Until Monday night!"

The others waved and dispersed to their respective carriages except Edward, who could walk to his office from *Chez Michel.* He politely declined Sir Paul's offer of a ride.

Edward watched until the carriages turned the corner and were out of sight before he headed toward the bank.

***

Edward

As he strolled along the street, Edward's thoughts swirled. *Lady Gabriella is a beauty, but a bit shrewish. Why do men marry, if women are so difficult?*

Although her temper repelled him, he felt compelled to face the truth: he was captivated by her passionate nature. Her analysis was flawed, of course, thinking that a musical play was an appropriate investment, but he had challenged her, and perhaps losing her temper was just her way of getting his attention. *Most ladies find me attractive, and Lady Gabriella is probably no exception. I must be on my guard, though. She has a way as no other woman to rouse my temper.*

To question a man's judgment was unheard of in Society. He would have to ask his father to have a word with Lord Ravenshire. Such easily aroused anger in the young lady did not bode well for the complex and cool-tempered skills necessary to direct commercial affairs. That task was unsuited to the weaker sex.

Still, Lady Gabriella Wyndward was a disorienting woman. Edward was well aware of her feminine lure, and wondered as to the shape of her body hidden by the current style of dress. As he had guided her out of the restaurant, he had placed his hand on her back and felt her firm young body beneath the frock. It had excited him physically, a sensation to which he was accustomed. But in this case, his mental state was also aroused by her. *Perhaps arguing is an aphrodisiac. Her ability to fence with her mind sets her apart from her Society peers. Perhaps she is the woman I should marry.*

She was beautiful and from a good family, and she could get him out of this tedious cycle of balls and dinner parties to meet the proper young woman. Once married, it would be inappropriate for her to act as Lord Ravenshire's agent, and she could occupy herself with running a household.

He would press his case with Lord Ravenshire Monday night, if he could get him alone. Surely the earl must be regretting his decision to make Lady Gabriella his agent, after today's unseemly outburst.

Perhaps sending her to the country after they married would be a solution, eliminating her from the account management process altogether. As her husband, she would have to obey him. Reaching the bank, Edward John Ashton James headed down the long hallway to his office, quite pleased with himself that he had solved the problem of Lady Gabriella Wyndward.

CHAPTER NINE

Saturday, March 9, 1811 – Interior of Lord Ravenshire's Carriage
Clarissa

In the carriage, Bri fumed. "That man is infuriating! He is an arrogant, self-absorbed, narrow-minded prig. Any woman who marries that man will regret it. Why did I ever agree to this Marriage Season?"

"He *did* try to apologize," said Clarissa. "He is quite handsome, and I think that you aroused his temper because he found you so attractive that he could not believe that you would not agree with him."

"Good looks pale in comparison to a good mind. I could never be attracted to a man with such a domineering manner. He is the type who would give orders to his wife!"

"Well, I am not as brave as you are when it comes to speaking my mind, but in the privacy of this carriage, I can tell you that you *are* attracted to him and it frightens you."

"I cannot be attracted to him, Clarissa." Bri's irritation continued to rise. "He is not a man that I would seek out for conversation, let alone love."

"We do not select those we love in a rational manner. The sparks that were flying between the two of you might ignite quite an *affaire d'amour*."

"Never! No matter what happens, I shall never have an *affaire d'amour*, as you put it, with that man."

Clarissa laughed at her friend's firm declaration. "I can hardly wait to hear about your first kiss."

Bri's cheeks became red with anger. "Why do you keep saying these things? Am I speaking to a deaf woman?"

"No, but I am conversing with a blind one. All of the rest of us at that table saw the attraction. You were so busy fighting your battle that you missed the fact that the war was over the minute you two looked into each other's eyes." Clarissa seemed amused by her own melodramatic rendition. "Stop fighting it. It will be divine to waltz with him at Thursday's ball. Do you think you will recognize him with a mask at the Masquerade Ball?" She answered her own question before Bri could respond. "Probably. It's a long way off."

"I will recognize his arrogance." Her tone revealed that she was not quite so sure of herself anymore. "I must admit, I was feeling a bit dizzy as he led me out the door, but I thought it was the dessert. Do you really think it could be love? Why would love disguise itself in argument? This is not the way I imagined romance. Although we have an understanding of financial matters in common, I shall have to beat him about the head to take me seriously."

"Remember that he is the product of Society. It is only to be expected that he be surprised and somewhat taken aback at your expertise."

"Oh, very well. Let us reserve judgment until we see what happens Monday at the theater. I must admit I am excited thinking about it! I shall be in his company all evening. Perhaps I *am* smitten."

Wistfully, Clarissa mused, "I wish I had a young man so handsome to dream about. But what if he did not love the theater? I am so drawn to it, yet I know it is considered risqué. The truth is my father has been unsuccessful in finding more backers. I do not want my father to lose part of his fortune due to indulging my dreams."

"Clarissa, as the unrecognized agent of my father's investment accounts, I am going to recommend that we take a small percentage of his monies, which actually is a substantial amount, to invest in new business ventures right here in London. By importing all these goods through his trading company, it seems to me that an interesting and lucrative sideline might be developing new companies. Your play may be just that type of investment." Bri appeared smug. "And Mr. Edward James, eminent banker, must do as I instruct, as Father is too big a client for the bank to refuse. All I have to do is convince Father.

What I will need from you are more financial details on the play. Can you have them ready Monday night?"

"Yes, I have prepared some papers that set forth the investment from the original plan that the composer presented to my father. I will bring them to the theatre. Your involvement in financial matters is quite unusual."

"And secret from all in the *ton* except you and my father's advisors." Looking out the window, Bri observed, "I see why the men were so concerned about our being in this area of town. These people on the side of the street look as though they have nothing, not even hope. Do you think they actually live on the streets?"

"So I have heard. We may be targets because of our wealth, so we are lucky to have Jean-Louis with us. "

"Why did Mlle. Bellerobe locate her shop in such an area?"

"The cost of stocking the shop was more than expected due to smuggling goods through the blockade, and the rents in the right part of town were too high. And, of course," said Clarissa in a more hushed voice, "her reputation preceded her, and some landlords would not rent to her."

"Well, maybe we can persuade some of those landlords who are our friends to revisit the issue. Look! I see the sign. It is just ahead."

The carriage pulled up in front of the shop. Under the hanging sign, a wide window was also painted with the shop's name: *Mlle. Bellerobe, Couturière Extraordinaire*. Bri stretched to see inside the store. "I expect that she *is* extraordinary, based on your description. I'm excited!"

As they exited the carriage, Jean-Louis held the door and scanned the immediate area. "I will wait out here for you. Do not wander from this store."

With a mock salute, Bri said, "Yes, sir," and then bowed.

***

Bri

Bri gestured to Clarissa to enter the salon first, as a doorman dressed in harlequin attire held the yellow door open. The multi-colored design also featured curled, pointed toe shoes and a rakish red beret. Epaulettes on the shoulders and brass buttons added a military flourish. Glancing sideways at Clarissa, she smiled, shrugged, and followed her in.

Entering the atelier, Bri admired the eclectic look of the furnishings. Unexpected elements worked well together. The same type of display cases and drawers as she had seen in Mme. Mottier's salon were in place, although they had clearly been designed for a different type of industry, and the old, worn wood gave an antique feel to the decor. Through yellow-and-blue printed chintz drapes came a woman younger than Mme. Mottier, with deep brown-black hair and a little too much rouge on her cheeks and lips. The combination of eyes outlined in heavy kohl and hair cut in a blunt style evoked an ancient Egyptian goddess. The woman's appearance presented a striking contrast to the demure buns and side curls of the women of the *ton*. For one of the few times in her life, Bri was at a loss for words.

"Welcome, Lady Clarissa." Mlle. Bellerobe spoke with a heavy French accent. "And this must be your friend, Lady Gabriella. What lovely hair, *ma chérie*. With the correct color palette, you could make an even more dramatic presentation."

"What do you mean by color palette?"

Taking one of each girl's arms, Mlle. Bellerobe led them through the curtain and into her salon, saying, "Well, *mes chères*, I believe that one's coloring determines the best colors to wear. For instance, our blonde Lady Clarissa cannot wear the deep jewel colors that I can, and likewise the pastels which shimmer on her would make you look quite ill, Lady Gabriella. It is a little game I play with myself, to design a series of colors in a palette that my clients should always seek, as well as those that they should always avoid. One must know one's own style and how to create the ideal image at first glance. I shall teach you both. Come along."

Nearly hypnotized by the French woman's manner, Bri and Clarissa listened mutely. Looking around, Bri understood Clarissa's description of walls of color. Huge swaths of fabric hung from hooks on the ceiling. *Walking through this multitude of hues, shades and tones of color is like being in the center of a diffused rainbow.*

"*Marie, viens ici avec la costume de Lady Clarissa.*" Mademoiselle's demand summoned a young woman who materialized from the folds of hanging fabric, holding a pale pink gown, trimmed with sparkling faceted beads around the neckline.

Clarissa gasped. "It's truly beautiful. The Austrian crystals look like diamonds, just as you promised. May I try it on?"

"But of course, we must make the final fitting. There is a screen in the corner. Your friend Lady Gabriella can help you out of your street clothes."

Momentarily caught off guard, Bri complied. *She is ordering me around as a Lady's maid.* She marveled at the dress. "Mlle. Bellerobe, this is truly a lovely creation. I now see what you mean about color. It is absolutely stunning on Lady Clarissa."

"*Naturellement,*" sniffed Mademoiselle. "For you, I would use fuchsia. Chinese powders from ground-up shells create this dye for silk. The same family of pinks and purples as the flower, but the appropriate shade for you. Very striking with your auburn hair. Not expected, and therefore more memorable."

Clarissa emerged from behind the screen and stood in front of the mirror as Mademoiselle and Marie adjusted the gown and the train. "Perfect," proclaimed Mademoiselle. "For your hair, we have a ribbon with a few more crystals. The shoes are also ready," she noted and called out, "*Marcel, les souliers de Lady Clarissa, s'il vous plaît.*"

A small, thin, middle-aged man appeared with a box which he held ceremoniously. As he opened it, Bri and Clarissa stared. Not only were the shoes covered in the same soft taffeta as the dress, but across the instep and on the heel there were bows with Austrian crystals in the center. Neither woman had ever seen such exquisitely beautiful slippers. With tears welling up in her eyes, Clarissa said, "Oh, Mademoiselle, you are a practitioner of magic. It is all so beautiful, beyond words."

"*Ah, oui,*" agreed Mademoiselle, smiling at the praise. "The other gowns will be ready for the next balls. You may have a choice at that time, but this is the one for Lady Elisabeth's ball on Thursday. You will look like a princess."

"Do you have any recommendations for me, Mademoiselle?" Bri strained to look beyond the draped-fabric walls that surrounded the particular section of the salon that they occupied.

Cocking her head to one side, Mlle. Bellerobe looked at Bri, squinted her eyes, looked up toward the ceiling, and then back at her client. "Follow me." While Marie prepared the pink ball gown for delivery, Clarissa and Bri followed Mademoiselle through a series of silk-divided sections like the one they had just been in, each designed around shades of color. They moved through yellow, green, pale blues, reds, blacks…every shade seemed to be represented. Finally, they came into an area draped in fuchsia and blue.

"I have a partially finished dress that a client left behind. She eloped to the Continent—how she managed to get there is a mystery of smugglers and bribery— and will probably not return, so it might be a fit for you, Lady Gabriella."

Marie reappeared, followed by another woman, as if in telepathic communication with Mademoiselle, with a midnight blue silk dress.

"Voilà!" Mademoiselle pointed to the screen in the corner.

Bri dutifully followed Mademoiselle's instructions, and Clarissa helped her put the dress on.

As Bri stepped out from behind the screen, Mademoiselle looked at her with a discriminating air, indicating with a whirl of her hand that Bri should turn around slowly in the dress. Once she had surveyed the lines of the garment, which had been cut on the bias with flair at the hem, Mademoiselle uttered a sound like, "Hmm."

A bit intimidated by the dressmaker's reaction, Bri looked at Clarissa who shrugged imperceptibly.

Mademoiselle missed nothing that transpired in her salon. "Ask questions. Don't be shy."

"I just didn't know what you meant by your 'Hmm'." *I feel like a foolish child.*

"I'm trying to decide what other colors would look best against your hair. Marie, bring me that new royal blue silk bolt from Paris and the striped one from Venice. Lady Gabriella, take off that dress and Julianna will bring another."

"Julianna, l'autre," ordered Mademoiselle.

Julianna returned with a fuchsia gown with puffed sleeves and a lightly-quilted silk bodice with pearl trim down the front panels.

Bri could not contain herself as she put on the second gown. "Mademoiselle, how do you import bolts of fabric from Paris and Venice through Napoleon's blockade?"

Mademoiselle tilted her head and stared at Bri. "Ask Jean-Louis."

Bri's head popped up. "You know Jean-Louis?"

"Everyone knows Jean-Louis, Lady Gabriella."

Another man delivered more bolts, and Mademoiselle selected the striped fuchsia, royal blue and white stripes of varying widths. From this bolt, the dressmaker pulled a long section of fabric, and began draping it over the fuchsia satin as an overdress with a tie under the empire gatherings under the bust line.

"The current rage is pastels, which only complement coloring like that of Lady Clarissa. Do you dare to be different, Lady Gabriella? To stand out?"

Clarissa laughed. "You are an astute judge of character, Mademoiselle."

The dressmaker continued to wave her arms, describing her vision. "We can add lace at the neckline and sleeves, just a *petite* ruffle, you understand, and use a fuchsia sash to tie it in the front in a bow with long ties, perhaps with tassels on the end." Thinking out loud, she added, "There are several possibilities here. We could create several combinations of these colors."

Setting down the length of striped silk, she picked up the bolt of royal blue silk. "We could embroider the dress in gold thread with *fleurs-de-lis* or some other design. Likewise, I have a bolt of," indicating with her hand to the assistant to fetch it, "gold silk for a sash."

Momentarily overwhelmed by the multiple options, Bri capitulated. "Make up whatever you think best. I leave their design to your judgment."

"*Bien.* Do you wish to have matching slippers for both gowns?"

"Why not?"

Clarissa twirled. "We will dazzle the men of the *ton* when we arrive in these gowns."

"That is the point, is it not? To dazzle and capture?"

Bri nodded. "I might as well dress as I like, for I fear that the men of Society are too tame for me, and quite incapable of sweeping me off my feet."

"Even your Mr. James?" Clarissa glanced at Bri out of the corner of her eye.

Ignoring Clarissa's comment, Bri bowed to Mademoiselle. "You are incomparable, Mlle. Bellerobe."

Mademoiselle shrugged. "*Oui.*"

Bri wondered if the colors would be too bold, but they looked so stunning in the salon that she abandoned caution. *My choice in clothes was a totally personal one and if Society disapproves, then so be it.*

The assistant returned with more selections. "Not necessary now, Jacques. Guide these young ladies through our maze to the front."

With a slight wave, she turned on her heel and disappeared among the hanging lengths of fabric.

Leading them, Jacques called out instructions over his shoulder. "To the left through the yellow silk...to the right through the white muslin...." Reaching the front of the shop, he added, "Will you need gloves, reticules, hair ornaments or undergarments?"

Embarrassed to hear a man mention undergarments, Bri blushed. "Whatever Mademoiselle thinks is appropriate will be acceptable. Here is my card. Please have her deliver the bill to my father's townhouse." Nodding, Jacques accepted the card, rang a small silver bell, and the harlequin-attired doorman opened the door for their exit.

Jean-Louis was standing outside the shop, casting a wary eye on the surrounding streets, maintaining a steady vigil during their sojourn at Mlle. Bellerobe's.

As Jean-Louis helped Bri and Clarissa into the carriage by Jean-Louis, Bri tilted her head toward him and scowled. "You know perfectly well who Mlle. Bellerobe is. Why didn't you tell me? How do you get these silks and luxurious fabrics to her?"

The Frenchman shrugged. "There are ways."

Bri shook her head in faux exasperation. "We must collect our new little dog and kitten on the way home. I should like for Clarissa to see that wonderful place."

"*Oui*. It is not far out of our way."

As they traversed the city, Bri related the tale of the injured dog and the abandoned kitten to Clarissa.

"Oh, how I would love a little kitten. Perhaps this doctor has found another for me to adopt."

"You can adopt this one, if you like. The puppy will probably keep me busy. The kitten is an adorable calico."

Clarissa beamed. "I can hardly wait to see her. Or it is a male?"

"I think it's a female."

Just at that moment, they pulled up in front of Dr. St. Cloud's store-front office.

Jean-Louis alighted from his driver's perch to open the carriage door for the two young ladies.

When Bri and Clarissa entered the veterinary office, the bell over the door announced their arrival. A voice called out, "I shall be right there." In the background, dogs barked, cats meowed and birds tweeted.

"Apparently Dr. St. Cloud has acquired more pets than I saw earlier this morning." Bri again examined the display of pet food on the shelves, wondering if it was better than the food scraps that most people served their animals.

Pushing aside the drapery that separated the inner office from the outer shop area, Dr. St. Cloud emerged. "Welcome back, Lady Gabriella. Your new pets await you. The puppy will need extra attention due to the broken leg, but it should be fully healed in about three weeks." Turning to Clarissa, he said, "And who is this young lady?"

As was customary, Bri made the introduction. "Lady Clarissa von Dusterberg, this is Dr. St. Cloud."

"Nicholas St. Cloud," added the doctor.

Clarissa extended her hand which he kissed lightly, in the Continental manner.

It was a normal gesture in Society when a man was introduced to a young lady, but Bri noticed that Clarissa seemed locked in a trance.

Bri broke the silence. "May I see my puppy now?"

Dr. St. Cloud smiled. "He's been patiently waiting. Please follow me." He led them through the curtains into a room with cages and an examining table. A young man stood nearby.

Taking him for the doctor's assistant, Bri's guess was confirmed when the doctor instructed him to unlock the puppy's cage.

"Here he is, Clarissa!" Bri reached out to take the splinted puppy into her arms. "I am going to call him Spotty." She glanced at the doctor. "Lady Clarissa would like to adopt the little kitten. I could not be so selfish as to take both pets when she so dearly wanted a kitten."

"I love cats myself, Lady Clarissa."

Clarissa blushed.

Unable to restrain her curiosity, Bri breached protocol. "Are you going to the ball next Thursday, Dr. St. Cloud?" *Her stomach wrenched as she realized her faux pas. What if he has not been invited?* Clarissa's face turned a deeper shade of crimson.

Spotty distracted Bri by licking her chin while she tried to come up with a reason to explain her blunder. "The ball would allow you to tell the *ton* about your adoption program."

"It is interesting that you should mention it. I received an invitation to the ball because my mother went to boarding school with Lady Elisabeth in Lausanne, but I hadn't decided whether or not to attend. If you two lovely young ladies would each save me a dance, then I *shall* attend."

Laughing, Bri nodded. "We accept, don't we, Clarissa?"

"I would be delighted to save you a line on my dance card, Doctor." Clarissa averted her eyes from his face. "May I see my kitten now?"

"Yes, she's just taking a nap. First you may want to look at the new type of food that I have developed for kittens, adult cats and elder cats." He led them back to the front of the store. "Each needs a different type of nutrition, and in my studies, cats in particular need certain nutrients that are not present in human table scraps. We must remember that cats are natural predators and carnivores. I have developed, according to the latest scientific techniques, a unique mixture of dry food that can be stored for up to a year before it loses its nutritional value. Would you like to try some?"

"Certainly, Doctor, if you recommend it."

"Is there a special food for puppies, as well?" Bri held Spotty who not only looked around the shelves, but reached with a paw to try knocking some bags on the floor. "Ah ha!" she said, "I see it over here." She walked over to a shelf with an assortment of choices.

"Of course." As Dr. St. Cloud assembled an assortment of cat and dog food for his new customers, a little meowing sound came from the back room. When he had placed the items in carrying bags, he said, "It is time to introduce you to your new kitten." Clarissa and Bri followed him into the area where the sick and adoptable animals waited.

The little calico bundle was standing in her cage, sticking her nose through the bars, crying plaintively.

"Oh, please don't cry, darling," cooed Clarissa in a soothing tone. "I'm going to take you home with me now."

"Cats do not like to travel as dogs do, Lady Clarissa. I recommend a carrying satchel that I have designed for this purpose. Cats can become frightened and may run away, breaking their guardian's heart as well as endangering themselves in traffic. Please accept this satchel as a gift from me to commemorate my first pet adoption."

Clarissa examined the satchel. "I see you have inserted holes for breathing. I hope it does not frighten her."

"It may, but if you talk to her in a soft, calm way, she will relax a bit. Cats like to know their territory. When you take her home, limit her to one room until she is comfortable. She may hide under your bed or behind a piece of furniture, but when she feels safe, she will emerge. Just continue to talk to her gently and she will respond. Try to pet her frequently so that you can develop trust between you. She has a soul. Though she cannot speak, she can communicate." He reached for some old newspapers, torn into thin strips. "Try to put these in a place where she can relieve herself, and it can be easily disposed of. Cats appreciate cleanliness."

"Oh. I hadn't thought of that."

"We are not in the country, and we cannot let pets out where they might be in danger. If you have a walled in yard, she can still jump on a wall and explore. Once she acclimates, she should return, but I don't recommend letting her wander freely outside."

Bri could not help but notice her friend's long gaze at the doctor. She broke the spell by saying, "We must hurry home now."

Taking her cue, Clarissa nodded and the doctor helped them out to the carriage, holding Spotty and carrying their food supplies. Jean-Louis helped the ladies, their new companions and their cargo into the carriage. As he closed the carriage door, Dr. St. Cloud asked, "What are you going to name your little kitten?"

Thinking for a moment, Clarissa called out the window as the carriage began to move, "Princess." She waved good-bye to the young doctor.

Once out of earshot, Bri smiled. "Now *you* are smitten."

"As are you, though you won't admit it. I *admit* that I find the young doctor appealing."

"Just appealing? You blushed the whole time we were there."

Clarissa's hands flew to her face and her eyes widened. "Do you think he noticed?"

Nodding, Bri laughed. "Unless he was dead, he noticed."

CHAPTER TEN

Saturday, March 9, 1811 – Interior of Lady Gwyneth's Carriage
Henry

As the carriage pulled away from *Chez Michel*, Henry shook his head and muttered to his sister, "Whatever are we going to do about her temper? She will never accept being in the background. She wants to be recognized for her own accomplishments—not an unreasonable desire—but one utterly alien to the *ton.*"

"What are you talking about, Henry? What accomplishments?"

Realizing he had opened Pandora's box, Henry flashed an apologetic glance at Gwyneth. "I should have let you know this sooner. Bri will be acting as my man-of-affairs, directing my accounts. All of her actions will be conducted in private. Only you and I and our bankers and barristers will know of her role."

Gwyneth scoffed. "Keeping this private will be difficult. In fact, a bit farfetched to even think it possible, wouldn't you say?" She directed her gaze at her brother. "It very nearly turned *Chez Michel* into a battlefield."

"She will not be parading around the *ton* as my agent."

"Now *you* are being naïve. You have chosen to ignore her independent nature. You acknowledged as much yourself earlier when you said that she would not willingly stay in the background. You have instigated a clandestine arrangement which may be revealed at an inappropriate time by an unknown person. It is a very foolish proposition invented, no doubt, by Bri, but set in motion by an even greater fool: You."

"Nonsense. James & Co. will maintain secrecy."

"Well," Gwyneth continued as if Henry had made no comment, "there is nothing we can do now, except try to limit the damage Bri can do to herself in public. We must impress upon her very strongly that she is to present herself as your agent in private only. Mr. James appears to be quite attracted to her. One cannot predict the ways of love and romance, and we must all take care until Bri learns how to control her temper and conduct herself properly."

Henry surrendered. "I shall speak to her tonight."

"We don't want to break her spirit, but her spirit may break her. By that I mean that it could cause irreparable damage to her reputation and lead to her being shunned. She still does not understand how harsh Society can be. Perhaps we have sheltered her too much and indulged her independence to a fault. It was amusing to see her flaunt convention when she was twelve. It is not so amusing at two-and-twenty."

"Bri responds to reason. This attraction to Young James, which she will deny, will no doubt have an effect on her view of the world. My guess is that she will be far more interested in attending the theatre Monday night and the balls in the *ton* now that she knows Young James is in the market for a wife. She may find the competition fierce for such a fine young man, but my sense of him is that he needs someone with her spirit rather than a simpering fortune hunter or an heiress looking for a handsome escort."

"He may not realize that yet, Henry." Gwyneth punctured Henry's smug assessment of the young man. "Few men do."

Having no riposte to that comment, Henry remained silent until Gwyneth's carriage reached his townhouse. "Rest assured I shall speak with Bri. I appreciate your taking her on today's shopping excursion. We'll see you Monday night at the theatre. Now that the Season is upon us, I imagine we should go to church tomorrow."

"Which one?"

"Although I prefer the Methodist meeting house, when I am in London, St. George's is the church whose flock attends with the specific objective of being seen."

Gwyneth laughed. "For you to attend St. George's is a real testament to your love of your daughter."

Henry shook his head. "I am no *devoté* of organized religion. Spiritual practices are more universal. Out on the ocean under the endless canopy of stars, the universe seems unrestricted by dogma."

"So I'll see you tomorrow at St. George's, and Monday night at the Haymarket. It should be interesting to watch Bri try to attract *and* ignore Mr. James all evening."

Henry exited the carriage, waved goodbye to his sister, and headed up the stairs to his townhouse, where the butler held the door open.

"Thompson, I expect Sir John for tea about five o'clock. Is Nashmir about?"

"Working in the greenhouse, milord."

"After I speak with him, I shall be at my accounts in the study."

The earl headed toward the back of the house and down the stairs through the Japanese rock garden that Nashmir had designed. He marveled at its serenity, which his valet and master herbalist believed would enhance the growth of healing plants. The greenhouse stood in the center of the garden. Looking through the paned glass, he could see the Tibetan bent over the old scrolls he'd brought with him from the lamasery. Henry always had the feeling that these scrolls were not meant to leave their libraries, but the earl was a practical man who believed in the greater good. Remedies locked in secret rooms in monasteries built on the highest mountains in the world were not useful to humanity. He knocked to alert Nashmir of his presence.

Nashmir looked up. "I am trying to isolate various stomach remedies to be ready to create a potion once I have examined Sir John."

"Very well, Nashmir. I shall bring Sir John to the greenhouse when he arrives. You are the last hope, I fear, for my old friend. He and Wolcott were close."

***

Nashmir

Nashmir returned to his research. He rolled up the scrolls and began to examine the multitude of medicinal plants he had cultivated for many years, selectively snipping bits of herbs and placing them into various small dishes. He kept jars of seeds he had dried and preserved himself from his Asian homeland, while others had been sent to him by like-minded research-oriented compatriots around the world, contacts he and Lord Ravenshire had established through the trading business, where Nashmir occasionally acted as a translator and interpreter.

Reviewing the selected cuttings on the sideboard, Nashmir lit a fire in the small burner he had installed for his medicinal work. Mixing herbs together in careful proportions, he began to brew a concoction according to a formula in a large red leather and gold embellished notebook that was his most precious possession, his life's work. This handbook was comprised of meticulously copied cures from obscure sects of lamas in the Himalayas, ancient Inca teachings from Peru, folk cures from parts of Africa as yet unexplored by white men, and the secret writings of European alchemists.

In addition, Nashmir had also secured rare texts from Hippocrates, whose early theories of "like cures like" were finally being rediscovered by men such as Dr. Hahnemann in Germany, with whom Nashmir maintained a regular correspondence, albeit under an assumed Western identity.

Nashmir had apprenticed as a healer in his native Himalayan mountain country in early childhood, when his instinctive selection of herbs demonstrated that he could cure sick and abandoned animals. He left the idyllic village after a dispute with the chief healer. Nashmir wanted to experiment with new combinations of herbal and breathing cures for the unknown diseases that foreigners introduced into their communities with the imperial thrust of the European and Asian powers.

Even an isolated village as theirs was no longer protected by geography, traders and wanderers brought illnesses that challenged the old ways.

But the chief healer did not believe in change, convinced of the overwhelming power of their centuries-old methods, passed down from healer to healer. Nashmir knew that the introduction of new diseases would mean the end of their society unless he learned how to cure the illnesses of western men and other foreign adventurers. Days after he left his village, trekking through unfamiliar valleys, he found shelter in a lamasery that followed the teachings of a mystical sect of Buddhism. Hidden from the outside world in a remote valley, he refined his natural gifts and embarked upon a spiritual quest for enlightenment. His native village was never far from his mind. He vowed to return when the chief healer was dead. By then, Nashmir hoped, he would have made progress in solving the mysteries of new diseases.

After a few years studying languages and sciences, especially biology and botany, from ancient texts at the lamasery, a chance encounter changed his life. As he was exploring a new area in the high peaks for a particular rare herb that grew only under unique rock formations, Nashmir found a man, collapsed and delirious, calling out in English for help. After providing instant relief for some of the man's symptoms of altitude sickness by administering some herbs he always carried with him in a small pouch, Nashmir blew the requisite calls on his carved yak horn, summoning bearers to carry the man to the lamasery. In that tranquil place, the Buddhist student ministered to the foreigner.

It soon became clear to Nashmir that the sick man, Walter Wolcott, suffered from advanced tuberculosis, made more critical in the rarefied mountain air, coupled with an opportunistic series of parasitic diseases. The combination of ailments proved to be afflictions too complex for Nashmir to cure without a longer period of experimentation than his patient's condition permitted. Seeing with his own eyes the growing threat to his pristine society that such new, virulent diseases represented, Nashmir discussed his fears with Wolcott during periods when the delirium that periodically seized the British expatriate was in remission. The spiritual discipline of the lamas and their ability to control their bodies and raise their vibrations to sustain health protected them from his patient's illness in the confines of the lamasery, but Nashmir knew that ordinary people rarely achieved such a level of synchronicity of body and mind.

Five years before being rescued by Nashmir, Wolcott had led a privileged life as medical doctor in London. One gentleman of the *ton* supported Wolcott's efforts among the poor of the city. Wolcott admired the discretion of this gentleman, whom he had known at university, for the philanthropist never wanted others to know of his largesse. This generous man also directed some well-heeled clients to Wolcott, which made him successful and well-known.

However, after a few years, Wolcott became disillusioned with his medical practice catering to the wealthy, and often irresponsible, aristocrats of the *ton*. One day he closed his office, placed his assets in trust under the guardianship of his benefactor, a man of impeccable integrity, and boarded a ship to India. He disclosed his intentions only to that guardian, Henry Wyndward, Viscount Ravenshire.

Once in India, Wolcott knew instantly that he had found his life's calling. After several years of trying to improve living conditions, one neighborhood and one hovel at a time, Wolcott contracted tuberculosis working among the poor in the squalor of Calcutta. Having been told over his years in India that miraculous healing could occur at remote monasteries in Tibet, he headed to the Himalayas. Once there, he became lost, wandering for several weeks from village to village, asking for directions to the places of healing, until the day Nashmir found him.

In one of Wolcott's brief periods of remission, when both he and Nashmir reluctantly assessed his condition as nearing its final deterioration, he suggested that Nashmir take over his identity as a medical doctor in order to further Nashmir's studies of disease. With no living relatives in Wolcott's family, Nashmir would be able to correspond with others as Walter Wolcott, M.D., using his medical diploma from Oxford to receive instant respect. Wolcott told him to seek out Lord Ravenshire and tell him the story of their friendship. Shortly before his death, which was peaceful and painless, he was able to write a letter of introduction for Nashmir to Lord Ravenshire.

Unbeknownst to Nashmir, he had also dictated another letter to Lord Ravenshire that the high lama transcribed for him. This letter instructed his old friend to make Wolcott's entire fortune available to Nashmir as his legal heir, to be revealed at whatever time Lord Ravenshire deemed appropriate. In the event Nashmir died in transit, Lord Ravenshire was instructed to establish a foundation for the medical care for the poor. It was with great strain that he made his fingers grip the pen to affix his signature to this letter. It was to be sent via the ancient post system of the lamasery, which might take a year or more to reach London. The lama agreed to put it with their other outgoing messages that were sent every few months to the outside world.

After Wolcott's death, Nashmir sent a letter to Lord Ravenshire referencing Wolcott and requesting to meet with him on the viscount's next trip to India. He received a reply, which, due to distance, took nearly a year from his original posting, giving him a time when the earl would next be in Bombay.

The following spring, with all his possessions in a small bag,

Nashmir made the harrowing journey to Bombay. A letter from the high lama gained him admittance to monasteries and homes of believers until he finally arrived in the city. His senses were bombarded by an amazing array of languages, colors, odors and exotic spices.

After sleeping in a small lamasery near the river, he washed himself in the cool waters and donned a clean set of clothes from his small bag. Loose trousers and a tunic of gray seemed out of place in the vibrant clothing of the people around him. He made his way a few miles farther down the river to the docks, where the offices of Wyndward Trading were located in a white-washed building.

He entered the doors with confidence that the man Wolcott had directed him to would help him. At first rebuffed by a clerk at a desk in the entryway, Nashmir persisted. He handed the letter from Wolcott that was addressed to Henry Wyndward, Viscount Ravenshire, to the functionary. Reluctantly, the clerk took the letter, pushed back his chair, and walked to the back of the offices.

A robust, confident man approached the youthful Nashmir, with the clerk scampering behind him. "I am the man you seek. Ask what you will of me, Nashmir. No request is too great after your kindness toward my old friend Wolcott."

Nashmir had considered such a moment. "Let me be your servant, sir, and pursue my studies under guise of being your valet. Under those circumstances I can travel the world freely with you, and I would be honored to be your servant."

The Tibetan would never forget the response of the then-viscount. "You are no man's servant, Nashmir. You are a talented healer. If this disguise is one you truly seek, then I will accept it. But in private I shall treat you as my equal. I abhor the divisions of Society and the arrogance of my British homeland and its doctrine of superiority. I have traveled enough to know it to be false. However, for you to achieve your dreams we must find a way to navigate in waters that are ruled by irrational mores. I shall support your studies with all my resources. I leave for London in a few days on my ship, *Diana's Wynd*. I insist that you be my guest until we sail."

"Lord Ravenshire, I am at your command." Nashmir's life had been fascinating and full ever since, but the dream of returning to his homeland was ever present.

Now, from his post in London, Nashmir corresponded with a

lama in a lamasery near his village who kept him informed of the conditions in their native country. Due to the length of sea travel and the seasons of land caravans, it took about six months for letters to reach that isolated area of the mountains. Nashmir knew that at some point he might return. The chief healer was ailing, but possessed of enough knowledge to keep himself alive and active for a while longer. But as the prospect of a return loomed closer, after an absence of nearly twenty years, Nashmir wondered where his knowledge might best be applied for the benefit of the most people. Perhaps a return to a small village in his native country was not the correct path.

In his daily meditations, visions of his pristine mountain village served to center and calm him. Yet Nashmir had to admit that part of him was exhilarated at the opportunities afforded him since he had left his far-off homeland. Already several articles had been published under the name of Walter Wolcott, Doctor of Medicine, generating a steady stream of fascinating correspondence from all over the world, filtered through the offices of Wyndward Trading to protect Nashmir's true identity.

Ending his reverie, Nashmir found the section of his notebook that covered ailments of the stomach, pancreas, spleen and abdomen. Convinced that he had an excellent selection of potential cures, with more available at his larger greenhouse at Ravenshire, should they be required, Nashmir prepared for his meeting with Sir John by studying specific symptoms.

***

Henry

Walking back into the house, the earl told Thompson to alert the cook about their dinner plans for the Monday night. "And ask Mrs. Jones to make tonight's meal light. *Chez Michel* was a rather rich treat for our mid-day meal."

***

Mrs. Jones

Nellie Jones, known affectionately as Cookie, was a robust woman in her mid-fifties. If truth be told, she had fancied the earl ever since she apprenticed to her mother in Ravenshire's kitchen. Her infatuation was satisfied by being often in his presence and anticipating his needs. She doted on Bri, whom she had spoiled since birth. After Thompson relayed the earl's message about dinner, Nellie decided that the chicken she was preparing could be chilled, mixed with spinach and doused in balsamic vinegar.

***

Henry

Nashmir was almost finished with his task when he was startled by the voice of the earl walking through the garden, "And Nashmir worked with a Japanese landscape designer to create this space. An idyllic spot."

"It invokes a sense of calm."

Greeting his visitors, the Tibetan led them to a table in the midst of the greenery. "I have been brewing some tea that helps me diagnose ailments. I must warn you, Sir John, that it may cause more pain in specific areas to help me make a more precise diagnosis of your condition. I have an antidote to stop this additional pain once the diagnosis is complete. Will you trust me?"

"Yes, Nashmir. My old schoolmate, Henry," Sir John touched Henry's shoulder, "has the utmost confidence in you. My son has been asking me to look into eastern practices of medicine, but I have resisted until now. I confess that my will to fight is being eroded by this constant pain. I put myself totally in your hands."

Recognizing the extraordinary nature of the banker's trust in him, Nashmir graciously bowed and poured a cup of the diagnostic tea for Sir John. "It should work almost immediately. You may double over in pain, but it is essential that you point to the exact area where the pain is most severe."

"Understood." Sir John sipped the tea. "Shall I drink it all?"

"Yes." His attention focused on Sir John.

Henry's apprehensiveness grew.

Sir John drained the cup. Within seconds, his face contorted and he grabbed his stomach, doubled over.

Henry caught his old friend before he hit the ground.

Nashmir knelt next to him. "Put my hand on the painful area."

Sir John pulled Nashmir's hand to his stomach.

"Is the pain throbbing or constant?"

"Constant there, but," Sir John gasped between breaths, moving Nashmir's hand to his lower abdomen, "throbbing pains here."

Pressing on the afflicted areas, Nashmir felt the areas carefully, pushing and probing with his fingers and fist. Satisfied, he pulled out what looked like a vial of smelling salts, held it under Sir John's nose for a few seconds until Sir John caught his breath. "Stretch out on the ground, take deep breaths, count to ten, and then try to sit up."

Breathing heavily, Sir John did as he was told, closed his eyes, and struggled to sit up. Henry and Nashmir helped him stand. When Sir John retook his seat at the table, he appeared disoriented.

Nashmir waited until Sir John's breathing returned to a normal cadence. "May I trouble you to ask a few questions, Sir John?"

"Of course. Fire away."

"How long have these stomach pains been apparent?"

"Over one year, but less than two."

"And the abdominal discomfort?"

"Just the last month or so, but the pains have been intensifying."

"Are they stronger or weaker upon awakening and eating?"

"Stronger upon awakening, and it varies when eating."

"Have you noticed that any particular foods ease or worsen the pain?"

"Yes, breakfast of milk and eggs lessens the pain, but lunches of meat and potatoes worsen it. Lately, I have considered taking milk and eggs exclusively."

"I believe that I can help you, sir. Have the Society doctors used leeches on you?"

"Once, but I put a stop to it. The surgeon wants to cut into my stomach, but I am aware of how few survive that operation, so I have refused to date."

"A wise reluctance, sir. You have two afflictions. First, I believe that you have been suffering from a diseased area, or ulcer, on the wall of your stomach, which has been caused by a combination of nerves and the western diet, which is disruptive to true health. It can be healed by a mixture of herbs I will prepare for you to brew as a tea and a change in your diet which I can outline in writing for you and your cook."

"Second, and more seriously, you have an obstruction in your intestine, where the pain is exacerbated by the ulcerated stomach. To treat this obstruction, we will dissolve it by another set of herbs to brew. Take both potions five times a day for the first three days, and eat no solid food. Normal tea is acidic and will harm your ulcer. Your system must be cleansed. Then, take these alkaline teas three times a day for the next seven days, while consuming only water, milk, and clear soup for sustenance. After one week of this regimen, I would like to meet with you again to determine the next phase of treatment. Will you abide by these requests?"

"Sounds reasonable to cleanse the system. Nerves, you say. Exactly what do you mean?"

"It has been my observation, sir, that western men labor intensively and place a high degree of value on the outcome of commercial transactions. There is little time for contemplation or relaxation, as they are considered frivolous. Nothing could be more untrue. As part of your treatment, I would like you to perform the following breathing exercises three times a day." Nashmir handed Sir John a paper with specific instructions. "I will deliver to your home the recipes tomorrow. The ingredients that are not standard will be provided in marked packets. I wish you good health, sir." Nashmir rose and made a slight bow.

"Thank you, Nashmir. You've given me hope."

"Perhaps you gentlemen would like to wait in the study while I prepare the alkaline tea mixtures. Please, Sir John," Nashmir reminded, "no milk in the tea, no honey or sugar. Drink milk separately before each meal. No alcohol or tobacco."

"Quite so, young man. I shall attend the ball on Thursday with no illusions as to culinary enjoyment."

"The tea packets I give you can be taken with you to the office or the ball to mix with hot water."

The earl put his hand on the herbalist's shoulder. "You never disappoint me, Nashmir."

Sir John and Henry walked back through the garden into the house, went into the study and sat in the armchairs before the fire.

"Jamesey, today, Edward, Sir Paul and I unexpectedly joined Gwyneth, Bri and one of my daughter's friends for lunch at *Chez Michel*."

"Edward told me about it."

"My daughter is possessed of an independent mind. She and

Edward got into a bit of a disagreement. Driven mostly by her lack of deference to Society, Edward made an unfortunate comment about women being unsuited for certain tasks. That type of comment is likely to anger many women, although most women would have had the good sense to keep it to themselves. Not my Bri. A woman of passion, John, and quite taken with Edward, although she would deny it if confronted." Henry leaned forward with his elbows resting on his thighs, with his hands clasped in front of him. "What I am trying to say is that I would not be unhappy if Edward and Bri were to marry."

"Interesting comment, Henry. Edward returned to the office after the lunch and noted that he had seen your daughter for the first time since he returned. He offered that she was lovely but quite opinionated. His solution is to 'tame' her by marriage. I believe he is smitten with her as well, but is trying to rationalize the attraction as a good business combination instead of dealing with his own feelings of passion. The fact that Edward would even speak of marriage astounds me."

"Let me warn you she has a head full of notions of romance. I have tried to dissuade her from such thoughts, but Edward would be well advised to court her in a romantic manner, or she may decline his proposal as she has countless other beaux. More than one of Ravenshire's eligible young men has been burned by the fiery barbs from her tongue."

"I understand he will accompany you to the theatre Monday night and host a dinner following the play. I shall pass this information on to him, but as Bri might ignore your advice, when it comes to women, I'm afraid my son thinks he has all the answers."

At that, Nashmir entered with his potent brewing packets. He gave Sir John the instructions, "The one marked in blue is for the stomach, and the one marked in green is for the abdomen. Mix one teaspoonful to a half-pot of tea. Drink all that is brewed. If stomach pains persist after the first day, double the amount of the blue potion. Be well." Nashmir bowed and stood as his visitors walked back through the garden and up the steps to the house.

Reaching the front door, Sir John gripped Henry's hand. "As always, I appreciate your counsel and I shall follow it."

Henry smiled and placed his hand on his friend's shoulder. *Please don't die yet. We have much to live through together.*

CHAPTER ELEVEN

Sunday, March 10, 1811 – Baroness Glasspool's Mansion
Charlotte

In the pre-dawn hours, Charlotte and Henry held each other after lovemaking. Henry's paramour—a designation she preferred to mistress—rested her head on his shoulder and sighed. Her raven locks covered his chest. Feeling loved and blissful, she opened her deep blue eyes. "You should probably leave soon to avoid any gossip."

"For fifteen years, we have been playing this game. Everyone knows we are lovers. Bri is about to embark on the Season, and husband or not, we can begin to plan our wedding after the Season is completed."

"Even if she does not wed?"

"She is intent on determining her own course, and if a man does not meet her standards, she has vowed not to marry."

Charlotte laughed. "That is our Bri. The young Mr. James seems just as sure of himself as he was when he insisted he could beat her at Whist. He has quite a courting battle to win. It will be fun to watch our Bri falling in love."

"Falling in love? Attracted, perhaps, but this Lord Byronesque obsession with love and poetry is not conducive to lasting marriages. Lust fades. Respect endures."

"Don't you love me?"

"Of course I care for you deeply, in my own romantic way." He kissed her deeply. "You are the woman I want to spend the rest of my life with."

"As well as the last fifteen years." She sat up.

He lifted himself up to a sitting position. "You're not angry with me, are you? Over mere words?"

"Mere words are the basis of civilization, Henry. *The Magna Carta. The Declaration of Independence.* Marriage vows contain the phrase, 'Wilt thou love her…' "

"Of course I adore you. Don't be ridiculous. Would I have been with you for fifteen years if I did not?"

"Would you? I don't know. I have not been demanding. I have met all your needs."

"You have the hospital for foundlings to oversee as well as the school for governesses, nannies and baby nurses. You are accomplished, determined and vibrant. I am devoted to you."

"Write me a poem."

Henry fell back into the pillows. "Must we do this now? I have to leave to get home."

She rolled on top of him and kissed him. "Not now. But before we marry, I want a love poem written by your hand from your heart."

"Very well, I shall try."

"No, you shall not *try*. You shall write me a poem expressing your love for me. Promise me. Promise me now."

Sighing again in resignation, Henry agreed. "I promise to write you a love poem by my own hand from my heart."

She rolled off and he rose to dress.

"I'll pick you up for church at nine o'clock."

"I'll be ready." She kissed him goodbye.

Will he write the poem on his own? Gwyneth is the writer…he may ask her for advice. Alone in the *ton*, Charlotte knew about Gwyneth's secret writing pastime.

As a young woman, Charlotte had been mistreated by a stepfather, narrowly avoiding his advances. Her mother, Lady Agnes, didn't believe her. One day, an old family friend, Jon Winters, the Baron Glasspool, an unmarried man of sixty, visited their country estate. He went for a walk after lunch, and heard a girl scream for help. He walked as quickly as he could with the help of his cane, and came upon Charlotte being assaulted by her stepfather. He was saying vulgar things to her and pulling down his breeches.

Winters wielded his cane as a weapon and fought off the attacker until Charlotte could scamper away. Just as her stepfather was bringing down the final blow on the older, infirm baron, he was hit from behind with a hoe by Charlotte. The strike split his skull. He spun around, spitting blood from his mouth, eyes wide as he realized what she had done. He sputtered unintelligible words and fell to the ground, dead.

Charlotte dropped the hoe and bent to help the wounded baron. When others came, he claimed he'd fought back with the hoe and killed the man in self-defense. No one disputed his version. Even Charlotte's mother accepted it.

Shortly afterward, Charlotte married the baron, escaping her mother and any future lascivious stepfathers. She was a mere sixteen.

Due to the baron's recurrent bouts of illness and infirmity, their marriage was never consummated. Charlotte didn't care. She lived eight happy years with a man who introduced her to the finer things in life, to libraries, opera, and books that only a city like London could offer. They rarely visited Glasspool.

Two years after Glasspool's death, at six-and-twenty, she met Henry Wyndward through his sister, Gwyneth, who served as a trustee on the Winters Foundling Hospital that Charlotte and the baron had established together. Mostly geared to provide for the illegitimate children of young working class women, Charlotte came to see that these women needed protection and professions or trades to escape a cycle of poverty, rape and childbearing. After meeting a woman who had established a school for governesses, baby nurses and nannies, Charlotte had worked with her to place unfortunate women in respectable positions after their confinement. Helping others filled her with joy. Though she had no children of her own, it gratified her that she could place healthy babies with families who wanted children. Unhealthy babies were cared for during their lives through a trust established by the late baron in a building adjacent to the hospital.

She'd entered Henry's life when Bri was seven. Henry's father, Neyl, and his uncle, Barryngton, had endured hell from a stepmother. Charlotte understood Henry's reluctance to marry when Bri was so young, having experienced her own horror under her stepfather's control. Charlotte and Gwyneth, as well as Rychard's wife, Aelwyn, functioned as a trio of mothers for Bri. When Aelwyn disappeared shortly after Rychard's death three years earlier, Charlotte felt she'd lost a part of herself.

She thought of Bri as a daughter. The curious young woman easily confided in Charlotte when she felt uncomfortable talking with her father or aunt. Charlotte laughed as she remembered discussing sex with Bri. So matter-of-fact, that child. And so practical about avoiding pregnancy. "How?" and "Why?" were asked a thousand times. Charlotte wasn't sure if Bri was still a virgin. She'd been doted on by boys at Ravenshire, but she was a level-headed girl. When she was ready, Charlotte knew Bri would ask the appropriate questions.

***

Sunday, March 10, 1811 – St. George's Church
Henry

As the congregation sang the last hymn that morning, "Rock of Ages, Cleft for Me," Henry inwardly winced. The bloody, gruesome lyrics offended him, but it was one of the most popular hymns in the Anglican church. As the last line was sung, "Let me hide myself in Thee," Henry slammed the hymnal shut, startling Bri on his left and Charlotte on his right.

After greeting their acquaintances following the service, they left Hanover Square to have lunch at Gwyneth's, their usual custom. Henry's large carriage accommodated four, and once they started moving, Charlotte asked, "Why did you slam the hymnal?"

"I detest those lyrics. I don't believe in blood curing sin, in coming naked to a cross to be saved or face eternal death, or that there's some throne in the sky."

Bri reached over. "Father, we're aware of your feelings, but why make a scene? Several people turned to stare at you."

Henry's ire rose, his faced reddening. "*I* made a scene? Look who's talking. All the *ton* will hear about your performance at Michel's."

Gwyneth shook her head. "No, they won't. Our booth prevented anyone from seeing or overhearing our conversation." She glanced at her brother. "It's something else. What's wrong?"

The earl sat back and rubbed his forehead. "I don't know. Today, the vicar's sermon, the condescending attitudes, the fakery on display, it all annoyed me. I've made my appearance for the Season. I won't be back."

"Fine. Discussion ended." Gwyneth brightened. "There's a lovely new *pâtisserie* that opened in the park. It has a special license to be open on Sundays. Let's walk over there for dessert after lunch."

Charlotte agreed. "A wonderful idea, Wynnie."

The use of Gwyneth's childhood nickname seemed to upset Henry again. "We're not children anymore. Why do you allow people to call you that?"

His sister leaned forward. "You are not yourself, Henry. Calm down."

"Don't tell me to calm down."

"Very well. Maybe you'll feel better after lunch."

The ride to Gwyneth's home was short, so the awkward silence passed quickly.

***

Charlotte

When they arrived at Gwyneth's, Henry went to splash water on his face. When he came back, he seemed normal again.

In the library, Bri looked through the volumes. She pulled one out and put it on the foyer table. "Aunt Gwyneth, may I borrow the book on Marie-Antoinette's Almanac, *Le Trésor des Graces*?"

"Yes, but I want it back. It was a gift from Luc's sister. Did you know that the hairstyles were so high at the French court that women had to bend over to walk under the chandeliers?"

"Why do you want to read that?" Charlotte picked it up and paged through it.

"It's for Jane Anne, my maid. She styles my hair. Not that I want to look like Marie-Antoinette—"

"Especially after losing her head," said Nambotha.

"Especially not." Bri nudged the giant man with her elbow.

After lunch combining Bri's favorite vichyssoise, veal in lemon sauce and buttered grilled squash, the group rose to walk through the park.

It was a rare sunny day, the kind that made Charlotte forget that London was such a rainy city. A multi-paned glass gazebo housed the *pâtisserie*. Glass cabinets held Napoleons, popular despite their name, dishes of *crème brulée*, cream puffs, an assortment of *petits fours* and ice creams in many flavors, made as the clients watched.

In many ways, it was a perfect afternoon for Charlotte. She was with the man she loved, the girl she loved as a daughter and the friend she loved as a sister. Her family. She couldn't remember the last time she felt her heart so full of happiness. The simple things: the clear sun-filled sky, the budding flowers offering the promise of spring, the quiet company of those she loved.

Bri and Gwyneth decided to walk in the park a little longer. "Guy will bring Bri home."

Henry nodded. He and Charlotte ambled back to where Jean-Louis was waiting. They watched him pop a cream puff into his mouth. "We didn't see you in the gazebo. How did you get that?"

Winking at Charlotte, the Frenchman opened the door to the carriage. "There are ways."

Inside the carriage, Henry took Charlotte's hand. "The first ball of the Marriage Season is next Thursday at Lady Elisabeth's. I think we should attend the second ball together, but for the first ball, I think I should attend with Bri alone."

Charlotte's heart contracted. Involuntarily, her hand went to her chest to stop the pain, to no avail. "Henry, I am hurt. I have spent the last fifteen years with you and Bri. A constant presence. We have traveled together as a family, with Wynnie, with Gio. I have been patient. I understand that your father told you to never trust another woman with your children, due to his painful experience, which I shared. But I love Bri as if she were my own."

"It's just one evening. It's not the end of the world."

"It is to me. I anticipated Lady Elisabeth's ball as our formal entrée to Society. Perhaps I've been naïve about many things."

Henry flinched. "What does *that* mean?"

"I am not a shrew. I never thought I wanted children. The foundling hospital lets me help so many children. But how much have I given up for you? You, a man as addicted to adventure as a glutton is to overconsumption."

"You are making too much of this one evening."

"Am I? In this moment, Henry, I feel utterly discarded. While I value my work at the hospital and school for governesses, I see now that I have deluded myself. I believed that you loved me. Not in a passionate way of the scandalous novels of the *ton*, but in a mature way, a sharing of our lives, a companionship that brought us both happiness.

"Perhaps we've used each other without knowing it. But now we are at a turning point. Bri is ready to start an independent life. That excuse is gone. By the end of this Marriage Season, you must decide. In fact, I may not wait that long."

"We talked about this last night—"

"This morning. Before dawn. In my bed."

Henry protested. "All these years, I thought we had an understanding. Eventually we will marry."

"Will we? Each other?"

"Of course. Who else would we marry?"

"I don't know. Someone who meets your requirement for convenience and acquiescence, as I did for so many years. Another wealthy widow."

" '*Did?*' You said 'did?' "

"I feel that I am no more than a tawdry mistress to you, one to be hidden from the *ton*."

"We just went to church together! The whole *ton* saw us together. You know you're important to me."

"Important?" Charlotte scoffed and looked out the window, away from Henry. She didn't want him to see the tears forming.

"I care for you."

"That's not enough."

"Are you harping again on the romantic poems of Lord Byron? Has your head been turned by such adolescent prattle? I told you I'd write you a damn poem."

"Now I'm a harpie? A 'damn' poem? I've given myself to you, Henry, and now I realize I was merely convenient. No need to seek out new partners, to change your life."

"Bri adores you."

"Don't use your daughter to blackmail me. Bri is a woman now, and she and I can have a friendship without you, if she so desires."

"You talk as if you've already decided to leave me."

"Leave *you?* A man who is addicted to leaving on ships, sailing into unknown unpredictable waters? A man who always pursues his desires and never looks back? I'm not leaving you. You were never really with me. Perhaps I shall go to Lady Elisabeth's ball with another escort. I have my own invitation, you know. Lady Elisabeth is a patroness of the hospital."

Henry's face drained of color. "But there will be talk."

"Talk? Is that all you care about? Talk? Do you not think that a widowed earl and a widowed baroness who have kept company for fifteen years are not already the subject of talk in the *ton*? Frankly, I should never marry you. I would lose control of my late husband's fortune by law. Perhaps I shall be a scandalous widow, seducing young virile men at my leisure."

Henry sat back. "Now you're sounding ridiculous."

"So only wealthy old men can seduce young women? There are those who seek what I have to offer."

"Charlotte! You, Bri, Gwyneth...all of you expect to change the world."

"So that is something only you are permitted to do? The puppet master who pulls all our strings?"

"Charlotte, I cannot believe you are reacting this way. It's simply a ball I will attend with my daughter."

"Without me. And it is simply a ball I will attend with another escort." *And I know exactly who it will be.*

Her last word to Henry was timed perfectly with their arrival at her mansion. She exited the carriage and didn't look back at him. "Be well, Jean-Louis."

The Frenchman tipped his black felt hat to her. When she was inside, he closed the carriage door and grimaced at Henry, shaking his head. "You don't know the first thing about women."

CHAPTER TWELVE

Monday, March 11, 1811 – The Theatre Royal Haymarket
Bri

Jean-Louis guided the white Arabians leading the earl's carriage to a gentle stop in front of the Theatre Royal Haymarket. Since tonight was scheduled for auditions and a rehearsal, only the center doors were opened. A uniformed doorman stood at the entrance with a list of names to confirm that a special invitation had been issued to anyone attempting to view the evening's events. Several curious passers-by had been summarily dismissed by the efficient guard.

After Jean-Louis descended from the driver's seat to open the door for his charges, the party exited. All were intrigued by what the evening held in store. Henry stood aside to let Gwyneth and Bri enter first. As promised, Clarissa had added the names of their group to the list.

Bri inquired of the list keeper, "Has Mr. Edward James arrived yet?"

The man nodded and pointed toward the front of the theatre.

Entering, Bri saw Clarissa in the lobby and waved to her.

Clarissa quickly walked over to the group. "Welcome, Lord Ravenshire, Madame la Comtesse, Bri. Mr. James is waiting for you."

Henry, Gwyneth and Bri followed Clarissa into the theatre.

Gwyneth leaned over to Bri and whispered, "Where's Charlotte?"

Bri whispered back. "Don't ask now. I'll explain later." Bri gazed upward at the detail of the interior candlelit chandeliers, shaped like stars. "Incredible workmanship."

Clarissa explained how the chandeliers could be moved up and down as needed, with a unique control system that was reputed to be an outstanding feat of engineering. The orchestra chairs were covered in deep blue velvet and gilded edges defined the outer margins of the box seats overlooking the orchestra.

Bri turned to gauge the design of the venue. "This is a thrilling atmosphere. I see why you are so drawn to the theatre."

"The auditions for the part of the wizard will start in a few minutes. After that, the rehearsal will begin. We are still working on the scoring of the signature love song. I anticipate we will be finished about nine o'clock." Somewhat embarrassed, Clarissa added, "The composer has not been able to get the melody exactly as I remembered it, and we've been arguing a bit. I want it to be perfect, and he thinks I am being petulant."

The earl waved his hand in an exaggerated theatrical way. "Artistic differences. You will come to a resolution by opening night. At the end of the process, it always comes together. Same in commerce."

Touching the earl's arm to get his attention, Clarissa said, "We were lucky to secure the theatre, as there was a cancellation due to a death. Now, we must whisper as we approach the stage so as not to distract the performers."

Reaching the row where Mr. James was seated, Clarissa motioned for the group to take their seats.

Standing, Edward whispered, "Good evening, Lord Ravenshire, Madame la Comtesse, Lady Gabriella." He bowed his head slightly in acknowledgment of each.

Nodding silently in return, they took their places. Bri had to be pushed surreptitiously by Gwyneth as she hesitated to take the seat next to Edward, but she recovered her demeanor and took her seat dutifully.

Bri adjusted her skirt to be comfortable. Her scarlet, black and purple wool plaid ensemble was trimmed with black fur. She clasped her black-gloved fingers.

Edward had donned a dinner jacket of velvet as jet black as his hair, with a light gray waistcoat that matched his eyes.

Their attention was drawn to the stage where a man began to speak. "Good evening. I am Herr Johann Kramer, the composer. Tonight we are auditioning for the role of The Wizard. As this role calls for some magic, we have three aspiring magicians who will perform here and we shall select one to bring the role to life. We are honored to beg the opinions of our specially invited guests in the audience tonight to help us make the choice. The scene will be one in which The Wizard speaks to The Princess. Lady Clarissa von Dusterberg will perform the role of The Princess for the purposes of the audition."

Polite applause accompanied his departure from the stage through the side curtain. From stage right, the first magician appeared.

He wore a red cape which he swirled with a flourish. Clarissa entered from stage left, and sat upon a cushioned recliner and began to read from a script, "I have requested your presence, Wizard, to divine whether or not my beloved Prince lives. Show me magic."

The first magician bowed and said, "I cast the runes. Let their signs reveal the truth." He cast the runes on the stage. "Ah, the decision is still in the hands of the gods. I shall send a bird to the Otherworld to bring us a further message." Opening his robe to reveal a black bird, he waved his hand and the bird disappeared, but clumsily, as they all saw him hide it under the other side of his cloak. "If the bird returns black, The Prince is dead. If the bird returns white, The Prince will live."

The actor then began to chant a nonsensical incantation, waved his arms, and two birds, one black and one white, flew out from under his cloak. He vainly tried to capture them, but they flew off into the theatre. He said, "They were supposed to obey. I don't know what went wrong. I know it can work...." Herr Kramer appeared to escort the hapless magician off the stage.

The second magician had an unfortunate stammer. Although his magic came off flawlessly, leaving those in the audience wondering how he switched birds, it was clear that he could not get through the dialogue.

The third magician came with a white wig and beard, and walked as though he were an old man. He wore a purple robe embroidered with half moons and a pointed cap embellished with golden stars. "He certainly looks the part," whispered Bri to Edward.

Clarissa repeated her lines, which the audience could practically recite with her on the third try, "I have requested your presence, Wizard, to divine whether or not my beloved Prince lives. Show me magic."

The third magician reached into his robe's pockets, brought out a handful of stones, and said, "I cast the runes," throwing them on the stage, but also causing smoke to rise with it, startling Clarissa as well as the audience. Raising his arms to the sky, he cried out, as if to the heavens, "Let their signs reveal the truth." Bending down to read the stones, he brushed his hand across them, saying "Ah, the decision is still in the hands of the gods." Rising, he again raised his arms. "I shall send a bird to the Otherworld to bring us a further message." Opening his robe to reveal a black bird, he waved his hand and the bird disappeared completely. "If the bird returns black, The Prince is dead. If the bird returns white, The Prince will live." The Wizard then began to move his hands in strange circular motions and began to chant in rhyme a foreign-sounding ritual spell. He whirled around and a white bird appeared on his hand, which he handed to Clarissa, looking directly into her eyes.

"Dr. St. Cloud!" Clarissa cried out without thinking.

The Wizard rose to his full height and nodded. "I was so surprised to see you here that I almost bungled my magic. It is a hobby, you see, and I thought it would be fun to try out for a limited-run play. I have practiced only before my animals until tonight."

Herr Kramer came running out, "You were wonderful! The part is yours if our audience concurs." He looked to the audience for approval. Loud applause confirmed his decision.

Dr. St. Cloud removed his hat and wig as the house lights came up. "Good evening, Lady Gabriella." He waved from the stage.

Bri smiled and waved back.

Edward's posture stiffened.

"How do you know this actor?"

"He is not a professional actor. Dr. St. Cloud is a veterinarian who saved Spotty, my new puppy." Bri called out to the stage, "What an interesting hobby you have, Dr. St. Cloud. May I introduce my Aunt Gwyneth, Comtesse de Merbeau, my father, Lord Ravenshire, and Mr. Edward James?"

"Good evening, everyone," said Dr. St. Cloud. "I suppose I don't look like such a dignified member of Society tonight." He offered Clarissa his hand as they came down the few steps from the stage to the orchestra seats.

"You must be the son of the late Comte and Comtesse de Villiers."

"Yes, Madame la Comtesse, I am."

"I knew your mother many years ago. We met in France on some of my husband's business trips, before Napoleon made travel impossible. As English girls married to French comtes, we spent quite a bit of time together. As I recall, her youngest son was off at school."

"So I was." A note of sadness marked his voice.

Before Clarissa could probe any further into the tone of the doctor's comment, Herr Kramer announced that the play was ready for rehearsal, and the house lights dimmed. Clarissa and Dr. St. Cloud took their seats in the row behind Bri's group.

The curtain rose on a classic scene from a European medieval fairy tale. A white castle was painted on a backdrop. A young woman, whom Bri surmised to be The Princess, stood on a balcony, which appeared to be part of the castle through clever *trompe l'oeil* painting. The balcony had been partially constructed earlier that afternoon, so that the supporting cross-beams were visible. The Princess was talking to no one, but dreaming out loud about The Prince, her dreams and the mysteries of love. She began to sing in a wobbly voice. The melody was liltingly romantic, and the lyrics did not fail to stir any of the listeners, even though her singing lacked power.

Each became absorbed in his or her own memories of lost or unrequited love.

When the singer ended her musical soliloquy, she came down from the balcony. Black-garbed stage workers pushed it aside while others pushed a new background of the throne of The King into view.

The Princess took her place next to her father's throne. The Wizard, played for rehearsal purposes by an older actor, stood on the other side of The King, and the trumpeters heralded an arrival. A page came to the throne, bowed, and announced, "A traveling Bard has arrived in the kingdom and offers his talents for Your Majesty's pleasure in exchange for bed and food."

"Ah, some entertainment to amuse the court," said The King. "And perhaps cheer my little princess. Let him approach."

The Bard entered by somersaulting his way to land cross-legged at The King's feet. Standing, he removed his traveling cape, revealing a black, red and white harlequin's costume. His red hat sported a red and black feather. He whisked his hat off his head with a flourish, and bowed. "I am Thomas, a poor Bard who travels far and wide to sing for his supper, great King."

Laughing, The King instructed, "It will soon be the dinner hour, Bard. After the repast, you will entertain us. For your current distraction, you have earned dinner and one night's shelter. After we hear your song tonight, we will decide if you may stay longer." Motioning to a page, The King commanded, "Show the bard to guest quarters in the East Tower."

The Bard bowed deeply, and turned to follow the page, with his knapsack over his shoulder.

Stage workers immediately appeared to clear the stage and set up the dining area. The stage slowly moved and the audience gasped, realizing that it was raised and on wheels to be moved to reconfigure the stage for the next scene behind the curtains.

Courtiers took their seats at a table shaped like a horseshoe, with The King in the center, The Princess on his right and The Wizard on the left. The Bard was seated at the far end of one of the horseshoe ends. There was no dialogue, simply murmuring and apparent toasts among the diners. Servers milled around the assembled group, taking away plates and bringing small cakes on platters.

Dinner appeared to be completed. The King rose and said, "Now we shall be entertained by our traveling Bard, Thomas."

On cue, The Bard took his place opposite The King where all could see him. He began to play his lute, singing a frolicking song of humor about the life of a traveling Bard. There was laughter and approval from the court.

As Thomas finished, The King and his court jumped to their feet applauding, "*Encore! Encore!*"

The Bard began to sing a song of courtly love, but stopped to tell the audience that the song was still being finished. He spoke the poetic lyrics aloud.

The listeners, both on stage and in the audience, were transfixed.

Bri looked around for reactions. She could see out of the corner of her eye that even Mr. James was exhibiting interest in the performance.

Gwyneth lightly touched Edward on the arm. "Are you enjoying the operetta as much as the rest of the audience?'

"Yes, Madame la Comtesse. Romance and courtly love are an invention of dramatists. Their entertainment value is predictable."

"Young James is not unaware of the fickle nature of women. Smitten by love one moment, walking away the next." Henry's tone sounded bitter.

The uncomfortable moment passed as Herr Kramer reappeared and announced, "The second act will begin."

The second act opened with the scene that had been auditioned earlier. Bri made a mental note to ask who played the part of The Wizard tonight. He was competent, though wooden. *Dr. St. Cloud will be triumphant in the role. And wouldn't it be delightful if Clarissa could play The Princess?* In Society, actresses were considered to be rather scandalous creatures. *It would be breaking precedent, but perhaps the world is getting a bit more tolerant.*

The scene they had watched three times for the audition was performed again. When the white bird appeared, the stage moved and the scene changed again.

Thomas the Bard was revealed in a dungeon with a small window. An old woman was escorted to the cell to visit him.

The jailer opened the door, and she entered. The jailer stood as though in a trance.

The old woman loudly stage-whispered to the Bard, "I am The Wizard of The King, sent by The Princess. My disguise and voice have confused the jailer. I have placed a spell over him. We have very little time. You must take this potion." The crone revealed a greenish, bubbling, misting vial that was hidden beneath her cloak. "Drink quickly, and obey me without fail."

"Is The Princess well? Does she miss me?"

"Stop prattling and drink, young man. Obey!"

"If it will bring me to my love, I shall." Thomas drank the potion. Coughing at the foulness descending his throat, The Bard bent over on the floor, and the old woman raised her cloak to hide him. Then she bent over and picked something up. Turning around to leave, the audience gasped to see that she had a monkey sitting on her shoulder.

"Jailer, I am ready."

The jailer complied, opening the door. His gait was stiff, moving as if manipulated by marionette strings.

The old woman hobbled up the stairs from the dungeon, singing softly as she went.

The stage moved again. The next scene showed the crone entering a forest, with the monkey on her shoulder. She made her way farther and farther into the dark forest. Eventually, she came upon a large tree. As she chanted magical words, the tree trunk parted. Taking the monkey off her shoulder, she placed him on the ground. Looking at him, she pointed her long, gnarled finger at him, "Stay."

Smoke rose from the floor and surrounded the tree. When the trunk opened again, The Wizard had returned to his original form. He motioned to the monkey to jump up on his shoulder, and he continued through the forest. "There is still much danger until you are free."

The stage moved again. This scene showed The Princess on her balcony.

The Wizard approached from a distance. He stopped and instructed the monkey, "Go to the balcony and sit. You will learn for yourself if The Princess truly loves you."

The monkey climbed the balcony and sat, tilting his head to one side, regarding The Princess.

"Hello, little monkey. Have you ever been in love?"

The monkey squeaked.

"Let me tell you a story of love, little monkey," and she began to sing the song that Thomas the Bard had sung on his first evening at the castle, but only the first few notes, as it was not finished. The trained monkey started jumping up and fell down.

The Princess leaned down and picked up the monkey and kissed him. Smoke and mists came up from the floor and surrounded them. When it cleared, Thomas the Bard stood in place of the monkey in the arms of The Princess. They began to sing their song of love together, announcing to the audience that it was not yet completely scored. They embraced in a kiss.

Just then, a group of knights appeared below the balcony, startling the couple. One knight's helmet also held the mark of a king. Thomas recognized the insignia of his father's coat of arms, and said, "Father, this is the Princess I wish to marry. I love her more than my life."

"My son, I have just come from the kingdom of Gravalon. They swear by all the gods that a spell was cast by an old sorceress to enable your escape from the dungeon. I have made peace on behalf of our families. His daughter also loves another and did not want to marry you under orders from her father. So, my son, you are free to marry for love as is your former intended."

Thomas the Bard and The Princess kissed, and the rest of the court appeared and sang a reprise of the happy song that The Princess and The Wizard had sung earlier.

The curtain came down, signaling the end of the play.

Silence hung in the theatre for a moment until the carefully selected audience exploded in applause, rising to their feet.

As the star-shaped gaslights glowed more brightly with the completion of the performance, the performers left the stage.

Edward said, "I have made reservations at *The Opera Café*, in keeping with this evening's theme. I would like to invite Dr. St. Cloud and Herr Kramer to join us." He went backstage to issue the invitation.

When the doctor, Clarissa and Herr Kramer finally appeared, the audience was gone. The logistics of the carriages took some management as they exited the theatre.

Bri wanted to ride with Mr. James, but there was only room for two in his small carriage and a chaperone would be required.

Dr. St. Cloud invited Lady Clarissa and Herr Kramer to share his carriage, as both had taken Hackneys to the theatre, while Gwyneth, Henry and Bri entered Henry's carriage and followed the procession to the restaurant through the gaslit busy streets of the city night.

CHAPTER THIRTEEN

Monday, March 11, 1811 – *The Opera Café*
Bri

Located about one mile from the theatre, the Opera Cafe was a relatively new establishment. When it first opened the previous spring, the *ton* was a bit put off at the lack of décor. Originally a wine cellar on the lower level of a mansion fallen on hard times, the main part of the house had been converted into showrooms for dealers in heirloom furniture, art and glasswork. The architect who oversaw the redevelopment of the property envisioned a restaurant to entice more shoppers to the showrooms.

The opera theme was a spontaneous improvisation by the waiters, who aspired to sing on stage. Walls were built of thick, heavy rocks gave the appearance of a dungeon or cave. Oil lamp sconces added romantic lighting among the oak tables, which were of varying sizes, but all constructed in the style of monks' tables, artificially aged by their craftsmen. Wood chairs held seat cushions of black velvet. The original floor, once covered over by moth-eaten carpet, was of mosaic tile, with the ancient Celtic swirl pattern in black on a white background.

The waiters, all of whom were men, wore black monks' garb, while the wine servers were all women, an affront to many in the *ton*. This major break with convention had increased patronage, as curious socialites came to see the women dressed in white robes with white fur-trimmed hoods. There was a raised platform in the middle of the room, with a pianoforte to one side.

As the group from the theatre gathered at the entryway, Edward said to the maître d'hôtel, "Our party is now seven persons."

The robust, but efficient, maître d' bowed deeply. "We can accommodate your group now, Mr. James." He led them to a long table near the rear wall with an excellent view of the entire restaurant. A pianist was playing classical selections softly, but the sound reverberated around the stone walls and mosaic floor, amplifying the effect.

Standing at the head of the table, Edward arranged the seating, saying, "Lady Gabriella, would you honor me by sitting to my right, and Lord Ravenshire on my left? Lady Clarissa, would you and Dr. St. Cloud sit next to Lord Ravenshire? Madame la Comtesse and Herr Kramer, please sit next to Lady Gabriella." When all were settled, Edward took his place and said to the assembled group, "I would like to take the liberty of ordering a special meal for us. Do I have your permission?"

As all were in agreement, Edward instructed the maître d', "We will have the Mozart special."

"It shall be done," said the maître d', who signaled to the wine servers to approach. "The first wine will be a dry white wine to accompany the grilled *shrimp en beurre* hors d'oeuvres."

Edward looked at Herr Kramer. "That was quite a polished dress rehearsal. When do you open?"

Herr Kramer, clearly relishing the attention, smiled at his audience and began, "Monday, April 22nd. Due to other commitments, we can only rehearse here on Mondays and Wednesdays, when the theatre is closed. We have to assemble and disassemble our stage machinery each day. Luckily, this theatre was built with storage space. There is a lot of pressure on our performers over the next few weeks to finalize the costumes, complete the script and finish the score. I hope that Dr. St. Cloud will accept the role of The Wizard." He looked to the doctor for confirmation.

"I would be honored to accept the role, Herr Kramer, even though it may scandalize Society. Perhaps I should adopt a stage name so that, under the wig and beard, I might remain unknown."

"An excellent thought, Doctor." Edward added, "One must be careful of one's reputation."

Bri was aware of Aunt Gwyneth's warning scowl to maintain her silence, and she pretended to adjust her napkin while the exchange between the doctor and the banker took place.

Edward tilted his head. "Let us help you select a name. It would be an amusing way to mark this dinner."

"Inventive, Mr. James." Henry warmed to the idea. "How about something from myths, like Merlin?"

"Oh, Henry, that's too obvious," said Gwyneth. "I would prefer something that evokes French ancestry, like Christophe de Christophe."

Herr Kramer joined in. "That does have a symmetry for the theatre marquee, but it is a long name."

Clarissa brightened. "How about a pun on animal names, like Terry Yorkshire?"

"Or Foxwell Hunter?" Henry led a round of guffaws.

Bri entered the fray. "In my opinion the name should be similar to that of Merlin, evoking a mystical mythical era, but perhaps a play on sounds, as well. How about Drew Wood?"

"Quite clever, Lady Gabriella. You invoke the mystical with the allusion to the Druids. I like your suggestion best. I am impressed."

Edward's air of smug approval annoyed Bri. "I am so glad, Mr. James. Impressing you was my one true hope." She turned to Herr Kramer. "What do you think, sir?"

"Clever, indeed, Lady Gabriella." Like most seeking approval, Herr Kramer fell back on flattery while evaluating the situation. "However, I think we should ask the doctor."

"I like Comtesse de Merbeau's suggestion, but I am amused by Lady Gabriella's idea. I think I shall be Drew Wood, and trust that those of you at this table will keep my secret."

Unanimous agreement was reached just as the shrimp course arrived. As the plates were being delivered by the monks, one of the wine servers took her place on the raised platform. The pianist began to play while the server sang selections from *The Marriage of Figaro.*

They ate to the musical accompaniment, and toasted Dr. St. Cloud's new stage name, "To Drew Wood, the eternal Druid," said Edward. After the toast, he said, "By the way, I do not know your Christian name, although I would like to see that designation changed now that I have a brother-in-law of the Jewish faith. It seems too restrictive. I prefer to call it a given name."

"Nicholas."

Edward raised his glass. "To Dr. Nicholas St. Cloud!"

The second course was a pasta dish served with a basil and pine nut sauce over very thin spaghetti. Asking its name, Bri was charmed to learn it was called *capelli d'angelo*, angel's hair. As the first plates were removed and the pasta presented, a waiter took the stage and began to sing a lament from *Don Giovanni*. The original sommelière approached to refill their wine glasses, and did not argue when patrons placed coins into the pockets of her robe.

The third course was filet of beef with Béarnaise sauce, with roasted potatoes and vegetables on the side. Tasting this perfectly seasoned beef, Henry proclaimed it to be one of the best he'd eaten in years. The others nodded in agreement as the tenor continued his aria.

After the singer accepted the applause of the patrons, Edward said, "The Continental flair for cooking is something we must pay more attention to in this country. Boiled meat and potatoes do get a bit tired. I will not debate the statement that the French and the Italians have won *la guerre de la cuisine*." Everyone laughed at their host's comment, as a waiter took the stage to sing from an unknown German opera.

As the remaining waiters cleared the table, and the sommelier refilled the wine goblets, Edward whispered to Bri, "I have requested a new dessert called 'crème anglaise with snow eggs,' and I will be most interested in your reaction."

The meringue and custard dessert was an unqualified success, eliciting whispered words of approval in deference to the singer. When the tenor hit and held the final note longer than expected, the room burst into applause, and he basked in the acclaim.

The pianist resumed playing more background music as the ensemble sipped Turkish coffee and tea. Edward announced, "I would like to thank you all for being my guests tonight, and now that I have seen the musical play, I must admit that I dismissed it without understanding the appeal of its story and the enchantment provided by its music. I hereby apologize to Lady Clarissa for offending her with my unthinking comments about investing in the play and also to Lady Gabriella, who rightly pointed out that I had made an uninformed judgment."

Clarissa smiled. "Thank you, Mr. James."

"I appreciate your willingness to admit your error, Mr. James." A nuance in Bri's voice suggested that she reserved full redemption for a later date.

The earl raised his glass to Edward. "To Mr. James, I thank you for your generous invitation to this most excellent dinner."

The group echoed, "To Mr. James!"

Edward rose, and the group prepared to leave.

Bri leaned toward Herr Kramer. "It might be a good idea to provide the pianist here with the music from the play before it opens. That way, people might ask about its provenance and you would build interest in the opening. In fact, getting a couple of the primary songs to be sung would be quite a marketing coup."

The earl approved. "Another excellent idea, Bri."

"I concur, Lord Ravenshire." Tuning to Bri, Edward added, "Your insights are clever, Lady Gabriella."

Irritated at his attempt to be ingratiating, Bri snapped, "I am a person of breeding and education, Mr. James, as are you. The fact that I can analyze business opportunities as well as you can, or better, should hardly be greeted with condescending praise."

Her aunt chided her. "Bri, I'm sure Mr. James did not mean his comment the way you have taken it. Please be as much of a lady as he has been a gentleman tonight and set aside this petty bickering."

Realizing that she might never be able to convince Aunt Gwyneth how annoying she found Mr. James, Bri surrendered. "Of course, you are right, Aunt Gwyneth." Turning to Edward, she said, "I apologize for my tone of voice, Mr. James. You have been a gracious host this evening."

Edward nodded his acceptance of her apology.

Within moments, goodbyes were said, and the dinner guests stepped into their carriages and Hackneys, heading into the fog-shrouded London night.

In her father's carriage, Bri could not get Mr. James out of her mind. *How will I be able to work with a man of such limited vision? Why does he irritate me so?*

CHAPTER FOURTEEN

Tuesday, March 12, 1811 – Lord Ravenshire's Townhouse
Henry

The earl sat in his study before breakfast, poring over the documents Bri had given him the day before. His solitude was interrupted by a jarring noise as Bri stomped up the back stairs, followed by clicking sounds made by the spurs on her equestrienne boots touching the marble floor.

Bri rode in the park with her Uncle Oliver, Lord Darlemont, her mother's brother, early every Tuesday morning. Darlemont, the late Lady Jane's youngest brother, and Henry maintained cordiality only to keep peace between the Wyndward and Pytchley families. The earl never asked about Bri's rides with her uncle. Although distrustful of each other, they shared a deep love for Bri.

"Am I late?" She looked at the clock.

"No, I couldn't sleep."

"When would it be convenient to finish our discussion about my ideas on investments? I will be meeting with Mr. James on Friday, and I want to be able to have your approval for the instructions I shall be giving him."

Removing his reading spectacles, Henry looked directly at his daughter. "Bri, if you believe that you will be giving Young James *instructions*, your meeting will be an unpleasant one. We have significant economic influence with James & Co., but they must be permitted to provide us with advice. You will need to persuade

Young James to adopt your recommendations. How you handle the relationship with James & Co. is also part of the test. Ultimately, the decisions are yours, but listen to your banker. Give him the courtesy not to make every conversation an argument."

Bri sputtered. "But Father, he is so dense and conceited."

"And quite handsome. I am not so dense as to miss the fact that there's more going on here than getting approval for business investments." The earl stood, put his arm around his daughter, and guided her toward the dining room. "Last night, Young James admitted a mistake in pre-judging the operetta as an investment. When you provide your detailed analyses of the investments and financial plans, he will be impressed. Occasionally, he will need to disagree to assert himself, but I predict that you will get what you want, my dear." He squeezed her shoulders. "You always do."

"Oh, Father, why can't I simply give him instructions? Do this and do that...it would be so satisfying. And after all, I am representing you, and I am therefore his client."

As they sat down to breakfast, the server poured the tea. "Just because I have capitulated to your every demand, don't think that Young James will. Remember that your role as my agent is quite unusual, and that you should be more circumspect. No more petty displays of pique at dinner parties."

Bri bristled. "You don't have to give me orders." She sighed, "I know you are right. I don't know why that man infuriates me so."

"It is often that way when one is drawn to another. I know Jean-Louis and you talked about my falling out with Charlotte. The subject of our disagreement, or misunderstanding or whatever we should call it, was about making a declaration of love. You expect the person you care for to understand and agree with you totally. When that person does not react as you expect, you become angry because you cannot control another person's feelings or actions.

"Learn now, Bri, and learn well—relationships are not about control. On the contrary, relationships are about respecting the other person enough to release your need for control. Let the other person be an individual and have different opinions, just as you expect to be respected as an individual for your opinions. True, Society does not treat women with the same degree of respect as men, but trust me: you will win more respect as people observe your competence than by forcing them to adhere to your particular standards of behavior at all times."

"Don't you believe in falling in love? Don't you love Charlotte? I know you love me…you tell me all the time. Why can't you tell Charlotte that you love her?"

"I don't know. Men are more practical than women, I suppose."

"Practical? Don't you believe people fall in love?"

"I believe they fall in lust. Love comes with time."

"You and Charlotte have been together for fifteen years. How is that not enough time? Are you afraid?"

"Are you afraid of Young James?"

Bri squirmed. "I might dance with Mr. James at the ball, just to be polite, but I hardly consider that falling in love." Bri looked at her food, avoiding her father's eyes.

The earl laughed and threw his head back. "Don't try that innocent act with me! I have traveled the world, and I know the signs of a young woman who believes she is in love. And what's more, I believe that Young James is quite taken with you. Any fool can see that you are beautiful. And Young James has observed your keen intellect."

"So you think that I *believe* that I am in love but I am really in lust?"

Her father shrugged. "Enough of this. We have work to do."

Finishing breakfast, Henry stood and signaled to Thompson, "We will be in the study." The butler nodded.

Taking his place behind his desk, Henry picked up his spectacles as Bri took a chair across from him. "After our meeting on this subject, I have been studying the books and concur with your suspicions. Before the rehearsal, I went into the office and collected a few more files for your review. I have glanced at them briefly, but saw nothing conclusive. We need to continue to dig. I don't want to give Blackie any indication that might change his behavior." Henry slammed his hand on a file. "Damn! I've always liked and trusted Blackie. I don't care about the money. I care about deception. I do not want to make accusations that cannot be proven."

Bri picked up the additional files. "I will study these and prepare a brief written report of my analysis. I must admit I was angry to be excluded from your meeting yesterday. Please understand, Father, how frustrating it is for me to be excluded solely on the basis of my gender. Perhaps I should disguise myself as a mythical Gabriel

Wyndward to attend these meetings."

The earl noticed her tilt of head, a sign she was analyzing something. "Don't get any wild ideas. That would be quite a ruse. But your private meetings with young James will gain you his confidence, and Sir Paul will comply. You will not have to resort to playacting."

"It was but a flight of fancy." Bri returned to the agenda she had prepared the day before. "The most important issue we have covered, questionable contracts. What did you accomplish with Sir Paul?"

"Sir Paul and Young James are both contacting their people in the places where we found the most egregious contracts. They will research the ownership independently, and then we will compare the results of their efforts. If both concur, then we can proceed. It is all due to your detective work, Bri. I have not paid as much attention to contract details as I should have, and in fact, my focus has always been more on developing business than the financial details. As long as we made a profit, I was satisfied. Blackie knows that and may have exploited my weakness. I bear the ultimate responsibility for inadequate oversight. These discrepancies did not cause sustained financial damage, although all commerce is affected by Napoleon. At least our activities in Africa and the Americas have provided new sources and markets. Your discovery underscores my confidence in you. Your first rite of passage has been a success."

Bri smiled. "Now to the estates." Income from the Ravenshire estates consisted of agricultural yields, income from land leased to farmers, rent from buildings in the village of Ravenshire, as well as land and building leases in the *ton*. Estates in Scotland, Ireland and Wales, from maternal ancestral inheritances, were maintained separately from income generated from those estates. "I have made an inventory of all your holdings so that we may compare results year to year. I noticed that we have not increased our rents for many years, and we should probably conduct a review of the market prices and make some adjustments, but slowly. We do not want to disrupt the income from these holdings or the long term tenants. Stability is a consideration." She handed her father her lists of holdings and accounting results.

He reviewed each parcel, and then gave Bri particular facts from his memory not recorded in the files.

"These details will help me develop recommendations as to

changes and adjustments." Several of his London flats were leased to widows of his school friends at very low rates, allowing them the security that their husbands' lack of financial resources could not provide. "You are very generous, Father."

Henry's rebuke was stern. "It is not charity, Bri, it is just. I charge something to allow them to maintain their dignity. Women do tend to outlive men, and few widows are as well provided for as Gwyneth. When I know I can be of help, I am. One does not lose by being generous. I believe that one increases one's wealth through helping others. Not all rewards are financial."

"Yes, Father, I understand. I shall endeavor to follow your example."

"You already do. I have noticed you measure your interest in people by their conduct as individuals rather than by virtue of their station in life, as one so often sees in Society. I am enormously proud of your character."

Momentarily overcome by emotion, Bri's eyes glistened with restrained tears.

"Thank you. I know I sometimes disappoint you with my impulsiveness. I am trying to think before I speak."

"Part of your charm is your directness, but when it descends into rudeness or insult, that is unacceptable."

Bri nodded. Returning to the agenda, Bri took a deep breath. "An approach to investments in small businesses is something I've been considering over the past few months. When you began the trading business, you had the advantage of substantial family income to provide investment capital. The profits from your trading as well as the estate profits have been wisely reinvested in land, buildings and general expansion of your businesses. Naturally, that reinvestment should continue. But I would like to suggest allocating a portion of profits to be used to invest in new businesses where the proprietors, or entrepreneurs, are talented and astute, but lack the family capital that you had."

Putting down his spectacles to listen, Henry cocked his head. "Interesting. Go on."

Taking a deep breath, Bri launched her pitch. "My proposal is that we take five percent of the profits of the trading business and invest in new ventures. Five percent is a relatively small percentage of total profits, but given the size of your operations, that percentage would provide a significant amount of capital on a quarterly basis. Through our contacts, and those of Sir Paul and Mr. James, we could select a few well-considered opportunities to finance in return for an ownership interest." Warming to her topic, she leaned forward. "The size of the ownership interests would vary by investment, depending upon the founder's character, business concept, stage of business development, financial resources and results, and collateral. I would structure each request with a complete plan for the business and analysis of its prospects, and provide advisors in specific areas as particular needs arise. What do you think?"

Mulling it over, Henry privately was enormously pleased at her ingenuity. *If she were a man, she could run the trading company better than I ever could.* "It is an excellent suggestion, put forth in your own extraordinary clarity of argument. I concur. Knowing you as I do, I can guess that one of our first investments will be in an operetta soon to open in the *ton*." He leaned back in his chair.

Bri's eyes sparkled as she sat up straighter. "Exactly! Last night, Clarissa gave me the original business proposal that convinced her father to invest. I asked her for the projected costs and profits for this run. When my analysis is complete, I will give you my recommendation."

"Not to me, my dear. The five percent is my decision. The investments are yours. I suggest that you discuss them with Young James." Henry raised both palms to stop her protests. "Not to second guess you, but to demonstrate to him your analytical business skills and to avail ourselves of his advice. Taking any objections of Young James into account will help structure the business direction to overcome potential pitfalls."

"But—"

"Bri, you will make the ultimate decision on any investment. That is agreed. But you must seek out the additional advice of Young James and Sir Paul for our own protection. Not all of these investments will be successful. Sometimes intelligent people with good ideas will fail, for a myriad of reasons. I don't believe we will be able to measure the success of our decisions for five years, so I want to have a record of your recommendations as well as those of Young James and Sir Paul. Then we will see if any patterns emerge. Any other ideas at the moment?"

"Yes. Jane Anne is a talented hair dresser. I believe a salon catering to the *ton* would be a success. They have such places in France. She could train others in her techniques and perhaps package and sell the special hair products she has developed from natural sources. At the moment, I am helping her find clients on her day off, to build word-of-mouth, and to see if she really likes the idea of being independent. That business is therefore a few months away from being activated.

"I have also talked with Dr. St. Cloud about some new dog and cat food that he has developed to meet their nutritional needs in a scientific manner instead of table scraps. While his inheritance is substantial, I was thinking that we could help him set up an export business through our shipping resources."

The earl smiled. "When you start thinking, you see opportunities that others miss, such as introducing the songs from the musical play into *The Opera Café*. You always cast an eye to the business angle." *Surely Young James must be as attracted to her mind as he is to her looks.* "Anything else?"

"Not now. I appreciate your confidence and approval of my recommendation for the investment operation. I thought we could simply call it Wyndward Investments. I look forward to helping these new businesses grow."

"Sounds fine. I am going into the office. Are you ready for the ball on Thursday? Should we practice our dancing tonight?"

"I have a few things to pick up today. I promised to meet Clarissa at the theatre for lunch on Thursday, but I believe I shall spend most of today reviewing the financial considerations for the play as well as the files you brought home from the office. But it wouldn't be a bad idea to review some dance steps. I don't want to make a fool of myself. On Thursday, Jane Anne will do the hair of two of my friends, and then return here at four o'clock to help me prepare for the ball. I am going to wear a wonderful green dress from Mme. Mottier's. I thought my first ball in the *ton* would be stifling, but now… who knows what will happen?"

"One more thing you should know. Blackie is going to attend the Season. Once I thought you and he might make a good couple."

Bri's face clouded. "I've always liked him. It is as disturbing to me as to you that he might have deceived us. But I don't feel the kind of attraction to him that I do to Mr. James. And he's too old!"

"So you *are* attracted to Young James." The earl strode out of the study and, over his shoulder, tossed out one more comment. "You have the same look that you did when you were six and pretended you didn't fall into the pond in your new dress chasing a butterfly. You can't fool me. You are smitten." He laughed as he heard her stand and stomp after him.

CHAPTER FIFTEEN

Tuesday, March 12, 1811 – Pelican's Beak Pub
Jean-Louis

Jean-Louis sat in his usual seat, with his back to the wall so he had an unobstructed view of the pub, frequented by men of questionable character under questionable circumstances. A man of medium height and what Jean-Louis would term medium features came in. *Average men are not noticed—they blend in.* "Thank you for coming." *The Bow Street Runners have a good man in Boyd.*

"Your note intrigued me. I must admit, I was surprised to hear from you. It's well known that you operate on the fringes of the demimonde and know every Hackney driver in London. But we've never tied you to a crime. You're generally looking for information, protecting your employer. I have no doubt that you are capable of anything. All men are. But you earned my trust when we investigated the death of Luc de Merbeau. So I came today."

Ale was brought to the table. After the server left, Boyd continued, "You think you have the culprit in your sights?"

"Perhaps. We may be wrong. But we suspect that one of the trusted associates of my employer may have been involved."

"What evidence do you have?"

"None, at the moment."

"What is the motive?"

"Partly money, but there is more we need to know. I believe the motive is buried in his sketchy early life. An orphan, no records, you know the profile. Events that pre-date my knowledge of the family. I have investigators in Scotland looking into some leads."

"A lot of speculation, Frenchman. Why involve me now?"

"I'd like to go back through all the reports of the comte's death. Maybe there's something we missed. Another body, perhaps. Maybe the mastermind killed the killer. No witnesses to a hired killer or footpad's demise. And the earl's younger brother died in the country a year before the comte in another *accident*. I'd like to know if any other bodies showed up in that area. Any sightings of Gypsies."

"Gypsies? Now that's an old canard. They're not all thieves and killers. In any case, that location is hours away in another jurisdiction. I have no authority there." He scoffed. "*You'd* have authority there. It's your shire."

"But I don't want to alert anyone of our interest. A bureaucratic review would be easier to ignore. I don't want our suspected culprit to know we're onto him."

"I'll help on the condition that we work together and that you keep me informed. Agreed?"

"Agreed."

They drained their mugs, and Jean-Louis left by the back door.

Boyd walked out the front.

***

Tuesday, March 12, 1811 – Winters Foundling Hospital
Gwyneth

The Winters Foundling Hospital was located in a working class area of London, near its main supply of foundlings. Gwyneth walked under the canopy that shielded so many babies left by mothers who felt they had no other choice.

First trying Charlotte's home, Gwyneth berated herself for not knowing that Charlotte would seek out a place where she felt safe, a place built from Charlotte's heart to help the unfortunate and make their lives better.

How could Henry be so obtuse?

The doorman recognized the comtesse and let her in. Gwyneth made her way through the brightly decorated foyer, through a long hallway with private rooms that provided anonymity to mothers awaiting childbirth, and into the back area where Charlotte's private office was located. She knocked.

No answer.

Gwyneth knocked again. "It's me, Charlotte. Please open the door."

"I'm over here."

Turning, Gwyneth saw Charlotte approaching.

"A baby was left by the side door. A little girl. We've settled her in." She opened the door and her friend followed her inside. "Please close the door."

The comtesse did as she was instructed. They sat down at a small table. "Charlotte…my brother is a fool."

Charlotte demurred. "I am the fool. Fifteen years gone. You and Bri are the saving grace." She shook her head. "I loved that man."

"Surely you still do."

"So what? He doesn't love me. I am too old for these courtship dramas."

"I don't know why he wants to take Bri to the ball alone."

"*I* won't be alone. I have another escort."

"Already?" Gwyneth laughed. "I shouldn't be surprised. You are a resilient and resourceful woman. May I ask who your escort is?"

"You'll see."

The comtesse raised an eyebrow. "I'm not sure Henry's ever lost something or someone he cared about, except by death. Your intent is to make him jealous, correct?"

"Perhaps."

"Perhaps? Ha! I cannot recall a moment where my brother didn't feel he was in control or couldn't bend the situation to his benefit. You have set him back on his heels. He thinks you said you would get another escort just to annoy him. The look on his face will be priceless."

"Gwyneth, I don't think you realize that Henry and I may never spend another moment together. I hope you and I will remain friends. I hope Bri will still see me as a friend."

Taken aback, Gwyneth leaned forward in her chair. "Always. I know I can speak for both of us."

Charlotte sighed, looked at Gwyneth and stifled a sob. Tears ran down her face. "I loved him, Wynnie. I still love him."

Gwyneth rose to her feet, walked over to her friend, leaned down and wrapped her arms around Charlotte, letting her sob until she was unable to shed another tear.

***

March 12, 1811 – Lord Ravenshire's Townhouse
Jean-Louis

After dinner, Jean-Louis pulled out his fiddle, and Thompson sat at the pianoforte in the parlor.

Henry and Bri bowed, and danced the steps of the Quadrille, the reel, and then tried a waltz. In a flourish of a twirl, Henry knocked over a stack of books on a side table.

"Let's start again. Keep your eyes on me."

"And knock over more things?" Bri stifled a laugh.

This time, they executed the steps flawlessly, bowing to their orchestra when they finished.

"One more time," Bri demanded. After the second waltz, she was out of breath. "I'm as ready as I can be. The orchestra probably won't even play a waltz."

Bri and Henry collapsed onto the divan.

"How will I have the energy to dance like this all night?"

"You're young. You'll have energy to spare. I, on the other hand, may have an apoplectic fit."

***

Tuesday, March 12, 1811 – Baroness Glasspool's Mansion
Charlotte

Charlotte had thrown herself into her work after dismissing Henry on Sunday. Seeing her friend Wynnie earlier that day had deepened the pain. *Wynnie and Bri are the closest people to me. I don't want to lose them even if Henry has hurt me so deeply.* She had found the perfect escort for Lady Elisabeth's ball on the fourteenth. *Henry needs to be taught a lesson—not to take me for granted. He is a selfish oaf.*

Late into the evening, Charlotte could not sleep, so she pulled on her robe and sat at her writing desk. The moonlight filtered through the window and her candle burned down until the wick floated in liquid as she read through her diary.

    After an hour, she began to write:

> Reading back over my entries, I see that I believed
> what I wanted to believe.
>
> I interpreted Henry's every action as confirmation of
> what I hoped, not what was. I read between lines
> where there was nothing to read.
>
> Oh, how we women delude ourselves, imagining a
> life with a man we love, assuming he wants what we
> want.
>
> I have been a fool, but no longer.
>
> No longer will I change my life to suit him.
>
> No longer will I wait to make plans, to travel, to dine until
> he and I have spoken.
>
> No longer will I think in terms of us. From now on, I will
> think in terms of me.
>
> No longer am I the leaf tossed by the wind.
>
> I am riding the wind.
>
> I am commanding the wind.
>
> I am the wind.

CHAPTER SIXTEEN

Wednesday, March 13, 1811 – Winters Foundling Hospital
Gio

Gio struggled to carry a large basket into the hospital. A nurse ran over and tried to take the basket away from the dwarf, but met resistance. Each struggled to overcome the other's tug.

"This is my job."

"And this is my lunch."

For a moment, the nurse's mouth dropped open.

Imagining that she was remembering horror-filled rumors asserting that dwarfs ate babies, Gio raised the top of the basket. "See? Wine? A baguette. Cheese."

The young girl's face turned a shade of scarlet. "Forgive me, sir."

"Lord Ostwold."

As an artist, Gio had seen every color in a human face, but this was the first time he could swear he saw violet in someone's cheeks.

The girl scurried off.

Gio walked back to Charlotte's office and knocked a special code.

The door opened. "My secret confidante. Thank you for coming." Charlotte leaned down and kissed him on the forehead.

The artist hopped onto a chair. "All is not lost. I've known the earl since he was twelve. You two have a camaraderie that is enviable. He is a man of the world, chafes at control, follows his own muse—a man of action as well as a deep thinker. He is loyal to friends, and tolerant. Give him some time to reflect. Yes, he may have taken you for granted. That's what we men do. A nudge may work."

"I have a nudge. Another escort for Lady Elisabeth's ball."

"Inducing jealousy. Clever, but fraught. Don't flaunt it. I shall be there. Wouldn't miss it now." He opened the picnic basket and Charlotte spread the food out on the table.

"Even a tablecloth. You are a thoughtful man. Maybe I should marry you."

Gio shrugged. "You could do worse."

"Why have you never married again, Gio?"

"Surely I am too cantankerous for any woman."

"No, you are talented, clever, and you love women."

Gio raised his index finger. "One little detail you're missing."

"You are a *famous* dwarf. Your worth is not dictated by your stature."

"Now who is being naïve? One good thing may come of your break-up."

"What's that?"

"You'll have time to sit for a portrait before I die. I'll immortalize you."

***

Wednesday, March 13, 1811 – Blackburn's Townhouse
Blackie

Not every night, but as midnight neared, and when the mood moved him, Blackie wrote in his diary. He'd adopted a code in the event his grandmother or her friend, the Gypsy witch, or a confederate they enlisted to find it, decided to snoop.

His black cat, Midnight, lay lazily on his desk, looking up occasionally as Blackie talked to her.

Trusting no one, a nonverbal keeper of secrets met Blackie's needs. She had come to him seven years earlier, of indeterminate age, as a stray. Watching him one night through the window, she pawed the pane to attract his attention. Intrigued, he opened the window and they took each other's measure.

"I expect loyalty, mousing and companionship."

The cat meowed.

Blackie smiled. "You agree to my terms?"

She rubbed her head on his hand.

"I submit to yours. Let me find you some food."

Accustomed to being alone at night, Blackie rummaged in the kitchen for cream and scraps of meat. He was about to move the bowls to the floor from the counter when the cat startled him by jumping up next to him. "You know what you want. I like that." He petted her short-haired coat and marveled at her amber eyes.

She looked at him.

"You know me, don't you?"

She held his gaze for a moment, and then went back to methodically licking the cream, covering her mouth with white foam.

Company. Silent, loyal and useful.

That first night they met, he'd written in his diary:

Tonight I met my first friend.

She will never betray my secrets.
She brings life to an empty home.
Her amber eyes shine in the darkness.

I am no longer alone...

***

Wednesday, March 13, 1811 – Lord Ravenshire's Townhouse
Bri

Bri opened the diary given to her many years ago by her tutor, Philip Laurence.

She flipped through its gilded-edge pages. Each was pristine. Untouched. No entries. Not a word had been written. Ever.

Bri's life was stored in her head, not on paper. Not for someone else to find.

Her father was a diarist, though primarily at sea with hours and hours of solitude. Trained to record his life by his tutor, Philip Laurence, who also tutored Bri, Henry had a musing, philosophical mind, as did his university friend, Nate Parker, known as The American. She'd met him during a long visit to America years earlier and argued philosophy with him for hours. She still remembered her arguments. They agreed to a draw.

The subject had been the nature of mankind: were killing, war and hatred the defining characteristics of their species or were kindness, empathy and love? She remembered Parker's novel approach: first each argued one side, then changed to become proponents of the other side. It formed the basis of her analytical approach: always understand the arguments of the countervailing proposition. To win a debate, one must understand the other point of view. A flash of insight gripped her mind. *Maybe that's where I'm wrong on Mr. James. I need to understand his point of view.* She quickly rejected that concept. *No. His thinking is flawed. I'm sure I can convince him with logic.*

Laurence always mentioned—or threatened—that he would like to write a history of the Wyndwards. Bri had scoffed at that notion. *Who would be interested?*

Although Bri was not a diarist, she was a letter writer, or more properly, a note writer—short and to the point on personal matters. Analytical reports, however, were a specialty—long and detailed. She was more at home with numbers than with emotions and she knew it.

Am I afraid to write down my feelings? Tomorrow is my first ball!

CHAPTER SEVENTEEN

Wednesday, March 13, 1811 – Lord Ravenshire's Townhouse
Bri

Muted light beamed from the gray, clouded sky into Bri's rooms as she dressed. *Only one more day until I see Mr. James again.* She chided herself. *I must get him out of my mind.* She had promised her father to behave.

At breakfast earlier that morning, the day before Lady Elisabeth's ball, Bri made the arrangements with Jean-Louis for Jane Anne's transportation to her appointments with Lady Penelope and Clarissa.

Once back upstairs, Bri sat at the antique kidney-shaped desk in her sitting room, reviewing the investment proposal for the operetta. In Berlin, it had run for four months and covered its initial costs in three, leaving a modest profit. Ticket prices in Berlin, however, were lower than in London, and theatre attendance was not as high. Furthermore, Bri noted, a great deal of the original cost was in development of the plot, music and rehearsal refinements before the play opened. Those costs were behind them for the London run, except for the general rehearsals and auditions now being conducted, which were minor.

The main obstacle that Bri saw in the investment proposal was that there was only a limited run possible at the Theatre-Royal Haymarket, as the Shakespeare Festival was due to begin three months after the operetta's opening date. This would mean either closing the operetta, or vacating the theatre so that the Shakespeare

Festival could have two weeks of uninterrupted rehearsal and production design before its scheduled opening. To extend the operetta's run, the only option seemed to be moving the entire production to a new venue on a very tight schedule. That expense would be significant and an alternative venue would have to be secured with a deposit before a full accounting of the play's finances could be completed. Bri estimated that with the right promotion in the *ton*, the run of the operetta could exceed six months. An abbreviated run of three months was not a viable investment option. Desperate for a venue, Herr Kramer and the count had compromised, but they had doomed their financial return.

In addition, the difficulties in leasing their current venue and delays in arranging financing had eroded operating capital more than projected. Bri felt that she could soundly recommend the financing necessary to mount the production in return for a modest portion of ownership, but the challenges surrounding an extended run would have to be solved.

The Haymarket was an excellent choice for the new play, but the Shakespeare Festival had a cachet and a following that she would have to consider. Perhaps there were other theatres that could be used or renovated in time to open their season. *I'll discuss this with Mr. James on Friday.*

Her thoughts turned to the banker. *Why does father think I am in love—or lust?* She didn't know how to describe her feelings for Mr. James, as they seemed to change constantly. One moment she admired him, the next she found him extremely annoying and petty. *He is handsome. Those gray eyes are intense, like the sky in a storm.* The jet black hair gave him an exotic air, even a little frightening at times.

When his gaze focused on her, she forgot what she was thinking. That had never happened to her before. *But that can't be love. Surely romantic love is instantly known to both parties, confirmed without any doubts. Maybe it is lust.* It was always that way in books. Her first thought was to ask Charlotte. Her stomach churned. *What if she doesn't want to see me again? She is like another aunt to me, a surrogate mother.*

Scandalous novels were surreptitiously passed among young ladies of the *ton*. Their themes were the same: one look from the hero and the heroine fell in love. No person, no story had prepared Bri for her complicated feelings. She considered herself an independent woman, although she knew she possessed a tremendous advantage by virtue of the freedom her father provided her. He made it possible for her to be whatever she wanted to be.

A proscribed life as a Society wife was not part of her life plan. Marriage was something she imagined far in the future, with an equal partner. Unwillingly, she found herself daydreaming about romance with Mr. James. Shocked at her own reveries, she could not prevent the random thoughts from entering her mind. The thought of seeing him at the ball that evening made her heart flutter. Her reaction embarrassed her. *Will others be able to discern my interest in Mr. James?* Clarissa said she noticed it. That would be humiliating. *Perhaps I have been too blasé about Society. Perhaps navigating the protocols of the* ton *will take more skill than I anticipated. Surely I am up to the challenge. None of those 'simpering Society types' could be more astute at this game than I. Could they?*

She loved the idea of dressing up for the ball, but admitted to herself that her peers had mastered a certain insouciance that she lacked. *Maybe attending the ball is not such a good idea.* To be evaluated based on what she looked like in her ball gown instead of her intelligence annoyed her. *I must admit I want to be admired for my appearance tonight. What is going on? Am I going mad?* She'd made a game of defying Society's rules, but would it backfire?

The clock struck eleven, and she realized she had arranged to meet Clarissa for lunch at the theatre. *Clarissa can reassure me.* Maybe that tea Aunt Gwyneth arranged was not so pointless after all. At least she would know a few other women at the ball. *Why did I agree to this? What if no one asks me to dance? Perhaps this, maybe that, what if that…I am going around in circles.*

Upset, Bri grabbed her reticule and dashed down the stairs. Remembering that Jean-Louis was assigned to Jane Anne today, she called out, "Thompson, would you please hail me a Hackney carriage? I need to meet Lady Clarissa at the Haymarket."

By the time she had put on her cloak, Thompson had secured a Hackney carriage. "Enjoy your day, Lady Gabriella."

"I shall return around three o'clock."

On the way to the theatre, her mind constantly reworked her dilemma. *Am I in love with Edward or merely infatuated?* What would it be like to be married? Would they live in town and occasionally visit Ravenshire? What about children? She could still manage Father's investments, but what did she know about children? How would she cope? Would they look like Edward or her? Maybe they could have

Sunday picnics with Father and Aunt Gwyneth, go to museums, the circus...then Bri abruptly stopped her imaginings, willing herself to come back to reality. *How will I survive tomorrow evening? Will I even sleep tonight?*

As the Hackney pulled up in front of the theatre, Bri got out. The guard recognized her and opened the door, saying, "Good morning, Lady Gabriella. Lady Clarissa told me to expect you. She is working with Herr Kramer on the stage."

Heading toward the stage, Bri saw Herr Kramer and Clarissa talking at the piano. Herr Kramer began the song that had not been finished the night of the rehearsal. The musical introduction lasted more than the few bars that had been played the night before, and then to Bri's surprise, Clarissa began to sing the lyrics to the haunting melody. Her a high, clear voice trilled unlike any that Bri had ever heard. The operas she had attended featured voices that were darker in timbre, more cloudy in expression. Clarissa's voice was lilting, strong and pure. The song touched Bri deeply, and she knew it would be the high point of *The Princess.*

Transfixed by Clarissa's performance, Bri was unable to move and watched and listened from the aisle. When Clarissa sang the final note, the silence was overwhelming. Bri could imagine the burst of applause, but the sound of her own hands clapping broke the spell.

Startled, Herr Kramer and Clarissa looked toward the aisle and recognized Bri. They smiled and waved her toward the stage.

"We thought we were alone, Lady Gabriella." Herr Kramer stood and clicked his heels. "What do you think of our little tune?"

"It is a masterpiece. Everyone in the *ton* will be singing that song. It is exotically beautiful and extremely romantic. You must prepare the music for *The Opera Café.*"

The composer gave a quick bow of his head. "That was an excellent suggestion, and one I intend to follow."

"Clarissa, you never told me that you could sing so beautifully. You should be the star of this production."

"I have been trying to persuade Lady Clarissa to take the role since the beginning, but she will not acquiesce, citing the dictates of Society."

"No woman of breeding would appear on the stage, and my father, although he enjoys the theatre, and has no objection to financing the operetta, would no doubt draw the line at his daughter actually performing in it."

Bri paced around the pianoforte. "Dr. St. Cloud's stage name gives him anonymity. Why should a woman be treated differently? Why don't you adopt a stage name? With a brunette wig no one would recognize you. You could be a young lady of the *ton* by day and a darling of the theatre by night."

"A clever solution." Herr Kramer tapped a key on the piano over and over. "A stage name…"

"Well, I will consider it and discuss it with my father tonight when he returns from Scotland. Perhaps a disguise would be acceptable to him. He might even enjoy playing a joke on Society, but it may be too daring. His main concern is my reputation, of course."

"You ladies come up with a name. I am going to prepare a copy of the score for *The Opera Café*." Herr Kramer clicked his heels with a slight bow and exited the stage.

"Will we see you at the ball tomorrow night, Herr Kramer?"

"Yes. I am going to provide piano background music during breaks from the dancing. I am going to play some of our score as another way to attract the *ton* to our operetta. I thought of it after your comment about giving sheet music to *The Opera Café*, Lady Gabriella. You have excellent ideas to attract an audience."

Bri beamed at the compliment. "I'm looking forward to hearing that plaintive melody again tonight."

Clarissa and Bri left the theatre, and climbed into Clarissa's carriage.

"Are you looking forward to seeing the doctor tomorrow night at the ball?"

Clarissa blushed. "I made a reservation at *Les Crêpes* for lunch, although I think I am too excited to eat."

"I never expected to be so on edge about something I once thought trivial. Aunt Gwyneth's tea was not a foolish waste of time, as I originally assumed. Now, I am glad we met some of the other women attending this Season. At least there will be a few familiar faces."

"And don't forget Mr. James and Dr. St. Cloud."

Bri shifted in her seat. "Clarissa, I don't know what I am feeling. One minute I am furious with Mr. James for being arrogant and narrow-minded, and the next minute I find myself dreaming of his kiss. How shall I survive the ball?"

"I am not annoyed with Dr. St. Cloud, but I am as nervous as you are. 'Is this romance?' I ask myself that question over and over. It is thoroughly frustrating."

They alighted from the carriage and went into the restaurant through a door painted in a welcoming shade of blue. Leaded panes diffused the early afternoon light from windows trimmed in white lace curtains that looked fresh against walls painted in the French blue of Provence. The proprietress showed them to a table under one of the windows. White tulips arced over the edges of blue and white Chinese vases at every table. The tables themselves were of sturdy wood, painted blue, with matching chairs upholstered in a blue-and-white checked pattern. White lace tablecloths matched the curtains.

"I would like a glass of wine, but I am mindful of Aunt Gwyneth's warning. My stomach may not be able to take too much excitement. I think chamomile tea is a better choice."

"I agree. I don't know how I could eat anything at the ball." Clarissa looked over the menu with little interest.

Bri leaned toward her friend and lowered her voice. "You don't. Aunt Gwyneth insists that I must eat at home so that I do not eat too much at the ball out of nervousness. You must have your cook prepare a small meal so that you can relax at the ball and 'just nibble,' as Aunt Gwyneth would say, so as to avoid spilling anything on your gown or making yourself ill in public." Bri laughed and leaned back in her chair. "When she first told me this, I thought it was ridiculous, but now it seems eminently wise."

"We thought we were so clever at that tea. The others knew we were making fools of ourselves."

The waiter appeared.

Bri ordered a mushroom and spinach crêpe and chamomile tea.

"Make that two," Clarissa echoed. "When the specter of the Marriage Season loomed ahead, I wondered if I would meet the man of my dreams at a ball and fall in love. It's already happened, before the first ball. All I can think of is Dr. St. Cloud. I fear I am in love with him and when I think about how I would feel if he were not in love with me, I become terribly sad. If he found romance with another, I would never want to attend another ball."

"It is clear that Dr. St. Cloud is already under your spell. Mr. James and I seem to be at each other's throats. Were he to spurn me, I would still have to see him. For one thing, he is a family friend. For another, he handles my family's banking needs. If Mr. James were to find another woman more appealing than I…I…would be desolated. I would have to see him with another woman. Why do I even let that thought cross my mind? Isn't falling in love supposed to be joyful? Half the time, I am nearly despondent. My feelings range all over the spectrum."

Their luncheon plates were delivered.

As they took small bites of their crêpes, they found the tea better suited their uneasy stomachs.

After finishing their meal, each promised to seek out the other as soon as they arrived at the ball to gain confidence by facing the *ton* together. Clarissa's carriage was waiting outside the restaurant. They climbed in, and continued to talk about their conflicting feelings on the journey home.

As they approached her father's townhouse, Bri turned to Clarissa. "Others have faced this prospect. I suppose it is a rite of passage that we will laugh about one day. At this moment, it seems decidedly unfunny."

Leaving the carriage, Bri looked through the window. "After tomorrow night it will be over." She shrugged. "Until then."

Clarissa waved farewell as her carriage pulled away.

CHAPTER EIGHTEEN

Wednesday, March 13, 1811 – Wyndward Trading Offices
Henry

As the earl's carriage headed to the offices of Wyndward Trading, he thought back to the early days, when his father Neyl oversaw the Ravenshire estates. His younger brother Rychard matched his father's love of the land, though Henry, as the older brother, would inherit the estates through the law of primogeniture. Then Viscount Ravenshire, Henry had longed for adventure away from the windswept foothills, pristine lakes and green fields of Ravenshire.

Obtaining his father's blessing to take two years to try to build a trading company with his inheritance from his late mother's family, Henry set off for London.

Neyl, the 10th Earl of Ravenshire, thought it best to tame his eldest son's wanderlust early. That lust was never tamed. No one foresaw the success of Wyndward Trading. In less than ten years, its annual returns exceeded the annual income generated by the vast Ravenshire estates. Memories flowed into Henry's mind. He remembered his first visit to this building, then fallen into disrepair, which now housed his operations.

***

Early June 1779 – The London Docks
Henry

Arriving in London from Ravenshire after graduating from Merton College, Oxford, Henry wandered among the warehouses near the docks, talking with the stevedores, day laborers, shipping clerks, whoever would give him a moment. Soon he knew which ships were sailing and docking and their cargo. He learned of a ship that had its sailing to the Caribbean delayed due to Lloyd's cancellation of its insurance, as too many shipwrecks in that area had occurred in this sailing season. Henry sought out the captain, and was directed to a warren of offices in one of the oldest warehouses on the docks. Once a grand building, it reeked of neglect, but retained the architectural character of the grand period of exploration nearly a hundred years earlier.

Making his way to the office marked *M. J. Kirk & Sons*, Henry knocked on the door and was greeted by a boisterous voice issuing a command. "The door's open, you fool."

A ruddy-complexioned man sat behind a desk covered with organized sets of documents. His still-robust physique was impressive for a man of his age, which Henry estimated to be over sixty.

"Well, what is it? Can't you see I'm busy?"

"Yes, sir." Henry aimed to be deferential. "I have come, Mr. Kirk—"

The weathered man barked a swift and abrupt correction. "*Captain* Kirk."

Henry recovered quickly. "Captain Kirk. I have been told that you've delayed your scheduled sailing to the Caribbean due to a lack of insurance. I am here to propose that I provide that insurance."

Throwing down his pen, and rising to his feet to take charge, the captain scoffed. "You don't look like a rich gentleman to me. And frankly, I have not the requisite twenty-five percent to put up to secure the insurance. I am very nearly at the end of my rope, so don't push me any farther."

"You will not need to put up anything, Captain. I propose that I provide the insurance bond in exchange for fifty percent ownership of your cargo profit."

Rage flushed the captain's face. "So bold, are you? What makes you think that I would even entertain that offer?"

"Because you cannot secure insurance under any other conditions, and because fifty percent of your cargo profit is better than no profit at all, Captain."

Mark Julius Kirk turned his back on the venturesome young man and stared out the dirty window at his ship, pregnant with cargo.

Henry remained silent. His grandfather, the Duke of Pytchley, had advised him long ago that silence was the best negotiating tool.

Captain Kirk turned around and stared at Henry. "If we are to sail, it must be tonight or I risk losing my crew. Can we make these arrangements now? You may be a fool, young man, but if you are a fool with the money that you purport to have, and can save my ship's cargo, then who am I to argue? I have exhausted all other options. Come over here, and let me show you the manifest."

Henry looked over the list of cargo bound for the Caribbean and discussed with the captain what they might procure for the return voyage to sell in England and Europe. Buoyed by Henry's explanation of his family background and offer of a letter of credit for any purchases that might exceed their profits from the consignments of goods destined for the Caribbean, Captain Kirk proved a ready partner.

Henry noted that some items had been ordered by British and Portuguese government outposts based on partial letters of credit, so that the shipment was secure. The balance was from wealthy landowners, many of whom had names that Henry recognized. Satisfied that the papers were in order, and that he could afford this transaction, the viscount extended his hand to the captain. "Let us go to my barristers and my banker to complete our transaction."

"Lead the way, Young Viscount."

Henry laughed. "That's what they called me at Oxford."

Captain Kirk filled a carrying case with the key documents relating to the voyage. "If you can make this work, I'll call you whatever you like."

"There's always the risk of interception by ships fighting the American Revolution." Henry wanted to know the captain's strategy.

"There's always a war somewhere, Young Viscount. Maybe you'll lose all your money. Maybe you won't. That's life on the high seas."

"Your sign says M. J. Kirk & Sons. Are there any sons?"

Kirk looked off into the distance. "There were. One died of

smallpox in the Caribbean. The other died in a shipwreck."

"I'm sorry to hear that."

"Not as sorry as I am to be reminded of it."

Leaving the building, they hailed a Hackney and Henry instructed the driver, "The offices of Gyfford & Wexford, Solicitors."

As they rode, Captain Kirk queried Henry. "Is not a young man like you supposed to 'do your duty' to the family estates? Are you the youngest son with no rights of inheritance?"

"No, sir, as a matter of fact, I am the eldest of two brothers, but it is my younger brother's love of the land that is compelling. I am hoping to build my own fortune so that he will be able to run the estates while I travel the world."

"Well, son," Kirk warmed to his story with a contagious enthusiasm, "a life on the sea is a life like no other. Once you get the ocean air in your blood, the open seas provide a feeling of unlimited horizons that nothing else can match. It is your wits you live by out there, not your breeding, Young Viscount."

"I've read a great many books on the explorers and seafarers, and I look forward to experiencing the ocean first hand. My grandfather's brother was a sailor and left me his logs. I became fascinated at an early age. I've sailed the Mediterranean as a passenger and to America once, before the war."

"Well, perhaps on one of my future voyages, we shall find a place for you."

"You misunderstand, Captain. I shall be on *this* voyage with you, protecting my investment and learning under your tutelage."

"Like hell you will! This is too much! I make the decisions, not some young whippersnapper." As the captain fumed, his face flushed to nearly crimson with fury."How old are you?"

"Nineteen. Treat me as any member of the crew on the trip over. I intend to learn the business from the bottom up. As for my role on the return trip, we can discuss that once we reach the Caribbean. I shall not usurp your role. I merely mean to learn, Captain." Henry remained calm. "And I *shall* sail with you. I am paying for the privilege."

Continuing the ride in silence, the captain stared out the window as the carriage pulled up to the building that housed Henry's solicitors.

Stepping out of the carriage, Henry paid the Hackney cabbie, and gestured for Captain Kirk to precede him into the building. As they entered the foyer, Henry strode to the clerk. "I am Henry, Viscount Ravenshire. I would like to see my family's solicitor, Sir Roscoe."

The clerk asked Henry and the captain to wait, disappeared, and then scurried around the corner, followed by Sir Roscoe. The solicitor appeared somewhat nonplussed. "I did not know you planned to meet with us this afternoon, Lord Ravenshire. What may we do for you?"

"Forgive me, Sir Roscoe, for not making a formal appointment, but I am here on a matter of some urgency." Gesturing to his companion, he introduced them.

"Let us seek privacy." Sir Roscoe led him to his office.

As they entered, Henry said, "The captain's ship, *Venture*, will be sailing tonight for the Caribbean. I have agreed to provide an insurance bond for the cargo in exchange for a fifty percent interest in the cargo profit. In addition, I have agreed to provide a letter of credit for additional purchases of cargo for the return voyage. We would like to draw up partnership papers that set out these terms, and then we will go to James & Co. to secure the appropriate letters of credit after you secure the insurance bond and set our agreement to paper."

As a tribute to his station and discretion, Sir Roscoe betrayed no indication of shock at these words. "I recently received a letter from the earl that you were coming to London to pursue development of a trading enterprise. You certainly have moved quickly."

Turning to Captain Kirk, the solicitor took his measure. "There is very little time, Captain. Ordinarily I would conduct a small inquiry into your background and experience. Given the time constraints, I must accept the viscount's assessment of you. We shall memorialize good faith in the documents and place our trust in each other. May I see the manifest?"

Sir Roscoe spent about twenty minutes reviewing Captain Kirk's papers. "I am satisfied that these documents meet maritime standards. Indeed, they are notarized by someone I know to be thorough and honest."

The solicitor rang a bell. When an attendant appeared, he instructed him to bring tea and biscuits for Henry and the captain while they waited.

"I will return in about a half hour's time with prepared documents for your signatures. Please make yourself comfortable here until then. Would you like to pen a note to James & Co. so that they can prepare your letters of credit before you arrive? We can send a messenger."

"An excellent suggestion, Sir Roscoe."

A clerk appeared with paper and pen, and waited while Henry sent a note to his school friend, John James of James & Co. Once the note was completed, the clerk dripped hot wax over the closure and sealed it with the solicitor's engraved stamp. He left the room.

The captain and Henry settled in for the wait. "Captain, I would like to hear more of your travels. This will be your seventh trip to the Caribbean?"

The captain beamed as he relayed his experiences. "The first trip was harrowing. We were first blown off course and then delayed in the Canary Islands, becalmed. By the time the winds picked up again, we were on the cusp of the bad weather, and barely survived a hurricane that blew us into a protected natural harbor on Barbados. It was a blessing of Providence, I tell you. That ship of mine can withstand anything."

"How did you make the contacts to obtain your cargo for the return trip?"

"Deliveries are to the landowners who want to replenish their supplies of items not available in the New World, luxuries as diverse as silk to books. However, they are actively seeking markets for their prodigious grain and sugar products as well as exotic shell jewelry. Some had their own trading companies that imported silver and gold from the southern continent, which we were able to exchange for the luxuries we brought. I decided that one-quarter government contracts, one-half private contracts and one-quarter speculative goods would be a good mix sailing from England, and I was right. What I have been unable to do as successfully is acquire goods to fill my cargo bays completely on the trip back. There was also a lesson to be learned in transporting perishable goods: it doesn't work except for feeding the crew during the voyage. I started at about fifty percent of capacity on the return trip, but it was still profitable. Until I met you, it had never gone over seventy percent. Your letters of credit will solve that problem."

Henry gathered his thoughts. "Captain, I know that you feel that I am something of an interloper in this situation, but perhaps you do not see the larger purpose in my participation. Completing a successful trip together in this first venture—in the *Venture*—coupled with my financial resources, we can buy another ship and send two ships per sailing season. There is no reason why we cannot one day dominate shipping between the United Kingdom and the Caribbean. When the war is over, we can sail to America and open new markets."

"Your determination and vision impress me."

They continued discussing ideas for potential routes and cargo. Henry came to see that the captain was an astute businessman as well as experienced sailor. When Sir Roscoe returned, they each read the documents, and signed where indicated on three separate copies. Sir Roscoe and a clerk witnessed their signatures. "We will keep one copy here for you, Lord Ravenshire. Another is for the bank, and one is for Captain Kirk." The formalities concluded, the gentlemen shook hands, and Sir Roscoe escorted them out to the front of the building. "The bank sent its carriage for you, as I was told you arrived in a Hackney."

Henry and the captain climbed into the carriage for the short ride to James & Co. On the way, Henry explained that John James was an old schoolmate of his, who had gained a good knowledge of shipping.

As they arrived at the bank, an elderly man at the front desk escorted them to the office of the Vice President. John's father was the Director, a firm believer in the principle of working one's way through all jobs in the bank to fully understand how it operated. Starting as a page, John then became a teller, followed by an assignment in the back office, processing loans, letters of credit and other transactions during school holidays. He had recently been given a private office and a few accounts to manage, mostly those of his schoolmates like Henry, Viscount Ravenshire.

As they reached John's office, he rose from his desk to greet them, "Ravenshire, good to see you," shaking his hand. "And you must be Captain Kirk." He shook the captain's hand with a firm grip. "May I see the documents?"

Henry handed the packet to the banker, who perused the papers. Motioning to the two guests to have a seat, John rang for tea.

The banker made a suggestion. "Given the time constraints, we can deliver notice of insurance bonds to your shippers by messenger. Most of them are our customers. I shall prepare the letters of credit.

Our name is well known in the Caribbean. We have established a small office in Bermuda to handle business in that part of the world, so you will have no problem securing cargo." Ringing for an attendant, John asked for several of the bank's standard letter of credit forms. Turning to Henry, he said, "My recommendation is to issue these in modest amounts rather than one total amount."

Henry and the captain readily agreed.

"Would five equal amounts suffice?"

The captain nodded.

"Very well." John filled in the amounts and affixed the seal of James & Co. When the paperwork was completed, John handed the letters of credit to Henry, and a list of shippers to whom the insurance bonds would be delivered. "Good luck on your voyage, Captain Kirk. We will await your return with great anticipation."

"I am going with the captain, Jamesey."

The banker appeared stunned.

"Would you please see that my father is informed of my journey? We should return in about four to six months' time."

"Of course, Ravenshire. Godspeed." John accompanied them to the front door, where the bank's carriage waited.

"I am to take you wherever you wish, sir," said the driver.

Henry glanced at the captain. "What last minute provisions do we need?"

"I have a list that I thought pointless to fulfill until now. And you will need some more practical clothes, Young Viscount. Gentlemen's garb will be of little use at sea." Putting his arm around Henry's shoulders, he signaled that they should get in the carriage, and they rode off to complete the list of errands, reviewing the details that needed to be completed before they sailed.

Later, on the ship in the harbor, just as the sun was setting, Captain Kirk assembled the crew on deck and said, "This is Wyndward, an unseasoned sailor. Teach him the ropes. Crew, we are about to embark on a great adventure. You have all been selected carefully for this challenge. Let us be off!"

***

Henry

Henry caught himself smiling at the memory of his first voyage with Captain Kirk as they drew up to that very warehouse where he originally met the blustery sailor. Now Henry owned the building. Fully restored to its 17th century elegance, the headquarters of Wyndward Trading always triggered a deep sense of pride in Henry as he approached it. Envious competitors pointed to it as a monument to his vanity. True, but it was a symbol of his achievement. He loved it.

Entering the building, the urgency of his task energized Henry. The idea that a trusted associate might be an agent of deceit filled him more with sadness than rage. The trading business was full of scoundrels. He did business with men he did not trust. He'd been kidnapped, ransomed, and wounded. He'd killed when necessary, and harbored no naïveté in the ways of men. If an employee took a commission here and there, he did not worry too much. The trading business was filled with risk, some of it life-threatening.

If Blackie engineered the illicit contracts, Henry resolved to uncover any duplicity. But the evidence must be incontrovertible. In his frequent absences on extended voyages, Henry had trusted his protégé with full governing authority. Until Bri had brought the array of unusual contracts to his attention, no reason had ever surfaced to doubt Blackie's character.

Now he was perplexed. Why would a man steal from the company he might one day control on a day-to-day basis? While ownership would rest with Bri if Henry died, Blackie had been designated as a co-trustee, along with Sir John, for the family's interest in Wyndward Trading. A piece of the puzzle was missing. A bad temper did not make a man a liar, an embezzler, a thief or a killer.

He walked past walls displaying paintings of each of the first five ships in the Wyndward fleet. Each ship was superimposed over an early map of the particular continent of its destination and the plotted currents. In the center of the far wall hung a life-sized portrait of Henry as a young man shortly after his second voyage, the company's success assured. Wincing at the memory of his lost youth, Henry grimaced as he saw the portraits Gio had done of him every five years. It was time for another, one of a graying patriarch. *No one escapes the relentless passage of time.*

The earl climbed the two flights to his third floor office. Blackburn's office had a partial view of the harbor, but it was not nearly as spectacular as the view from Henry's corner office, which also included a view of the ever-higher buildings of the city.

***

Blackie

For years, Blackburn had worked side-by-side with the 11th Earl of Ravenshire, who was called "Lord R." by everyone at the trading company. He had devoted himself to gaining Lord R.'s trust. He knew that his temper was a source of concern, so he terminated anyone who might report his angry outbursts. Still, he knew that Lord R. had some loyal employees who might speak the truth. Lately, he had scrupulously adhered to a policy of self-restraint to avoid any unnecessary confrontations when he was so close to his goal.

It was a goal planned many years earlier, when as a young clerk in Lord R.'s employ, he had seen no true rival for ultimate control of the company. Lord R.'s younger brother, Rychard, was four years older than Blackie, and preferred running the country estates. He had no interest in the trading company. Lord R.'s daughter, Bri, was quite clever, with a mind for commerce, but no woman would ever run such a large enterprise. Even though Lord R. had given Blackie every indication that he would be the lead director of the trading company "someday," Blackie had seen other trading companies fail when the owner died. The Wyndward family had a dark secret, which only he knew. Rychard's tragic riding accident four years earlier had eliminated any competition for family succession from Lord R.'s generation. But progeny were a risk. The earl's sister's husband, the Comte de Merbeau, had been killed two years earlier in a runaway carriage accident. It was not bad luck. Both deaths were part of a decades-long plot.

The issue of overall inheritance, however, was an impediment to Blackie's vision of himself at the helm. Bri, whom he always referred to in public as Lady Gabriella, was a beautiful woman. A husband might take too much interest in the trading operations in the future. No amount of interest would be to Blackie's liking.

As insurance against future interference, he had entered into contracts under his authority as lead director of Wyndward Trading with new suppliers, suppliers where he served as a hidden partner. This way, he could build himself a small fortune, outside the scrutiny of Lord R., accessible in foreign banks should he need to leave London on short notice.

He had planned his moves over many years, and now the final piece was to be placed on his chessboard. In order to finally secure his position with Lord R., he intended to propose marriage to Bri, marry her and produce a male heir. His son would one day inherit all of Lord R.'s enormous wealth, which Blackie would control until the son's majority. He was congratulating himself on his perfect plan when, to his surprise, Henry walked into his office.

"Lord R., I thought you might be home preparing Bri for her first ball tomorrow night."

"Ah, right you are, but that is a task for tomorrow. I've come to talk to you about some financing arrangements that I am making with James & Co."

"Our bankers? A new financing arrangement?" Blackie's wariness was evident in his voice.

"Yes, Young James, Sir John's son, has returned from an extended period of travel abroad and will be working with us to modernize our accounting and financing activities. As part of this exercise, he will be in on Monday to discuss our overall operations, and I would like you to spend the better part of the day with him to bring him up-to-date on our current and historical operations."

"What is the purpose of the new financing?"

"I am considering doubling our size, so that instead of six ships a year to each continent, we can make twelve. Napoleon's wars will end and I want to be poised to take advantage of re-opened markets as we did when peace was signed with the Americans after they won their independence. In order to commit the necessary capital, the bank needs to update its familiarity with our overall operations."

"Excellent." *I can expand my secret supplier network to take advantage of this additional volume.* "I don't have a problem with that."

"Any new developments lately?"

"Yes, Lord R. We have had tremendous success with our African imports, and have exceeded our profit estimates for those shipments. Tomorrow night will be an indication, because Lady Elisabeth will be displaying selected African goods at the ball. I was able to persuade her that this particular type of display would give the ball an exotic flavor. I hope you approve."

"I don't need to approve. I trust you, Blackie. 'Tis an excellent idea to show the *ton* the breadth of our imports."

"It occurred to me that we could turn some of the empty space on the far side of the building into an emporium to sell items. We could call it Wyndward Emporium or Wyndward Novelties or another name that appeals to you. If it works, we could expand."

"I like that concept. I've always said that you have an excellent mind for commerce, Blackie."

"I appreciate your confidence. I am looking forward to the ball tomorrow night. I hope Lady Gabriella will save me a dance."

"You know she has her own mind. You'll have to navigate that sea on your own."

"Understood."

"I have a few hours before I must return home, so let us review our shipping schedule and cargo for the next three months."

Always efficient and prepared, Blackie reached for a file on his desk. "I have it right here: ships, routes, dates, cargo and potential markets."

CHAPTER NINETEEN

Thursday, March 14, 1811 – Lord Ravenshire's Townhouse
Bri

A flurry of activity swirled around the townhouse, interrupting breakfast several times. The usually unflappable Thompson lost his temper when a footman dropped a glass pitcher of water, breaking it.

"Get out!"

The chastened footman disappeared and another took his place, silently cleaning up the debris.

Henry turned toward the commotion.

"Forgive me, Lord Ravenshire."

The earl waved his hand to dismiss the request. "No need to apologize, Thompson. We're all on edge today, aren't we, Bri?"

Lost in her own thoughts, Bri didn't hear her father's comment. Ball gowns expected yesterday had been delayed until this morning, and her mind was darting in different directions at once. *Will my gown be perfect? Will I remember the dance steps? Will I commit a faux pas in front of everyone?* She tried to focus on her detailed investment proposal for the operetta, but the irritating Mr. James kept popping into her head. "Leave me alone!" she cried out aloud, startling herself.

Henry leaned back, took off his spectacles, put down the newspaper and stared at her.

"Not you, Father."

"To whom else would you be speaking?"

"Someone who won't get out of my head."

"Ah," her father nodded. "The inimitable Young James."

Bri pouted.

"If your grandmother were here, she'd say—"

" 'Pouting is unrefined, unattractive and undisciplined. Cease it at once.' " She laughed.

Spotty barked.

"You agree, I see. I didn't mean to alarm you." Bri leaned down to pet Spotty. "I need a diversion." She sat up straighter. "I know just the thing!"

"Dare I ask?"

"No. Let me surprise you."

"Now you have me worried."

Bri rose and looked toward the figure in black who was finishing his toast. Many in the *ton* would be shocked to know that Jean-Louis frequently ate at the earl's breakfast table. More than a driver and bodyguard, he was a friend and trusted advisor. "Well? Is my carriage at the ready?"

The Frenchman stuffed his last bite of toast into his mouth, pushed back his chair, stood, and bowed. "On a moment's notice, as always. He held out his arm. "To the stables?"

Bri nodded, kissed her father on the forehead, and accompanied Jean-Louis down the back stairs, through the garden to the stables where she waited while the team was harnessed. She couldn't help but notice that the young apprentice to the stable master, Ali, the orphaned son of an Arab guide that the earl had taken in after his father had died on one of the earl's treks, was absorbed in stitching two pieces of tanned leather into a saddle bag. A paper with a design was propped up in front of him between other items of horse tack. Bri stood behind him, looked at the design, and leaned closer. "That is ingenious. Hidden compartments, weapon sheaths. Is this your own design?"

The shy Ali nodded.

"Have you come up with other innovations?"

"Yes, Lady Gabriella." He pulled out a pile of papers showing intricate drawings of saddles, stirrups, bridles, halters, reins, bits and more. "Our supplier said he couldn't make these, so I've been working on prototypes."

Bri twisted her neck around to catch the eye of Jean-Louis.

Turning back to Ali, she smiled. "When are you meeting with the supplier?"

"Probably next week when I have a few things to show him."

"Let me know when. Jean-Louis and I will accompany you."

"Of course, milady. But why?"

"Because I have an idea, Ali. Keep me informed."

The team was harnessed, and Jean-Louis held the door for Bri. As she climbed in, she whispered, "So that's why you brought me to the stables to wait."

Jean-Louis closed the door and shrugged. "I'm sure I don't know what you mean, Lady Gabriella."

"To quote someone we both know and love, 'There are ways.' I'm intrigued."

"Where to?"

"First, Dr. St. Cloud, and then Atelier Maximilian."

"As you command, my queen."

"I expect nothing less than total obedience."

"Even from Mr. James?"

Bri scowled at the Frenchman. "Get to your perch, driver."

Jean-Louis tipped his hat and followed her command.

***

Dr. St. Cloud's Veterinary Care Clinic
Dr. St. Cloud

Dr. St. Cloud's shop was bustling this morning. He waved at Bri.

She waited until he had taken care of two clients who had arrived before her.

"How may I help you today, Lady Gabriella?"

"I want a large dog that likes water and is known for loyalty. It is to be a surprise gift for my father. His last dog, Homer, died a few months ago, and he misses the companionship. He dotes on Spotty, but he is my lap dog. Father needs a dog to ride with, hunt with, and sail with."

"You are in luck. We have a pair of young Dalmatians that were brought in for adoption. I must say, word is spreading quickly around the *ton*. I must have you to thank for that."

"I mentioned it to my grandmother, the Duchess of Pytchley, on

Monday at lunch when she met Spotty. That's akin to putting it on the front page of the *Times*."

"Well, the owner of these dogs died, and his son's dog didn't like them. He attacked the male. Their fights concerned him, so he brought them to me. I've looked over the male, and he's healing quickly. The female is fine. Would you like to see them?"

"Yes. I hope they will not be skittish around other dogs. I'm sure Spotty wouldn't fight."

As he guided Bri to the back cage area, he answered over his shoulder. "Probably not. However, there is always a period of adjustment when additional animals are introduced in a home." Reaching a cage with two Dalmatians, he stopped. "Here they are."

The dogs rose from their resting position and stood, noses pressing on the cage and tails wagging.

"Dalmatians love to run with horses and are excellent guard dogs. Which one would you like?"

"Both."

The doctor laughed. "Why am I not surprised? Let me give you complimentary leashes."

"I insist on paying an adoption fee to help support your work. Consider it a donation."

"That's very generous. I need more cages, and more space."

"Let me know if there is nearby space. Perhaps we can work out an approach where adoption activities are donation-based and the expansion of the food products is set up as an investment arrangement. We can talk more about it over the next month or so."

"Between balls?"

"Yes, to keep my sanity."

"I thought attending balls would be an annoyance, but I find myself thinking about their etiquette constantly, worried about making a *faux pas* in front of Lady Clarissa."

"You are not alone. It's a type of performance, isn't it?"

Dr. St. Cloud cocked his head. "I never thought of it that way, but you're right."

When the dogs were leashed, Bri held both grips in one hand and led the dogs, or rather, they led her, happy for adventure, out into the street where Jean-Louis stood, leaning against the carriage.

The female dog leapt up and looked at him adoringly.

The Frenchman petted her and looked at Bri. "I should have

known."

"Really? I thought you knew everything." She laughed. "Looks like the female has chosen you. The male is for Father, but he is still healing, so he can ride with me. She can ride with you if you think you can handle her."

Jean-Louis tilted his head. "As if I couldn't handle anything or anyone."

Bri shrugged. "As if."

Holding the door as Bri and the male climbed up the steps, Jean-Louis closed them in. He looked up at his driver's perch, then back at the dog. The female looked at him, looked at the perch, jumped to land on the driver's mounting step perfectly, but lost her balance.

Jean-Louis caught her and lifted her to the driver's bench. "I'll have to see if Ali can fashion steps for you on the side of the carriage. You have reflexes like a cat." He stepped on the mounting perch. "Move over."

The female Dalmatian did as instructed.

He petted her. "*Ma chérie*, we are meant for each other. I shall call you *Chérie*."

***

Atelier Maximilian
Bri

Atelier Maximilian had grown from the original gallery and teaching studio of Madame Nicolette Victoire, who had been Gio's patron and employer during the years his family pretended that he did not exist.

When Mme. Victoire retired, Gio's prominence ensured the continuation of her vision. She chose the name Atelier Maximilian, after Gio's son, whom she raised and introduced as her orphaned grandson.

By the time Gio's lordship was restored, his reputation as a portraitist was known throughout Europe, and the atelier thrived.

Over the years, they had taken over nearby shops for art studios and galleries where exhibitions were constantly changing, featuring their students as well as emerging artists who had fled Paris under Napoleon.

Hearing the bell, the director looked up and recognized his visitor. "Lady Gabriella, we weren't expecting you."

"I came on a whim. Is Gio about?"

"Yes. He's back in his studio, muttering to himself, as usual."

"I know my way." Bri walked back through the wide hallway, passing rooms where artists were working on restorations, a lucrative side business, as well as studios of artists who needed space. When she reached the back area splashed in northern light, she found Gio, his back to her, looking out the window in silence.

Gio didn't need to turn around. "I'd recognize that confident heel click anywhere, Bri." He was one of the few family confidants who could address her in such an intimate manner. "Ready for the ball tonight?" He twirled on one foot to face her, and then bowed. "I am quite the dancer, you know."

"Nothing about your capabilities would surprise me." Bri plopped down in the portrait subject's chair. "To answer your question, I am nervous, excited, terrified...I surprise myself. I was so blasé about these balls, an annoyance. Now...I worry that I may stumble, literally as well as figuratively."

"You have a lot to deal with. The attentions of the young banker—"

Perplexed, her brow wrinkled. "But—" The truth came to her, and she raised her hands in surrender. "Of course! You know everything."

"Correct. And Charlotte is deeply wounded. In nearly forty years, I've never known your father to be deliberately cruel, but he has broken her heart."

"I don't know what to think. Charlotte has been like a mother to me and I love her. I need her." Bri's voice cracked.

Gio walked over and hugged her as she shed her tears. After a few moments, he lifted her chin to him and dried her eyes with his finger. "That's better." He sighed. "We men can be cads, Bri, but I think Henry is unmoored by your Season."

"What? How would that affect him? And why break off with Charlotte?"

Moving back, Gio pulled a stool over and sat opposite her. His voice softened. "He is losing you, Bri. You have been his life. Another man will claim your heart. He is lost, facing an uncertain future."

"But Charlotte and he planned to marry after my Season."

The dwarf tilted his head. "There are inflection points in life where the curve of events is altered. Henry, perhaps for the first time in his life, is uncertain of the future. As a young man, the Young Viscount, as we called him then," Gio smiled, "was precociously certain of himself. As a sailing man like Henry would say, he faces uncharted waters. Not the waters of the sea, to be conquered by intellect and skill, but the waters of emotion. Waters he has let carry him forward during your life. But now, as you prepare to chart your own course, he spins like an untethered buoy, his future direction unknown."

"Are you saying it's my fault that he and Charlotte have had a falling out?"

"It is no one's fault. He is at odds with himself. You have been the driving force of his life. To men, change is chaos. You women bend like trees in the wind. Men break."

"Now you're saying he's broken?"

"You are far too literal, Bri. You father is emotionally brittle right now. Men don't admit to weakness or ask for help. You must let him come around. I have told Charlotte the same thing. But she is deeply hurt and channeling her pain into dubious action."

"The escort?"

"She told you?"

"My grandmother did."

"Of course. The duchess knows all that happens in the *ton*. But you must have patience, Bri. Henry and Charlotte are well-suited to each other. In time, they will see that, unless—"

"Unless what?"

"Unless he sails away. That is what men do. And when they return…all may have changed."

"I've thought about sailing away. America seems more open than here. I felt an all-encompassing energy there, a surge of creativity. An intoxicating belief that all was possible."

"So you were in New York. Energy is its defining characteristic. I loved it too."

Bri scanned the studio and saw Blackie's portrait. She leaned toward it at first, then stood and approached it to peer more closely. "Is Blackie looking over trees? Is that what the blob of green is?"

Gio sat back, rose to his feet and stomped over to her. "It's not finished! That 'blob of green' will be the Brazilian rainforest."

"The timber contract. The one that sealed Blackie's position." Bri kept moving her head as she examined the likeness. "There's something about him—"

"It's the jaw line."

Bri shook off the notion. "Many men have jaws like that."

"They say that people start to look like their dogs after years of being together. Maybe it's the same with Henry and Blackburn."

Bri threw back her head in laughter. "Gio, you always make me laugh."

"A moment ago, I made you cry."

She nodded. "Laughing is better."

"How much time do you have?"

"A few hours."

"Sit for me. I'll have food brought to you and Jean-Louis. He's with the carriage, right?"

"As always, but with two companions. Dalmatians."

"Then soup bones are in order." He rang for his assistant. "We have a small kitchen here and the cook is quite clever at coming up with unexpected meals."

When the clerk arrived, he explained what he wanted. The clerk seemed ill at ease, uncertain.

"Is something bothering you?"

"One of the restorers has a question for you. I said you were busy, but she's quite insistent."

Gio sighed. "Very well. Send her in." He raised his arms in a shrug to Bri. "You see, my work is never done." Taking her arm, he said, "Now, sit in the chair."

Doing as she was told, Bri let Gio arrange her arms and head as well as drape her dress and place one foot outside the hem. "There. Let me sketch you."

"Actually, Gio, I was wondering if you would paint me in a ball gown as a way to commemorate my season. A portrait to hang at Ravenshire alongside my mother and both grandmothers."

"Done. This will be a study to capture color and light to prepare for the more formal portrait—"

"Lord Ostwold?"

The dwarf turned to see his youngest restoration expert standing with a small painting in hand. "Come in, Miss Rybicki. Lady Gabriella Wyndward, this is Miss Bettina Rybicki."

The women nodded their greetings.

Bettina walked over and showed Gio the painting. "I'm concerned because when I began to remove the grime in the varnish from the fire, I may have taken off too much. The color underneath is very different."

The white-haired artist took the framed canvas over to a table and removed the canvas from the frame. Walking over to the window, he held it against the glass. "I think the artist painted over another canvas." He turned around. "That's what starving artists do. This is a pleasant little oil landscape done by the son of our client. He passed away. Many of his other paintings were untouched, and we took this commission with the caveat that restoration might be impossible. Continue removing the grime and varnish. Do just the right side, and then let's take another look together."

"Thank you, Lord Ostwold."

After Bettina left, Bri tilted her head at Gio. "It's unusual for a woman to be an art restorer. Are you breaking with the conventions of the art world?"

"Don't I always? Am I not evidence of a breaking with convention?" He pointed to himself. "And I am partial to redheads."

Bri smiled. "We are fiery and unpredictable."

"You're broken your pose." He walked over and repositioned her, lifted out a medium-sized canvas and began to sketch in charcoal.

"Tell me about the portraits of my mother and grandmothers."

"Your grandmother Wyndward, Lady Rebecca, sadly, was already ill when I met your grandfather. I painted the children—you know that portrait—but even then, Lady Rebecca had few days where she felt strong enough to meet with visitors. A year or so after she died, your grandfather commissioned a portrait of Lady Rebecca in her wedding gown."

"But how? She had died."

Gio shrugged. "It's not an unusual request, I've learned over the years. People intend to do something, but the time is not right, the moment passes, and then it is too late. I had small reference paintings of Lady Rebecca to capture her likeness. I see much of her in Wynnie—the blonde tresses, the high cheekbones. But I needed a model in the wedding gown to drape it properly, so the 10th Earl asked Rychard's nanny, Brigid, to put on Lady Rebecca's dress to pose for me.

Hair as black as night, I recall. I came one day and luckily captured all the folds and details of the gown. It fit her perfectly, but when I came back a week later, she was gone. She'd left in the middle of the night with no note, the same night that I'd sketched her. Rychard was devastated.

To lose his mother, and then the nanny, a replacement mother…it was hard on him. Wynnie and Henry also missed her. Just the nearness of a caring woman comforted them after the loss of their mother. So, I persuaded another housemaid to don the dress, but it didn't fit her nearly as well. That one day with Brigid made that painting work."

"My grandmother's death was devastating for all of them. Your portrait of her as a vibrant presence gave them great comfort."

The artist nodded. "It helps the pain to see the person you loved in a painting. You forget the warts and see only love."

"Warts? I should know when you start to sound sentimental that an unexpected blow is coming. My grandmother didn't have warts."

"How do you know?"

Bri scowled at him.

"Regain your pose. I was speaking figuratively. As I said earlier, Bri, you take things too literally. That will be important with the young banker. I look forward to seeing him tonight. Didn't he come to your family's Summerfests? A tall, lanky young man?" Gio sat back and laughed. "He's the one you beat at Whist! I remember his jaw set in anger and humiliation. He stormed off and threw stones into the pond. I think he visualized you as a target. I sketched you that day, you know. It's here somewhere."

Bri looked around at the piles of sketches and canvases and laughed. "Will I ever see it?"

"Maybe, if I live long enough to catalogue all of this. When I die, all my work will be even more desirable. That is my burden." He emitted a faux sigh. "I must paint to ensure a proper inheritance for Maximilian and Charles."

"You protest too much. The Ostwold estates are sufficient."

Gio shrugged. "I will always paint. I hope to keel over at my easel with a brush in my hand."

"Or a barb at the ready."

"Why not both?"

***

Lord Ravenshire's Townhouse
Bri

Returning from her outing, Bri took the male Dalmatian's leash, and laughed at the look on Thompson's face. She put her finger to her mouth to let him know to remain silent. Her eyes sparkled as she imagined her father's reaction.

Hiding the dog behind her, Bri found her father in his study, hand on his forehead, reading through the documents he had brought from the trading company, making notes on another piece of paper. Absorbed in his work, he didn't realize she was there.

She cleared her throat.

He jumped, startled out of his concentration. He cocked his head. "What does that mischievous look on your face mean?" He sat back and put down his pen.

Releasing the dog, she watched him run toward Henry, jumping up, putting his paws on her father's shoulders, licking his face.

"They ride next to horses, love water and are excellent guard dogs. And you need a companion."

Her father smiled, and then furrowed his brow. "How?"

"I went to Dr. St. Cloud. He also had a female from the same litter that fell in love with Jean-Louis. A *coup de foudre*. He's named her Chérie."

"I'll have to rack my brain for another ancient name from Greek mythology." He laid his head back and rested it on his chair back. "There's been Demeter, a female found on that first trip with Captain Kirk. Then Atlas, a male from Crete, followed by Electra, a female from Africa. And then my beloved Homer, from Scotland. I have it—Hector. The honorable Trojan."

"He lost."

"But he was noble."

"He died."

"We all die."

"You win, Father. Hector and Chérie. She has a grayish nose instead of charcoal, and he is a bit larger, so they should be easy to tell apart."

Spotty came in and Hector sniffed him. Spotty sat patiently while Hector licked the lap dog's ear.

Relieved, Bri smiled. "Instant friends. My work here is done. I am off to a nap and a bath. I will need all my wits about me tonight."

"You will be the belle of the ball. Fortune hunters will follow you like Spotty."

Bri grimaced.

Henry laughed. "Off with you." He rose to embrace her. "A thoughtful gift. I think I'll take Hector for a ride. I need some air." Looking at Hector, Henry tilted his head toward the door. "Ready?"

The dog took off, pulling Henry by the leash.

***

After Bri's nap, she bathed and put on a dressing gown for the brief supper, planning to dress after eating. Bri intended to heed her aunt's advice to eat before Lady Elisabeth's ball. She trusted Cookie with the informal meal that she, Aunt Gwyneth and her father would eat before they left for the ball. After years of loyal service, their cook knew exactly how to please the earl and his daughter.

Bri bounded into the kitchen, trying to divert her attention from the evening ahead. "What's on the menu for tonight, Cookie?" The earl addressed the cook properly as Mrs. Jones, even though he had known her as a girl from Ravenshire, where her mother had been cook. Bri had called her Cookie since childhood, and Nellie didn't mind. She doted on Bri and still called her by her nickname when they were alone.

"In the last few days, Bri, both your aunt and your grandmother made a point to instruct me on the proper pre-ball meal, as if I were ignorant. I know how important it is to make a correct impression at the first ball of the Season. Do they think I learned nothing in my years at Ravenshire, then working as scullery maid to the duchess before I came here as cook for your mother?"

Bri nodded. "They worry because they know I am not overly cautious and speak my mind too often without thinking. The gossip rags are ever-ready to pounce on any *faux pas*." Bri pulled up a stool and watched Nellie cut vegetables. "Cookie, do you think the notion of romantic love is foolish?"

"Not all women find a fairy-tale prince, Bri. Young ladies of the *ton* may dream of romance, but their families still must approve of their selected mates or they risk being disinherited. Your parents were lucky." Nellie's eyes misted over as she thought of Lady Jane. "Your mother adored your father. Their marriage was expected, but not ordained. They loved each other, but that is not always the case in Society marriages. Follow your heart, I say."

"I know I must be careful tonight. As Grandmother instructed—Bri mimicked her grandmother's voice perfectly—'You must always conduct yourself with unimpeachable discretion.' "

She loved making Cookie laugh, watching the rolls around her middle shake. Bri watched for a while as Cookie prepared their spare dinner: asparagus drizzled with herbs and butter accompanied by a cold chicken salad mixed with apricots and mayonnaise.

Jane Anne walked into the kitchen, having just arrived home.

"How did it go with Lady Penelope?"

"She looks beautiful. Her hair is thick and lustrous, like yours. She babbled on and on about the baron." Jane Anne lowered her voice. "I've seen him here. Isn't he the same age as your father?"

Bri nodded. "Lady Penelope is besotted with him. He told Father he is finally ready to marry." She frowned as she noticed a glance passing between Cookie and Jane Anne. "What?"

They looked at each other, then at Bri, feigning innocence.

"Don't be coy. What did that look between you mean?"

"No need to trouble your head with ugly gossip." Cookie dressed the asparagus.

Jane Anne turned to leave.

Bri caught her arm. "Oh, no. You can't run away from this."

Nellie sighed. "You must promise never to mention this and nor ever tell your father."

"Now you are worrying me. I promise. What is it?"

The cook took a deep breath. "There have been rumors for years about the baron and his sister."

Unable to comprehend their meaning, Bri was perplexed. "Are you worried that Lady Penelope might be competing with a mistress? Do they have secret lovers?"

"It is whispered that *they* are secret lovers. Lady Davinia's son looks exactly like the baron."

Scoffing, Bri shook her head. "Family resemblances are common. This type of gossip is cruel and unfair. I insist that you stop engaging in such ugly talk. They are sister and brother!"

Jane Anne shrugged. "Half-sister and half-brother."

"Cease this immediately. Lady Penelope must be protected from such nasty chatter." Bri scowled at them, turned on her heel and left the kitchen. *It can't be true.*

***

Lady Gwyneth's Townhouse
Gwyneth

As she dressed for the ball, Gwyneth couldn't help but marvel at the freedom of today's fashion versus her experience when she attended her first balls in the previous century. She had been laced into stiff-boned corsets fitted over heavy brocade dresses that made it difficult to breathe or move due to the sheer weight of the gowns. She thought back to her first ball.

***

More than thirty years earlier, the highlight of Gwyneth's first ball was her dance with Jamie Craigfell, a nephew of the Duke of Pytchley. She had adored Jamie since their childhood gatherings at holidays with the duke's family. A handsome, dashing figure, Jamie was an accomplished horseman and master of the ways of the wealthy leisure class. A year younger than Gwyneth, he attended the ball at sixteen to Gwyneth's seventeen in 1780.

Recently returned from school in Switzerland, Gwyneth had been presented to the king and ready to attend the Marriage Season. While no prospective engagement had been formally arranged between her parents and the duke and duchess, it had been discussed.

Gwyneth had considered but rejected romantic overtures by Nathaniel Parker, a university friend of Henry's. She had felt completely at ease with Nate. He had lived with them at Ravenshire, as had Aelwyn, a stowaway on a boat Henry and his tutor, Philip Laurence, had sailed on during a brief tour of Europe and Africa. Nate and Aelwyn had been her best friends growing up. While she liked to travel, the thought of going back to America with Nate, being so far away from everything she knew, frightened her. Like many young women of the time, she had led a sheltered life.

In early adolescence, she had shared her first kiss with Jamie.

Henry expected to marry his distant cousin, Lady Jane, the duke's daughter. Family connections were important to the Wyndwards and

Pytchleys.

Jamie charmed people, and he danced better than most men. Indeed, young Gwyneth had felt like a princess of the court as they danced the Quadrille. After three balls and several chaperoned afternoon teas, Jamie asked her to marry him. She was deliriously happy that day. Her dream had come true. The marriage came quickly, but the happiness soon faded.

Overuse of wine by her new husband unleashed a belligerence that bordered on cruelty. A few days after their marriage, Jamie slapped her for no reason, slurring his words. "Don't look at me with those accusing eyes." He did not have his own home yet, and they had taken up residence with his father, Montague, a ne'er-do-well second son. Jamie's mother, Wisteria, reveled in striking out verbally. She showed a particularly truculent streak of animosity toward Gwyneth.

A man with no ambition beyond entertaining himself by sporting, hunting and accumulating mistresses, Jamie also liked to gamble all night at his club. Often, he would leave a ball with Gwyneth, only to instruct his driver to deliver him to his club before taking his wife home. His primary occupation seemed to be waiting for his father to die. When home, he drank excessively and hit Gwyneth periodically. Worse, he would physically force himself on her in the middle of the night. Humiliated, she was left to fend for herself with her formidable mother-in-law, who criticized Gwyneth's every action and was quick to label the young wife as inadequate to keep her husband at home to fulfill his duty.

After a year, she could no longer hide her bruises and her pain. Because Henry was gone for extended periods of time building his trading company, she never knew when he would return. To ease her pain, she wrote a letter to him, posted to his London office, telling him of her husband's drinking and the episodes of striking, but she could not bring herself to discuss the repeated rapes. She told Henry the horrifying truth that her miscarriage was due to Jamie knocking her to the floor and kicking her in the stomach. As a married woman, she had no recourse to prevent such abuse. Sex, forcible or not, was considered a husband's marital due. The assault could not be proven. In her letter, she begged Henry to take her away and let her live in London with him. She knew that he would support her financially no matter what Society might say. He had always been her protector.

Subterfuge was needed to mail the letter. On the pretext of a shopping trip, she used the rare moment of freedom to post the letter through a shopkeeper.

The day in 1782 when Henry received her letter, he had just returned from North Africa and planned to leave for Brazil on another voyage in a few days before returning to marry Lady Jane at Christmas. He postponed the sailing, over the vehement arguments of Captain Kirk, and paid all the crew to remain in London until he returned. He rode his horse, a strong steed, all day to reach his sister, stopping only to feed and water the horse. As darkness fell, he arrived at the home of Montague Craigfell, where his sister was being held against her will.

Henry pushed aside the butler. "Where is my sister?"

Hearing his voice, Gwyneth gathered a small bag she had packed with Wyndward family jewelry, and fled downstairs.

Lady Craigfell tried to block her exit. "Where are you going, you ungrateful girl! How dare you turn your back on your husband? I shall ruin you in Society. Your family will be destroyed!" Rage caused the veins in her forehead to pulsate as her face reddened.

Calmly, Henry gathered the sobbing Gwyneth into his arms. "You are safe now. And as for you, Lady Craigfell, you will never socialize with my family again. I will reveal all to the duke and duchess. You will not attend my wedding. Were it not for my love for Lady Jane, I would see the ruin of you and your family for the abuse your lazy, worthless son has directed toward my sister. He is a disgrace to all gentlemen."

With that, Henry escorted Gwyneth out the door and jumped up on the horse, lifted her up behind him, and headed back toward London. With more weight to carry, and a long's day's ride already behind him, the horse could not travel as fast. Riding until nearly midnight, they stopped to spend the night at a small inn. Acquiring two rooms next to each other for propriety's sake, Gwyneth collapsed on the bed in one room. The other room remained empty for the night, as Henry slept on the floor of his sister's room after barricading the door against the possibility of a chase by Gwyneth's husband. Neither slept more than an hour.

In the morning, they went downstairs for breakfast in the inn's dining room. As they sat down, the proprietor came over.

"Lord Ravenshire and Lady Gwyneth, I would like to extend to you my deepest sympathies."

Gwyneth tensed. "Whatever do you mean?"

"Oh, I assumed you knew. Forgive me, then, for being the one to bring the sad news, milady. Your husband was thrown from his horse near the crag about a mile from here last night. He was dead by the time other travelers on the road found him."

Henry and Gwyneth were stunned.

The proprietor brought tea, toast and eggs, and left them in silence.

Gwyneth leaned in to whisper to her brother. "We must go back for the funeral. It is the proper thing to do."

Her brother shook his head. "No. We shall not be hypocrites. Send a note if you must, but you no longer owe that husband or his family any courtesies."

"I suppose they would resent my presence, or even bar me from the estate. In all candor, I feel nothing but relief."

"As well you should. He can no longer hurt you or anyone else, for that matter. Sail with me to Brazil. By the time we return, the circumstances of his death will have faded from gossip."

***

An insistent meow from Mozart roused Gwyneth from her remembrances of so long ago. She petted the demanding Siamese.

Standing, she examined her reflection in the full-length mirror. *Do I look my age of eight-and-forty? I am wiser than the seventeen-year-old girl I once was, but my mind feels the same.* Descending the stairs, she saw Nambotha waiting with her cloak.

"Guy has pulled the carriage around for you. You look beautiful, Madame la Comtesse. Enjoy the evening."

"I shall."

Nambotha escorted her down the steps to her carriage.

When she arrived at Henry's townhouse, Thompson greeted her. "The earl is dressing. Lady Gabriella is in the parlor."

Bri stood, tightened the ties on her dressing gown, and kissed her aunt on the cheek. "I am trying to think of anything except the ball. I'm terrified."

"Nonsense. You've never been terrified of anything in your entire life."

They sat on the settee next to each other.

"Last night I practiced dancing with Father. It's been months since I last danced at Ravenshire. I hope I don't stumble."

Henry's booming voice startled them. "You won't stumble."

"Henry, you look quite handsome.*" I hope Charlotte attracts a lot of attention tonight.* Seeing the dog, she was taken aback. "Who is this?"

"Hector. A surprise from Bri."

Henry strutted around the room in his black velvet jacket, saying, "I still cut quite a dashing figure," followed by Hector at his heels. "I should think many young ladies will want to sign my dance card."

"As if men had dance cards." Gwyneth shook her head.

Spotty limped into the room. He'd adjusted to his cast and nuzzled up to Bri.

Bri froze. "What if no one signs my dance card?"

Her father scoffed. "Young James will, and Blackie will."

"At least I can talk to Blackie without feeling pressured."

"I've warned you he has an eye to courting you as well as Young James."

Bri shook her head. "He's too old. He's like an uncle, not a beau."

Gwyneth rose from her chair and put her arm around Bri's shoulders. "It's only a dance."

Thompson announced, "Supper is served."

"Come along, you two. Put something in your stomachs. Then Bri can avoid fainting and Henry will have the energy to sweep young ladies around the ballroom."

Bri took only a few spoonfuls of the meal, nibbling at the asparagus and chicken. It wasn't long before she excused herself to find Jane Anne and dress for the ball, leaving Henry and Gwyneth alone.

Henry squirmed in his chair, adjusting the apron Mrs. Jones had set out for him before they sat down to eat. "Wherever did Mrs. Jones get this apron?" Henry's mutterings betrayed his irritation. "I feel like a schoolboy."

"Oh, hush. This is Bri's evening and we must help her through it. If she loves Mr. James it could be quite difficult for her if he does not return her feelings. It might be the first time she didn't get what she wanted."

"It is a bit more complicated, Gwyneth. Blackie told me today that he wants to court Bri."

"Then Blackie might spark jealousy in Mr. James. This will be a very interesting evening." *Not to mention you and Charlotte.*

Rising from the table, Henry took off the apron.

Gwyneth noticed it was stained with remnants of the meal.

Henry shrugged.

His sheepish look confirmed to his sister what she already understood: Mrs. Jones knew her earl.

"You look quite lovely, Gwyneth. Regal, I should think."

Gwyneth smiled. In her silver linen dress trimmed with royal blue, with upswept graying blonde hair, Gwyneth was still an attractive woman. She enjoyed her role as Bri's mother figure along with Aelwyn and Charlotte. Aelwyn was presumed dead and Charlotte and Henry might never reconcile. Her closest friends, gone.

"Dance with me, Gwyneth." Henry hummed a waltz as he guided his sister around the room.

Laughing together as they fell into the settee, Gwyneth kissed her brother lightly on the cheek. Hearing footsteps, they looked toward the door. Both momentarily stopped breathing at the sight of Bri.

Resplendent in her pale green moiré gown, wispy curls circling her face as her thick red hair was arranged on top of her head, Bri looked stunning. A forest green velvet ribbon trimmed with pearls was interwoven among strands of hair. The small ruffle around the neckline and the pearls on the bodice were elegant touches. Around her neck, she wore opera-length pearls that had belonged to her mother, with matching earrings and a ring with two pearls. Aunt Gwyneth had let her borrow a gold bracelet that Henry had bought for her in China to complete her jewelry for the evening.

"Perfect." Gwyneth's eyes misted.

"You will steal the hearts of all the young men tonight, and some of the older ones, too." Her father extended his arm. "Shall we be off?"

At the carriage, Jean-Louis bowed to Bri. As she climbed into the carriage, he whispered, "I always knew you were a princess living secretly among us."

"If I look calm, it is all an act. I am quite truly terrified."

"I thought you said you couldn't act. You seem quite accomplished at hiding your terror."

Jean-Louis closed the door after Henry and mounted his driver's perch, along with Chérie, to drive his charges to Lady Elisabeth's ball.

CHAPTER TWENTY

Thursday, March 14, 1811 – Lady Elisabeth's Ball
Bri

Situated in Kensington Gardens, the Pepperell mansion was a massive gray stone edifice, with a stone-paved drive leading to a covered *porte cochère*. The first story of the house was fifteen feet high, with black shutters framing each large, multi-paned window, and a huge black door carved with the triple-fox crest of the ancestral Pepperell family estate at Wilshire.

A winding line of carriages stretched toward the entrance. From the carriage window, Bri caught glimpses of gowns and top hats as earlier arrivals alighted and were greeted at the door. Her excitement grew. She took a deep breath as their carriage pulled into the area where they would disembark.

The Pepperell footmen wore uniforms of black and silver. Courtly in appearance, wearing white wigs, one of them opened the Ravenshire carriage door, extended a hand first to Gwyneth and then to Bri, helping them exit. After Henry stepped out of the carriage and donned his top hat, another footman directed Jean-Louis to the waiting area, then bowed and gestured to the group to enter the mansion. The doorman stood at attention. "Invitation, please."

Henry handed it to the gatekeeper. "Lord Ravenshire, the Comtesse de Merbeau and Lady Gabriella Wyndward."

Turning to the butler standing in the foyer, the doorman repeated the names.

The butler wore a uniform similar to that of the footmen and doorman, but it was styled in a more subdued manner, wearing buckled shoes instead of boots. "Of course. Lord Ravenshire, Madame la Comtesse and Lady Gabriella. Good evening." He instructed the waiting footmen to take the cloaks and hats of the guests, inserting pre-lettered cards with their names in the pockets of the cloaks and bands of the hats.

The butler bowed. "This way, please." He led them to the receiving line where he was about to announce them when Lady Elisabeth interrupted.

"Lord Ravenshire needs no introduction." To her guest, she said, "Henry, I'm delighted to see you here tonight." Having known the earl since childhood, she was one of the few people who dared address him in such a familiar way.

The earl gallantly kissed Lady Elisabeth's hand. "As I am to see you, Lis."

"And Gwyneth, how lovely you look tonight." She hugged her old friend from school in Switzerland. "And Bri, you exquisite creature, welcome. I think you will have a very successful Season, my dear. Your dress is *au courant* and the color is a striking complement to your hair. Enjoy your evening." Smiling, Lady Elisabeth turned to greet her next guest while Henry greeted the distinguished Ambassador Gerhard Dietrich Pepperell, once posted to the Austro-Hungarian Empire before Napoleon's wars.

Bri proceeded down the receiving line of the large and influential Pepperell family, renewing old acquaintances and being introduced to prominent people. She lost count of the times she repeated, "Delighted to see you again." *How will I ever remember the names and titles of all these people? I have been too dismissive of etiquette. I must strive not to embarrass Father and Aunt Gwyneth.*

At the end of the receiving line, each young lady was handed a dance card with five spaces. A braided white silk loop and tassel slipped on each young lady's wrist, allowing her to dance. Young men were given a pencil engraved with the Pepperell triple-fox crest.

A waiter appeared with a tray of Champagne glasses, and each guest took one.

Henry led the way into the parlor, which was about equally divided among attractive young people of Bri's age and more mature members of Society who served as chaperones for their progeny.

Well-dressed, bejeweled matrons and fat-bellied, red-faced gentlemen appeared to be the rule among the older set, setting Henry and Gwyneth apart as unusually attractive exceptions.

"Ah, there is Lady Penelope," said Bri. "Jane Anne set her hair for tonight and it is quite lovely. I think I shall compliment her on it."

"Enjoy yourself, and remember to sip."

"Yes, Aunt Gwyneth." Bri walked through the crowd to Lady Penelope. "Good evening, Lady Penelope. Your hair is lovely."

"Jane Anne is a treasure, Lady Gabriella." She introduced Bri to her father. He bowed and left the two young women to speak alone.

Lady Penelope whispered, "I have tried many times to put my hair in this style but could not quite make it work. Using the combs was rather clever, and I've had several compliments on it already. I hope Jane Anne will be able to help me for every ball this Season. And I hope the baron likes it."

"I'm sure he will." Bri was about to explain about Jane Anne's dream of opening a hair salon when she was tapped on the shoulder.

"Lady Gabriella, you promised me a dance, I believe." Dr. Sr. Cloud bowed his head.

After she introduced Dr. St. Cloud to Lady Penelope, he signed the fourth line on Bri's dance card and the second on Lady Penelope's. Bri scanned the room. *Has Mr. James arrived? What if I have no spaces? Would that make him jealous? What if there are too many empty places on my dance card and he thinks me unpopular?*

Bri glanced at Lady Penelope's dance card. Three lines were already filled. She felt a pang of jealousy when she noticed "Edward James" written on the first line. *So he is here. Does Lady Penelope know Mr. James? Is she a rival?* Baron Beauchamp's name was on the third line. "Is Lady Clarissa here yet?"

"No, I have been looking for her." Dr. St. Cloud looked around the room, and his eyes lit up. "There she is. Let us greet our friend."

Clarissa was in her pink gown from Mlle. Bellerobe's, with her blonde locks arranged to fall in curls on one side of her head. Jane Anne had created a truly a dramatic look and made Clarissa the center of attention, as all wanted to know her hairdresser's name. Accompanying Clarissa was a tall, blond mature gentleman that Bri assumed must be Count von Dusterberg. Near her father's age, the count carried himself with military bearing.

Bri and Lady Penelope walked over to greet her.

The plump effusive Lady Penelope smiled. "Lady Clarissa, your hair looks marvelous."

"So does yours. Jane Anne has a definite flair."

Clarissa turned to her father. "Father, you remember Lady Gabriella who stayed with us in South Africa. Let me introduce Lady Penelope Firth and Dr. Nicholas St. Cloud, the veterinarian who helped me adopt our little kitten, Princess."

The count bowed slightly, clicked his boot heels in true Teutonic fashion, and said in only slightly accented English, "Lady Gabriella, I understand you have been very kind to my daughter. I would like to invite your family to dine with us. Would Saturday one week from now be open for you? And I'd like to invite you as well, Dr. St. Cloud. My daughter has told me of your interest in Herr Kramer's operetta, and I am most anxious to hear your thoughts on it."

"I would be honored, sir," said Dr. St. Cloud, "and, if I may, I would like to sign Lady Clarissa's dance card before it is full." He signed the last line on her dance card. All the young ladies knew that if a man signed his name on more than one line, that gesture was tantamount to a proposal of marriage.

"Father and Aunt Gwyneth are here and looking forward to seeing you again." Bri scanned the room and caught her father's eye, waving him over to their group. Her wave stopped in mid-air when she noticed Mr. James speaking with Lady Patricia. She recovered quickly, and hoped no one had noticed her reaction.

When her father and Aunt Gwyneth joined them, they and the count renewed their long acquaintance.

The count bowed. "I appreciate the courtesies you have shown my daughter while I have been in Scotland this past week. Please honor us by being our guests for dinner Saturday in one week at our home. I have also asked our young veterinarian to join us. I hope you are free."

Henry and Gwyneth agreed that dinner at eight o'clock on the twenty-third of March would be delightful.

Glancing around the room, the count shook his head. "It has been some years since I attended any balls. Since Clarissa's mother died, I have been somewhat of a hermit. Perhaps this Season will be one to make new friends for myself as well as my daughter. I understand you have seen a rehearsal of Herr Kramer's operetta. What did you think of it?"

"It was very enjoyable. I believe it will be quite a success here. The score was varied and compelling. My late husband, Luc, Comte de Merbeau, was a composer. I believe that the *ton* will be talking about *The Princess* throughout the Marriage Season."

"As we are both without partners, Lady Gwyneth, perhaps you will agree to dance with me this evening. I shall try not to be too clumsy."

"I would be delighted, although I have not danced in quite a long time myself. Henry and I fell into the furniture when we danced a bit earlier tonight."

The count bowed and escorted the doctor and his daughter to greet some old friends.

Duff Blackburn appeared "Good evening, Lord R., Madame la Comtesse." Turning to Bri, he bowed. "Lady Gabriella, might I have the honor of signing your dance card?"

Unable to refuse by protocol, Bri smiled and handed him her dance card. "Of course, Blackie." *What if Edward is not available for the same dances I am?* To her horror, Blackie signed in the last space. She was hoping to reserve the last dance for Mr. James, but there was nothing she could do but smile.

"May I get you more Champagne?"

Bri laughed. "I have quite enough at the moment." She introduced him to Lady Penelope and he signed her dance card on the second line.

Bowing slightly, Blackburn excused himself.

A voice she did not recognize came from behind her. "Lady Gabriella, may I sign your dance card?" She turned to see a man in a military uniform with an eye patch. "My sister, Lady Melanie Thornton, told me you were here. We haven't seen each other since we were children."

"Lord Lt. Thornton, I remember you, of course." Bri handed him her card, and he signed on the first line, nodded his leave, and disappeared into the crowd. *Dr. St. Cloud, Blackie and Lord Lt. Thornton. Only two spaces left. Where is Mr. James?*

After the military man left, Bri leaned toward her aunt. "Must all the spaces be signed before the dancing begins? Will I be a failure if I have empty spaces?"

Clarissa nodded. "I am wondering, too."

Gwyneth smiled warmly at the two nervous young ladies. "Your dance card can be filled at any time. Remember, men are also a bit intimidated by this process. My dear friend Lady Elisabeth has planned the evening to be split into four parts. The first part will consist of three dances. Then, a cold buffet will be offered in a room adjacent to the ballroom. A period of entertainment will follow dinner where Herr Kramer will play the score of *The Princess* on the piano while accompanied by a harpist. Then, the last two dances will take place. After the last dance, guests may linger or leave, but it is considered ill-mannered to stay past the hour of midnight."

"It relieves my queasy stomach to know what to expect." Bri sighed. "I am but a step away from a *faux pas.*"

The count came back to stand with them.

"No need to be worried." Her father put his arm around her. "The count and I stand at-the-ready to fight the dragons and protect you from the wolves of Society, eh, Lord von Dusterberg?"

"Quite correct, Lord Ravenshire. If your dance cards are not filled, we will dance with you ourselves. As neither of us is married, it might create speculation as to our interest in a young bride. It may make your young men jealous, and who knows? It may attract some young ladies to entrap the mature specimens that we are. Are you open to entrapment, Lord Ravenshire?"

"If I must throw myself to the young ladies of the *ton,* so be it."

Aunt Gwyneth scoffed. "You two are quite amused at yourselves, I see. Perhaps you are not quite as mature as you imagine."

"Everyone here seems quite amused by something." Bri recognized the voice. She felt her heart stop and could not breathe for a moment. Turning to see Mr. James, she introduced him to the count.

Extending his hand to the count, Mr. James said, "It is an honor to meet you, sir. Your daughter invited us to a preview of *The Princess* and we found it quite interesting."

"Thank you, Mr. James. In return for your including my daughter in your dinner party after the theatre, I would like to invite you to dine with us Saturday evening in one week at eight o'clock."

Bri's heart beat at a rapid rate. *Will Mr. James agree?* Clarissa must have told her father to invite him. She would have a business meeting with him Friday morning and a social occasion the following night! *I feel dizzy.*

"Thank you, sir. I would be delighted to join you. Lady Clarissa, may I sign your dance card?"

Turning a bit pink, Bri felt her emotions rising as he signed it. But then he turned to her and said, "Lady Gabriella, are there any spaces left on your dance card?"

"Yes, Mr. James," she said, handing it to him. He frowned as he saw the last dance was taken, and she was momentarily pleased that he seemed irritated. He then signed the third line and handed it back to her. "Thank you." *Only one space left.*

"If I may take my leave of you, I must have a word with my father."

Henry scanned the room for Sir John. "Ah! He's with the baron. I'll join you." Henry followed Mr. James.

"And I see an old friend." The count clicked his heels and left.

"Baron Beauchamp is a handsome man…perhaps he and Lady Penelope will be a match. He's waited so long to marry. I supposed it's never too late." Gwyneth looked around the crowd. "I see Mildred Greywold. I think I shall speak with her."

Bri remained with Lady Clarissa and Dr. St. Cloud.

As she swept her eyes around the room, Bri noticed a short, rotund man staring at her. To her horror, he smiled at her and began to move toward her group. She turned to talk to the others, but he intruded.

"I know we've been introduced, but I do not know your name. I remember your hair. You are the loveliest young lady in the room. May I have the honor of signing your dance card? I am Fitzgibbon, Viscount Clyr." His voice was weak and high-pitched.

Bri remembered him. "I remember meeting you at the Duchess of Pytchley's Christmas party, Lord Clyr." Hesitating a moment too long, she handed her dance card to him.

"Ah. Lady Gabriella, now it comes back to me. A lovely name. A lovely name indeed." He signed the second place on her card. Without bothering to introduce himself to the others in the group, he walked away. They could overhear him say to Lady Melanie, "I know we've been introduced, but I do not know your name. I remember your hair. You are the loveliest young lady in the room. May I have the honor of signing your dance card? I am Fitzgibbon, Viscount Clyr."

Bri rolled her eyes as the others laughed.

A young man approached Bri shyly. "You d-d-do not remember

me, Lady G-G-Gab-b-briella," he stuttered, "b-but we took r-riding lessons together in the p-p-park near your aunt's house when we were children. I am George Banningford, Viscount A-A-Armstrong."

Smiling in remembrance, Bri extended her hand. "Of course, I remember you, Viscount Armstrong. You were the best student in the riding class. You must be the leader of the hunt club by now."

Grateful for her warmth, he took her hand, and said, "I am definitely b-b-better at riding than I am in Society. May I sign your d-d-dance card?"

"I'm so sorry, but it's full. I'll save you a space at the Masquerade Ball, I promise. There will be seven dances that night. I know because my grandmother, the Duchess of Pytchley, is the hostess."

The viscount nodded and quickly disappeared, his face flushed with embarrassment.

Lady Clarissa was now separated from Bri by several people, and Bri was free to wander about the room. She decided to greet Lady Patricia and find out how well she knew Mr. James, but was stopped in her quest by Blackburn, who was holding two glasses of Champagne.

"There you are. I noticed that your glass is empty. So I brought you more Champagne."

Is it empty? Bri looked at her flute, remembering Aunt Gwyneth's words. It was clear to her now how easy it would be to have too much Champagne in this atmosphere.

Bri accepted the glass. "Thank you, Mr. Blackburn."

Blackie smiled and tilted his head. "Moments ago I was Blackie. No need to be formal, Lady G. You are fascinating, the most beautiful woman here. All the men in this room want to sign your dance card, but they are intimidated."

Bri smiled, not knowing how to respond.

"As you know, I put off marriage in lieu of building my career with your father. We've always had an easy banter between us and interest in the finer points of commerce. Now that you are grown, I find you enormously attractive as well as charming. I hope it doesn't shock you that I would like to court you. May I call on you on Sunday afternoon?"

Stunned, Bri stammered. "Mr. B-Blackburn—"

"Blackie."

"Blackie," she breathed deeply, recovering her composure, "the

Marriage Season is a new experience for me. I expect it will be full of surprises and new discoveries. As we are acquainted with each other now, perhaps we should take things a bit more slowly. Sunday afternoon seems too soon for me to be accepting courtship offers. Shall we defer this conversation for a few weeks or a month?" *I must appear calm. I do not want to offend him or arouse his incautious temper.*

Blackie bowed his head for a moment. "Of course. I don't want to rush you. I just wanted to make my intentions very clear at the outset. I hope I shall not have to duel for you, but if so, I am considered an excellent shot."

Shocked at this comment, Bri spoke before thinking. "Dueling has been outlawed, Blackie. Surely you wouldn't risk your life for me. I do not love you."

Duff Blackburn rose to his full height. "I take my statements seriously, Lady G. Outlawed or not, one way or another, I shall fight for you. It makes the challenge so much greater, and the prize so much sweeter. And what is love but a woman's foolish fantasy? Marriage is more of a rational decision than a romantic inclination."

Bri stiffened. "I am not a 'prize,' nor will I marry a man I do not love."

Confident, Blackburn stood his ground. "You can learn to love if it is in your best interest. I can be rather charming. And I can teach you a few things about love."

Disturbed by the look in his eye, Bri felt her face reddening. Behind her, the voice of Mr. James interrupted her conversation with Blackie. "What's this about love?" He extended his hand toward Blackie. "Mr. Blackburn, I presume. Are you passing yourself off as a romantic?"

After shaking Edward's hand, Blackburn adopted a more combative stance. Annoyance in his voice was apparent as he was forced to look up at James, who was more than two inches taller. "Don't tell me a hard-hearted banker like you, Mr. James, is a believer in the nonsense of romantic love? Surely as the scion of a wealthy family, you favor a match that is socially appropriate more than one that feeds your baser instincts. What is love but dressed-up lust? That is for your mistress, not your wife."

Mr. James delivered a calm and measured retort. "Mr. Blackburn, I'm sure that Lady Gabriella is not interested in talk of mistresses. Romantic love fills the heads of young women, but you don't need to insult them. Their harmless fantasies will evaporate soon enough."

At that comment, Bri felt anger toward both of them. "Listen to me, you two self-appointed experts on women—love is not lust. And romantic love is not to be dismissed as a harmless fantasy. Any man that wants to court me will have to prove his love to me before I will marry him. And if none can, then I shall not marry."

Shocked, Edward scoffed at her response. "That is a ridiculous statement. Fall in love yourself, if you must, but why insist that a man, who is infinitely more practical than a woman, must likewise fall in love? Do you want a husband to be truthful or to feed your romantic fantasies? Marriage is a more serious endeavor than romance."

Blackburn shrugged. "Lady G., if you want me to say that I love you, then I will say that I love you." He began to make exaggerated gestures with his arms. "I love you more than the stars in the sky, more than the light of the moon and the rays of the sun. I will write poetry to you and sing songs of love. Then will you permit me to court you?"

"Court her? Exactly what is going on here?"

"I simply asked Lady G. if I might court her. Specifically, I requested to call on her Sunday afternoon next. She has deferred that meeting. I have told her that I am prepared to duel for her. Am I correct in assuming, Mr. James, that you are also interested in courting Lady G.? Shall we meet at dawn to settle this?"

Edward's voice sounded icy. "Perhaps it will come to that."

"How dare you men presume that my choice of a marriage partner be decided by you in some silly duel? You may kill each other for all I care. Set your sights elsewhere." Bri stomped off, leaving the two men staring at each other.

CHAPTER TWENTY-ONE

March 14, 1811 – Lady Elisabeth's Ball
Bri

As Bri made her way toward Lady Clarissa, she was relieved by the fact that she would not be sitting out any dance, although she was angry and uncertain as to her feelings about Mr. James. Aunt Gwyneth had been correct in her prediction that Mr. James would exhibit jealousy toward Blackie and vice versa. If Blackie indeed turned out to be deceiving her father, he could turn into a very dangerous man if cornered. The reference to a pistol should not be taken lightly. Involuntarily, she shivered at the thought.

Spotting Clarissa, who was talking with Herr Kramer, Bri joined them.

The composer appeared buoyant about progress on the operetta. "It is nearly perfect. All it needs, Clarissa, is your voice. Will not you please consider the wig that Lady Gabriella suggested?"

Bri put her hand on Clarissa's arm, saying, "Have you spoken about this to your father yet?"

"No, I am hoping to ask him on Monday, as we are both going to be at the theatre that day for rehearsals. I am worried, though. Investment is one thing, performance is quite another."

An idea popped into Bri's head. "Why not surprise him? Tell him you need to work on things backstage while he sits out in front. Put on the wig and play the role. At the end, pull off the wig and ask his permission."

Herr Kramer brightened. "It could work. No, I know it would! Once he saw your talent he could not refuse. A stage name would protect his honor and bring you fame. It is a once in a lifetime chance. Please take it!"

"Well, if he believed the disguise—"

"He will!" Bri had no doubt.

Clarissa mused, "It might work. I guess it is better than not trying, and at least I can play the role once in rehearsal. I shall do it!"

Bri beamed that her suggestion was accepted. At the same moment, a bell rang.

After silence descended on the room, Lady Elisabeth announced, "The first dance is about to begin. May I call your attention to the displays of African masks, pottery and artifacts that are displayed around the room? I wanted to create an exotic ambiance and thanks to Mr. Blackburn of Wyndward Trading, we dance surrounded by treasures. Find your partners and join us in the ballroom."

Clarissa and Bri looked at each other for reassurance, understanding each other's fears and excitement.

Dr. St. Cloud appeared to escort Clarissa into the ballroom, and Lord Lt. Thornton walked up at the same time, offering his arm to Bri. The opening dance was a reel, and Lord Lt. Thornton danced well. Bri was grateful that she didn't make any mistakes. The dances were long, lasting fifteen to twenty minutes. Her energy began to wane after ten minutes. *I must practice more.*

Lord Clyr approached her for the second dance. Grateful it was the Quadrille, with specific steps, she did not have to look at the corpulent oaf much. Even her gloves became damp from his sweaty hands. Her skin crawled. He smelled as a man who bathed rarely and covered body odor with cologne. The scent was overpowering. Relief washed over her as the dance ended.

There was an interlude of about ten minutes between dances. Edward approached with two glasses of punch. "I thought you might appreciate some refreshment."

Grateful that it wasn't more Champagne, Bri accepted the glass. "This is exactly what I need."

Looking into his eyes, she caught herself wanting to sigh, and realized that it would be too revealing of her feelings. *Relax. Breathe, as Nashmir counseled.* She realized that she was concentrating so hard on relaxing and breathing to remain calm that she was not listening to what Mr. James was saying.

"Are you preoccupied, Lady Gabriella?"

"Forgive me, Mr. James. I am unaccustomed to dancing and I need to catch my breath."

A bell rang, signaling that Lady Elisabeth would make an announcement. "I have a surprise for you all. The next dance will be a waltz, as is my prerogative as hostess."

"Daring." Bri knew many in the *ton* did not approve of the waltz, bringing men and women into such close contact versus the steps of the reel or the Quadrille.

"Why else do you think I signed the third line?"

"You knew? How?"

"Lady Elisabeth is my godmother. And whoever signs the dance card before the break escorts his partner to dinner."

"But you waited. I could have had that line filled by the time you saw me."

"Did you expect me to run to you as a pet dog?"

Bri bristled. "You are the most infuriating man. Why do you want to dance with me when you are so free with your criticism?"

"I like to see how you react. It gives me insight into your mind."

Squinting as her cheeks flushed, Bri spoke slowly. "Are you saying that you believe you can elicit expected reactions by deliberately provoking me?"

Edward shrugged. "I don't know what to expect. That is the point. I'm learning about you."

"So I am some kind of scientific experiment to you? Do you intend to test this statement, or that retort, to draw a conclusion? I do not react as chemicals mixing in a vial."

"No?" Mr. James displayed a smirk that increased her frustration.

She finished the punch. As she looked around for a place to put the cup, Edward signaled a waiter.

Taking the glass, the waiter placed it on his serving tray while Edward set his next to it.

The orchestra began to tune up, an indication that it was time to move into position for the third dance.

Extending his arm to Bri, Edward moved them into position for the waltz. He took her right hand in his, she placed her left hand on his shoulder, and he reached to hold her back with his left hand.

She felt her breathing quicken. Her heart fluttered. As Nashmir had advised, she immediately loosened her muscles and felt Edward pull her closer. She worried that her face would turn scarlet with excitement, telling a tale she did not want told.

***

Edward

Edward felt protective toward Gabriella. *What is Blackburn up to?* Knowing, as did she, that Blackburn might be dishonest, Edward vowed to himself to do everything he could to prevent such a man from courting Gabriella. If that required a duel, so be it. Edward's initial reluctance to marry her to fulfill his duty by his family gave way to an overwhelming desire to possess her. He desired more than her body. He desired dominion over her heart, her mind, her soul. He wanted to possess her completely.

His mind raced as they swirled around the ballroom floor. Although he wanted no other man to dance with her, he knew he could not prevent it. Perhaps he should propose soon, but given her earlier protestations to Blackburn, he would have to get beyond her fixation on romantic love. *Is romantic love a salve constructed to obscure mere lust?* True, he felt incredible physical attraction to Gabriella. *She is a beautiful woman, but there are other beautiful women at the ball. None move me on so many levels.* His attraction was deeper than the involuntary physical desire that a man felt whenever he saw an attractive woman. There was a connection, an understanding, a compelling influence that was building between them. He knew she felt the same, or she would not have let him pull her closer to him. He wanted to kiss her, and wondered where they could go. As they approached the doors to the verandah opposite the ballroom, he whisked her off the dance floor into the night air.

He continued to dance with her, but searched for a way to whirl her out of sight of the others. Guiding her to a spot between the windows for total privacy, he pulled her to him and kissed her gently. She did not resist, and pushed herself closer to him. Parting after the kiss, he looked deeply into her eyes and knew that she desired him as he desired her. "I find you an intriguing dance partner, Lady Gabriella. I trust that we will dance together often this Season."

Gabriella stared at him but said nothing.

"We must rejoin the dance before we are missed." Edward swept Bri back into the ballroom at the next open window, as if they had been dancing in and out of the verandah.

***

Henry

Henry watched as Edward and Bri danced out to the verandah. He smiled, hoping that Bri was happy in Edward's arms. Concerned that others had noticed, he looked around and frowned. The only one looking in that direction was Blackie.

***

Bri

Bri was disappointed when the music stopped. "Thank you, Mr. James. That was very enjoyable."

"For me as well, Lady Gabriella. Let me escort you to dinner."

"Very well, Mr. James."

***

Blackburn

Blackburn had not missed their exit, vowing to do the very same thing on his dance with Lady Gabriella, the last of the evening. *She will not elude me. I can feign romance with a beautiful woman. If she wants to live, she will marry me.*

***

Bri

A giant ice sculpture of two swans whose necks intertwined stood as the centerpiece of the long buffet table. Lady Elisabeth had created an appetizing supper for her ball guests with iced assortments of fish and cold meats arranged on both ends of the table. A variety of potato dishes were displayed on either side of the swans. For dessert, a gourmet selection of *petits fours*, cream puffs and small éclairs was tempting. Most of the men filled their plates as they made their way around the buffet, while the ladies, in accordance with Aunt Gwyneth's description, took only small portions or simply one *petits fours*.

Grateful that her aunt had made her eat something earlier, Bri was too excited to eat. Edward took a selection of all the buffet offerings while she picked out a small selection of meats and a single *petits fours*.

A voice came from behind her. "Ask for lemonade instead of Champagne." Bri turned to see Gio, bent down and kissed him. "Mr. James, I'm sure you remember my family's dear friend, Lord Ostwold."

"Indeed I do. The last time I saw you—"

"Was at the Wyndward Summerfest about six years ago. Shortly afterward, you left for the Far East, I believe. What did you learn there?"

Edward gestured that they sit at one of the tables, open for anyone instead of being regimented with place cards. "The Far East is an exotic place with mores that vary much from our own, as well as kingdom to kingdom. I traveled from Vietnam, the ancient Annam, initially thinking I'd retrace the steps of Marco Polo. I had the great good fortune of being able to travel at will, with local guides who served as interpreters and bodyguards. I learned a smattering of many languages: the poetry of Vietnam is written in their language, but most commerce and administration is conducted in Mandarin, as the Chinese ruled them for over a thousand years. Then into China, seeing the Great Wall…an unbelievable achievement. It extends for more than thirteen thousand miles, and portions of it have crumbled, so once it was longer. It was built over a period of eighteen hundred years, inconceivable to us. The Chinese planning encompasses a minimum of one hundred years. Its population is the largest on earth, its people industrious and clever. Do you have an idea what was used for mortar?"

Gio shrugged. "Rice?"

Bri scoffed. "That's ridiculous, Gio."

"No. Not ridiculous. Correct. The 'sticky rice' they eat is what holds that wall together."

Gio sat back. "A guess. Perhaps I really am as smart as I think I am."

"Where else did you visit?" Bri leaned forward.

"Mongolia, the ancestral home of Genghis Khan, as well as Nepal, Tibet, the Himalayas. Do you know that the Himalayas house the world's largest salt mines?"

"Yes. We import it. Pink sea salt is a delicacy mined for millennia." Bri smirked.

"I didn't know that, and I'm not ashamed to admit it." Gio tilted his head as if perplexed. "If the highest mountains on Earth house salt mines, what does that mean? Were they once at the bottom of the sea? Has the earth slipped on its axis and waters flowed to a new leveling point, leaving deserts that were later raised to mountains? An unending cycle of destruction and renewal?"

"Now that *is* ridiculous," Edward laughed.

"But were it true, would that knowledge make men humble? If the geography of the world could change that dramatically, what might be in store for us mere mortals?"

Bri smiled. "Gio the philosopher...I'm not surprised. An interesting theory—"

Edward sputtered. "—Surely you jest. The world does not topple around on its axis. Seas do not dry up and thrust the earth up to become mountains."

"Don't be so certain. Mapmakers have noted the outlines of the continents fit together like puzzle pieces. Maybe the history of the earth is yet to be understood." Bri sipped her lemonade.

The conversation changed as others joined them: Henry, Gwyneth, Clarissa, Dr. St. Cloud and Count von Dusterberg. While the topics were of general interest and pleasant, Bri had vowed to not argue with Mr. James. Every time she looked at him, she thought of their kiss and wondered if there would be a verandah at the next ball. *How can I long for his kiss and yet find him so irritating at times?* She had always imagined that falling in love would be so instant, so clear, so effortless. This situation was confusing, yet her attraction to him was difficult to resist. She kept a polite ear tuned to the conversation around her while she was absorbed in analyzing her own situation.

She had been bored by her country suitors, never taking any of them seriously. *Why couldn't we have stayed friends?* The men became irate when she spurned their advances. This Society crowd was far more sophisticated, and yet she found most of the men to whom she had been introduced tonight, almost without exception, as boring as those in the country. Instead of talking about their herds and crops, the men of the *ton* seemed steeped in discussion of men's fashion and their gambling skills.

Suddenly she saw what had been obvious to those who knew her best, and why they kept telling her that she was smitten by Mr. James. *He does not bore me.* In fact, he fascinated her and angered her simultaneously, bringing forth emotions that she had never felt before. He had the manners of a gentleman, and apologized when he realized he had done something offensive. He shared her interest in commerce and investments and yet had traveled abroad like her father, so he was an adventurer, not a narrow-minded provincial prig. She looked at Mr. James differently in that moment, a bit puzzled. *Is this the feeling that inspires poets? Does this man interest me enough to consider marriage? Does he feel the same way about me?*

As the waiters served tea, Lady Elisabeth invited the guests to bring their tea cups into the ballroom, where a pianoforte and harp had been placed in the center of the floor. Herr Kramer and the harpist appeared. Lady Elisabeth introduced them. "I have asked Herr Kramer to play some of the music he has composed for the new operetta *The Princess* which will open in the *ton* next week. My cousin saw it performed in Germany last spring and highly recommended it. For the London premiere, Herr Kramer has added a new melody which I find quite enchanting. I hope you enjoy this little interlude before we recommence the dancing."

While Edward was engaged in conversation with her father, Bri moved into the ballroom. There, for the first time at the ball, Bri spotted Charlotte. *She's with him? Father will not like that.* Part of her felt her father deserved to be shocked. The man her father called The Nemesis had his arm around Charlotte's shoulders.

Her father was walking toward her. *Where is Mr. James?*

"Did you see Charlotte?"

"What?" Her father's brow furrowed.

He must not have believed she'd get another escort.

Bri inclined her head toward Charlotte. "Look whom she is with."

Henry paled, and then his face flushed to a dangerous wine-red.

Bri recognized the signs of anger swelling up within him.

"That man is a scurrilous political manipulator. And worse."

"He is a powerful man, Father. I know you don't like him."

"He is a man who gathers secrets that he uses to extort victims. He trades in gossip that ruins lives. He is scum."

Raising Bri's discomfort, Charlotte and The Nemesis were walking toward them.

Henry turned on his heel and walked away.

Bri stood frozen in place.

Aristotle Drummond was called "The Nemesis" by her father. She didn't know the reason for her father's deep-seated hatred, but his visceral reaction to Drummond was so extreme, she was wary to meet him.

Charlotte greeted Bri warmly. "Bri...Lady Gabriella, have you met Mr. Aristotle Drummond?"

"No, sir," extending her hand, "but your reputation precedes you."

Drummond nodded, appearing amused at her retort. "Let me get us some Champagne, Charlotte. It was a pleasure to meet you, Lady Gabriella."

Once he was out of earshot, Bri whispered to Charlotte, "What happened between you and Father? Is it irrevocable? I need your advice about Mr. James."

"I shall always be your friend, Bri, and always available to you. I think of you as the daughter I never had. I don't want you to be angry with your father. He and I have had a falling out over this ball and our accumulated misunderstandings of each other. My advice to you on Mr. James is simple—be careful. Don't persuade yourself that you are in a romance that exists only in your head."

"But I know Father loves you."

"He has never said the word, 'love.' He *cares* for me. Perhaps as he might care for a dog. On second thought, many men love their dogs more than their wives." She took another sip of Champagne.

"You sound bitter."

"Fifteen years are gone, Bri. Let this be a lesson to you. Don't waste your life on a man who takes you for granted. You have made assumptions about your father, as I have. I just say to you," sweeping her hand in a gesture around the ballroom, "do not delude yourself that men think as we do. Don't make assumptions about Mr. James. If you fall in love during this season, make your paramour say he loves you. Don't assume it."

With a kiss on Bri's cheek, Charlotte slipped away to rejoin

Drummond.

Bri returned her attention to the entertainment portion of the ball, thrilled to see that Herr Kramer would be playing selections from the score of *The Princess*.

After acknowledging polite welcoming applause, Herr Kramer and the harpist played interludes. Bri gauged interest by watching faces, noting smiles and seeing other indications that people found the music captivating. She felt Mr. James come up behind her.

He whispered in her ear, "Your promotional ideas are being implemented."

When the composer finished playing the interludes, he played the signature melody that would be reprised throughout the operetta. In looking around for reactions to this particular melody, Bri glanced at her father, standing next to her aunt. He appeared transfixed, as if in a trance. The color had drained from his face and, for a moment, Bri feared for his health. Seeing that he was swaying, she nudged Mr. James and silently directed his attention to her father.

Edward squeezed her hand, as if to give her comfort. When she turned again to her father, she could see a tear running down his cheek. She had never seen him react that way to any piece of music. When Herr Kramer finished and the room broke into applause, Gabriella walked over to her father and put her hand on his arm. "What is it, Father? Are you unwell?"

"I must speak with Herr Kramer. I must know where he learned that melody." Henry moved toward the piano.

"He learned it from me, Lord Ravenshire." Clarissa responded to the earl's quizzical look that seemed to beg for an explanation. "I learned it from a woman in Madagascar. Sold into the Sultan's ranks of slaves, she became his spiritual healer. In her native land, she had been some kind of priestess or princess. She used to sing this song, as well as others, in the evenings, accompanying herself on a lyre. This was my favorite, and I remembered it well enough to help Herr Kramer put it into a composition."

Their intimate group waited for Henry to speak.

Barely at a whisper, he asked, "Her name. What was her name?"

"Taita."

"I thought she was dead," exhaled Henry. "Lost at sea after a volcanic eruption and a violent typhoon. A ship of the slave trade must have found her adrift. She lives. I must find her."

The count cleared his throat. "The Sultan is visiting for the opening of the play, with his entourage, his favorite wives and Taita. He never travels without her."

"Taita? Coming here?"

Bri remembered his talk of a lost love. "Father, is this the woman you loved who died?"

Her father nodded. "So many years." His voice was barely audible.

"When I asked her about the song, she talked of a lost love. She said the gods had separated them. It must be you of whom she spoke."

"Count, would you see Lady Gabriella home? And Young James, would you escort Lady Gwyneth home? I need air and time to think."

"Of course."

Kissing Bri good night, Henry whispered in her ear. "I hope you enjoy the rest of the ball." He left the room before she could respond, stopping briefly to thank Lady Elisabeth.

Watching him leave in silence, the count spoke first. "Taita is an ethereal creature. I have seen the results of her healing powers. She is a woman worthy of Lord Ravenshire."

"The fourth dance is about to begin," announced Lady Elisabeth. "Please find your partners."

Dr. St. Cloud bowed his head and extended his hand. "Lady Gabriella?"

Before she could reach out, Edward gave a signal to the doctor and pulled Bri aside for a tête-a-tête, whispering in her ear, "I will watch Blackburn's every move as you dance with him. It is more than mere jealous irritation. You may be in danger."

"Jealous irritation, Mr. James?" Bri tried to act coy. "Do you resent another man's interest in me?"

"Lady Gabriella Wyndward, I intend to marry you. Do not trifle with me."

"Oh, you intend to marry me. Do my wishes enter into this matter or is it totally your decision?"

"Don't be difficult. Of course I expect you to see the logic of this course. We have similar interests, our families are well-acquainted, and we are attracted to each other. Once you have considered these things, you will agree to marry me."

"Well, I have considered 'these things' as you refer to them, and I agree that we have a great deal in common. However, I shall never marry a man who does not love me."

"Romantic love is a fantasy. Mature love can grow from respect and similarity of temperament. Don't expect me to throw myself at your feet, declaring unending pain unless you agree to be my wife. I am making an honorable proposal of marriage. It should not be confused with the fantasies of an arrested adolescence influenced by cheap novels and the poetry of lovesick bards."

"Have you learned nothing about me to date, Mr. James? Certainly you must have realized this simple fact—lecturing me is, to use the phraseology of my grandmother, 'unnecessary, unimaginative and unsuccessful.' My father is clearly torn by love for Charlotte and his memory of love with Taita, though he, like you, will not admit it. Do you intend to lecture him that he is acting like an adolescent? Or your parents, who are still quite affectionate with each other, even in public? Are they not still in love with each other?"

"You are confusing the issue. They are not foolish people."

"So only foolish people fall in love? Are you saying that my desire to marry a man who loves me is foolish?"

"Must you take a rational discussion and turn it into an argument? You are foolish if you persist in clinging to fantasies about love. One of these Society fops who talks so eloquently of love would bore you after one week, and you know it. You need a strong man to match your strong nature."

"And no strong man can fall in love?"

"Why do you insist on irritating me with this talk of love?"

Laughing, Bri understood. "Of course! Now I understand why this talk of love irritates you so much."

"What are you giggling about?"

"You have been protesting too much, Mr. James. You have fallen in love with me and you refuse to admit it. That is why this topic arouses such anger in you. Love is an emotion you cannot control, just as you cannot control me."

"Do not analyze me, Lady Gabriella. Your amateur philosophy of human behavior is laughable. We shall end this discussion until you have resumed a rational frame of mind. However irritated I am by this discussion, I shall still watch your dance with Blackburn with concern. Please set aside this childish coyness and recognize the danger you may face with him. Give him no reason to guess your suspicions."

Quickly regaining her composure, Bri nodded in agreement. "I recognize the danger, and I will be careful. I've known him forever. I feel comfortable with him."

"Perhaps a duel is not out of the question." Edward scanned the room. "I must find Lady Penelope." He nodded adieu and walked away.

Bri smiled at Dr. St. Cloud. "Forgive that interruption, Doctor. Family business and all that."

Dr. St. Cloud escorted her to their position for the reel. "I'm not blind or deaf, Lady Gabriella. I think it's more than 'all that'."

Bri felt a sensation that someone was staring at her. She turned to see Blackie smiling in a way that made her uneasy. *Did he see Mr. James take me to the verandah? Does he know that Mr. James kissed me?*

Bri didn't have time to consider him any longer, as the music began for another reel. She wasn't sure her stomach was settled enough for the twirling and fast footwork. There was no time to talk during the demanding movements.

Afterwards, there was a brief time between dances. She wanted to delay her time with Blackie, so engaged the doctor in further conversation. "Did you and Clarissa enjoy your dance?"

"Yes, I must say I am smitten. I am indebted to you for bringing her into my life. If the dog had not been hit and you had not come into my shop, I might never have met Lady Clarissa."

"You are forgetting your magician's audition. Fate decreed that the two of you would meet. You owe me no debt. Clarissa's happiness is what is important."

Dr. St. Cloud agreed. "I hope to speak with her of my feelings soon. Her father is a bit forbidding. Do you think he will approve of courtship?"

"He is a formal man, used to the protocol of the diplomatic corps. But if the two of you truly care for each other, he will give you his blessing. Of that I am certain." *I hope I am right.*

The last dance was with Blackie. Bri didn't see him. Walking around the perimeter of the crowd, she found it striking that the men's attire, shades of gray and black punctuated by white silk or linen shirts, contrasted with the spectrum of color displayed by the women's ball gowns. The styles ranged from overly frilly little-girl fantasies to the elegant mature look epitomized by Aunt Gwyneth.

Most had their trains tied up so they wouldn't trip while dancing.

Bri noted particular design elements of the gowns that appealed to her. In the midst of this exercise, she caught herself imagining how she would look at future balls and wondering if Mr. James would like this or that feature of a dress. Annoyed at her preoccupation with his opinion, Bri vowed to develop her own style and stop worrying about his approval.

A hand touched her shoulder.

She turned to see Blackie.

"The last dance, Lady G. Will you go out to the verandah with me as you did with Mr. James?"

"The waltz led us there. We danced in and out of the windows. The dance determines the steps, Blackie." She tried to smile in a coquettish way.

"Then we'll see where the steps take us, won't we?"

CHAPTER TWENTY-TWO

March 14, 1811 – Lady Elisabeth's Ball
Edward

Edward stood close enough to overhear Gabriella and Blackburn. *She's pretending to be a little too eager.* When he had noticed Blackburn's name on Gabriella's dance card for the last dance, he had deliberately signed no other dance card on that line, intending to watch over her. Observing from the sidelines, Edward reviewed the information he had collected about the earl's protégé. The reason for a vendetta, if it existed, lay in the past. He would set an investigator on the trail of Blackburn's past immediately. As Blackburn danced with Gabriella, Edward felt pangs of jealousy rising within him. His rival was holding Gabriella closer and longer than necessary. It irritated him that she seemed to be amused by Blackburn's conversation. *She is such an exasperating woman. Too sure of herself, unaware of the danger Blackburn presents.* And yet, he wanted to protect her and hold her safe in his own arms. Surely this was just physical attraction. Her fixation on romantic love contrasted with her analytical mind. *My instinct to protect her from a predator such as Blackburn falls into the range of standard male biological behavior. I will never submit to her demand for a declaration of love.* Her romantic exuberance must be tempered by his rational control. He would not compromise his principles.

Still, it was like torture to watch her dancing with Blackburn. It required all of his training in the Asian arts to shield his emotions from view. *This is the last time I will watch her dance with another man. She will be mine and mine alone.* He wondered what Gabriella and Blackburn were discussing in such an animated way. Could she maintain her acting for the entire dance? *One slip of the tongue and Blackburn will be aware of her game.*

When the dance finally ended, Edward lost no time in reaching Gabriella's side. "In accordance with her father's wishes, Blackburn, Count von Dusterberg will escort Lady Gabriella home."

"I saw Lord R. leave in haste. What caused him to depart early?"

Gabriella smiled. "It is a personal matter, Blackie. Nothing that concerns the trading company."

Ignoring her taunt, Blackburn bowed his farewell. "I look forward to continuing our discussion about African spices, Lady G. Thank you for a lovely dance."

Edward firmly took Gabriella's arm. "Good evening, Blackburn."

"Good evening, Blackie," Gabriella called over her shoulder as Edward pulled her away.

Guiding Gabriella through the crowd, Edward could not hide his irritation. "Why do you call him 'Blackie,' as if you are close?"

"I've always called him that. I've known him ever since I can remember. He is my father's most trusted associate. He always looked out for me when Father was on long voyages."

Pulling her to the back of the foyer, waiting for the others to retrieve their cloaks, Edward continued his interrogation of Gabriella. "What were you talking about during that long dance?"

"I kept it to neutral topics such as new products from the trading company's different markets and which ones he thought would be successfully introduced this year. I actually learned a couple of things."

"Surely you're not suggesting that you enjoyed talking with him?"

"Well, ignoring my suspicions and being rational, as you have been insisting, I must recognize that Blackie's grasp of the trading company's operations is impressive."

"Impressive? I can't believe that I am hearing this." Edward's voice rose in volume with each word.

"You are speaking too loudly, Mr. James."

"You're right."

"As usual."

Edward ignored her retort. "The man is very likely stealing from your father's company and you are falling under his spell. The next thing you'll be saying is that you are in love with him."

"Ridiculous." Gabriella fumed and appeared to force herself to whisper even though her temper flared. "I am simply following your instructions. From a business perspective, the man has insight that could be useful in the future. I am simply stating a fact."

"This man has no insight except in discerning how to seduce you, except he does it with talk of business instead of poetry. And you are the one touting romance. Would you have me recite statistics to impress you?"

"He wasn't trying to seduce me. No one is trying to seduce me except you, with a stolen kiss." She tilted her head at him and leaned closer. "You just admitted you seek to impress me."

His gaze intensified. "I did not notice any resistance from you, so that kiss was not stolen."

Gabriella looked away.

"Marry me and put an end to this game of wits. Stop harping on this topic of love. We have much in common. Many marriages have been built on less."

"True. But mine will be built on love."

"You have set up an impossible situation. If I said I loved you right now, you would not believe me. How long must this charade continue?"

"Until you can tell me you love me and I can believe that the words come from the deepest part of your heart." Bri's voice softened. "For you must understand, Mr. James, I am falling in love with you. And I cannot marry you unless I know that you feel the same passion for me."

"Perhaps it is I who am foolish to ridicule your romantic concepts. I have built my life on rationality and sound judgment. I care for you."

"That is not enough." Bri realized the staff was holding their coats and the count and her aunt appeared irritated at the delay. "We have a business appointment tomorrow at ten o'clock, as I recall." She raised her voice loud enough to be overhead. "Good evening, Mr. James.

Walking with her to get their cloaks, he said, "And good evening to you, Lady Gabriella."

As he watched the count's carriage pull away from the

townhouse, he silently cursed himself for losing his temper. *No woman has ever had such an impact on me.* His Tibetan and Zen training in Japan had not anticipated a force such as Lady Gabriella Wyndward. His mouth dropped open as he realized what he had said to her: *I proposed marriage to her tonight. Twice. Am I losing control of myself?*

***

March 14, 1811 – Lord Ravenshire's Townhouse
Bri

Bri let Thompson take her cloak, and asked, "Has Father returned?"

"No, I was expecting him with you, Lady Gabriella. Is something wrong?"

"We must find him, Thompson. He left the ball more than two hours ago, saying he wanted time to think. Has he ever spoken to you about the woman he once loved who died?"

"Once, many years ago."

Bri related the story of Taita's song and the inexplicable twists of fate that would bring the woman that her father had long thought dead to London within the week. "Father was stunned to learn that she was alive, as you might imagine. He was almost in a trance. Where would he go to be alone to think?"

"Either to the docks or to Ravenshire. Is Jean-Louis with him?"

"Yes, he asked Count von Dusterberg to take me home, and Mr. James escorted Aunt Gwyneth to her townhouse.

"Then you may rest well, milady. Jean-Louis would guard the earl with his life. Your father has most likely gone to the docks to watch the ships prepare for their voyages. He finds it a compelling sight and one that gives him perspective. This would not be the first time that he sought solace where he found his path as a young man. I will ask Nashmir to prepare a special tea for him so that he will have a dreamless sleep and awake refreshed."

"Do you really think so, Thompson? Shouldn't we search for him?"

"Lady Gabriella, a man of your father's age would no doubt be offended that we thought he could not survive life's surprises. He is a man, and you must let him be one. Sometimes men simply need to retreat into themselves until they are ready to re-emerge to meet their fate."

204

"I will defer to your judgment, Thompson. I can't help but be concerned about him, though. I've never seen him act in such a manner. First encountering Charlotte with The Nemesis tonight," nodding to answer Thompson's unasked question, "and then finding out his lost love lives." Bri sighed. "Perhaps I shall drink some of that tea myself."

Bri climbed the stairs to her rooms and met Jane Anne in the hallway.

"Oh, milady, you still look so beautiful! Tell me about the ball. I've always imagined how it must be."

Talking as they walked into her room, Bri sat down on the edge of her bed. "It was a structured evening, very formal for the most part. There were five dances, including a waltz with Mr. James. I found him attractive and appealing but arrogant and annoying at the same time. Lady Penelope and Lady Clarissa were thrilled with your styling of their hair. They will be steady clients, I am sure. We will figure a plan for you, but give me a few days.

"Something else happened with Father. After a rift with Charlotte, who attended the ball with another escort, a long lost love he thought dead was revealed to be alive. I don't know what to think. The baroness will be distraught when she learns of it—and she will. Word will spread like a grassfire. I need sleep. Tomorrow I must resolve other pressing matters."

"Yes, milady." Jane Anne helped Bri out of her ball gown and into her nightdress. She unfastened the hairpins and brushed Bri's hair until it was smooth and softly curling around her shoulders.

A knock on the door announced the arrival of Nashmir with his specially formulated tea.

"Nashmir, your breathing techniques calmed me tonight."

The Tibetan nodded acknowledgment of her comment, and then left, followed by Jane Anne.

Finally alone with her thoughts, Bri picked up her cup of tea and carried it to the window. Spotty slept on the floor next to her, his leg wrapped in fresh bandages with a clean splint. *Nashmir is a treasure, healing people and pets.* Sitting on the velvet cushioned window seat, she looked out over the courtyards of the adjoining townhouses. There were a few gaslights on in the city. The moon was bright and stars were in abundance. Bri could see Nashmir working by candlelight in his greenhouse, the only activity apparent in the hour past midnight.

So much had happened tonight. Blackie's interest in her was disturbing. *He has the trading company at his fingertips. Does he want my fortune as well?*

Bri froze in mid-thought. *I like Blackie, but I don't love him and will never marry him. But Edward proposed to me tonight. Twice. Am I wrong to want romance? Is it such a foolish notion?*

Father had lost a love five-and-twenty years earlier. As she considered his quandary, she recalled the voyage that had long ago entered Ravenshire lore. Her father had been lost for over a year in 1785 and 1786. Something nagged at her. With a start, she remembered her parents had married in 1782. *Father was married to my mother when he met Taita. I never knew my mother, and now I learn, by accident, that he betrayed her with some island woman.*

Bri stood and paced around her room. *How can I consider marriage when my own father broke his vows? How could he? First the breach with Charlotte and now this island woman from the past?* Never had Bri doubted her father's love for her. *The stories of his shipwreck and saving several members of his crew made him seem like a hero. But he betrayed my mother. Did he not love my mother?*

Nashmir's tea could not counteract the rage, confusion, disappointment and pain building in Bri's heart and mind. She sipped but remained fully lucid.

Not only did he betray my mother...what about Charlotte? Baroness Glasspool had been her father's constant companion for years, and Bri assumed they would marry someday. *Her heart is near-broken now. When she finds out about Taita, she will be inconsolable. I hope she doesn't do something rash, like marry The Nemesis for revenge. I thought love brought joy, but I am confronted by only pain.*

Another realization washed over her. *Father's lost paramour is a slave. A slave!* Belatedly, she considered the fact of the woman's race. Would Society ever accept such a union? What if the Sultan would not release the woman from slavery? Would Father buy the woman's freedom? Could one actually buy another human being? If the Sultan refused to release the slave, would her father kidnap Taita and sail away to another tropical island? Fear gripped her as she realized that if that happened, she might never see her father again. *Will he abandon me?* Losing him would be more than she could bear.

Life in the *ton* was supposed to be predictable and boring, and she often ridiculed those who relished its stability. Now, however, confronting the turmoil of her own life and of those she loved, she was unsettled. Spontaneity and unpredictability did not seem as appealing.

She heard horses outside, and saw Jean-Louis pull the carriage into the stables. Shortly thereafter, she watched him walk to Nashmir's greenhouse. Jean-Louis carried a candle to light the way for Nashmir as he carried a tray with his special brew into the townhouse.

Father has returned. Bri grabbed a robe and slippers and went down a flight to her father's room to wait for him.

***

Jean-Louis

"I hope that tea is potent."

"It should induce sleep." Nashmir entered the house from the garden. Jean-Louis turned up the interior gaslights. "I'll wait here."

The earl, who'd dallied in banter with the stable master, came up behind Nashmir and climbed the stairs.

The Frenchman walked over to a bench and gazed at the silent moon.

CHAPTER TWENTY-THREE

March 14, 1811 – Lord Ravenshire's Townhouse
Henry

The earl trudged up the stairs to his room. His legs felt like logs. Hearing footsteps behind him, he was relieved to see that Nashmir held a tray with tea. *Probably a potion to help me sleep.* He strode to his chest of drawers, pulled off his cravat and let Nashmir remove his jacket when Bri's voice startled him.

"Nashmir, I must speak to my father alone."

Turning to acknowledge her, Henry nodded at the valet to leave. "I'll leave my clothes on the chair for you to tend tomorrow." The earl sat on the edge of the bed. "I wandered around the docks trying to make sense of it all." He ran his fingers through his hair. "I'm stunned to learn Taita is alive."

"You were married when you met Taita. How could you betray my mother? Are you not the man I have looked up to for my whole life? Are you not a man of honor?"

The pain he felt was clear in his voice, as the memories flooded back into his consciousness. "My ship was blown off course by a tropical storm. Many men died. Fewer than ten of us were left, clinging to pieces of the ship. A pod of porpoises nudged our make-shift rafts toward an uncharted island. Those of us who'd survived the storm washed up on a beach surrounded by rocky cliffs. We thought we were alone. We had not the strength to climb the rocks. Three men died that night. Many of us, including me, had lost a lot of blood.

"The next day, a double-hulled outrigger canoe appeared with six men onboard. The men chattered in a language we did not understand. To our relief, they gave us water. Two stayed with us while the others went to get more natives. Vultures were circling the dead. We hoped our rescuers were friendly, but many South Sea islands were rumored to be inhabited by cannibals. There were also fables of ghostly ships sailing over the waters, monsters of the deep and cities of crystal floating in the sky, but the tall tales of sailors were not always to be disbelieved."

"I've hear that story a hundred times. You always left out the part about a romance with an island woman."

Henry stared her into silence and continued, haltingly. "A contingent of double-hulled outrigger canoes arrived, led by a young woman who gave the natives orders. She knelt by each of my injured crewmen, pulled pouches with liquids out of a bag she carried over her shoulder, determined the extent of their injuries and treated each one. She knew how to set broken arms and legs, as well as how to clean and stitch deep gashes with a needle fashioned out of coral.

"As a matter of duty, I insisted on being last to be seen. By the time she got to me, I knew the poultices stung from the reactions of my crew, but I hoped that meant her medicines would stanch any infection. I feared I might lose a leg. Her care saved me and all the remaining living members of my crew.

"I was lost in delirium for several days. Healing took weeks. After recuperating, we learned the rudimentary words of the language of our hosts, hunted for birds and rabbit-like creatures, caught fish, and survived. The near-perfect island environment offered abundant waterfalls, fruit trees, cocoanuts, pineapples and small game to sustain us. My crew included all races and nationalities from many sailings. The natives had never seen white, black or brown men before. There was no fear, and all were accepted. We felt safe.

"Seeing signs of the typhoon coming before the shipwreck, I had strapped my ship's logbook and diary to my abdomen, and sewed my astrolabe, nocturnal and scale into my pocket, so I could calculate our position if I survived. Once healed, imperfect and partially damaged as my instruments were, I determined our location was over 2,000 miles from any other known land. I doubted we would ever see a European, or even Asian, sailing ship in such a remote part of the

Pacific Ocean. I had to come to terms with the fact that my life as I had known it was over. I believed I would never see Jane, Gwyneth, Rychard or my father again. I felt totally alone.

"Our lives became a daily ritual of finding food, learning to build thatched roof huts from palm fronds, making rope from plants to tie on the fronds. The natives fashioned adzes made from volcanic rock, other tools carved of coral or bone. I asked them to show me how they did it. With time, I mastered their painstaking process. They marveled at my instruments, but told me how they navigated by the points in the heavens and knew which islands were located under which stars. The rumblings of the island's volcano, which they attributed to the mere groans of their gods, occasionally woke us, but the people said it was as a burp after a meal, nothing to worry about. 'You will know when the gods are angry.'

"The young woman, Taita, was the island's princess, daughter of the chief. She was a healer who could *feel* the illness of another. Kneeling beside an injured or ill person, she would sway, as if hit by a wave carrying a message from the sick person's body. I watched her from a distance. The people treated her as a goddess. The chief and I formed a bond, and he asked me if I wanted to marry his daughter. I explained that I had a wife back in my country, across many seas.

"He said, 'You have been granted a new life by the gods. How you choose to live it is up to you. If my daughter wishes to have a joining with you, I shall not refuse.'

"After a few months, Taita wished for us to have a joining—what the tribe considered marriage. She wanted this even though the future was uncertain. I told her that if a rescue ship appeared, I would have to leave. That was my duty to my family. She said she would not stop me from doing what I must do, but she could not come with me. She owed the same bond to her people as I did to mine. The tribe held the joining ceremony. We pledged ourselves. In that time, in that place, I chose the honorable path for her and the tribe."

Bri's voice quivered. "So the time and place determine the basis of your ethical decisions? The joining ceremony might have been the honorable path for Taita and the tribe, but it was not honorable for you. You were already married, pledged to another until death parted you. Of what value was either pledge? You left Taita, too. And Charlotte? Who has been loyal to you and loves you? Are you going to leave me too?"

"I am not asking for your approval. You have been the focus of my life since your birth. I can only hope that your understanding will come with time. I don't know what will happen with Charlotte or Taita. I don't know what to think about anything right now."

"How long after your joining did the cataclysm happen?"

Henry looked off into the distance as he remembered. "Not even a month after our joining, the volcanic rumblings became more pronounced. The typhoon season was not over, and the people were fearful. When the flames started shooting high into the sky, most ran to the rock caves to seek shelter from the volcanic lava flow, out of the wind. The people believed the wind from a volcano delivered death. When the volcano appeared to be on the verge of a massive eruption, Taita's father was hunting on the other side of the island. I stayed to be sure all the people were safe in the caves, while she sailed to the other side of the island to bring her father back. We thought there was time." His voice cracked. "We missed the signs of another typhoon.

"The volcano erupted, the island was cleft in two, and the seas raged for days. When the typhoon passed, we emerged from the caves. I led a search party to find anyone on the other side. We found only bodies, including the chief's, strewn among high rocks. Others were wrapped around tree tops, pierced by stray palm fronds or drowned, tossed by nature onto the beach. Taita's body, as well as those of several others, never appeared. We assumed they had been swept out to sea. To find out now, more than five-and-twenty years later, that she lives…"

"My head is splitting. I cannot hear another word." Bri stood and swayed. She fell back into the chair, unconscious.

***

Nashmir

Returning from the house, Nashmir sat on the bench across from Jean-Louis. "Lady Gabriella was waiting for him. Something is afoot. Thompson mentioned something about a long lost love. Tell me what ails the earl."

"I left Chérie to guard the carriage and slipped into the ball, lingering on the edge of the room to watch. All went according to expectations until the interlude of music from *The Princess*, the operetta that Bri is sponsoring, was played. One song caused the earl to pale. He signaled to me that he wanted to leave immediately.

"All of us have heard the story of his shipwreck and how the islanders saved him. Apparently, he omitted another part of the story. An island princess, a healer, saved his life as well as the lives of the remaining crew. Certain he was marooned forever, never to return to England, he joined with her in a ceremony that passed for marriage on the island."

Nashmir grasped the situation. "So when the volcano erupted, he thought her dead. And the song reminded him of his lost love?"

Jean-Louis pushed his black felt hat back on his forehead. "Worse. The island princess taught the song to Lady Clarissa on a visit to Madagascar. Taita was rescued by the Sultan and is his slave, now, to this day. She lives."

"And Lady Gabriella knows, and has determined that—"

"Her father was married to her mother when he married the island woman. The earl has fallen off his pedestal."

"Confronting the foibles of one's father is the beginning of maturity."

"Confronting the foibles is traumatic. Accepting those foibles is the challenge."

The window of the earl's room was thrown open. "Nashmir! Bri has fainted."

Nashmir and Jean-Louis bounded up the stairs to the earl's room.

The Tibetan checked her pulse. "The tea has taken effect. She is asleep. Please drink your tea, Lord Ravenshire. Sleep will come." Nashmir left the earl alone with his pain.

Jean-Louis lifted Bri into his arms and carried her upstairs to her room.

***

Jean-Louis

After settling Bri into bed, Jean-Louis went down the steps to the garden, followed by Thompson and Nashmir. Over the years, they had established the pattern of conducting private conversations in Nashmir's greenhouse.

The Frenchman pushed the rim of his hat farther back on his forehead as he sat on the bench. "We are in the middle of a gossip rag story-in-progress. We must act quickly to keep this quiet. A bribe has worked before to keep it out of the papers, but the *ton* will talk."

Nashmir shrugged. "That is your area of expertise."

The Frenchman raised an eyebrow. "Bribery? Or fixing a problem. I am unsure how to proceed at the moment. The link to Taita is the count. And the rift with the baroness will spread faster than a speeding arrow reaches its prey. She was escorted to the ball by The Nemesis."

Thompson appeared inscrutable. "Lady Gabriella told me."

Nashmir clenched his jaw and narrowed his lips into a line.

Jean-Louis turned his eyes to the butler. "Thompson, he will listen to you."

The butler scoffed. "And just what would you have me say? Don't cause a scandal? Think of the baroness? Follow your heart? Don't cause an international incident with the king's favorite spice capital?"

The former trapper shook his head. "I'm thinking of the servant network."

Thompson demurred. "I don't deal in gossip."

"I've said it before and I'll say it again—gossip is the life's blood of the *ton*." Jean-Louis threw his head back in frustration.

The Tibetan weighed in. "We must allow the earl to manage his own life. We are not his minders. All will develop as it should."

Standing to pace, Jean-Louis was losing his patience. "Not that Fate drivel again, Nashmir. Man acts, man has free will, man changes what he can for a better outcome."

"And who is to say what a better outcome might be?" Nashmir tilted his head, waiting for a response.

The Frenchman looked at Thompson. "Do you also propose we do nothing?"

The butler nodded.

Nashmir stared at Jean-Louis. "I do not believe it is my role to interfere. Advise, perhaps, but that is a delicate undertaking. The time for such a private moment may not present itself."

"*Foutre!* We each have his ear and his respect. Together we can persuade him to tread with caution."

"It's a bit too late for that. Would you tread with caution if your lost love appeared?" The butler eyed the Frenchman.

Jean-Louis felt a twitch in his cheek. *Foutre! I've given myself away.* He knew when he was beaten. The trick was never to fight to the death, but reserve action for a later date.

Thompson set the tone. "For now, we watch. We do not interfere. The earl is accustomed to dealing with obstacles. Nothing will prevent him from pursuing his goals. Members of the Wyndward family do not recoil from action." The butler left the greenhouse.

The Frenchman stopped pacing. "Thompson knows something we do not. His family has served several generations of Wyndwards."

"It is not our place to ask."

"Stop pretending to be so passive. You cure people, don't you? You could let them die. That would not be interfering with nature. It is always our place to ask or act when disaster lurks."

"Frenchman, you are enamored with conspiracies. You imagine danger approaching from all angles." Waving his hand in a dramatic gesture, Nashmir was unusually demonstrative. "The *ton* is not the hunting ground of predators."

"Isn't it?"

"Act with prudence."

"You just told me not to do anything."

Nashmir sighed. "In twenty years, I've never known you to take any man's advice. I don't expect you to start now. Your insights are invariably astute. We differ on whether you should act on them. As a trapper, you know the value of patience."

"A trapper lies in wait for his prey. Wild animals are more predictable than gossip rag purveyors. An attack by a wild animal is terminated by action or avoided by retreat. We cannot retreat from a newspaper story. We must stop it today, tomorrow and every day that follows."

"Then you must give them a better story."

"No. I refuse to trade in information that hurts innocent people."

"No one is innocent."

"Still, I have my principles."

"As you said earlier, a bribe may work. It is a straightforward offer."

Jean-Louis shrugged, tilted his hat in adieu, and strolled toward the stables for what he expected would be a fitful sleep.

***

Blackburn's Townhouse
Blackburn

After the ball, Blackburn wrote in his diary:

> Henry left the ball early, clearly disturbed.
> I must learn what has upset him.
>
> My love, Lady Gabriella, seems infatuated with the
> foppish Mr. James.
>
> He is no match for me, though younger.
> She must choose me.
>
> A duel may be in order.

He looked toward the drawer that held his weapons. *My pistols are ready, my knives hide in my boots, and poison is concealed in their hilts. If I must eliminate Mr. James to gain Lady G., so be it.*

CHAPTER TWENTY-FOUR

Friday, March 15, 1811 – Lord Ravenshire's Townhouse
Edward

E dward arrived a little before ten o'clock for his appointment with Gabriella, buoyant about the memory of their kiss the night before and looking forward to seeing his client.

The butler was not expecting any visitors. "Mr. James, I was not aware of your appointment. Both the earl and Lady Gabriella are still asleep."

Perplexed, Edward's brow furrowed. "The evening was not overly late."

"No, Mr. James. Other events intervened. You may wait, but I have no idea when they may awaken. Nashmir provided a sleeping potion for each of them."

"May I see Nashmir? I'd like to talk to him about my father. If Lady Gabriella is not awake after our discussion, I will leave."

Thompson nodded. "Follow me."

Edward walked to the back of the house, down the stairs and out through the garden to find Nashmir talking with Jean-Louis in the greenhouse. He knocked on the window pane to alert them of his presence.

"Apparently both the earl and Lady Gabriella are under the influence of one your potions, Nashmir. I wanted to speak to you about my father." Jean-Louis moved to leave them alone, but Edward put up his hand. "Please stay. I'd like your advice too."

Nashmir motioned for them to take seats on the benches inside the greenhouse.

"It's only been a couple of days, but my father seems in better spirits. He still has pains, but he said they are less intense."

The Tibetan nodded. "That is as expected. Within about two weeks, there should be a marked reduction in the frequency and intensity of pain. It is important for him to eat the special diet I have suggested. One of the teas, as you have guessed, is a mood elevator."

"What happened here last night that the earl and Lady Gabriella needed sleeping potions?"

The herbalist directed his gaze to Jean-Louis.

The Frenchman shrugged. "It was not what happened here, Mr. James. It was the music at the ball that affected them both. The earl learned that a love he thought lost still lived, and Lady Gabriella learned that her father had a secret love. She was already upset about the rift with the baroness."

"Lady Gabriella didn't seem that upset at the ball."

Jean-Louis sighed and tilted his head. "That was before she calculated the timing of the island event. At first, she assumed the earl met Taita before he married Lady Jane. Alas, it was not so."

Edward threw his head back as the truth dawned. "Ah, and her adoration of her father, and the likely behavior of all men by extension, is now thrown upside down." He paused, remembering the earl's story from the previous night. "But the earl was shipwrecked and presumed dead. He had no way of knowing other ships would see the volcano and explore the area."

The Tibetan raised an eyebrow. "When one's assumed history of another is called into question, and long-cherished assumptions are dashed to dust, it is unsettling. Lady Gabriella is a devotée of the notion that romantic love conquers all. Being confronted with the truth of her father's actions has shaken her to the core. And the apparent ending of his relationship with the baroness, who loves Bri as a daughter, all happened at the same time."

Jean-Louis glanced at Nashmir. "Most of us encounter disappointment early in life. We have protected Lady Gabriella, perhaps too much. We are at fault." He directed his gaze to Edward. "You may have to scale a cliff of doubt, approbation and distrust that did not exist last night in your courtship. Tread carefully. Be steadfast and she will come around."

"I assume Lady Gabriella likes to ride. She told me she rides with her uncle every Tuesday morning. Do you think she'd enjoy a ride in the park?"

The Frenchman nodded. "Lady Gabriella is an accomplished horsewoman and very competitive, as you might imagine. And there is still ice on the skating pond. She used to love ice skating as a little girl, but hasn't skated since Christmas at Ravenshire. Her skates are in the stables."

"I have skates somewhere. Maybe physical exertion will boost her outlook."

"Don't expect an overnight transformation." Jean-Louis stood to leave. "You have the mettle to meet her on the battlefield of wit. Be patient. You are well-matched."

"I agree with Jean-Louis, Mr. James. You have an open and agile mind. She bristles at control, as does a fine horse who knows his head. Patience will reward you."

"I'm not going to mention you compared Lady Gabriella to a horse, Nashmir. Something tells me that analogy would not be well received."

"There's hope for you." The Frenchman tipped his hat and left.

Nashmir bowed his head.

Edward walked toward the house.

A window opened overhead. "Mr. James! I overslept. Can you wait a bit longer?"

He saluted. "Yes, milady. I await your command."

***

Bri

Spotty whimpered a greeting and looked at Bri with love in his soft brown eyes.

That potion worked. I can't believe I overslept. She rang Jane Anne's bell.

While the maid drew her bath, Bri opened a drawer to select an appropriate outfit.

She decided on a navy blue overdress paired with a thin white wool chemise, selecting a simple strand of pearls and single pearl earrings. She added one of her mother's pearl rings to her array, and went into the bath area while Jane Anne carried Spotty downstairs to

218

perform his morning ritual outside.

The water was warm and relaxing, with bubbles from the French bath oils that Aunt Gwyneth had given her the previous Christmas surrounding her in the deep tub. Ordinarily, these were moments of luxurious privacy where her mind could roam unfettered, but last night's revelations had shaken her faith in her father and the life she thought lay before her. Thinking of Mr. James, her heart fluttered. *He proposed marriage. It happened.* But no matter how practical such a match would be, she would never consent unless he declared his love for her. *If my father can set aside his vows, how can I trust any man?*

The banker's kiss had thrilled her. Brief but passionate, it unleashed in Bri an undiscovered desire for physical fulfillment. *I must set aside such emotions and stick to the commercial aspects of investments.* It would take all her will power to maintain a business demeanor in this morning's meeting with him. In fact, she realized that she had better make some specific mental notes so that she would remain focused on the points she wanted to make. Knowing that she had her father's approval to insist on her investment options, she conceded that it would be best to persuade Edward to her point of view.

As a man, he would probably have to change certain things to put his imprint on her recommendations. The earl had explained, in Asia this was referred to as "saving face," avoiding embarrassment in front of another. She could present her case in such a way as to permit him this courtesy. But if he became too difficult, she knew that ultimately she would be in control. As the estate's and trading company's agent, she could simply give him orders. Such a course would not advance her romantic objectives, however, and she resolved to concentrate on persuading with facts rather than dictating her wishes.

Finished with her bath, Bri hurriedly dressed.

Jane Anne braided her hair in the French manner and fastened it with a navy silk ribbon.

Gathering her notes for the meeting with Edward, she went down the stairs, hoping to avoid her father.

His door was closed. Relieved to have avoided him, she continued to descend.

Reaching the landing, Spotty jumped up to kiss her hand, despite his injured leg. He hobbled behind her, wagging his tail.

"Mr. James?"

She found him in the parlor. "Will you join me for breakfast?"

"Why not?"

An odd response.

Without being asked, the server brought eggs, scones, jam and bacon. Thompson poured tea, an orange cinnamon flavor. Spotty lay at Bri's feet.

Edward smiled. "Navy blue is a striking contrast to your hair. You look lovely today. I trust you slept well."

"Flattery is not necessary, Mr. James. I overslept due to a potion from Nashmir." She buttered a scone, spread jam on it and took a bite. "I prepared an agenda for this morning."

"I expected no less."

She halted in mid-bite. "Are you mocking me?"

"No, I thought I was confirming my respect for your thorough approach to commerce."

Bri stared at him. *Can I trust you? Will you always love me or will you treat marriage as an inconvenient necessity?*

"These eggs are perfect. Is this dill?"

"Yes. With a pinch of chives."

When both were finished eating, Bri put down her napkin, indicating that breakfast was over. "Let us go into the study."

Edward followed her.

Gesturing to him to be seated, Bri sat behind her father's desk.

Edward gazed around the room. "An impressive collection of books."

"My father always says that one needs to be surrounded by books on long ocean voyages. His agents in foreign lands are always seeking rare books for him, and he has some exceptional volumes." *And secret love affairs with Polynesian princesses.*

Edward commented on the intricate carvings on the oak desk. "These are Celtic symbols—"

Anticipating his comment, Bri explained her father appreciated the irony of the Celtic designs defacing the oak.

Bri lost no more time on small talk. She handed Edward the agenda she had prepared.

"I see the first order of business is for me to brief you on the investigation of Blackburn's potential diversion of monies. Unlike you, I did not sleep well, being preoccupied with questions. My investigators are processing the audit. Let me take our discussion in a different direction. How many people close to you have died unexpectedly?"

Surprised by this question, Bri thought for a moment. "My mother died birthing me. Uncle Rychard died in a riding accident near Ravenshire and his wife, my Aunt Aelwyn, disappeared the same day. We feared suicide from grief, but her body was never found. Uncle Luc, Aunt Gwyneth's late husband, was killed by a runaway carriage while crossing the street. He turned to wave goodbye to Aunt Gwyneth, and as he stepped into the street, the carriage careened around the corner and he was trampled by the horses. Neither the driver nor the owner of the carriage was ever found. It had been hired for the day. We were devastated by so much death. Aunt Gwyneth was inconsolable for months. She's just starting to come out of it after two years. My grandfather died at the age of one-and-seventy. Surely you don't think Uncle Rychard and Uncle Luc's deaths could both be the work of Blackie, do you?"

Grimly, Edward stared out the window, and said, "We must examine all possibilities and eliminate none. Let us assume that he was behind both deaths. What is his purpose? Last night I thought I had an inkling. The death of your Uncle Luc makes my theory plausible."

Bri's patience waned. "Out with your theory, Mr. James."

"The piece of the puzzle that is missing is Blackburn's motive. His position in your father's trading business is both powerful and lucrative. It gains him entrance into Society. I am not familiar with his name or background in any other context, but I will know soon. I set my investigator on the trail of Blackburn's past before I came here this morning. Consider this: neither your father nor Rychard left a male heir. If the Comte de Merbeau and your aunt had produced a son, he would ultimately have inherited the Wyndward holdings, assuming your granduncle Barryngton either renounced the title or died. As a result of the deaths of both Rychard and Luc, no male heirs exist. While Lord Ravenshire or the Comtesse de Merbeau might marry again and have children, it is unlikely at this point. We will never know how many murders Blackburn would have been willing to commit. Be that as it may, circumstances now leave you as the only link to the Wyndward fortune. Whoever marries you might well father a son who will inherit. Until then, your husband could conceivably control a successful international trading business, which, when coupled with the vast Ravenshire estate holdings, is a prize some would kill to possess. That is why I think Blackburn is intent on courting you. It would gain him respectability in Society as well as great wealth. I see him as an extremely dangerous adversary."

Bri was silent for a few moments. "I find it difficult to comprehend that Blackie planned this so long ago. What kind of mind could conceive of something so evil?"

"A criminal one. The diversion of monies from the unauthorized contracts is no doubt an insurance policy. He could leave the country at any time and have access to funds in several foreign cities, eluding authorities and escaping virtually without a trace. Only your close attention to those footnotes uncovered this scheme. Lord Ravenshire does not examine the numbers that closely and even your account clerks would accept such disclosure as satisfactory. He was hiding the truth in full view, but only you bothered to ask the right questions. Luckily for you, he is not aware of our investigation into the ownership of these companies. If he gets desperate with fear of discovery, he may try to harm Lord Ravenshire." He paused for effect. "Or you."

"Why would Blackie harm me if he thinks I am his key to wealth?"

"Because your refusal of his advances would unravel his long-plotted scheme. He will have to flee the country, but if he knows he has been found out, he will want revenge. Although he probably has secreted money away in places other than those we have identified, that amount will pale in comparison to what he hopes to control through you. As a last, desperate act, he may want to punish all those who stood in his way, and by rejecting his courtship, you would have doubly wounded him. I warn you, until we have more answers and can either prove or discard this theory, you must take care not to offend him overmuch. While it pains me to say it, you must flirt with his courtship offers, and make him believe that it is possible. If he thinks his scheme is achievable, he may let down his guard and give us time to find the answers. This is a dangerous game. We must make certain that your safety is assured."

Bri's temper exploded. "How dare you suggest that I should flirt with a man who might have killed my two uncles, possibly Aunt Aelwyn and grandfather? Were I to accept your theory, he would not hesitate to kill me if he found me out. Is this the type of game you would request your wished-for-fiancée to play?"

Edward spoke slowly and deliberately. "It is no game. I was wrong to label it as such. It is a battle where death will surely come to one side or the other. Be assured that I will do all in my power to protect you from harm. I will not hesitate to kill him should the situation require it."

"You, Father, and Jean-Louis will protect me—" Bri's voice was soft and low. "But who will protect you? As an avowed suitor for my hand, you would be the logical candidate for immediate removal."

"Immediate removal. An interesting euphemism, Lady Gabriella. Would it pain you to have to face my 'immediate removal'?"

Stricken, Gabriella blurted out the truth. "Of course, you fool. I am in love with you." Regretting her outburst, she walked to the window to try to regain her composure.

Edward rose, walked to her and put his arms around her shoulders. "I know, Lady Gabriella. I am honored. You are very, very dear to me."

Relaxing her shoulders, Gabriella continued to stare out the window. "You are afraid to say you love me."

Irritated, Edward twirled her around to face him, "Stop these adolescent ravings." He touched her face. "You may be in danger. Do not force me to mouth words that are meaningless. My devotion to you is real." He pulled her closer and kissed her deeply.

She could feel his heart beating next to hers. She pulled away. "For a moment, I felt safe with you. But I felt safe with Father and he is not the man I thought him to be. How can I trust any man now? Perhaps my mind is playing tricks. Blackie has always been good to me. Granted, he is too old for me and the courting situation is awkward, but I can't believe he has a penchant to murder at will. I don't know what is real and what is imaginary."

The doorbell rang. Thompson's voice was louder than usual. "Your Grace, we weren't expecting you."

Bri's eyes widened. "My grandmother, the Duchess of Pytchley." Leaving the study with Edward at her heels, Bri walked to the parlor. "Grandmother, what a surprise."

"Hardly. The *ton* is abuzz with your father's bizarre departure from the ball. Is he mad? Such behavior is unacceptable and unbecoming of his station." She stared at Edward. "Just who is this young man?"

"Grandmother, this is Mr. Edward James."

Edward bowed his head slightly. "It is an honor to meet you, Your Grace."

"Sir John's son. You have your mother's eyes. A lovely woman. What are you doing here?"

"Calling on Lady Gabriella."

"Why were you not in the parlor? This is unacceptable, young Mr. James."

"I was showing him Father's library, Grandmother."

"Your reputation is paramount, Bri." Turning to Mr. James, she added, "Remember that, young man. You should be thinking for her. Lady Gabriella is a headstrong young woman. Takes after me in that regard. But I am a duchess and I can get away with it. She cannot." Turning to Bri, she asked, "Where is your father?"

"I think he might still be asleep."

"At this hour? Has he become indolent?"

Thompson cleared his throat. "The earl is bidding at *Tattersalls* horse auction this morning."

The duchess frowned. "As is your Uncle Oliver. I hope they don't come to blows over horseflesh."

Edward looked puzzled, but made no comment.

The duchess missed nothing. "My son blames Lord Ravenshire for the untimely death of Lady Gabriella's mother. His blame is misplaced. Oliver adored Jane. She died in childbirth, as do too many women. Her delicate constitution and predilection to melancholy pre-dated her marriage. While Lord Ravenshire's penchant for extended voyages and embracing danger contributed to her unhappiness, he was not responsible for her death." The duchess glanced at Bri. "Tea, dear? Have I taught you nothing?"

Bri rang for the server.

"Run along, Mr. James. I want to hear the unvarnished truth about the ball from my granddaughter."

Edward bowed. "It is a pleasure to meet you at last, Your Grace."

Waving her hand dismissively, the duchess concurred. "Of course it is." She eyed him with a squint. "You comport yourself well, Mr. James. You know when to listen and not insert yourself unnecessarily into the conversation. I like you. Now leave."

"Good day to you, Lady Gabriella."

"And to you, Mr. James."

"I'll see myself out."

As soon as the door closed, the tea arrived. The duchess took a sip, frowned in surprise. "This is provocative. A hint of vanilla, orange and cinnamon." She sniffed. "International trading has some benefits." Putting down her teacup, she tilted her head. "Now, Bri, tell me all about the ball. What is the real problem with Henry? How could he let that despicable man escort Charlotte to the ball?"

***

Friday, March 15, 1811 – Tattersalls
Baron Beauchamp

Tattersalls buzzed with activity. Henry spotted Beauchamp and his sister, and walked over to them. "How many race horses does one man need?"

"Can't ever have enough."

Davinia, Beauchamp's older sister, still lovely in her late fifties, grabbed the earl's arm and pulled him closer. "Henry, you are still a dashing man. What happened between you and Charlotte? It's all over the gossip rags that she was escorted to the ball by Tottie Drummond. And why did you leave Lady Elisabeth's ball so abruptly last night?"

Henry cringed. "Let's table that discussion until lunch after the auction. Tell me, my dear Lady Portchallont, how do you manage to look younger than Beauchamp and I?"

"A combination of black magic and secret potions, of course."

The baron looked over *Tattersalls* printed auction list. "I need a few more racing horses for the Season. Which ones are you leaning toward, Ravenshire?"

Shrugged. "Just wanted an outing. A diversion."

Beauchamp, known as the blond baron in his youth, still sported a full head of hair, though tending more toward white than blond at this age. He raised an eyebrow at the earl's revelation. "I hear several men are in pursuit of Lady Gabriella."

Linking arms with her brother and Henry, Davinia pulled them forward. "Let's go look at the horseflesh up close."

Dutifully, the men allowed themselves to be escorted toward the preview stalls.

Jean-Louis placed a hand on each of the horses, stall by stall.

***

Darlemont

Darlemont looked over the auction list. He planned to purchase a team to race in the upcoming season. With luck, their wins would result in high stud fees. Walking over to the stalls to examine the horses before bidding, he noticed the earl's former trapper. The Frenchman's distinctive black garb and hat made him stand out among the dandies of the *ton*. *His affectation of dress is almost as annoying as his attitude. Still, I remember his devotion to my sister. And I recognize that he is protective of my niece. But he regards me with disdain. 'A man of leisure,' he called me, as if leisure equated indolence. Where the Frenchman lurks, the earl cannot be far distant.*

From behind him, his brother-in-law's voice proved him right. "Oliver, will we be bidding against each other?" *Feigned cordiality in public must be observed, Mother would say.*

He turned to greet Henry. "Perhaps. Abigail implored me to acquire a more winning team for our stables. She prefers chestnuts, not the whites that you select, so I doubt we'll be bidding against each other." He turned to the earl's companions. "Lady Portchallont, you look lovely." He nodded to the baron. "Lord Beauchamp. How is the Marriage Season treating you?"

"My feet hurt. But there is a multitude of lovely young ladies."

"Young, indeed." *Odd for a man to enter the marriage market at his age when he is not a widower. Most thought him a molly all this time. He's certainly pretty enough and spends a lot of time with his sisters.*

Henry intervened before the baron could respond. "I assume we will see you at the Masquerade Ball. What is your costume?"

"I shall withhold that information to surprise you. And you?"

Henry shrugged. "A corsair."

Darlemont raised an eyebrow. "A pirate, eh? Some would say such a disguise is not far afield."

"Some."

Tipping his hat, Darlemont bid them adieu and headed toward the bidding stands.

***

Davinia, Lady Portchallont

Davinia shivered. "Frosty as ever, that one."

"We cannot choose our families." Henry shrugged. "Oliver dotes on Bri and takes her riding every Tuesday. He is her only remaining uncle."

"Your tolerance is admirable." Cocking his head toward the crowd, the baron redirected their attention to the crowd. "Let's pick our horses and then take our places with the bidding throng and join the fray."

Again linking arms with Lady Portchallont between them, the baron and the earl headed away from the stalls to the bidding stands, followed by a silent Jean-Louis.

Davinia tilted her head, watching him. "I've heard your stories about this Frenchman for so many years, but this is the first time I've been close to him. He's placing a hand on each horse's neck. Is he communing with their spirits? Is he some *magus* for horses?"

The baron laughed. "Jean-Louis is famous for many things. He killed a polar bear in northern Canada with merely a knife. Some say it was with his bare hands, but exaggeration is how legends are born."

"Maybe I should drop you foppish gentlemen and chase after a real man."

"He may be the only man immune to your spell, Davinia." Her brother exchanged a glance with the earl. "Jean-Louis is a cipher. Ever present. Vigilant. Reflexes like a jungle cat."

"Shot one of those on safari with a bow and arrow. The beast was in mid-air leaping to attack our bearer." The earl shook his head. "That leopard skin blankets him at night, head and all. He used to put it on to play with Bri."

"And she wasn't afraid?"

"Not many leopards growl in French."

Davinia had a high lilting laugh. Henry could see how she had captivated the late Peter Portchallont, whose wealth their son, David, inherited, also bequeathing a generous annuity for his widow.

Jean-Louis came toward them, having examined all the specimens. He had marked his selections on the list and handed it to the earl.

Henry compared it to Beauchamp's. "Let's avoid a bidding war between us for the palfrey and the Arabian. Which do you prefer? Your choice."

"The Arabian, of course. But others will want that palfrey, too."

"True, but I would feel no guilt winning against another."

"Nor would you if you bested me."

"No, but I am being polite to curry favor with Lady Portchallont to help me deal with my problems with women."

"Lunch is a given, Henry, but I might not reveal *all* my secrets."

"Perhaps not, but I shall ask all the same."

The bell rang, signaling the auction would begin in two minutes.

"To the bidding stands, gentlemen."

***

Chez Michel
Baron Beauchamp

Sitting under Henry's caricature, Davinia teased her brother. "Why are you not important enough to have your portrait here?"

Henry laughed. "I'll have Gio do it as a favor."

Davinia laughed. "Beau couldn't sit still for a portrait when he was younger. Gio painted me and now I look over my parlor, eternally youthful."

The blond baron tilted his head toward the wall. "Perhaps seeing my portrait here would impress Lady Penelope."

The earl raised an eyebrow. "She appeared impressed enough at Lady Pepperell's ball. She has an infectious laugh, and warmth that is instantly endearing."

"A bit plump, is she not? After a baby or two, she may fill an entire carriage." Davinia sipped her wine.

Beauchamp glared at his sister. "I am enthralled with Lady Penelope. Do not insult her again."

Davinia brushed away his comment with a dismissive wave of her hand. "It was a jest."

The earl shrugged. "If Shakespeare taught us anything...well, you know the rest."

Staring at Henry, Davinia honed in. "While our meals are being prepared, Your Excellency," using the baron's youthful sobriquet for the earl, "tell me what happened with Charlotte and why you left Lady Elisabeth's ball early."

Henry took a deep breath. "My first *faux pas* was to suggest to Charlotte that I escort Bri alone to her first ball. I didn't think she would mind, but she was hurt and broke off our companionship of fifteen years. I thought it would blow over, and then to see her with Drummond, a man I call The Nemesis, cut me to the core."

The baron had never told his sister the truth about why Henry and Drummond hated each other. It was one of the few secrets Beau kept from Davinia.

"That explains why you vanished." Davinia grimaced.

"No. That would give Drummond too much satisfaction." Henry explained his shock at finding out that Taita lived. "And so, you see, I am trapped in a mire of uncertainty. I must tell Charlotte about Taita. No step will free me from hurting one of them."

Lady Portchallont twirled her wine glass as she considered his situation. "Uncertainty is untenable. You must resolve the uncertainty surrounding the island woman or it will poison your future with the baroness. The baroness has been patient, understands you and your social demands, and accepts your love of adventure. She is the mature choice. Yet you remember the lost passion you felt with the island woman. That memory is as fresh as the new throes of love. Into your ordered life appears a ghost, a perfect ghost. No history of arguments, demands, or disappointments mars her image. Someone once said to me—you, Your Excellency—that we should not put anyone on a pedestal because one so vaulted can only fall. Heed your own advice."

"You must tell Charlotte the truth before the purveyors of salacious gossip spread it around, but you must also see the island woman," agreed the baron. "You must know your true feelings. At some point, we all must make mature choices."

Davinia shot him a look of puzzlement. "Is your barb directed at me?"

Their conversation was interrupted as the server brought their meal.

Once the server was out of earshot, the baron looked at his sister. "No barb was directed at you. I am merely recognizing that I have avoided choosing a wife for all these years. Many women have offered themselves to me, but I finally feel ready. It is my own journey to maturity to which I refer. You and our other four sisters married, had children, and made yourselves a family life. I occupied myself with hunting, traveling, pursuing the urge of the moment. I realize now that I lack a connection to a family of my own. I am uncle to many, father of none."

His sister sighed. "Back to you, Your Excellency. How do you intend to resolve your dilemma?"

"Taita will be in London when the play opens. I intend to see her and ask the Sultan for her freedom."

"Dear God, you don't intend to buy her?" Davinia pointed at him with her fork. "No woman would accept that offer as anything other than being traded from one man to another!"

"I was hoping he would voluntarily free her. Then she could return with him of her own volition or stay with me."

"Ravenshire," the baron cautioned, "you assume she remembers you with the same ardor as you remember her. Ask for a private meeting, perhaps, but do not offer up an ultimatum to a man who is used to ruling a land of subjects. Any demand will backfire."

The earl looked off into the distance. "You both have given me excellent advice." Hearing his own words, he echoed with a smile, "Most excellent advice."

"Tread carefully." The baron took a sip of wine. "Charlotte is real. Taita is a phantasm of your imagination. To be frank, she would not be accepted by the *ton* except by old friends like us. I know that matters not to you. But think before you act on or speak of this. Your path is fraught with traps."

CHAPTER TWENTY-FIVE

Friday, March 15, 1811 – Interior of Lord Ravenshire's Carriage
Bri

On her way to her aunt's, Bri looked out the window of the carriage, but saw nothing, lost in thought. Edward had proposed marriage. Blackburn might be the murderer of her uncles. Two men sought her company—one steady, if a bit too practical, the other diabolical. It would take her most accomplished acting skills to succeed at Lady Baxter's costume ball on the 30th. Still, a lot could happen in two weeks.

How much should I tell Aunt Gwyneth? After a moment's hesitation, she decided that her aunt must be made aware of the full details. Bri hoped it would not make her suffer too much. Aunt Gwyneth had so loved her brother, Rychard and her husband, Luc.

Believing herself to be immune to harm, she feared for Edward's safety. What if Blackburn tried to kill him? Was Edward really so accomplished a fighter? Would he survive when her uncles had perished?

Torn by these thoughts, she had a look of deep concern on her face when she arrived at Aunt Gwyneth's townhouse. As she exited the carriage, Jean-Louis admonished her. "Perk up. Don't scare your Aunt Gwyneth."

Bri nodded. "You're right, of course. It has just been a series of such shocking discoveries."

"Some discoveries, some theories. Evil will meet evil, Bri. Should

Blackburn be proven guilty, he will meet a just fate. I am your shadow, and you are safe."

"It helps to know you are nearby."

Nambotha appeared at the door. "Miss Bri, what a surprise! Your aunt was just about to have lunch. I'm sure she'd like you to join her."

Aunt Gwyneth came out of the dining room to greet her. "How lovely of you to stop by. Dominique will prepare a plate for you. Come join me."

Giving Nambotha her cloak, Bri followed her aunt toward the dining room. The server returned with another table setting and then vanished.

"How is Henry? I was so worried about him when he left the ball after finding out that the island woman still lived. That shock, in addition to the rift with Charlotte, is a lot to absorb."

"He went to the docks to wander and think. After all these years, he wonders if she will still love him as she did long ago." Bri sighed. "Did he ever tell you about her?"

"No."

"You must have realized by now that he was married to my mother when they met. I am so disappointed in him, I am undone. How can a woman ever trust a man?"

Gwyneth took a moment before speaking. "Henry is an adventurer. He was devastated by the deaths of two children. The second one died just before that voyage. He was wrong to leave your mother alone, but he didn't plan to fall in love. I don't know what I would have done in his position. Women are different than men in many ways. You'll notice, as you get older, that few widowers remain unmarried for long. Men crave validation from a woman. He thought he was lost forever. I always wondered if he had met a woman on that island...he never spoke of it until last night, but I sensed something had happened that he kept hidden. You cannot change the past, only how you react to it."

"I'm not reacting well, and I'm taking it out on Mr. James."

"Your father has been diminished in your eyes as a result of decisions he made when he thought he'd lost everything. If the volcano had not exploded, and the Dutch ship had not gone to investigate what remained, Henry would have been lost to us forever. But Edward is not to blame for your father's actions."

"My faith in men is at low ebb." Bri took a deep breath. "That is not all. I came here today to tell you something else."

Gwyneth sat back and waited.

"Blackie is probably a thief and may be a killer."

"Blackie? I don't believe it. Who do you suspect Blackie killed?"

"Uncle Rychard and…Uncle Luc."

Her aunt's face paled. "You are not yourself, Bri. You've let Henry's romantic betrayal affect your thinking. What you suggest is impossible."

The server returned with their luncheon plates. Out of habit, neither Bri nor Gwyneth spoke while a servant was in the room.

"What is the basis for this wild concoction?"

"To be certain that no male heirs to the Wyndward fortune would be born. The theory Mr. James put forward is that Blackburn's plan is to marry me, have a son, and control Wyndward Trading and Ravenshire estates through our child. Furthermore, Mr. James may be a target. Blackie knows that Mr. James is pursuing me, and his jealousy is aroused. If he knew that Mr. James had proposed marriage to me, he would become even more desperate."

"What? Did you just say that Mr. James has proposed marriage to you?"

"Yes, but no one else knows of it. I have told him that unless he is in love with me, I will not marry him. He says I am lost in a muddle of adolescent fantasies, but I believe that he loves me. I need to hear him say the words 'I love you,' or I shall not marry him."

"Bri, Mr. James is clearly in love with you, though he may not know it yet. Give him time, and I believe that he will say those words. But stop insisting on it. The more you push a man, the less willing he is to give in, even if it only means giving in to his true feelings. Men elevate rationality over emotion, fearing it weak to talk of love. Do not make the dragon too big for him to slay."

"Surely you don't think that I should marry him if he will not say that he loves me?"

"I believe that he loves you. I can see it. You can see it. Be patient."

"Charlotte was patient for fifteen years. Father never told her he loved her. I told Mr. James that he is afraid to say that he loves me."

"Oh, Bri…do not criticize a man like that. He will consider it a challenge to his manhood and you will have a battle on your hands.

Praise, not criticism, is what works." Her aunt sat back in her chair. "I can't believe Blackie killed Rychard or Luc. I know Blackie, I've traveled with him for months at a time. This may be some fantasy concocted by Mr. James to tether you to him."

"Someone at the trading company is setting up new accounts and diverting funds. We think is it Blackie."

"Because you want it to be him. Blackie is a convenient target. He should be your last suspect. He is Henry's most trusted associate. You are wrong."

***

March 15, 1811 – Baroness Glasspool's Mansion
Henry

Henry took a deep breath and rang Charlotte's bell. He'd planned what he would say in the carriage ride after having lunch with Beauchamp and Davinia. *Will she see me?*

The earl noted that Charlotte's butler, Morgan, stared at him with more than the usual level of contempt. *Does he know only that Charlotte and I have broken off or has he heard about Taita?*

"The baroness does not wish to see you, Lord Ravenshire." Morgan moved to close the door.

Stopping the butler, Henry shouldered his way into the foyer. "I must see her now."

"She is napping."

A voice came from the parlor. "No, I'm not, Morgan. Show Lord Ravenshire in."

Henry followed the butler into the parlor and watched him close the double French doors. He took a seat across from Charlotte in the grand room. "I wanted you to hear directly from me—"

"That you had an *affaire du coeur* with an island woman once upon a time? And that she will soon visit London, as the slave of a Sultan? Very exotic, Henry. So we would have been broken one way or the other. Nothing has changed."

"Charlotte—"

"Fifteen years, Henry. And you never thought to tell me of your dalliance? Were you married to Lady Jane at the time?" She paused. "I can see the answer in your face. My God, Henry, you are a cad! I am a greater fool that I ever imagined possible."

"Please listen to me. I met Taita when I thought I would never return to England. And after the volcanic eruption and typhoon—"

"Yes, your famous heroic tale left out the most important detail. Well, now you are caught, Henry, and a red-hot topic in the gossip rags. Best to sail away as you always run from life. Sail away and don't come back."

The muscles in the earl's jaw flexed as he tried to restrain his temper. "I thought Taita died in that cataclysm. I do not deny my actions. But can't you understand—"

"Yes, I can understand. And I would have understood if you'd told me sometime in the last fifteen years. But now, in front of the *ton,* you vanish from a ball, abandon your daughter, and cause a scene that will consume the gossip-mongers for weeks, at a minimum. Granted, on a certain level, it makes you more human. An actual weakness has been revealed about Henry Wyndward, the man who can do no wrong."

The earl cast his eyes downward then directed his gaze at Charlotte. "I never claimed to be perfect."

Charlotte scoffed. "Why are you here? To tell me the truth? I've heard it. Please leave."

"Charlotte, I must see her again. I must know how I feel. Then we can talk about the future."

The baroness stared at him. "The world revolves around *you.* What *you* must do. How *you* feel. What *your* future will be. One thing is certain, Henry. Your future is yours alone. It will not include me. Do not call on me again."

Henry stood. His regret and anger vied for control. "And Drummond? You had to flaunt that blackguard? He has secrets, too, Charlotte. Dark and ugly secrets you will never know. Don't trust him."

"As I trusted you for fifteen years? I no longer have illusions. Go."

The earl nodded and went to the door. He turned and said, "I've not given up on us, Charlotte."

"Of course you haven't. It's all about you, Henry. I, however, *have* given up on us. *Us* is not *you.*"

***

Sunday, March 17, 1811 – Winters Foundling Hospital
Bri

On the third Sunday of every month, the Winters Foundling Hospital held what Charlotte called Enrichment Day. She invited people to set up tables in a former ballroom of the large mansion that served as the hospital. The women in confinement would need jobs when they left, and enlightened employers came. In the beginning, only one person showed up—Bri.

Bri found places for the women to work at Ravenshire or Pytchley estates or in the London homes of the duchess, her father or her aunt. She persuaded other family contacts to help the unfortunates. "How would you feel if you were totally abandoned? The mother is no different than the child. Alone, bereft of family, hopeless." For most, their sense of charity prevailed. Not all, but Bri didn't give up. She invited them every month. Sometimes she was successful. Sometimes not.

Today, she was pleased to see several tables set up. She peered more closely to the corner of the room and walked over. "Gio?"

Without turning, he answered the voice he recognized. "There might be a budding artist among these young girls. I've convinced Maximilian that we should have an art school and dormitory in part of the unused buildings we've assembled on the block." He turned around to see Bri smiling at him.

"You *do* have a heart, after all. You're not all clever banter and social connections."

"As a green-eyed sorceress with wild red hair once said to me, 'What good are social connections if one cannot exploit them for contributions to a worthy cause?' "

"So it worked. Finally."

"You have a way with men, Bri."

She scoffed. "Tell that to Mr. James." Looking around the room, she noted, "Each month, Charlotte's attracting more tables."

"I heard my name." Charlotte put her hand on Bri's shoulder. "Thank you for coming."

"I look forward to these events. What happens between you and Father will not affect my commitment to the foundlings and the women in confinement." Bri embraced Charlotte. "Tell us about the other table sponsors."

"A milliner has two openings for women who might like to fashion hats from felt—supplied by a certain intrepid former trapper we know."

Gio raised an eyebrow.

"Yes," Bri answered the unasked question. "Jean-Louis remains influential in the North American beaver pelt trade."

"A legend, no doubt. How many of those stories are true?"

Bri shrugged. "I gave up trying to figure that out long ago."

"A school for chefs seeks scullery maids."

"Why couldn't women become chefs?"

A wry smile came over Charlotte's face. "One step at a time, Bri."

"And over there, for the first time, a school for young women is seeking students. It has developed a comprehensive curriculum to train women to be governesses, nannies, nurses, ladies' maids, and so on." She lowered her voice. "Their name is not revealed so as to preserve the anonymity of these applicants. A new start should not carry forward the brand of the past." Bri looked toward the table and thought she saw a familiar figure. After briefly speaking to the middle-aged woman at the table, he disappeared through a side door. "Was that—"

Charlotte held a finger to her lips. "He prefers to be an anonymous donor. Orphaned into the care of his grandmother, he has a soft spot for abandoned children and mothers who cannot care for them."

"So it was he. I never knew—"

"And you must never mention it." Turning to the dwarf, she repeated her warning. "That means you, too, Gio."

"Isn't life interesting? Just when you think you have someone pegged, he—or she—reveals unsuspected depths."

Maybe Aunt Gwyneth is right and we're wrong to suspect Blackie.

CHAPTER TWENTY-SIX

Monday, March 18, 1811 – Berkeley Crescent Park
Gwyneth

The clear spring day without a hint of clouds cheered Gwyneth as she walked through the park across the street from her townhouse. A gazebo had been turned into a coffeehouse and *pâtisserie*, a hidden and beautiful gem of privacy among the flowering gardens. *La Pâtisserie entre les fleurs* featured small café tables for two, ideally suited for intimate private conversations. The comtesse arrived to find Gio sketching the bakers as they worked. As her art teacher years earlier, the dwarf had inspired her and refined the talent that her father saw in his daughter's sketches. Immersing herself in art had helped her cope with the untimely death of her mother. Today, she glanced over Gio's shoulder at his work-in-progress. "Never an idle moment."

"The eye must constantly be challenged." He didn't pause, turn or stop until he'd finished the outline of his composition. When he was ready, he turned to greet his friend. "We have the table in the corner."

"The better to see everyone."

"Of course."

Every time Gwyneth thought about Gio's past, she wondered how she could have forgiven such abandonment and cruelty. Giovanni da Garfagnini had been born in 1743 to Lady Ianna, the only daughter of Ian Conall, the Viscount of Ostwold. To her family's shame, she had fallen in love with an Italian sculptor, Giancarlo da Garfagnini, with no money, but undeniable talent. Lord Ostwold finally acceded to their marriage. Gio was the eldest son born to the couple, but as a dwarf, only his parents loved him. His grandparents hid him as much as possible, but word got out. When the second son, Pietro, was born a child of normal proportions, the grandparents insisted that his name be Anglicized to Peter, and ignored Gio. After the death of his father when he was sixteen, despite his mother's protestations, Lord Ostwold threw Gio out on the streets. "You are disinherited."

The abandoned dwarf fell in with a group of artists, married one of them, and had a son, Maximilian. His wife succumbed to consumption. To his great surprise, as well as that of his grandfather, he became infamous and then famous. Infamous as a chronicler in paint of the demimonde and theatre, Gio became famous as portraitist to the aristocracy, starting with the family of Neyl Wyndward, 10th Earl of Ravenshire. Several years after painting his first portrait of the earl's family, Lord Ravenshire brought his only daughter, Lady Gwyneth, to the art studio Gio shared with Madame Victoire. Gwyneth was Gio's wealthiest student, and the saddest, when he first met her. After the death of her mother, Lady Gwyneth lost herself in sketching and painting lessons and became an accomplished artist.

Taking to his celebrity with gusto, Gio was always the spark at any party. He never looked back until the tragic accidental death of his younger brother, who had not yet married, caused his mother to beg her ailing father to name Gio his heir. On Lord Ostwold's deathbed, he complied, dying at peace with his daughter, grandson, great-grandson and great-great-grandson by his side.

As Gwyneth recalled the trajectory of his life, she was grateful to have counted him as a confidant since the age of nine, when he taught her watercolors. He was her best friend.

"I took the liberty of ordering orange-cinnamon tea and two croissants with raspberry jam." Gio looked through the paned gazebo. "Spring flowers are popping up. After our talk, let's find some specimens. I see crocuses, irises, tulips and daffodils."

"Maybe a quick sketch. I don't have time to paint." Gwyneth shook her head. "This Marriage Season for Bri has just begun, and I am already exhausted. She has the son of our banker interested as well as Mr. Blackburn."

Their conversation was interrupted as the server brought their order.

Gio wrinkled his face in a thoughtful grimace. "Blackburn? I'm painting his portrait. An edge of arrogance comes through. Interesting eyes show an unusual tinge of aqua. Bone structure reminds me of the earl." He sniffed. "I'm not one to say any man is too old for any woman, but he is too old for Bri."

Gwyneth laughed. "Not one to say, indeed. Bone structure? Blackie shows no resemblance to Henry."

"My eye for detail sets me apart. You know I'm always right."

"You suggested this meeting, Gio. What did you have in mind?" She sipped her tea.

"Besides a little spring color?" He smiled and took a bite of his croissant. "You are starting to be yourself again after a long period of mourning for Luc. I think it's time to move beyond the secret scandalous novels you write and publish your faerie stories and alphabet book. The mechanics of printing have improved. We might be able to create engravings from your artwork."

"We?"

"I'm here to help."

"My publisher is interested only in novels, not art and poetic flights of fancy."

"So create your own publishing company. You run a museum. Museums have art. Call it," he searched his mind before brightening, "Musée de Merbeau Press. You might also consider publishing the autobiographies of famous artists."

"Artists become more famous when dead."

"You wound me, Madame la Comtesse."

"Are you more interested in seeing me publish my work or your autobiography?"

"Both." He raised both palms in the air in a shrug. "I am nothing if not a diplomat."

"Closer to nothing than a diplomat."

Their banter was interrupted by the sound of a glass breaking.

A female voice cried out, "I cut myself. I'm bleeding."

A man from across the room got up, carrying a medical bag and hurried to the injured worker.

Gwyneth squinted, peering closely at the man, and then got up from her chair and walked toward the commotion behind the counter. "Dr. Northcliffe?"

He glanced away from the wound he was tending and recognized her. "Lady Gwyneth, I just returned from Africa and planned to call on you." He turned back to the injured girl, picking glass out of her wound and then bandaging the cut. "It shouldn't leave a noticeable scar. Here is more gauze. Clean the wound with mild soap and change the bandage for the next two days, then remove the gauze."

The proprietor reached for the cash box to pay the doctor, but Dr. Northcliffe stopped him. "No need. 'Tis a simple cut."

Packing up his bag, he tilted his head toward Lady Gwyneth. "I didn't see you come in."

"I'm with Gio. Join us." She pointed to where the dwarf artist sat.

"I guess my mind was preoccupied or I would have noticed you with such a well known figure."

The proprietor sent a server scurrying to place Dr. Northcliffe's half-eaten meal on a tray and added a chair to Gio's table.

Guiding Dr. Northcliffe to their table, Gwyneth introduced him to Gio, and then explained, "Dr. Northcliffe is from Ravenshire and looked after our family, as did his father before him. A few years ago, he decided to do medical missionary work in the Cape Colony and just returned." They sat.

"I lost my wife there to a tropical disease. I have three young daughters, and thought it best to leave the bad memories behind and return to England for their education, although Africa gets in your blood. I miss it already."

"I'll never forget the safari I went on with Lady Gwyneth and the late Comte de Merbeau. Though it was in East Africa, not the Cape Colony, I imagine it's the same. Everywhere you look offers a subject for an incredible painting. The variety of wildlife in the Ngorongoro Crater and the savannahs of the Serengeti made me think God might be real."

"Ignore my heretical friend." Gwyneth dismissed Gio's comment with a wave of her hand. "I'm sorry to hear that Claudia has died. Please accept my condolences."

"Thank you. It's been a year now, and I'm thinking of attending the Marriage Season. My girls need a mother."

Gio smiled. "We were just talking about that. Lady Gabriella is in the throes of the *ton's* rite of passage."

"I'm sure someone as lovely and clever as Lady Gabriella will attract many suitors."

Gwyneth nodded. "Our banker and Mr. Blackburn are pursuing her."

"Mr. Blackburn? He is quite a bit older."

Gio feigned shock. "We mature men are to be preferred to young fools."

The doctor laughed. "The last time I saw Blackburn was the day we found Rychard's body. Tragic death. And then, as I recall, Lady Wyndward disappeared shortly afterward."

Gio's tone became serious. "Rychard as a small boy was curious. A delight. He pestered me with questions and made suggestions as I painted that nanny who vanished without a word. He was hurt by her unannounced departure so soon after his mother's death."

"I miss Rychard every day." Gwyneth sounded as wistful as Gio. "And we all loved Brigid."

Dr. Northcliffe frowned. "I didn't mean to bring memories of death into our reunion."

"Death is part of life." Gio took a sip of tea. "No doubt I shall soon be on the other side of life myself." He glanced at his former pupil. "But fear not, Lady Gwyneth. I intend to haunt you until the end of your days."

"I would expect nothing less, Gio."

The doctor looked preoccupied and distant.

Noticing his discomfort, Gwyneth leaned forward. "Doctor? Are you unwell?"

"No, forgive me. Something has always bothered me about the day we found Rychard's body. Blackburn arrived as I was leaving Lady Wyndward. She was expecting Rychard, and became distraught when Blackburn said he hadn't seen Rychard along the road. He delivered something from Wyndward Trading, and then offered to help me look for Rychard. A thunderstorm was underway and we wondered if Rychard might have taken shelter in a hunting lodge along the way or in the town."

"What bothered you?"

"I had a notion to look by the stream, but Blackburn dissuaded me, saying Rychard wouldn't take such a dangerous route in a storm where waters might rise precipitously. Hours later, after the storm subsided, we found Rychard's body by the stream. Now that I think about it, there was no need for him to make that delivery himself. A messenger from Wyndward Trading came regularly to Ravenshire. Blackburn happened to be in the area at the precise time when Rychard died."

Gwyneth blanched. "What you're suggesting, Dr, Northcliffe, is simply not possible. Henry trusts Blackie more than anyone else in the trading company. He's been my brother's closest associate for over twenty years." *Could Bri and Edward be right?*

Gio's brow wrinkled as he grimaced. "Arrogant, yes…but a killer? Can't say as I've known any murderers." He shrugged. "The nature of murderers is one of the few things on which I am not an expert." His eyes narrowed and he tilted his head. "I don't see Blackburn as a killer, but maybe that's how killers are. They fool you. I suppose in this world, all things are possible. Any of us may kill given the right circumstances and motivation."

Gwyneth sat back in her chair, confused. "That is hardly comforting, Gio."

***

Monday, March 18, 1811 – Inverness, Scotland
Mirela

Mirela absent-mindedly shuffled her Tarot cards and spread them on the table. She frowned. "Unrest being at Ravenshire."

Catherine looked up from her kneading.

"Of what sort?"

"Something about a woman. The earl and a woman. Not the daughter. A love coming from the past. Their paths will crossing again."

"Were he to marry again, our plans would be ruined."

"Facing many obstacles. When the time being right, the cards will telling us."

The former baker's assistant punched her dough to work out the air bubbles. The pounding sounded as if Catherine used more than her usual force. "Don't tell me, I know. The cards never lie."

"Don't killing the brioches with your fists."

CHAPTER TWENTY-SEVEN

Tuesday, March 19, 1811 – Lord Ravenshire's Townhouse
Edward

After the duchess's dismissal of him on the previous Friday, Edward and Bri rescheduled their meeting to Tuesday morning to discuss investment opportunities. On a foggy morning, Edward arrived early on the designated date.

Thompson opened the door. "Mr. James, you are early. Lady Gabriella is riding with her uncle. She should be returning shortly. I'll show you to the parlor."

Edward walked to the window and looked out over the manicured neighborhood of privilege. *So she likes early morning rides. I shall suggest that soon.* He walked around the room and examined the varied artifacts from the earl's world travels. *Each one must have a story. I'll remember that in case there is a lull in the conversation or an awkward moment.*

He heard the click of Bri's boots on the Italian tile floors. *I think of her as Bri now. I must be careful not to say it out loud.* When she came into view, his heart jumped. Her auburn hair under her riding hat was windblown. He wanted to reach out and tuck it back into place. Her face was flushed from the vigorous ride. Jealousy welled up in him. *I want to ride with her.*

Bri was startled to see him. "You are early, Mr. James." She unstrapped her riding hat, lifted it off her head, and handed it to Thompson. "I never eat before I ride, so I'm famished. You'll have to join me for breakfast before we begin our discussion."

"If I keep eating two breakfasts whenever I see you, I shall be as portly as the florid Lord Clyr."

"That would be unfortunate, Mr. James. Dancing might tax you into apoplexy. I should miss your wit." She turned to walk toward the dining room.

Edward followed. "No need to plan my demise at this stage, Lady Gabriella."

She tossed a comment over her shoulder. "I am so relieved." She sat down and gestured to Edward to do the same.

"I don't believe I've met your uncle, Lord Darlemont."

"Uncle Oliver and I ride every Tuesday morning. He and Father have a strained relationship, as the duchess told you. She must like you, you know. She would rarely volunteer such information to a stranger." Gabriella sighed. "I breathed my first breath as my mother breathed her last. I love hearing stories about my mother as a child. Uncle Oliver adored her and I have learned what she was like through his eyes."

Thompson brought their meals.

Bri bit into her toast as if ravenous.

"Don't eat too fast."

"I don't need your advice." She took another bite and began to hiccup.

Edward remained silent at first, but the hiccupping did not subside. He rose and pulled her from her chair.

She resisted, flailing her arms.

He put his hand on Bri's stomach and forced her to bend forward, momentarily stopping the air flow. The hiccupping stopped. He removed his hand and she stood, catching her breath.

"You didn't need to manhandle me."

"Shall I apologize for helping you?"

"You overreacted. People hiccup. It is not life-threatening."

They finished their meal in silence, and then walked to the study.

Edward closed the door and took a chair. "How is your father?"

"Distracted and distraught. I am trying to accept his actions, but they are profoundly disturbing to me."

"If you can't concentrate, we should reschedule our meeting."

Bri bristled. "I can hold more than one thought in my head at one time, Mr. James. We need to discuss issues at the trading company as well as a new company we are forming, Wyndward Investments. But before we begin, what action did you and Sir Paul plan to take to investigate Blackburn's foreign activities?"

"We cannot communicate quickly with our foreign counterparts. Even under the best of circumstances, however, it will take six to eight weeks for a response."

"As our banker, you must be aware of the confidential fact that Wyndward Trading has a fleet of homing pigeons we use to communicate with far-flung offices. It gives us a competitive advantage."

"I was not informed of this option."

Bri shrugged. "I will speak to Jean-Louis. It is something he instituted long ago with Father. He learned about the practice while serving in the French army."

Edward nodded. "Aside from that, the option that offers the most rapid result would be an audit of the company's files, which my clerks began the day after we last spoke. I intend to visit the trading offices later today to check on their progress. Given the perilous nature of our current situation, we need answers immediately. It is a delicate task to undertake such research without alarming Blackburn." Edward leaned forward. "Protecting you is more important than mere financial misappropriation. We must know more about whether the deaths of your uncles and your grandfather were accidental or intentional."

"You must take care also. I don't want you to be the victim of another so-called accident."

Edward's lips narrowed. "I am no victim. Should Blackburn try to kill me, he will get more than he expects. My years in the Far East have taught me fighting skills that are largely unknown here. I do not wish to dwell on this topic, but I can react with brutal swiftness and deadly force if threatened."

Bri absorbed his words and took a deep breath. Glancing down at her copy of the day's agenda, she noted, "The audit is the first item on my agenda. The second point is establishing investment parameters for new ventures. Father has agreed with my proposal to invest five percent of the trading company profits in Wyndward Investments. I believe that the distribution of investments should cover a range of commercial activities, such as the funding of scientific projects that can result in patented products or processes, the founding of small businesses and the backing of theatrical productions. What I would like to discuss with you," making it clear that the basic decision to invest in new ventures had been made, "is the creation of parameters to evaluate each type of investment on a consistent basis."

"Why do I suspect that the first funding of a theatrical production has been committed in the absence of the establishment of such parameters?" Edward raised his eyebrows.

With a slight smile, Bri shrugged.

"Would I be wrong in imagining that *The Princess* is the first candidate for this investment program?"

"No, you would be quite correct. As we both know, *The Princess* operetta is a proven commodity in Germany, received an initial injection of capital from Count von Dusterberg, and can be promoted during the Season. The music is enchanting, as was demonstrated at Lady Elisabeth's ball." She pointed to a file on the desk. "Here is a complete presentation on our proposed return on investment."

Edward picked up the file and read through it. "According to this report, in order to generate the kind of return necessary to recoup any additional investment by Wyndward Investments, the play must run at least four months. And to a crowd that fills the theatre to a minimum capacity of seventy-five percent, assuming the standard rate for tickets in the *ton*. The contracted length of run in the Haymarket is a mere three months. We will need to either extend the run at the Haymarket by finding another theatre for the Shakespeare Festival or selecting another theatre to move the production of *The Princess*. The time frame is unworkable." Edward slammed the file shut with a thud.

"We have the Haymarket and that gives us time to find a new venue. Do you abandon all opportunities so easily? I was given to believe you had an eye for commerce. Was that impression incorrect?"

Edward sat back. "I have an eye for *viable* commerce. Tell me your thoughts." He crossed his arms over his chest. *Let's see how you respond, Lady Gabriella.* He couldn't resist taunting her.

"I happen to know that certain theatres are secretly owned by some of your banking clients. It seems to me that you should consider contacting them to take on this production."

Edward sat up straighter and anger flared in his face. "And just how do you know about our private clients?"

Bri leaned back in her father's chair. "I attend dinner parties in the *ton*, Mr. James. At Ravenshire, we are not without weekend visitors. People talk at dinner parties. Some people are circumspect, others brag. Are you unaware that my family has a wide range of contacts?"

She trapped me. "No. I am not unaware of that fact."

"I find it odd that you have theatrical connections, but were dismissive of their operating characteristics when the subject was introduced."

"Theatres charge rent whether tickets are sold or not. Some productions succeed, more productions fail."

"Will you undertake to find another theatre or shall I? Count von Dusterberg is willing to continue to back the production, but would welcome a partner."

"Let's table that discussion until we have reviewed your *full* agenda."

Looking down at her list, Bri checked off the theatre issue. "Next, I want to invest in the opening of a hair styling salon catering to the *ton*. After that, there is the expansion of a new line of specially formulated cat and dog food. I will be preparing full proposals on these investment options in the next couple of weeks."

"I assume you mean Dr. St. Cloud for the latter project. How can he appear in a production while simultaneously maintain his practice and formulate special food? He needs to make a decision about the course of his life's work."

"Perhaps you can only do one thing at a time, Mr. James. It would be short-sighted of you to think all others have such limitations."

Anger rising within him, Edward stared back at her, willing his temper to remain unrevealed. "If your approach to our collaboration is to insult me with each suggestion, this conversation will have a short duration."

Bri tilted her head. "Perhaps I was unclear. Dr. St. Cloud has already formulated the cat and dog food, and he is working on bird feed. His performance obligations are in the evening, really no different than the commitment required for any dinner party in the *ton*. The operetta will be over within a few months. It is a diversion for him, not a new career. The food formulation has an existing and growing market. It is not as if the total life span of the investment will expire within the period of the run of the operetta. But if that was not *clear,* then I apologize."

"I look forward to your investment analysis. What's this about a hairstyling salon? Ladies of the *ton* have their hair done at home."

"Modern women are more adventurous than dowagers. This is not uncommon in France, and the French do lead in fashion."

A note of sarcasm crept into his voice. "May I remind you that we are at war with France?"

"Their fashion standards still rule. Look at the dramatic change in women's clothing compared to twenty years ago. Dress styles are loose and flowing. Women are no longer laced in and restricted. Fashion is a metaphor for change, Mr. James."

Staring at her in disbelief, Edward sputtered. "An investment in a hair styling salon? Are you mad? All styles, whether in hair or dress, go in and out of fashion. What is the long term viability of such an operation? A substantial fixed investment will require constant clientele. Barbers are different. Men need frequent hair cutting and styling, for their own hair and their wigs. But women's hair length is much easier to maintain."

Bri's face flushed. "Since when are you an expert on the maintenance of women's hair? Just because hairstyling is now done by servants in the home does not mean that it cannot be done in a salon setting. There may be ancillary products, such as specially formulated hair soap and Egyptian henna coloring mixtures that can be sold. Manicures and pedicures can be given, with adequate training. You know nothing of what a woman's grooming requires."

"Then educate me. Put the facts in your proposal and we will discuss facts. What do you suggest for investment parameters?"

"Simple. There must be a market or an unmet need for a service or product. There must be a way to reach that market. The proprietor or proprietress must have a special skill in his or her field and be of good character. The financial plan must be sound under multiple scenarios."

"If it were so simple, Lady Gabriella, then all businesses would succeed. Unfortunately, most new businesses fail. Furthermore, am I to understand by your use of the word 'proprietress' that we might be dealing with a business where a woman will be in charge?"

"Yes." Bri's tone was defiant. "The proprietress will be Miss Jane Anne Kelly."

"An Irish girl? Why do you believe that the ladies of the *ton* will accept her?"

"Because she is highly skilled at hair styling and she will be providing a service. Whether a hair stylist be Irish or Chinese makes little difference to a woman who leaves a salon looking and feeling more attractive. This is a relatively small investment. You need not lose any sleep over it."

"I will not. Does Miss Kelly have existing clientele? Does she work at a barber shop now?"

Bri gave him a defiant stare. "She is employed as my personal Lady's maid."

"Miss Kelly is your Lady's maid?" Edward rolled his eyes. "You cannot seriously be considering entrusting your investment funds to an Irish girl who runs your bath and makes your bed."

"You complimented my hair last night. You danced with Lady Penelope and Lady Clarissa. Did people not come up to them in your presence and praise their hair?"

"I assume by your question that Jane Anne arranged their hair."

"Yes."

"I concede that there were many compliments. As with all of your suggestions, I shall await your analysis. I hesitate to ask, but is there is anything else on your agenda?"

Bri nodded. "I am interested in scientific projects requiring investment. I assume that you may have suggestions. The future is fast upon us, and will be one of machines and scientific invention. I would like to see some of Wyndward Investments be positioned for that future. My father's uncanny ability to spot trends in other cultures that translated well to ours or others on his shipping routes have brought much success. It is a common mistake to prepare for the future based on the past. I want to anticipate the future and prepare for the unknown."

"Sometimes when you speak so knowledgeably of commercial and financial matters, I forget that you are a woman."

Putting down her pen, Bri took a deep breath. "Are women biologically unsuited to understand commerce and finance? I think not. In fact, I believe that if women were in commerce in equal numbers to men, there would be an overall improvement in the world."

Exasperated, Edward threw up his hands. "Just when I think you are beginning to be reasonable and think logically, you come up with another ridiculous notion! Women in commerce? It will never happen."

"Civilization is an inexorable march of progress. The male need to dominate has caused war and misery throughout the world. Someday women may change the world into a more compassionate place. That would be progress. War is not progress. It is destruction."

"Then let us not war with each other. True, the history of England and Europe is a bloody one, and battle is never kind. I shall surrender to your premise, and hope that the world will, indeed, someday become a more compassionate place. I admire your faith and optimism.

"I also agree that a longer run is essential and that *The Princess* will likely be a success. I was wrong to dismiss the investment initially. And wipe that smug grin off your face. It is not often that I admit defeat in the area of investment analysis, but I did not give this production adequate attention. I shall refrain from making an uninformed judgment again, Lady Gabriella. And I shall make inquiries as to theatre availability for the period after the Haymarket run ends."

Bri smiled. "So you accept my proposals?"

"I will consider them. Are you accepting mine?"

Cheeks reddened with embarrassment, Bri raised her head. "Not until you say that you love me. My condition has not changed."

Edward remained silent. "Then I believe we have concluded our affairs for today."

"Indeed we have." Bri stood. "Good day, Mr. James."

CHAPTER TWENTY-EIGHT

Tuesday, March 19, 1811 – Wyndward Trading Offices
Edward

Entering the Wyndward Trading building, Edward approached the watchman in the warehouse area, handed him a letter from Lord Ravenshire explaining he had full access to the facilities, and was admitted. He walked straight back through the marbled entryway toward the workroom where his clerks and investigative team were pouring over the records. Under instructions to utter no words as to their true mission in the trading offices, they conducted their examinations in silence.

The head clerk handed Edward an envelope marked, *Edward James, Confidential*, and indicated by raising his eyebrows that Edward would find it informative.

"How much longer do you expect the audit to take, Jaspers?"

"About one or two more weeks, sir. We have examined practically all of the files on this floor, and there are two more floors. We are proceeding in accordance with our standard auditing procedures." The head clerk's answers were in compliance with previously scripted codes in case they were overheard.

"I am anxious to see that the audit is completed as soon as possible. As you normally work a half-day on Saturday, I am authorized to double your pay if your crew will work full days on Saturdays. However, I expect no shortcuts in audit procedures should you finish early."

The investigators were buoyed at the thought of extra money and unanimously agreed to work as requested.

Edward addressed them all. "Thank you, men." *Such an innocuous phrase would irritate Gabriella—she would no doubt like to see women doing this work.*

"Thank you, sir!" they echoed as one.

Briefly, Edward caught himself thinking that Gabriella could probably sort out the trading anomalies faster than his group of clerks. He immediately dismissed the thought as too dangerous for her. The concept of women working as banking clerks was ludicrous. Always alert to the processes of his own mind, he recognized Gabriella's protests of equality must have influenced him, and vowed to himself to monitor his thoughts more carefully. *I might inadvertently implement one of her ill-conceived headstrong notions.*

"Jaspers, may I have a word with you outside?"

"Certainly, Mr. James." Jaspers rose, and before leaving, addressed another clerk. "Simpson, you are in charge until I return. Remember, no discussion of your work."

Edward was silent until they were outside. Lowering his voice, he said, "Jaspers, I appreciate the willingness of you and your crew to undertake this detective work for me."

"Yes, sir." The head clerk adopted what appeared to be an awkward stance.

"You know what type of evidence we are looking for in the audit. The man is no doubt a thief, but new information has surfaced which suggests he may be an even more dastardly character than we had feared. It is possible that he has killed members of the Wyndward family for personal gain."

Swallowing hard, Jaspers stood taller, declaring, "You can count on me, sir. I shall be very careful."

Edward put his hand on the head clerk's shoulder. "Thank you, Jaspers. There will be a special bonus in this for you."

"You are a generous man, sir, but you already pay me very well. I do not want to profit from helping you discover a murderer. I will do it because it is the right thing to do."

"You are a credit to our bank, Jaspers." Edward gestured for them both to go back into the building. They made their way soundlessly past the watchman, save for the scuffling of their shoes against the smooth marble floor. Once back in the workroom, Edward opened the envelope to review the information within.

***

The clock struck nine times.

Edward sat back in his chair and ran his fingers through his hair. Leaning forward, he looked at the last file he'd reviewed, and slammed it shut.

Jaspers jumped, startled by the noise.

"Sorry, Jaspers. It's late. We should return tomorrow with fresh eyes. I've found nothing yet. Have you?"

The other workers had been dismissed hours earlier, but Jaspers had remained. He stood and stretched. "I've been reconstructing the earl's and Blackburn's travel records over the last twenty years, since the time Blackburn was hired, and cross-checking the dates against when the contracts-in-question were signed." He motioned to Edward to join him at a large table with a roll of paper spread over it.

"This looks like a printing roll." He examined the mechanism. "You can pull it and then rip it off."

"It is. I have a friend at the *Times* and we bought a discontinued roller. I thought it might come in handy for other purposes, and it was within the budget you gave me."

Edward shrugged. "I haven't had time to review your expenses, but I commend your ingenuity." His eyes swept over the information detailed on the long paper.

Pointing to the left side, Jaspers explained that the trail began in 1791, when Blackburn began as a clerk at age nineteen. "As he learned the business, he must have impressed Lord Ravenshire, because the earl took him on a voyage the first year, to Africa. They were gone for six months. In 1792, they sailed to America, accompanied by the Comte and Comtesse de Merbeau and Lady Gabriella."

The banker smiled. "The earl told me Lady Gabriella insisted on traveling with him after that long trip to Africa. She was barely three years old and lectured him the moment he returned."

"A third trip the following year to Brazil took another six months, again with the Comte and Comtesse de Merbeau and Lady Gabriella. The fourth trip was to Asia, this time with Philip Laurence, Lady Gabriella, and a maid. After that, the earl and Blackburn traveled at alternate times to cover more of the world. I'm still compiling the information, but as we move forward, Blackburn became more and more connected to the major international exporters."

"And with the family. No wonder they find it difficult to imagine Blackburn could be guilty of such heinous crimes. Keep up with your charts, Jaspers. Good work. But enough for tonight."

They extinguished the candles and locked the door.

Edward's carriage was waiting. He dropped Jaspers off at his home, and then continued to his club.

***

Tuesday, March 19, 1811 – Edward's Gentlemen's Club
Vaux

Vaux spotted Edward as he walked into the bar adjacent to the card room. The clock had recently chimed ten times.

"Hanforth, take my place."

The blond African hunter, who had been watching over Vaux's shoulder, balked. "I know not what has preceded." Nevertheless, he shrugged and picked up the cards.

The other players, Banfield, Khan and Durwood, continued their game without stopping.

At a nearby table, Viscount Waltham and someone Edward didn't recognize played backgammon.

Vaux caught up with Edward and put his hand on his friend's shoulder. "Hold, James. Come play a round of cards."

"Long day, Vaux. Come have a brandy with me. I need to unwind and eat something. Banking banter can be mentally exhausting."

"I don't know how you do it. My eyes glaze over when my agent talks numbers."

They took seats at the bar.

"Two brandies and roast beef sandwiches." Edward tilted his head toward his old university friend. "Things are changing, Vaux. You need to develop a facility for numbers or they will choke you. An agent with too broad authority might bankrupt you. Your penchant for updating interiors is a very expensive hobby. We need to get together to develop your budget for Lady Haley's project."

Their brandies arrived. They swirled the coppery amber-tinged liquor around in their snifters.

"No argument, James. Another wealthy dowager has approached me."

Raising an eyebrow, Edward considered the idea. "Word-of-mouth is the best advertising, but people like to see similar rooms for inspiration. Will dowagers invite strangers into their homes?"

"Doubtful. I was thinking about some kind of warehouse done up in sections, showing differing room treatments."

"Have you the spare capital?"

"Spare capital. A banker's phrase." Vaux sighed. "In a word, no. My agent says there's pressure on rents, and the renovations I've done in our food halls will take years to be recouped, whatever that means."

"You know what it means—you simply don't want to pay attention." Edward turned in his chair, directing his gaze toward Vaux. "I may have an investor who would provide the funding for your design company for a percentage of ownership. Would that type of arrangement work for you?"

"You mean that you think my idea has merit?"

"We would have to develop a budget, projections, and test it out with a client, but yes, I have seen your design work and I think such a concept is viable."

"Who is this investor? Not knowing his identity is unsettling. I won't be second-guessed on design."

"Let me suggest the idea to my client first, and then we can meet at the bank to discuss it. I cannot reveal the name at this time."

"Mysterious, James. But whatever you recommend, I will do." Vaux sipped his brandy. "How goes your courtship of Lady Gabriella? You looked quite intertwined at Lady Elisabeth's ball."

"As did you with several young ladies, clearly captivated by your banter. A man as handsome as you, Vaux, should have no trouble. Women fawn over you. You have looks, money and a title. What more could they want?"

A man who could love them. "You know I've never had much confidence around women. I put on quite a show, but they terrify me."

"They're not all as imperial as your mother. Perhaps she's put you off the gentler sex."

"Perhaps." *Would you remain my friend if you knew the truth?* "Come say hello to the old crew."

Carrying their brandies, they walked into the card room.

Hanforth threw his cards down. "Damn that Vaux."

"That Vaux is here."

They looked up to see Vaux and Edward. "James! Pull up a chair."

Edward and Vaux took two chairs from an empty table and moved them to the game.

Banfield smirked. "Rumors are that you and Lady Gabriella Wyndward are smitten."

"She is beautiful," said Khan, an Indian married to the cream-and-cherry-complexioned daughter of a land-rich and cash-poor earl. "We met her last Christmas at the Duchess of Pytchley's party. Opinionated, as I recall."

"That may be an understatement. She is a challenging woman," added Durwood. "She tore me into little pieces on the topic of women being allowed into the university."

"Why shouldn't women be admitted?" Hanforth shrugged. "They are more docile and probably would adjust to a don's lectures far better than I. I ached for adventure, not pedantic exercises."

Durwood laughed. "Hanforth, have you ever met Lady Gabriella? 'Docile' is not a word anyone would associate with her."

Edward smiled. "I've known Lady Gabriella since childhood, though I hadn't seen her since a Summerfest before I left for Asia. Let me put it this way—we have spirited debates. It makes life interesting."

"As in engagement?" Banfield sat back. "Am I hearing that the daring Asian adventurer Edward James has met his match?"

Vaux watched Edward's face flush with embarrassment. *He is in love.*

CHAPTER TWENTY-NINE

Wednesday, March 20, 1811 – Lord Ravenshire's Gentlemen's Club
Henry

Henry waited in the library of his club for Edward to arrive to update him on the audit. In a high-backed leather wing chair, he read the paper. He was startled to hear the voice of The Nemesis.

"Ravenshire, you caused quite a scene at Lady Elisabeth's ball last week. It's the talk of the *ton*."

The smug, self-satisfied tone irritated him. Henry's lips narrowed into firm line as he stared at the speaker. "The *ton* has little of substance to talk about if my behavior is of any interest."

"Far be it from me to offer advice, old friend, but Charlotte is not over you."

Henry stared at Drummond. "If you hurt Charlotte…" *I will kill you.*

"Go ahead, Ravenshire, say it. You've always wanted to kill me. We both know why."

"That's only part of it. Your blatant manipulation of vulnerable people for political expediency is contemptible. You are a cancer on our way of life."

"Grow up, Ravenshire. Politics is people. People are corruptible. I corrupt them to my ends, as you would to yours." He stood to leave. "And on a personal level, you are the one who has hurt Charlotte, not I."

The Nemesis headed toward the exit.

Edward entered and passed Drummond.

Drummond nodded to Edward in greeting. "Congratulations, James."

"For what?" Edward stopped and stared at Drummond.

Turning, Drummond said, "For capturing the heart of the heiress of the Season. Word is you and Lady Gabriella will soon be engaged. And here you are with her father at his club. That's confirmation."

"I am Lord Ravenshire's banker. We meet for other reasons."

"Really? No commerce is to be conducted at this club. Are you and the earl in violation of its precepts?"

"No."

"Then it is personal."

"Personal, to my understanding, Drummond, means the purpose of our meeting is none of your business."

Drummond smirked. "Whatever you say, Mr. James. Good day."

"Good day."

Henry's jaw was rigid when Edward reached him and took a chair. The earl demanded, "What did that snake say to you?"

"He wanted confirmation of my engagement to your daughter. I deflected his comment, but I can see why he holds such a Machiavellian reputation."

"Subtlety is not one of his strengths. His threats are clear." Henry cleared his head. "You have news for me?"

"Only that we have found nothing definitive in the first week of our audit. Did Bri tell you of my concerns about the untimely deaths of your brother and the comte?"

"Yes, and there's more. Two people who worked under Blackie died under mysterious circumstances, and Gwyneth ran into an old friend from Ravenshire, Dr. Northcliffe, who also thinks Blackie might have killed Rychard, or been involved in his death.

"Blackie visited Ravenshire the day of Rychard's death. He and Dr. Northcliffe found the body together, but only after Blackie discouraged him from looking where they actually found the body."

Henry shook his head. "Gwyneth doesn't believe Blackie is capable of murder."

"Neither does Lady Gabriella, although she confessed concern for my safety. It is possible that I may be jumping to unsubstantiated conclusions, but I do not trust Blackburn."

Henry sat back and shook his head. "I've trusted Blackie for so long with so much. We think alike on so many levels. For years, I thought of him as another brother. Now that sounds naïve."

"No, it's human. You have similar interests and work closely together. We may be wrong. That possibility must always be acknowledged."

"We don't have all the puzzle pieces, but the image that is coming into view is dark and dangerous." Henry leaned forward. "Talk to Jean-Louis about sending messages by our pigeons. We keep it secret from most, but we can communicate across vast distances in an efficient manner by bird. He developed the skill in the French army. We have dovecotes in all our offices and at Ravenshire."

"Lady Gabriella mentioned something along those lines. I'll speak to Jean-Louis."

"The messages must be short, to fit on a narrow scroll of paper, but it might go faster than Sir Paul's missives."

"Understood." Edward rose to leave.

Henry stood and shook his banker's hand. *He would be a fine son-in-law.*

In preparation for his next meeting in the same club parlor shortly, Henry reached into his pocket to retrieve a folded list of companies domiciled in foreign lands. His contact would search for hidden ownership with his cohorts in the specified locations. The earl placed the list between the pages of his newspaper, which he put down on the side table.

His guest, Malcolm, the foreign officer, set his newspaper on top of Henry's.

A waiter came by with two glasses of sherry.

Malcolm took a glass and leaned toward the earl and spoke *sotto voce.* "Take care in your shipping plans. We may come to war with America over the issue of impressment of sailors."

Henry was taken aback. "How many wars do we intend to fight at the same time? Napoleon is controls all of Europe. Now we will fight another war across the Atlantic? The last one wasn't a success."

"I make no defense. I simply am informing you of what may come."

Henry sighed. "We can redirect our fleet."

"There will be ample room for the odd intrepid blockade runner."

"There always is." Henry drained his sherry.

"Sorry to hear about you and Charlotte. Would you like to know what I know of the Sultan?"

Taken aback, Henry asked, "Does everyone know?"

The foreign officer nodded.

Henry sighed. "Of course, I'd like to know what you advise."

Sipping his sherry before talking, Malcolm, a distinguished-looking gray-head, sat back in his chair. His staccato delivery sounded as if he were reading from a file. "Absolute ruler, responds to flattery. Treats slaves well unless they challenge him. Appears jovial, but a despot lives beneath the veneer. Tread carefully. If all else fails, you could petition the king to detain the woman in question on some pretext, but I warn you: the Sultan controls the trade in spices that the king considers superior to all other sources."

"I know. I am the shipper."

"Not for long, should you incur his wrath."

Henry frowned, stood, and took the top newspaper, while the foreign officer took the lower one that Henry had placed on the table.

***

Thursday, March 21, 1811 – Outdoor Skating Pond
Jean-Louis

Jean-Louis and Chérie jumped down to open the door to the carriage. Gwyneth, Bri and Edward climbed out.

The footman brought the skates for Bri and Edward and handed a pair to Jean-Louis.

Edward tilted his head and leaned toward the Frenchman. "You skate?"

"There is ice in Canada, Mr. James."

"Jean-Louis trekked the far north where ice never melted." Bri walked toward the pond.

Edward followed close on her heels. "And killed a polar bear with his bare hands, I heard."

Bri turned to Edward and scoffed. "Don't be silly. He used a knife."

The Frenchman signaled to the footman to stay with the carriage, and he ambled after his charges, accompanied by Gwyneth. "You are a busy chaperone."

Chérie trailed behind.

"I shall be grateful when she becomes engaged." Gwyneth tilted her head at Jean-Louis. "What do you think of him?"

"He is a decent sort, and can spar with language better than most."

The comtesse nodded. "She denies the attraction."

Jean-Louis laughed. "Beyond her protestations lies the truth."

Gwyneth and Jean-Louis sat on a bench while he put on his skates.

Edward and Bri were already on the ice.

The spring thaw had chilled and the pond seemed solid. "This is probably the end of the skating season." Gwyneth looked over the skaters. "At least fewer are out, and there is more room to turn without bumping into another skater."

Jean-Louis leaned forward. "Bri is easy to spot."

Wearing a fitted red jacket with white arctic-fox trim, Bri's red-and-black plaid skirt swirled as she skated.

"Edward skates well," added Gwyneth.

The Frenchman shrugged. He fastened the leash on Chérie. "Let's see how you like the ice."

Chérie bounded onto the ice, pulling her trainer. Once on the solid surface, she slid, fell, rose to her feet and fell again.

"I think we need to try something else." Jean-Louis took off his scarf and placed it on the ice. He picked up Chérie and sat her on the scarf. "Hold on." He skated, pulling her along.

She looked around, and then barked.

"You like it?" He sped up and twirled her around the pond's clouded and glassy frozen top layer. He kept looking back at her. "Happy?"

Chérie barked an answer he assumed to be, "Yes."

Edward and Bri were holding hands, as much for stability as closeness, while they skated around the pond in a broad circle. They laughed when they saw Jean-Louis and the Dalmatian entertaining the other skaters.

Another couple executed a lift in a ballet-like move.

Bri and Edward were transfixed by the lift and missed a curve, crashing into another couple.

Gwyneth stood, trying to see if anyone was hurt. Without skates, she could not go out on the ice.

Jean-Louis skated toward the group. No one was badly hurt. The other couple skated off, but Edward appeared to have injured an ankle. Jean-Louis supported him to a bench on the sidelines, took off his skates, and maneuvered the damaged foot in different directions. "It's not broken, but no more skating for you today."

"Mr. James, you can watch Chérie while Jean-Louis and I skate a bit. We'll be right back."

Gwyneth's mouth fell open. She moved to sit next to Edward.

The Frenchman suppressed a laugh, handed the leash to Edward and whisked Bri away. "You've wounded your fiancé, literally and figuratively."

"I didn't wound him. And he is not my fiancé."

"Yet. And you have a lot to learn about a man's pride." Jean-Louis whirled Bri around the ice, knowing he was showing up Edward's level of skating skill.

Nearly breathless as they spun around, Bri chided her protector. "Now who's wounding a man's pride?"

"That's different. Men expect other men to taunt them. They expect their fiancées to cater to them."

"I cater to no man."

"An unnecessary statement if I ever heard one." Jean-Louis sped up as he led Bri to the other side of the pond. With Bri firmly in his arms, they executed a flawless series of spins, twists and pirouettes, traversing an invisible diagonal path across the ice, ending up at Edward's feet.

"You're amazing together." Edward's voice betrayed no evidence of jealousy.

Bri sat on the bench to unlace her skates. "Jean-Louis taught me to skate about as soon as I could walk."

Chérie whined.

Jean-Louis smiled. "*D'accord.* One more sweep around the pond, and then it's time to go."

***

Thursday, March 21, 1811 – Edward's Gentlemen's Club
Edward

Flushed after his day ice skating, Edward limped into the bar area of his club.

Rogers spotted him. "James, what happened?"

"A minor skating injury. My ego got ahead of my skill."

"Trying to impress a woman, eh?" Rogers waved to a server to bring two whiskeys. "Lady Gabriella, I presume." He laughed. "The gossip rags are following the two of you on a daily basis."

"How delightful." Edward winced as he sat down.

"Is it the ankle or the gossip rags?"

"Both."

"Come gamble with me tonight."

"Not tonight. An early evening for me."

"I have a new racing carriage—it's like riding the wind."

"Open?"

"The night air is invigorating."

"Too fast over a bump and you could fly out, to your death."

Rogers leaned forward and patted Edward's arm. "James, always so cautious. One little sprain and you're cowering at speed." He looked away. "Ah, there's a crowd I know. Like me, they are partial to dice and cards and ladies of the evening." He got up and moved to join them, saying over his shoulder, "Feel better, James."

"Take care, Rogers."

CHAPTER THIRTY

Friday, March 22, 1811 – Wyndward Trading Offices
Blackburn

Blackburn proceeded through his agenda, covering new routes, revenues and estimated profits for the next few sailing seasons, during a meeting with top trading area directors when the earl arrived. Henry motioned to Blackie to continue, and took a seat.

"If only we could predict hurricanes in the Atlantic and typhoons in the Pacific. But we can't. We can't risk sailing in certain months to certain destinations. Even though we have experienced captains and bring them together periodically to share their knowledge so others may learn how to respond to crises, we can't risk losing cargo by ignoring sailing seasons."

Henry listened for a while, and then raised an eyebrow, signaling to Blackburn that he wanted to speak. "We're blockade-running in the Channel and elsewhere, which entails evading warships, cannons, and trained military officers. Perhaps we should formalize training for our officers, as if our trading ships were part of a military operation. In many ways, we already have the components in place. We could have a week's induction set up quarterly to be certain that each officer had at least one training session per year. Any comments?"

Sheldon shook his head. "That's delaying sailing or taking from their off-time."

Blackie disagreed. "They'd be paid. It would take several hours a day for a week or so. We can make it work."

The others murmured agreement.

"I'll put together an outline of the curriculum and circulate it for all of you to comment on." Blackie tilted his head. "We cannot avoid storms at sea. Not sailing in hurricane season is only one strategy. We must constantly improve our knowledge."

Henry had the attention of all when he spoke. "I met with someone in a position to know something few others do, and I must ask all in this room to not repeat what I am about to say to anyone but those of us sitting here. It may be talked about in some circles soon, but we have some advance knowledge and should act on it expeditiously." He took a deep breath. "We may be at war with America again within a year or two. The issue of impressments of their seamen is boiling over."

Blackie frowned. "Why fight another war against a country who won their independence across an ocean to the west when we already have Napoleon to fight in the east?"

"That is what I said," Henry conceded. "But my contact believes that options to avoid conflict are dwindling. We should redirect traffic over the next six months and let partners in South America transfer goods to avoid attack. It will cost us, but not as much as losing the entire fleet that services North America. We will still need to send a few direct ships with our most experienced captains…enough to distract our competition from our strategic repositioning."

Fong slammed down his hand on the table. "Planning is pointless but essential. The unpredictable human element impedes progress."

Gonzales agreed. "It was ever thus. Complacency brings death to men and ships."

"Carry on." Henry rose and left the meeting.

***

Friday, March 22, 1811 – Interior of Lord Ravenshire's Carriage
Henry

After being told of Bri and Edward's concerns about the deaths of Rychard and Luc, and listening to Gwyneth's tale of Dr. Northcliffe's suspicions, Henry still couldn't believe Blackie's complicity. *I've detected no change in his behavior. But I have to take precautions. If he is a master at deception, I have been a fool.*

Heading toward the storage warehouse, Henry was torn. *Would Blackie have been so foolish as to leave a trail?* Henry hoped that his suspicions of Blackie were unfounded. Proof was essential—incontrovertible proof. *How could I have trusted a traitor, a killer? Am I such a poor judge of character?* He needed proof.

Reaching the warehouse, Henry instructed the driver to wait for him, and he unlocked the door. He found the watchman at his desk, asleep. Loudly clearing his throat, Henry woke the man.

Shocked to see the earl himself, the man begged for his job. "I didn't mean to fall asleep, Lord R.—"

Henry put up his hands to indicate to end the pleas. "How many hours have you been on duty?"

"Twelve, sir. My relief is due soon. Please, Lord R., I need this job to feed my family."

"When did the shifts change from eight to twelve hours?"

"About three years ago, sir. Mr. Blackburn said it was a cost-saving measure."

"Well, it will be changed back to eight. I need you alert. Lack of alertness is what will cost too much, not another watchman. Does Mr. Blackburn come here often?"

"Not at all. He sends messengers with work notices."

Henry nodded. "I will speak to Mr. Blackburn."

"Yes, Lord R."

Henry walked to the file rooms. Each bank of file drawers was organized by decade. He intended to search for vouchers or travel itineraries for dates around the date of Rychard's death. He found a voucher for delivery to Ravenshire. There was an inventory of goods delivered to Lady Wyndward. *Aelwyn saw Blackie that day. Dr Northcliffe was right.* All accounting seemed to be in order, recorded in the proper manner. *Blackie pays attention to details.*

Looking for the year of Luc's death, he found nothing. He returned to the watchman.

"Tomorrow, report as usual and your new schedule will be posted. Your shift will be reduced from twelve hours to eight hours, but your wages will remain the same. Furthermore, I think we should have two watchmen on duty at all times."

"Thank you, Lord R."

Maybe Blackie is just misguided, looking for efficiencies in operations. But all our company information is here. It should be better protected.

Returning to the trading company, Henry told Blackburn of his decision. "Have two men on duty at all times. Our company information needs to be secure."

"You're right, Lord R. It was a foolish way to cut expenses. We had just lost a ship to Napoleon and I overcompensated for our losses. Wages for a few men don't compare to the loss of cargo. I was wrong."

He says all the right things. Am I going mad?

***

Friday, March 22, 1811 – Mlle. Sabine's Brothel
Mlle. Sabine

Lying in bed after sex, Sabine looked at Jean-Louis. "Your Bri, is she engaged yet?" She referred to Lady Gabriella that way because he had always talked of Bri as a daughter.

"Not yet, but the young man seems up to the challenge. I like him."

She smiled. "I wasn't sure you could ever let her go."

He shrugged. "Neither was I. But it's not as hard as I thought. He's a good man. And she's having an impact on him. He's seeing the world differently."

"You've told me she's secretly helping women start businesses. I had an idea I thought she might be interested in. It's something she could import, so it would benefit the trading company, and it would be invaluable to young women to control their own destinies. You've said she's independent and non-judgmental. Do you think she'd agree to meet with me?"

"I don't know. A meeting could be arranged. Perhaps at her aunt's home."

"Let me know. I think she'll find it very interesting."

"Shall I ask what—"

"It's a woman's conversation, *mon amour*." She wrapped her arms around him and they lost themselves in each other.

CHAPTER THIRTY-ONE

Saturday, March 23, 1811 – The Hanforth Mansion
Bri

Gaslights gave an ethereal glow to the long walkway that led to the count's mansion. Set off the street by fifty feet, the imposing white edifice had been in the family of Clarissa's mother for generations, willed to her in a specific bequest.

The butler's military bearing and strong German accent struck Bri as theatrical. Dressed in a red jacket with gold buttons carved with the von Dusterberg family crest, black jodhpurs and shiny black boots, he opened the door, clicked his heels and bowed his head as Lord Ravenshire approached. "Good evening, Madame la Comtesse, Lady Gabriella, Lord Ravenshire, Mr. James. I am Wolfberger, butler to the Count. May we take your cloaks?"

Another uniformed servant stood slightly behind Wolfberger. He accepted the cloaks from the new arrivals and ferried them to a room just off the marble foyer.

The butler led them into the parlor, paneled in an unusual light wood. A large painting of the count and a woman whom Bri assumed to be Clarissa's mother, Lady Melissa, hung over the marble fireplace. Queen Anne chairs upholstered in English chintz were adjacent to the fireplace, whose crackling logs took the chill off the spring night.

Bri smiled, noting that the Count was seated with Clarissa and Dr. St. Cloud, engaged in animated conversation when they entered. She was pleased to see that the count and Dr. St. Cloud seemed to be cordial with each other, allaying Clarissa's jitters about a more intimate meeting than the ball.

Rising to greet his guests, the count poured the chilled Champagne himself, and handed a flute to each guest. "We have an announcement to make tonight, and we would like you to be the first to hear it. Doctor?"

Taking Clarissa's hand, Dr. St. Cloud beamed. "Clarissa and I are engaged to be married."

Lord Ravenshire raised his glass. "May I offer a toast to your happiness?"

The guests echoed, "To your happiness!"

Bri hugged Clarissa. "I am so happy for you."

Dr. St. Cloud glanced at Bri. "We would not have met if you had not been concerned about the injured dog and brought him to my shop."

"Then it was our driver, Jean-Louis, who should get the credit because he knew exactly where your shop was and drove me to it."

"Then we shall invite Jean-Louis to our wedding." Clarissa knew that such a statement would raise eyebrows throughout the *ton,* although not in this room.

Gwyneth smiled. "I'm sure both your mothers would be thrilled were they here with us. I miss them both. When is the wedding date?"

"We are still discussing the date. Since we have just met, we felt a longer engagement would be in order. While we are certain of our feelings, we want to concentrate on the operetta's success. The wedding can wait."

"A special license would be faster, but all the wedding pomp is seductive." Bri turned to the count. "Speaking of the operetta, Mr. James and I reviewed financing its projected run today—"

Her father interrupted. "Not now, Bri."

***

Count von Dusterberg

Wolfberger announced, "Dinner is served."

The guests followed the count into the dining room. Its pale wood paneling led Bri to comment, "Count von Dusterberg, this is such an unusual type of wood. Was it imported from Prussia?"

"Precisely. This is a species of aspen that grows only in the north country of my homeland. Clarissa's mother, Melissa, decided to use it when we renovated the house after many years away in embassies. After Prussia joined with Napoleon, we emigrated from Prussia to her country of birth. My late wife was also partial to a palette of pale colors, and commissioned these oriental rugs to her own design, made for us in the near east."

"They are magnificent. And this table is so unusual, too. Is it a monk's table? Aunt Gwyneth has one from France."

"Ah, yes, it is a monk's table, but from Italy. Actually, it is two tables joined at the center because they were so narrow. Some think it too rustic, but we liked to think that monks in the past may have illuminated manuscripts at these very tables." The count enjoyed explaining the various renovations to the home, and enthralled his dinner guests with tales of the discoveries made during the two-year process.

Dinner was pleasant, full of conversation about the wedding, the operetta and the upcoming balls—Lady Baxter's Ball and the Masquerade Ball at the palace of the Duke and Duchess of Pytchley.

As the group sipped cinnamon tea and enjoyed dessert, an apple tart with fresh whipped cream, the count revived Bri's earlier topic. "Before dinner, Lady Gabriella, you mentioned the projections for the financial performance of the operetta." The count knew from Lord Ravenshire and Clarissa of Lady Gabriella's facility with financial and accounting matters and her proposal that Lord Ravenshire become the count's partner in financing the operetta, but he was a Prussian male, and appeared somewhat taken aback by her direct approach. Still, his breeding had ingrained in him restraint of emotional reactions, and he listened with a calm exterior. "By all means, continue, Lady Gabriella. I am interested in your analysis."

As Gabriella explained her reasoning, Edward would join in from time to time to add to her points.

A team. They bolster each other's reasoning. He couldn't resist a smile at their obvious competitive spirit.

When they were finished, the count looked into his champagne glass and said, "These are all excellent ideas. If you can put these pieces together, I will agree to your business transaction, but we have very little time. This is the twenty-third of March and the operetta is due to open in a month."

Edward nodded. "We believe that the opening and initial run can go on as planned. Although we intend to have a verbal understanding on an extended run by opening night, the paperwork may not be completed by then. However, in the event that we are unsuccessful, we have the financing available to move the play to an entirely different theatre. Count von Dusterberg, I was wrong in my initial analysis of the operetta's potential success, and now I want to assure its best prospects for the future."

The count, impressed with the young man's forthrightness, nodded his approval to the banker. "Keep me informed."

While the other guests continued to talk, Henry leaned closer to the count. "May I have a word with you in private?"

"Of course." The count and Henry excused themselves and walked into the library and closed the door.

As in the other rooms, the light wood set off the colorful bindings of books in German, Latin, French, English and what Henry recognized as Arabic. "You are as well-read as a don at Oxford."

Indicating that Henry should take a leather chair opposite him, the count laughed. "Well, in military campaigns, one is advised to understand the enemy. Although a diplomat, I confess to a lifelong love of books on military strategy."

"As must I. Given long sea voyages, one must read or go mad." Henry clasped his hands, looked down at them and then back at the count. "I wanted to talk to you about Sultan Sarduba of Madagascar and Taita."

"I thought as much." The count offered Henry a brandy.

Henry took the brandy and swirled it in the snifter. "What I want to know is, what kind of a man is this Sultan? I find slavery abhorrent, but I have traveled throughout the world and I know that there are degrees of slavery. I want to get a sense of the man before I approach him."

"He is quite urbane, having studied at Cambridge as a young man, as do many wealthy young men from around the world. The British Empire has fostered a reverence for education that is admirable. The Arabs began the slave trade. It is lucrative. The Sultan is a fair man. He cannot change the ways of his society in one generation, but he is trying to instill principles of respect and tolerance. However, he is a ruler with absolute power."

"I assume you know the story of my shipwreck."

"I do."

"Until I heard the song that Herr Kramer and Clarissa created for the operetta, I thought Taita had died long ago."

The count lowered his eyes for a moment, and then directed his gaze at the earl. "I can understand the shock of learning that she lives. You must be wondering if time has changed her feelings, and what her life has been like in the Sultan's palace. I can assure you that she is not among his harem. The Sultan recognized her healing powers and the Arabs revere spiritual values, so she has been placed on a pedestal. She is a slave, but she is not treated as a lesser participant in the Sultan's household. He values her counsel."

"If she wanted to be free and stay in England, would he let her remain?"

Thinking for a moment, the count shrugged. "He is a man of his culture. He would have to be approached in the right manner to agree to free her. In one respect, it would be easier in England, away from the pressures of his local kinsmen and advisors. He might expect an offer of money for her freedom, but I will need to confirm this in advance, as it might offend him. He may consider the gesture of granting her freedom as evidence of his generosity as Sultan and a devout religious man. According to his tradition, heavenly rewards await those who perform altruistic earthly deeds, and releasing her from slavery might fall under that precept. I will look into this so that I may advise you from a more informed perspective."

"Whether she still loves me or not, the idea of her remaining a slave...is unthinkable. England may not please her. I am gratified to know that she is not of his harem and has been well treated. There must be an angel watching over her, both from the terrors of the volcano and typhoon as well as the horror of slavery. If she wants to return to her island, I will take her there."

Remaining silent for a moment, the count respected Henry's unusual acknowledgment of his private pain. "I cannot begin to imagine the shock of this discovery and the agony of uncertainty you must be experiencing until you see her again. His ship is due to arrive just as the operetta opens. He and his entourage will be my guests. Accompanying the Sultan will be his two most favored wives, the crown prince, Taita, his vizier, the foreign minister and several scimitar-wielding bodyguards. I am hosting a reception for them here on the evening after they arrive. Your family and Mr. James are hereby invited. I shall ask the Sultan for permission for you to visit with Taita in private. As he is my guest, his culture compels him to grant his host's wishes, within reason. I will also speak with Taita to request her agreement to meet with you. I will send a messenger to your home as soon as this is arranged, so that you will not have to spend another moment in torment."

"Thank you. I will be forever in your debt."

"Not at all. I am pleased that my daughter and Lady Gabriella have become such good friends and brought our families together." Standing, he walked to the window, stared at his brandy glass for a moment, and then looked at Henry. "Your sister, Lady Gwyneth, is a fine woman. I enjoyed dancing with her at the ball last night. It has been a very long time since I danced. I had forgotten how delightful it can be. What I am trying to say, sir, is that I would like to see your sister on a social basis, and I was wondering how you would view my clumsy attempt at courtship."

Henry smiled. "It has been two years since her husband died in an accident. I want only the best for Gwyneth. You do not require my permission. As you have observed, the women in my family make their own decisions."

"Thank you. It is odd to feel like a schoolboy again," said the count. "When I was a young man, I did not believe that men of our years could understand the lure of romance. How wrong I was."

Nodding, Henry agreed, "The 'arrogance of youth' was a phrase I dismissed as the jealous carping of old men." They laughed, left the library, and walked down the hallway to join the other guests in the parlor.

As they approached the parlor, Clarissa was saying, "but Father does not know, so you must keep this a secret until we can prepare him properly."

The count frowned. "Prepare me properly for what?"

***

Henry

Clarissa blushed with guilt and looked at her fiancé.

Dr. St. Cloud stood. "Count von Dusterberg, I have a hobby of performing magic for children who are confined at hospitals in the *ton*. On a whim, before I met your daughter, I arranged to audition for the part of The Wizard in *The Princess*. Herr Kramer thought I was the best candidate for the part. I auditioned in a wizard's garb, totally disguising my features. I have selected a stage name, and would like to fulfill my obligation to Herr Kramer, with your blessing."

Gwyneth spoke up. "We saw the audition, Count von Dusterberg, and the doctor really is an extraordinary magician."

The count's face flared into a crimson hue. "Am I to understand that I am the only one in this room who does not know about this? What is next? Clarissa, do you intend to perform as well?" Reading the answer in the look on her face, the count glared at Herr Kramer. Pointing to him in anger, the count's rage was barely contained. "This is your doing. Taking her to the theatre at such an impressionable age was supposed to instill in her an appreciation for the dramatic arts, not a desire to perform. It simply is not done in Society. Opera, perhaps, but an operetta is considered fanciful and actresses do not enjoy the reputation that I wish my daughter to have."

"Father, I have not agreed to perform. When the doctor auditioned for the Wizard, I played the part of the Princess as a foil in the audition. It seemed to me that with a black wig, costumes and a stage name, no one would recognize me. Since the doctor and I are engaged, I do not need to attend all the balls, and the play is performed only four nights a week. Will not you please give this your consideration when you are not so angry?"

Clearing his throat, Henry suggested, "Perhaps we should depart so that this discussion can be conducted in private."

"That will not be necessary, Lord Ravenshire. I would like your opinion. What would you advise me to do?"

"Ah, there is no escape for me, I see." Henry hoped to lighten the tone of the conversation. "Let us consider this logically. Lady Clarissa is engaged and so her marriage prospects will not be dimmed by her yearning to perform. Her future husband must not object because he is planning to perform himself. In a disguise, she may not be recognizable. Therefore, her privacy and yours, Count von Dusterberg, may be protected. On the other hand, I have heard Lady Clarissa sing and she has a lovely, lyrical voice. Once introduced to the public, she may become a 'light of the stage' and be in demand for future performances. Performing may not be a one-time flight of fancy. It may lead to more recognition than you are prepared to face."

"I, for one, do not believe that such talent will produce scandalous talk for long," added Gwyneth. "At first, I was taken aback by the doctor's desire to perform, but he is quite good at it and seems to enjoy it as a hobby to his serious practice of veterinary medicine. I realized then that I was unfairly prejudiced against the theatre. If I enjoy watching a performance, then why should I dismiss the players as socially unacceptable? Perhaps we can be on the forefront of changing the perception of those in the *ton* who are similarly prejudiced."

Bri joined in, "Clarissa has undeniable talent. Is it so wrong to pursue her singing? Her true friends will remain and the others are not worth thinking about."

Edward leaned forward. "I must temper the arguments of Madame la Comtesse and Lady Gabriella by saying that prejudice against theatrical performers clearly exists. Most people in the *ton* are intolerant and unlikely to alter their perceptions."

Bri scowled at him with evident disagreement.

The banker continued. "I agree with Count von Dusterberg that performing may damage Lady Clarissa's reputation, although her engagement, as Lord Ravenshire points out, tends to mitigate any immediate damage to her marriage prospects. The Comtesse makes the excellent point that enlightened people can change their minds." Edward began to pace around the parlor, thinking aloud. "Given the reactions of the people in this room, it occurs to me that the best approach to this issue may not be to disguise oneself and hide from the *ton*. I am just exploring options, you understand, but what if Lady Clarissa's performance were not disguised, but rather publicized? What if the backing of Count von Dusterberg, Lord Ravenshire, and James & Co. were openly revealed? What if we persuaded the theatre critic of the *Times* to write of the changing mores of Society and the acceptance of the theatre as a legitimate enterprise? What if we created the perception in the minds of the *ton* and the public at large that talent had a language all its own that bridged diverse cultures and societies? What if we used publicity to change the prevailing opinion of the theatre, as essayists have done for centuries to change political opinions? What if we made it appear that to be prejudiced against the theatre was narrow-minded and unsophisticated?"

Lord Ravenshire cautioned, "That is a lot of 'what ifs,' Young James."

Gwyneth nodded. "It is true that the *ton* values sophistication and it is true that publicity can be managed to mold public opinion. But what is the best venue for this effort? Dare we make an announcement at the Masquerade Ball? Bri's grandmother would have to be informed in advance. Is that what you are thinking, Mr. James?"

"Yes, but we would need to map out a detailed plan to control the dissemination of the publicity."

"Just a moment." The count held up his hands to halt such speculation. "Let us not get carried away by fanciful notions of publicity. I care naught for the effect on me, for I have a record that will withstand any stones thrown by the *ton*. But it is Clarissa who may be harmed, and we cannot let the thrill of the game cloud the impact that such a course might have on her."

The doctor spoke up. "I believe that you have isolated the key barrier, Count von Dusterberg. We are all concerned about Clarissa's reputation. Perhaps Clarissa and I should be married immediately so that there is never a question of her standing in Society as a marriageable young woman. Then, part of the burden is removed from you, sir, as I will be her husband and presumably the target of any such criticism."

Bri looked around the room and said, "It is ultimately Clarissa's decision, is it not? We can define all sorts of plans for publicity campaigns but since she is the one who will rise or fall based on the success of these plans, it is she who must decide. With your blessing, of course, Count von Dusterberg."

The count glanced at the ceiling, then back at his daughter. "What is your desire, Clarissa?"

First looking at her father, then Dr. St. Cloud, Clarissa returned her gaze to her father, and said, "I have always loved the theatre and the feeling I had on the stage as I sang was indescribable. If I were to let this opportunity pass for the sake of bending to the restrictive perceptions of the *ton,* I would always wonder what might have been. You have always taught me that we must be true to ourselves. I would like to perform in the play, with your blessing. But I am not prepared as yet for the publicity outlined by Mr. James. I would prefer to begin in anonymity."

Softly, the count agreed. "Then you may follow your heart, my darling. Your happiness is my only concern."

Turning to Dr. St. Cloud, the count said, "As for your offer to marry Clarissa before the play opens, I think it a bit rushed, but let that be Clarissa's decision, as well."

Clarissa smiled. "There is no rush. I am confident that Dr. St. Cloud will not change his mind."

"Mr. James, your suggestions are interesting. Let us refine them together during the run of the operetta, and consider them as potential actions for the future. Such as," he paused to look lovingly at his daughter, "Clarissa's next starring role."

"Yes, sir, I will be honored to accept that responsibility if I may count on the help of Lady Gabriella."

"Of course you may, Mr. James."

The earl stood. "On this happy note, the hour is late and we must be going. Dinner was delightful, and we look forward to seeing you at the Baxter Ball."

CHAPTER THIRTY-TWO

Sunday, March 24, 1811 – Lady Gwyneth's Townhouse
Gwyneth

Bri, Edward and Henry came for a mid-day meal on Sunday after church.

As soon as they arrived, Henry continued his complaints about the morning's service. "The high Anglican service is too much for me. I said I'd go once during the Marriage Season for Bri's sake. Today marks twice. Not again."

"I'm a Dissenter too, Father. The Methodist Meeting House in Ravenshire has a completely different atmosphere. I love to sing the hymns of Charles Wesley. Maybe there should be a service where people just sing. Then it's their voice direct to their Creator without any other intervention. That sermon infuriated me."

Gwyneth shrugged. "I don't see why we need to parade ourselves through church for Bri's sake. We're known Dissenters. Who are we fooling? No one."

Edward threw up his hands. "Don't look at me! I was invited."

Nambotha led them into the dining room and disappeared to bring the platters.

"That sermon was so insulting. To think that there are two full volumes of *Fordyce's Sermons to Young Women*. It's inconceivable. The vicar read that prattle to the entire congregation...the self-righteous opinions of an unmarried man dictating how a young Christian woman must conduct herself to be 'worthy' of a husband...is, in a

279

word, 'unChristian.' To 'deserve' to win a man's offer of marriage?"

"Let us change the subject, Bri." The earl gave her a direct look.

Bri sat back and crossed her arms.

Edward put down his fork and gazed at Bri. "You may be surprised to hear, Lady Gabriella, that I actually agree with you. The world is changing in commerce, in mores, in expectations. I see things differently now after being bombarded by your constant arguments. My initial reaction was that your ideas were preposterous. With your prodding, however, I have observed that women are not treated equally. Women don't need to be protected from life, they need to be prepared to deal with it, as men are."

Bri's challenge came immediately. "Then petition Oxford to admit women."

Henry's head fell to one side as if being battered by a boxer. "One step at a time."

"That's easy for you to say—your freedom is not restricted in any way, other than limits you put on yourself."

Gwyneth dipped her spoon in the vichyssoise, signaling them all to begin eating. "I think there's one more thing you should do before the Masquerade Ball."

Edward watched Bri's shoulders slump.

Bri didn't speak, but raised her eyebrows in an expectant and challenging look.

"You should ride Rotten Row in the late afternoon at least once this Season. Henry can get the baron there, and you can bring Lady Penelope. See and be seen, that is the game."

Scoffing, Bri brushed the comment aside. "Games? I do not want to play games."

"Why not? You're quite adept at Whist." Edward avoided her eyes.

"And why corrupt the French *route de roi*? People in the *ton* speak French."

"The name is irrelevant. Let's pick a day and set the plan in motion." Gwyneth brooked no more discussion.

"I'd like to accompany you if Lady Gwyneth will approve."

"Of course I approve, Mr. James. How about early April?"

Bri perked up. "Let's ride this week, on Thursday morning with the baron and Lady Penelope. After that, we can consider an afternoon ride."

"Very well." Gwyneth glanced at Henry.

Bri smiled. "Lady Penelope is having a trousseau party for Clarissa on April 6th. The banns have been read on the last three Sundays, including today, so now they only need to set the wedding date."

Nambotha removed the soup dishes and brought a cheese plate with fresh baguettes.

Gwyneth nodded to the butler to bring tea. "I thought it best to keep lunch light."

Bri took a section of a baguette and spread some Brie on it. She smiled. "Bri eating Brie." She popped the bite into her mouth. "The opening of *The Princess* is set for Monday, April 22nd."

Edward nodded. "Before you ask, I have almost concluded negotiations to move the Shakespeare Festival to another theatre and extend the run for *The Princess* for as long as a year."

After lunch, Gwyneth smiled. "Henry and Edward, how about if the two of you go into the Music Room? I need to speak with Bri alone."

Bri blanched.

***

Bri

What have I done now?

Gwyneth led Bri into the back sunroom, out of hearing.

***

Henry

Henry and Edward took a glass of sherry from Nambotha. Standing in front of the floor-to-ceiling library shelves, Henry smiled. "Luc and Gwyneth shared a love of books."

Edward took a sip of sherry as he gazed at the titles. "How did they meet?"

Henry thought back to his first meeting with Luc more than twenty years earlier.

"I was on a trading mission to French Canadian territory, and had just engaged Jean-Louis as my guide.

"We were in the far north of Canada, at the height of the fur season, examining pelts to meet the stringent criteria of the trading company clients, some of the finest British, European and Asian furriers. In the middle of a very spirited negotiation with another trapper in the town's fur market over excellent pelts of white fox, commotion distracted me. Two sleds drawn by barking white huskies roared into the town square, one edging ahead of the other as they passed a frozen fountain. A small crowd had gathered to watch what appeared to be the end of a spirited race.

"I finalized the purchase of the pelts, left Jean-Louis to complete the paperwork and see to the securing of our new inventory. I trudged through the snow to find out the results of the race.

"As I approached the milling crowd, I observed quite a bit of money changing hands. The victor was being congratulated. The loser yook it good-naturedly. I heard him say, 'I will not bet again that a French comte can't hold his own in a dog race against a native *Canadien*. I recognize that my opponent has excellent natural skills.'

"The winner graciously bowed to his opponent. 'You proved to be a fierce competitor. Your newly acquired humility is gratifying.' The crowd laughed.

"I made my way to an oddsmaker who was busily settling wagers. I asked what the race was all about.

"One of the losing wagerers explained. 'François opined that nobleman could never do a real job, such as steer a dog sled to deliver food to the next town. He said only a working man would have the stamina to make the trip from this town to the next and back. The comte took him at his word and challenged him to a race. We all thought François would win handily, but that comte fooled most of us.'

"I asked who he was.

"The man shrugged and said he didn't know much about him. 'He's a Frenchman, not a *Canadien*. Didn't think they had dog races in France. Thought all they did was drink wine and watch dancing girls.'

"The comte overheard our exchange, came over and put his hand on the man's shoulder. 'Not so, my friend. I grew up racing horses, so this was not too far afield. But today is much colder than any day in France, I can tell you that!'

"I held out my hand and introduced myself. 'May I buy you a drink, comte?'

"He agreed and said, 'I am Luc, comte de Merbeau.'

"The wagerer nudged me. 'He's a real comte.'

"I laughed and added, 'And I a real viscount, but that means nothing here in the North Country. We are visitors in your white wilderness. Guide us to a fire and some ale.'

"The comte laughed, agreed, and we followed the wagerer to the local watering hole.

"By the time Jean-Louis appeared, the comte had agreed to accompany me to Montréal and on to New York City to sail back to England. He told me, 'I've been traveling around Canada for half a year, and it is time I returned to see if my younger brother has managed the family vineyards and racing stock into oblivion.' Luc shrugged and said, 'Actually, he is an astute vintner and he was happy to get me out of his way. I've never been much interested in the family business, so I suppose it was an error of Fate to make me the eldest son. My interests lie in philosophy and music. I wanted to see the New World and I've spent some fascinating time with the Cree Indians. Their spiritual foundations are quite extraordinary. I might write about what I have learned on this trip.'

"Jean-Louis also spent time with many native tribes. The two Frenchmen spent the better part of the night informing me of various tribal beliefs and practices. As dawn broke, I asked Jean-Louis if we had any other commerce to conduct.

" 'Just the red fox order. I have arranged that negotiation for tomorrow morning, so we can leave by mid-day.' Turning to the comte, the trapper said, 'I see that we have our driver for the sled caravan.'

"I laughed and said, 'Shall we race all the way to Montréal?'

"Luc demurred. 'I've had enough racing in this frigid climate. Can we light a fire in the sled without going up in flames ourselves?'

"Jean-Louis shook his head. 'We must wrap ourselves in fur pelts and ride on the wind.'

"And so we did."

***

Edward tilted his head. "And that twist of Fate led the comte to Lady Gwyneth."

"I could not have hoped for a better husband for my sister. She suffered through a terrible first marriage. Widowed after her first husband died in an accident, Luc proved a wonderful partner for Gwyneth until the runaway carriage took his life. To think that it might have been Blackie's work—"

"No proof."

"I've known him for so long. Never would I have imagined he could murder Luc or Rychard. At the time, Jean-Louis suspected foul play, but an investigation of the Bow Street Runners turned up nothing."

"We have no more now than you did then."

***

Jean-Louis

Outside, Jean-Louis spooned up the soup brought to him by Dominique. "The comte's recipe is only part of this delicacy, Dominique. For years, I've wondered what it is that makes your concoction so much better than even a French chef's creation. It just came to me. You've pureed the potatoes to an astonishing degree. The secret is the smoothness."

"*Peut-être*, perhaps. I'll never reveal my secrets, even to you."

"Wise."

Dominique unwrapped a towel covering a bone for Chérie, who jumped up and took it out of her hand, hiding under the carriage to preserve it from any nearby hungry dog.

"We are not going to take your bone, Chérie." Jean-Louis laughed.

"You like having a companion." Dominique smiled. "I must get back. *Au revoir.*"

"*Au revoir.*"

***

Bri

In her private study, Gwyneth wasted no time in broaching the subject she'd pulled Bri aside to discuss. "I assume you and Edward have not yet had relations."

284

"You mean—"

"You know what I mean."

"Yes. I mean, we have not."

"Good. I want you to make an excuse to stay after the others leave. We need to discuss matters appropriate for the ears of women only."

Bri shrugged and they went out to rejoin the men. *I knew this conversation would come someday. I grew up around animals. Does she think I'm totally ignorant?*

***

After Edward and Henry left, Bri and Gwyneth went into the Music Room. Moments later, the doorbell rang.

Bri frowned. "Who could it be at this hour?"

Nambotha's voice told her. "Your Grace."

Bri stood. "Grandmother?"

"I thought they'd never leave. Your aunt and I agreed you need to be educated as to matters of marital intimacy."

Blushing, Bri remained silent.

"There are devices to prevent becoming with child. These conversations are a bit indelicate for your aunt and me, so I have arranged for you to take a little ride to speak with a disinterested third party."

"Now?"

"Now. Let us depart."

Aunt Gwyneth escorted them to the door. "The duchess will take you home afterward."

Puzzled, Bri shrugged and followed her grandmother to her carriage.

Once inside, the duchess waved to the driver, and reached for Bri's hand. "Better to discuss these matters than have a hasty wedding. I have no illusions about the desires of young people. Believe it or not, I was young once. I am a firm believer in consulting experts on all matters. Tonight we are going to consult a professional." She looked out the window. "It's not far."

"Here? Near where Aunt Gwyneth lives? Are we going to see a friend of hers?"

The duchess scoffed. "I should think not. She is not of our

station, but she is an expert in her field."

"And what field might that be?"

"She runs the most exclusive brothel in London."

Bri sat back on the carriage bench, speechless.

When the carriage stopped, the duchess signaled a doorman. Shortly afterward, a woman with a hooded cloak approached the carriage and got in.

She pulled back the hood and bowed her head. "Your Grace. And you must be Lady Gabriella."

"This is Mlle. Sabine, Bri. She has a commercial proposition for you as well as a gift."

Bri raised an eyebrow. *My grandmother is on friendly terms with a brothel owner?*

Mlle. Sabine pushed back her lustrous dark brown hair in the latest style. Her kohl-outlined eyes exuded warmth. Her lips and cheeks were not the red hue that Bri had expected, but a pale pink. "Lady Gabriella, I had an importing arrangement through one of my employees who has recently left the country unexpectedly and left me without a source for a very important product." She pulled a sponge out from her cloak. It had a string attached.

"Sponges? Pardon me, Mlle. Sabine, but that does not seem so unusual."

"Sponges from the Red Sea are best. When soaked in vinegar and sprinkled with lemon, they provide an effective barrier to becoming with child. They are inserted prior to relations, and removed within three hours afterward by pulling on the string. Rinse them in water and they can be used over and over again."

"Ingenious. How long have these been used?"

"Since ancient times. It has been a secret of Jewish women for millennia. That is how I came to learn of this use, from my former employee. Nothing else works as well. You can cut an orange in half, clean it out and insert it to prevent the male juices from penetrating your womb, but results vary. Many don't insert it properly, or far enough. In any case, I need replenishments. As you might imagine, we use these rather heavily compared to a typical woman."

Bri blushed. "Yes, I can understand that. As I recall, we have a source near the Red Sea who provides coral. They are coral divers and sponge divers, but I didn't know about the efficacy of this product. I'm sure I can arrange to import these for you. It takes a few months to set up a new distribution system. I trust you have enough until the new sponges can be delivered."

"Yes, I have enough for about six months, but I like to plan ahead."

"So do I."

"How are these cords attached?"

"Simply tied. Braided silk works best."

"We have a source for that too. Is this device used widely?"

"Not that I know of. It is exclusive to my operation."

"Perhaps we could arrange a partnership to import and distribute larger quantities. This is a naturally occurring and regenerating resource. Let me place an initial order. How many do you require over a six month period?"

"About two hundred."

"I'll order five hundred and we'll set up a small operation of women to assemble them. I have a friend who runs a foundling hospital. The unfortunate women in confinement there need a way to earn money. This could help them."

"I heard you were unusual, Lady Gabriella. That you believed in women helping women. And that you would even speak to someone like me."

Bri reached over and squeezed her arm. "Stop. You are an enterprising woman with a product that is in demand. 'The world's oldest profession' has lasted for a reason." Looking at the duchess, she smiled. "You never cease to surprise me, Grandmother."

Mlle. Sabine pulled her hood up. "Then we are in agreement?"

"Yes. I will submit a proposal to you within a few days." Bri handed the sponge back to Mlle. Sabine.

She pushed Bri's hand back. "A gift. A sample to test. Remember, soak in vinegar with a few drops of fresh lemon." Mlle. Sabine exited the carriage.

The carriage began to move again.

"How did you meet her?"

"Let's just say I needed some advice about the duke, so I went to an expert."

CHAPTER THIRTY-THREE

Monday, March 25, 1811 - James & Co., Bankers
Edward

The Monday after dinner at the count's, Edward rode in his carriage to the bank. *Will we ever find proof of Blackburn's theft—or worse, murder?* He wanted to get to the bank offices early to prepare the letters he hoped would allow *The Princess* to either remain at the Haymarket or move to another suitable venue.

Edward addressed his first letter to Sir John Sullivan, whom he knew socially, suggesting that the Shakespeare Festival consider using the Royal Theatre, Wellclose Square, citing its history in the performance of Shakespeare's plays, in lieu of the Haymarket.

The second letter was to the Earl of Brookvale, the current owner of the Royal Theatre, Wellclose Square. As renovations were being made there, Edward suggested the earl consider naming the Shakespeare Festival as the Royalty's permanent troupe, guaranteeing both the troupe and the theatre of consistent seasons and ticket sales. As the earl's banker, Edward knew that the financial advantages would be very persuasive to the commercial focus of his client.

The final letter was to the owner of the Haymarket, requesting that he consider extending the run of *The Princess* if Edward could arrange a renegotiation of the Shakespeare Festival's contract. As *The Princess* was paying a higher fee than the Shakespeare Festival, Edward expected that the owner would agree, subject to avoiding any negative publicity. The owner of the Haymarket was also one of the bank's clients. Edward stressed the success of *The Princess* in Germany. He dispatched a messenger with these letters, hoping to get a response within a day or two.

He then wrote out a proposal for advertising and promoting *The Princess*. When the messenger returned from the earlier deliveries, he dispatched the proposal to Lady Gabriella for review. In his note to her, he said that he would be at the trading offices later that day to check the progress of the audit.

These tasks completed, he left the bank and instructed his driver to take him to the local parish magistrate, his old friend Rudy Aldrich, who studied law and had a passion for administration of justice. He first met Rudy on an African safari when they were children. They were nearly mauled by a lioness outside their tent. Later, as schoolmates at Merton College, Oxford, they'd forged a lasting friendship. Edward had written to Rudy during his travels in the Far East and had looked him up immediately upon his return.

Edward was ushered into a large room with rows of desks. He looked around the busy office of investigators. Watchmen and constables patrolled some areas of the city, but Aldrich's group was an experiment to try to apply scientific principles to the solving of crimes. Edward hoped that this group could help him locate any information on Luc de Merbeau's death.

Judge Aldrich appeared and shook Edward's hand warmly, asking, "What brings you to the halls of justice? Bank fraud?"

"Perhaps, Aldrich." Edward corrected himself. "Judge Aldrich. Where may we speak in private?"

Aldrich escorted Edward to his office and closed the door. "This is no social call."

"No. I have reason to believe that a death labeled 'accidental' in 1809 may have been murder. I believe that I know who the murderer is, and I am trying to help the slain man's relatives prove it. The case to which I refer is Luc, Comte de Merbeau, killed by a runaway carriage. The carriage was found abandoned. The constable learned that it had been leased for the day, but the stable owner would not tell me the name of the man who leased it without an order from a judge. Hence here I stand."

"James, you are a banker, not a trained criminal investigator. This type of thing can get dangerous. De Merbeau was the brother-in-law of the Earl of Ravenshire, of course. Ravenshire's driver is more than a driver—Jean-Louis is a legend in the *ton* to those who know of his exploits. I have no doubt he can handle the devil himself, but you are not a military man. Don't protest. I know all about your Asian fighting arts abilities, but please don't take the law into your own hands. Perhaps my office can work with the Bow Street Runners to help."

"A Bow Street Runner named Boyd looked into the case after the Comte's death, and my client has contacted him to assist us."

"I know Boyd. He is a good man who follows the trail no matter where it leads. The tentacles of politics have tangled and tarnished many an investigation. Tell me what you need and speak of this to no one else."

"Aldrich, the woman I love may be in danger from this very same murderer. I cannot wait for the wheels of justice to turn. I need answers now."

"Understood. We have instituted new rules here in the last five years. Case details are kept in an orderly manner. We should be able to find it in our archives in the basement, second level. Come with me."

The magistrate led Edward down several flights of stairs to the basement. As they descended, Edward realized he had described Bri as "the woman I love." *Damn! She has influenced my mind. I must be more careful. Aldrich must think me a fool.*

When they reached the second level of the basement, Aldrich instructed the guard to unlock the door and light the oil lamps. They found the section housing files from 1809, and scanned the alphabetized list of case files. Impatiently, Edward looked over Aldrich's shoulder. "There. Merbeau, Luc de."

Aldrich noted, "File 23, drawer 3."

Retrieving the file on de Merbeau, Aldrich's curiosity got the better of him. Instead of waiting until they were back in the office upstairs, he glanced through the file. "This confirms your information. They traced the carriage back to its owner. A Gypsy leased the carriage that day. The owner charged double the normal rate because he didn't like the man's demeanor."

"In other words, he didn't trust a Gypsy."

"A reasonable assumption."

"Not all Gypsies are criminals."

"You misunderstand my reference. I meant that your conclusion was a reasonable assumption about the prejudice of the stable owner." Aldrich returned to the file. "A witness saw the carriage gather speed and head for the comte with deliberate intent. Perhaps Boyd can find the Gypsy. Let's get back upstairs, review this file together, and I'll issue an order for the stable owner to open his records to you."

***

Leaving Aldrich's office with the judge's order in hand, Edward looked at his pocket watch. It was now nearly three o'clock. He gave his driver the address of the stable.

He walked in, and the stable owner recognized him and put up his hands. "I told you, nothing without an order from the magistrate."

Edward pulled the order from his pocket. "Here it is."

The man's face fell, and he read it over and gestured to Edward to follow him to the back. A table served as his office.

"How do you find anything in this mess?"

"Do you want my help or not?" The owner adopted a defiant stance. "I know where everything is." He tossed papers aside, revealing a stack of ledgers beneath. He looked at each until he found the correct year. He sat down and paged through it. "Here it is. Date, time, cost. Paid in cash. Name: Rajko Bihari, Gypsy. No address, of course. Damned scum, they are. That's why I charged him double."

"Why did you write down 'Gypsy'? Is that your custom when you lease a carriage?"

"Only when my gut tells me I should." He pointed to other entries. Some were identified as Ethiopian, Molly, Spaniard. "It fixes their image in my mind for the next time, if there is a problem."

"Do you have a particular hatred for Gypsies and foreigners?"

"Why not? This is not their country. They are wanderers, travelers they call themselves. Nomads. Thieves, I say. I was lucky to get my carriage and horses back."

"What about the term 'Molly'? Why would a man's private proclivities impact his ability to pay for a carriage?"

The man spit on the floor. "I don't like them, that's all. I take their money and charge them more for the privilege. There ain't no law against it."

"Perhaps there should be." Ignoring the man's grunt of

disagreement, Edward had one more question. "Did you ever see this Bihari character again? On the street, in the neighborhood?"

"I assume he was the one they fished out of the river the next day."

Edward leaned in closer. "What? How would you know it was the same man?

The owner shrugged. "I don't. I just added it up. The body was dressed as a Gypsy under a driver's cloak. That body was found the day after my carriage was abandoned...abandoned with another man's body trampled by my horses and pressed beneath the rims of my carriage's wheels—I am unlikely to forget that. They found the Gypsy's body very near the scene of the accident. Nobody ever came to see me about it. I told the local constable."

"What did he say?"

" 'The only good one is a dead one.' "

Unused to open avowal of unvarnished hatred, Edward was taken aback, but refrained from debating the stable owner. "Do you remember the constable's name?"

"No. But he was a decent sort."

Not to my way of thinking. Edward betrayed no emotion, and thanked him for his assistance. Leaving, he fumed. *Damnation! The trail spirals into a series of dead ends. Did Blackburn kill the driver after engaging him for the murder of Luc de Merbeau?*

CHAPTER THIRTY-FOUR

Tuesday, March 26, 1811 – Lady Gwyneth's Townhouse
Gwyneth

Gwyneth's groom helped her ascend her sidesaddle, to ride aside. At Ravenshire, she had ridden astride with her brothers until her father had reluctantly instructed his stable master to commission a sidesaddle for her. Originally, she had chafed at its restrictions and dangerous instability at a fast trot, but unless she was riding in a hunt, donning breeches as a man and riding astride at a gallop over the fields, city riding resembled a palace procession where one assumed an ambling gait, more to be seen by the *ton* than riding for pleasure. Still, Gwyneth looked forward to these weekly outings, taking in the fresher air in the park, even in the rain. She especially liked the rain. The smell of it invigorated her and the washing of the air made her feel that her troubles were being washed away at the same time.

As she waited for Oliver, Lord Darlemont, to arrive for their weekly ride with Bri, Gwyneth reflected on the trap of family entanglements. Oliver had adored his older sister, Lady Jane, Bri's mother, who had been close to Gwyneth. He had little respect for his cousin, Jamie, Gwyneth's late first husband. He might not have known the extent of Gwyneth's unhappiness in that marriage, but he was well-acquainted with Jamie's indolence, drunkenness and general deportment. "A disgrace to all gentlemen," he'd muttered once. Darlemont's facial features exhibited more than a passing family resemblance to her first husband. Despite the passage of time, Gwyneth's heart always contracted in a spasm of fear when Oliver's face came into view.

These weekly rides offered a short respite from the bombardment of events during the hectic pace of the Marriage Season. Still, Gwyneth could not quiet the thoughts flying through her mind. Bri and Edward…the triangle of Henry, Charlotte and Taita…Blackie perhaps the murderer of her brother and husband. The incessant mental turmoil needed to be calmed. And now Count von Dusterberg had invited her to dine out. *Am I ready for a romantic interlude? Should I discourage him or see how I feel?* The prospect of intimacy with a man after Luc's death remained inconceivable.

The rain didn't deter Wyndwards or Pytchleys from riding. *If I only rode on sunny days, I'd no longer be skilled at it.*

***

Darlemont

Despite his mother's oft-expressed dissatisfaction with most of his habits, Oliver had always been an early riser. Being born at 3 a.m—a Gypsy fortune teller once told him—meant that his energies would always be highest in the morning. Not that he frequented fortune tellers, but his mother would visit the caravan camps in disguise, dressed as a servant. On one occasion, she had dragged him along. It was unusual to be invited to accompany his mother anywhere as a child, so he was thrilled at the adventure and the event remained a highlight of his life. Instructed to remain silent—the better to cement her disguise—he never forgot the day.

Enthralled by the garish colors of her tented wagon, he followed his mother's instructions to remain silent on that bleak, windy day. Gusts buffeted the tent. And then it happened. The Gypsy turned over the Death card. The next one was a woman. He began to cry, fearing his mother would die. But his mother still lived. In retrospect, Oliver assumed the portent must have been the death of his sister. *Many women die in childbirth. It would not be an unusual prediction to come to pass.* He discounted it now, believing the Gypsy used predictable events to appear a true seer to her gullible clientele. Oliver put little trust in reading the stars or a crystal ball. He meant to make his own destiny, not wait for it to appear. The unfortunate truth was that, as the only surviving son of a duke, he was forced to wait to assume his life's work. It would not begin until his father died.

He dismissed his remembrances, relishing the morning's pale light as he rode through the near-deserted streets. He arrived at Berkeley Crescent to find Lady Gwyneth pacing her horse in front of her townhouse. Her hat didn't shield her hair or pale blue riding habit from the soft drizzle. *I've always admired her spunk. I regret not knowing of the pain my cousin caused her.* How women could ride aside baffled him. He'd tried it once on his sister Jane's horse and had fallen off. Ever since then, he'd marveled at the balance and grace of a woman on a horse.

After their greetings, they rode side-by-side to gather Bri, and then to Hyde-Park. Even though the *ton* generally rode in the early evening before dinner, the Wyndward-Pytchley clan rode alone in the morning, away from the gossip rags and disdain of the self-appointed leaders of Fashionable Society. Even so, it would not have been fitting for Bri to ride alone with her uncle. A woman chaperone was required to maintain Bri's reputation. As a result, Gwyneth was as much a hostage of the Marriage Season as his rebellious and brilliant niece. Bri didn't look like her mother—Jane had been a delicate blonde—but Bri had a sparkle that reminded him of Jane as a young girl, before the pressures of the *ton* had worn her down and melancholy had descended over her soul.

Like her aunt, Bri was ready when they arrived, and they headed toward the park.

"Ready for the Baxter Ball?"

"To be paraded like a prize cow at a country fair is hardly my idea of an exciting evening."

"It's not as bad as all that, Bri." Gwyneth exchanged an amused look with Oliver.

Bri sighed. "All the rules, all the chaperones, all the expectations…it's exhausting."

"I hear Edward James is interested in you. As is Duff Blackburn."

"Blackie's too old."

"And James?"

"He's arrogant, condescending and extremely annoying." She spurred her horse to ride ahead.

Oliver laughed. "He's getting under her skin. Are they a good match?"

Gwyneth nodded. "He can parry her wit and their interests are similar. Everyone who's seen them together knows it. They're fighting the notion of inevitability."

"She'll put him through his paces, just like a horse." Oliver winked at Gwyneth. "Sparring with Bri always makes my day more interesting. James will come around."

"I'm chaperoning them riding here on Thursday, along with Lady Penelope and Baron Beauchamp."

"The baron is Henry's age. But who am I to predict the course of true love?"

**

Wednesday, March 27, 1811 – Wyndward Trading Warehouse
Edward

"Damn!" Edward slammed down the report Jaspers had prepared. "The man is too slippery for us. All can be explained as an oversight here or there. No proof."

Jaspers hung his head. "I am so sorry, Mr. James."

"I am not angry with you, Jaspers. Your work is thorough. My frustration is with Blackburn's damnable cleverness. He knows how to cover his tracks." Edward frowned. "We can terminate the 'audit' process and get your clerks back to regular bank tasks. There will be a bonus for all of you for working long hours in such a diligent manner."

"What about the other concerns?" Jaspers swallowed hard. "The murders?"

"No proof there, either. We're working on it."

**

Thursday, March 28, 1811 – Rotten Row in Hyde-Park
Baron Beauchamp

The baron blinked the sleep out of his eyes as he spurred his horse into a canter to reach the spot in the park where Ravenshire had told him to "accidentally" run into Lady Penelope when a chaperone would be present. Not an early riser like his friend, he had made a special effort to make this rendezvous. Lady Penelope's warm exuberance enticed him. She was different than any other woman he'd met. And his sister, Davinia, was coming around. *I want a life of my own, with Lady Penelope.*

In the distance, a group of riders rode in his direction. Beauchamp recognized Lady Gabriella's red hair, pulled back in a ponytail. *Apropos.* Soon, Lady Gwyneth, Lady Penelope and Young James came into view. The French former trapper came up the rear, trailed by a Dalmatian. *He's always around. Like a bodyguard.* The baron slowed to an ambling gait and they stopped to greet each other.

"Good morning, ladies." He tipped his hat to them and nodded to Edward. "James. How's your father?"

"Improving, Baron Beauchamp. Lord Ravenshire's herbalist is to be highly recommended."

"The earl has quite a web of clever retainers surrounding him."

Bri bristled, although she called him by his nickname. "We prefer the term 'associates,' Baron Beau. "The word 'retainers' suggests a class of servitude."

The baron shrugged. "Do you pay them? Call them what you will. I know the earl treats all men equally."

"And women."

"And women, Bri." The baron's winning grin dissolved any remaining tension. "You're looking quite lovely this morning, Lady Penelope."

She blushed. "Thank you, Lord Beauchamp. It's the spring day. I think we may be on the cusp of sunshine." As she spoke, the clouds parted and the air warmed with the full sun beaming on them.

Edward smiled. "You have spoken, Lady Penelope, and the gods have answered."

"Will I see you all at the Baxter Ball on Saturday night?" *My interest cannot be disguised, but I shall roll the dice.*

"Oh, yes!" blurted Lady Penelope a little too quickly. The others echoed her response.

"May I ride with you awhile?"

He didn't think Lady Penelope could blush more deeply than she had earlier, but he was wrong. And pleased. He turned his horse around and they kept their horses at a gait where they could talk without exertion.

***

Thursday, March 28, 1811 – Darlemont's Gentleman's Club
Darlemont

Playing cards at his club, the Earl of Darlemont sighed. *Bad hand.*

Sir Reginald, a diplomat in the Foreign Office played his card. "Unrest in Africa adds to the continent's instability."

Tottie Drummond discarded and drew another card. Drummond relished his role as a political mastermind who advised powerful men in government. "Africa is always unstable. The unruly, unwashed, illiterate masses resist control by their educated betters."

Nigel Norman, a Member of Parliament, concurred. "They don't know what's best for them."

Darlemont shrugged. "We can't subjugate the whole world. We disrupted millennia of village life, imposing our will on the unwilling. Why are we surprised when uprisings develop?"

The diplomat laughed. "Darlemont, you sound like you are supporting an argument for revolution."

"You're the diplomat and a student of history. Do you not see that revolutions are a matter of history? All governments fail. The French Revolution felled a monarchy and birthed Napoleon. War is the way of men."

The political manipulator, a student of Machiavelli, shrugged. "War is a tool of the prince. There are princes of nations and princes of commerce. Your relative, the Earl of Ravenshire, is a prince of commerce. Does he not resort to a war against the competition? One wielded with economic weapons instead of swords, cannons or guns?"

"You know I hate the man. I believe his neglect killed my sister."

The Member of Parliament disagreed. "Women die in childbirth, Darlemont. Your animus is misplaced."

Drummond shot his client a glance warning him to remain silent. "I share your disdain for Ravenshire, but for other reasons."

Sir Reginald changed the subject. "Darlemont, we're all looking forward to your mother's annual Masquerade Ball. Dare anyone discuss his disguise?"

Darlemont tilted his head at the diplomat. "You start, Sir Reginald."

"I am coming dressed as an Ottoman. The ambassador is lending me a scimitar for the evening."

The political master smirked. "I hope you don't cut a swath through the crowd. Remind me to keep my distance. I doubt the Duchess of Pytchley would appreciate blood staining her marble floors.

The diplomat furrowed his brow. "I never thought of that."

"I thought diplomats advised others to think before acting." He played a card and picked up another. "I plan to come as Machiavelli."

Norman laughed. "That's no disguise at all. And who can tell one 15th century Florentine from another? You could be mistaken for Lorenzo himself."

The Machiavellian shrugged. "Perhaps, but I know who I am. Who will you impersonate?"

"Henry VIII."

"You have the girth for the role." Darlemont leaned back in his chair. "My mother is partial to ancient Egypt and Rome. She is coming as Cleopatra with Father as Julius Caesar."

Sir Reginald raised an eyebrow. "Neither came to a happy ending."

"I made the same observation, to no avail. I will be coming as Augustus."

"Better than Mark Antony. That would be rather scandalous." The political schemer picked up a card, discarded, and declared victory.

CHAPTER THIRTY-FIVE

March 29, 1811 – Mr. Khan's Mansion
Edward

Edward arrived for a dinner party hosted by Khan, his university friend from India. Scheduled just before the Baxter Ball. Khan had planned the evening to make interactions at the ball more relaxed for their circle of friends. Edward meant to arrive early for a pre-dinner sherry, but was the last to join Khan, Durwood, Vaux, Banfield and Hanforth.

Khan held up his glass. "Before the festivities begin, a moment of reflection. To old friends, new loves and the future."

"Here! Here!"

"We all know Edward is enamored of Lady Gabriella, she of the tart tongue. My family's estates in India ship though Wyndward Trading. I have never met a woman like her. Not exactly deferential to men. Banfield, what about you?"

"So far, no one has swept me off my feet."

Vaux laughed. "I think we're supposed to sweep *them* off *their* feet, Banfield. I fancy Lady Melanie, but she doesn't seem to go anywhere without that unusually tall Lady Clementine."

Hanforth shrugged. "Two at once, Vaux. I didn't know you had it in you."

Durwood smirked. "There's a retort there, Hanforth, but I'll let it pass."

The blond safari aficionado ignored the comment. "My cousin,

Lady Clarissa, has been away in South Africa, so she doesn't know any of these young ladies well."

"Lady Patricia has a naughty look," offered Banfield. "Tempestuous eyes."

"I heard she was secretly seeing Lord Merrick." Hanforth looked around for confirmation.

Vaux looked perplexed. "Then what is she doing here?"

"Secretly, Vaux. That is the operative word."

"Lady Marianna talks a prim line, but her dresses are a bit too tight." Banfield tilted his head in Hanforth's direction. "I noticed her staring at you, Hanforth. Perhaps she likes your rakishly long hair."

The doorbell rang.

"No more gossip, friends. The contest begins." Khan went out to greet the new arrivals.

As the room filled with guests, Khan's wife, Lady Alice, and Durwood's wife, Lady Rose, entered from another room. Once all arrived and any introductions made, the butler led the group to the dining room and they walked around the table to find their names on place cards.

As soon as they were seated, Lord Lt. Thornton stood to offer a toast to Mr. Khan. "To our host!" The others stood and echoed his words.

The toasts went on in order, as was the custom, until the soup was served. A soupy concoction with lumps and dabs of color appeared before them. A basket of *bhatura*, a bread, was passed around. Not everyone broke off a piece. "*Kheer*, rice with milk and dried fruit is like a soup." announced Lady Alice. "Tonight we are offering you Indian cuisine. We hope you enjoy it!"

Edward glanced at Bri. Watching her take the exotic food, he detected no change in her facial expression *Does that mean she likes Indian food or that she is disguising her distaste for it?* He watched as she swallowed a morsel of bread, then dipped her spoon in and tasted the *kheer*.

Bri's eyes widened. "It's delicious. Spicy, as expected."

Edward tried the soup. Despite his years in the Far East eating mysterious mixtures of unknown ingredients, it took all of his training to not gag visibly. He swallowed and his throat felt as if it were on fire. He took some wine, but it did not quench the burning. *Can I spit it into my napkin? Probably not.* He glanced around the table.

Banfield seemed to enjoy the soup.

Hanforth, the safari-loving trekker, appeared unperturbed. *He must eat rats in the wild.*

Vaux reached for the wine, panting. "It's so hot! I wasn't expecting it to burn my throat."

"There's a trick to it," offered Bri. Tearing off a piece of *bhatura,* she demonstrated. "A bite of *bhatura,* followed by a spoonful of *kheer.* It absorbs the fire of the spices."

Lady Alice laughed. Signaling the butler, she said, "Be sure there's *bhatura* for all."

Those who had passed on the bread raised their hands to alert the server to fill their plates.

Edward berated himself silently. *Of course she's been to India. Khan is my friend and I've never eaten his native food. Am I provincial?*

Lady Rose opened the topic on everyone's minds. "What do you think of the Marriage Season and how would you change it?"

Lord Lt. Thornton was the first guest on whom her gaze settled. "For me, it is efficient. I am often away on military matters and have little opportunity for socializing."

Lady Melanie spoke next. "My brother has a tendency to see everything through a military lens. For me, as a shy person, it is helpful to have friends like you around me as I go through this. Waiting to be asked to dance or getting one's dance card filled unnerves me."

"Would it be better for a marriage to be arranged by your parents?" Vaux shrugged. "Some people are lucky to experience a *coup de foudre*—a thunderbolt, love at first sight. Other of us must wade into love. And by the way, Lady Melanie, it's just as nerve-wracking to have to ask for a dance as it is to wait."

"But a woman cannot decline a dance without shaming herself." Lady Patricia scoffed. "Come now, Vaux, you can banter with the best of them. You have to learn how to play the game, make it work for you."

Lady Clementine appeared uncomfortable. "A game for your entire future? Isn't that a bit cavalier?"

Lady Patricia leaned forward. "How else could one tolerate the rules, the protocols, the gossip?"

Lady Marianna nodded her head. "One misstep and the gossip rags will ruin your reputation."

Banfield demurred. "No one reads that trash."

The rest of them laughed.

"Everyone reads that trash." Durwood shook his head. "Test the gossip mills at your peril."

The server reappeared with *aloo gobi*, a cauliflower and potato mixture flavored with curry and turmeric. *Dal,* a pureed mixture of lentils, followed. Finally, Tandoori chicken, tinted a red hue by its spicy sauce, was served.

"More bread?" Lady Alice signaled the butler before hearing the answer.

"Yes!" all responded at once.

Edward watched Bri again. *She didn't hesitate. I am impressed. Bri is unflappable.* Catching himself, he realized he was thinking of her as "Bri." *I'd better watch myself. That is too intimate a way to refer to her.*

Bri frowned. "Some say, 'Gossip is the life's blood of the *ton,*' so we all must be mindful of our actions."

Hanforth smiled. "Perhaps I should develop a new approach to the young ladies of the *ton:* 'Leave it all. Come with me to Africa. Forget your ball gowns. Trek into the unknown.' "

Laughing, Bri agreed. "I think you have it, Lord Hanforth. A new continent, a new life."

Khan leaned back in his chair. "I left India to escape an arranged marriage. My family disowned me. I had to build my own world. Now my brother and I are in business, but it's taken many years to repair the rift within my family. You have more freedom here than you recognize."

After finishing a bite of *bhatura*, Bri could not restrain herself. "Men do. Women are still treated as accoutrements to a man's choices."

Here she goes. Should I stop her? Edward waited.

Vaux disagreed. "Men are circumscribed too. Our behaviors and choices are limited as much as yours."

The men at the table nodded in agreement, unprepared for the vehement disagreement by the women at the table.

"Untrue!" claimed Lady Clementine.

"Oversimplified!" cried Lady Melanie.

"*Men* are hardly restricted by convention, Vaux," countered Lady Patricia.

"Men's choices are not as limited as those available to us," said the more restrained Lady Marianna.

Bri took a deep breath. "I cannot ride alone in the park. I cannot sit with a man in a carriage without a chaperone. I cannot engage in commerce without being tainted as a wanton woman. I cannot travel alone. I cannot make choices for myself. Decisions are imposed upon me, albeit by well-meaning relatives. Were I to marry, all my assets would be controlled by my husband. Women are not free." She stared at Edward.

Edward lowered his head, and then looked directly back at Bri. "Perhaps, in the future, the rules of society will change. I hope so. I think men and women functioning as equals in all areas of life might make the world a better place."

"Are you just saying this to pretend to agree with me?" Bri squinted at him.

Will squinting help her discern the truth of what I say? "No. I have come to see things differently after our spirited discussions."

Sitting back in her chair, Bri crossed her arms. "Hmm."

The spell was broken as the footmen removed the dishes and the butler brought bread pudding with sliced almonds. "Don't worry. This is not spicy," said Lady Alice.

Edward didn't take his eyes off Bri. *What is happening to me? I am changing. Is she?*

***

As the dinner party guests left, Edward escorted Bri to her carriage. Jean-Louis was throwing sticks for the dog to catch.

Chérie jumped up on Edward when she saw him. He knelt down and let her lick his face.

Bri laughed and petted Chérie's head.

"You're kneeling. Are you going to propose again?"

"Again?" Jean-Louis shook his head. "You're a brave man, James."

"Why not?" Edward spread his arms wide and the dog jumped up on him again.

"Are you proposing to me or Chérie?" She reached down and took his hands. "Stand up. You're not entirely hopeless, Mr. James. I'll see you at the Baxter Ball." She leaned over and kissed him on the cheek.

"Until Saturday, Lady Gabriella."

Bri climbed into the carriage.

Jean-Louis closed the door, lifted Chérie up to the driver's bench before he climbed up himself. He picked up the reins, calling softly to the horses in French to move out.

Edward watched as the carriage vanished into the fog.

He felt a hand on his shoulder and turned around to see Vaux. "You were kneeling. Did you—"

"Not tonight."

Banfield and Hanforth walked over.

"Let's let Vaux take us to the club in his elegant carriage. A brandy to cap off the evening."

Vaux signaled for his driver to pull forward to pick them up. Once inside the carriage, Banfield sighed. "My father is pressuring me to rent or buy a townhouse to be ready for a wife. The thought of it makes my stomach churn."

"Don't say 'churn' after that meal." Edward stifled a burp.

"You acted perfectly nonchalant. Good job." Hanforth threw his head back and laughed. "The meal tasted much better than I expected. And Lady Gabriella's tip came *after* I'd taken a morsel of bread, unlike you, James."

Edward winced. "My throat may never recover."

Vaux put his hand on Banfield's shoulder. "I might have a house that would interest you. It just became vacant and I was going to redecorate it. It was rented for twenty years and needs some work."

"Did someone die there?"

"It happens." Vaux shrugged. "The rent will be fair…for an old friend."

"Set it up. I'll look. You can design it all, but I need a music room. Is there room for a pianoforte and a harpsichord?"

"Of course. Why do you think I thought of you? I have another one opening soon with a massive set up of stables in the mews. The entire block belongs to this house. I was thinking that Rogers might want it for his collection of carriages."

Edward shook his head. "A man can only drive one carriage at a time. I can see the attraction to a sporty phaeton, in addition to a larger carriage with protection from the weather, but the Hackneys work well around the city. How many does Rogers have now, after he crashed his phaeton? Six?"

"Eight." Vaux shrugged. "A man has his passions."

"Rogers has too many." Banfield scoffed. "Drink, gambling and women will be the death of him if a carriage accident isn't. He narrowly avoided a duel after Lady Elisabeth's ball."

"What? You didn't tell us, Banfield. Spill." Hanforth leaned back and took another sip of brandy.

"He was in his cups after the ball. As people were leaving, he staggered over to Lady Clementine and insulted her about her height, saying, 'No man wants to look up to a woman.' Lord Lt. Thornton, who was escorting his sister and Lady Clementine's maiden aunt, Baroness Mitchell-Jones, called him out. Only the intervention of Lord Clyr, who was passing by, ended it."

"Lord Clyr, that fat, florid, flaccid prig?"

"You're a bit too fond of alliteration, Vaux. Apparently, the diminutive Lord is well-connected and persuaded Lord Lt. Thornton, who would no doubt have prevailed, to stand down. He shepherded Rogers away." Banfield swirled the brandy in its snifter and sighed. "There may not always be someone to save Rogers from himself."

Edward nodded. "Sometimes people can have too much money. They think it gives them impunity for their actions and voids the necessity of self-control."

Hanforth put down his glass. "Time for me to turn in. I'm exhausted by social banter. Give me a wild animal to stalk any day rather than be stalked by marriage-obsessed women."

"Maybe you'll find a woman who likes to go on safari. The beautiful women who fall for your long blond locks may not take to the deprivations of life on the savannah." Vaux stood.

"Unlikely," Hanforth conceded.

"But not impossible." Edward smiled. "Stranger things have happened."

"Like you falling for Lady Gabriella?"

The others laughed at Edward's sheepish look and rose to leave.

***

Later that same night – Mlle. Sabine's Brothel
Jean-Louis

The Frenchman climbed the back stairs at one of the most exclusive brothels in London. Admission to Mlle. Sabine's was only by introduction. Politicians, ambassadors, dukes, marquesses, earls, viscounts and knights of the realm passed through her establishment. All were guaranteed complete privacy. On occasion, someone died, either as a result of overexertion for his age, or as a trick gone wrong. When that happened, Mlle. Sabine would send for Jean-Louis, who would remove the body to another location to avoid any unfortunate publicity. Once a patron strangled a girl. The Frenchman dealt with the offender in a permanent manner.

Jean-Louis and Sabine had met as young people shortly after he first arrived in London when he accompanied Henry's father, the 10th Earl of Ravenshire, to a soirée at the brothel where she worked. Henry, then a viscount, never knew about his father's visits to the brothel. The earl always arranged them privately with Jean-Louis. He told the Frenchman that he would never marry again, but that all men needed the companionship of a woman occasionally. One night he confessed to Jean-Louis that he had once taken advantage of an innocent young woman and never wanted another such lapse on his conscience. A woman who had chosen life in a brothel signaled consent. That first night, the earl had procured a companion for the Frenchman as well as himself. Sabine was the one chosen by Jean-Louis and they had become confidants.

Jean-Louis told Sabine upon their first meeting that he had a love far away to whom he would return someday. As he remembered it, she had smiled, touched his arm, and said, "I chose this profession. Someday I will have my own establishment. I do not want a conventional life."

Now, close to twenty years into their arrangement, Sabine had her own establishment in which Jean-Louis was a silent partner. Nodding to one of the guards posted on every floor, hired and trained by him, Jean-Louis knocked on Sabine's office door. She opened it, smiled, and took his hand and led him into her chambers.

***

Mlle. Sabine

Wrapped in each other's legs, Mlle. Sabine sighed.

"You were right about Bri. She and the duchess and I met." She pulled away and looked at him. "Should I be jealous of you and the duchess? She speaks of you in a possessive way."

"I remind her of a lover from her youth, nothing more. She is a remarkable woman."

"She and her granddaughter are both remarkable. Not what I expected. I can see why you have adopted this family."

CHAPTER THIRTY-SIX

March 29, 1811 – Pelican's Beak Pub
Jean-Louis

Jean-Louis pulled the carriage off the main street next to a brick building.

Henry exited into the dark alley. "What hellhole is this? It looks like a backstreet for cut-purses."

Jean-Louis gave the footman a knife. "Kill anyone who approaches."

The footman nodded.

Henry stared at him. "You hire killers as footmen?" He stared at the footman. "Smith?"

The footman shrugged.

Jean-Louis stood his ground. "Not all are killers. But all are trained to kill if necessary."

"How did I not know this?"

"You charged me with the protection of your family. I do what is necessary."

"Where do you find such men?"

"There are ways." The French former trapper swept his eyes over the earl. "You are not far off in your assessment of this area. Take off your coat. You look too rich for this place. Remove your cravat. The pub is frequented by the demimonde. Cut-purses, footpads, killers-for-hire, a motley lot of reprobates and outcasts sit within. 'Tis a place to disappear." Jean-Louis put the earl's discarded clothing into the carriage. Frowning, the Frenchman shrugged. "We'll make it work."

Entering the pub, the barkeep nodded to Jean-Louis, who walked to a table in the back corner. He tilted his head at a man at the bar. Taking their seats, the barkeep brought two ales, and Henry looked up.

"Did we order?"

"They know me."

The man from the bar came over and sat down. Looking at Henry, he observed, "You look out of your element, even without the cravat."

"It was an attempt to appear un-rich."

"Didn't work. You'll need an escort out of here." Noting the Frenchman took umbrage, he countered. "Yes, Frenchman, even you. The target is too tempting."

"Then it's good we have a Bow Street Runner to protect us."

Henry stared at the man. "Here?"

"Where else to find out what the underworld is up to?"

"This is Boyd. He investigated the death of the comte."

"You must be the man who found this trapper in the wilds of Canada."

"That would be true."

"As I mentioned in our last meeting, we have reason to believe that the comte's death was not an accident, nor that of this man's younger brother." Jean-Louis took a swig of ale. "And possibly more."

"Deaths in the past are difficult to investigate. Leads are lost, memories fade, and witnesses disappear."

The earl leaned forward. "We may have the murderer in our sights."

"Explain."

"We suspect a man who has a vendetta against my family, for a reason I do not know. A man I have trusted for twenty years, a once-considered friend, whom I now suspect of the most depraved deeds. Part of me is shamed by my thoughts, while another part of me believes that he played a role in their deaths. And my brother's wife disappeared shortly after his death. I feared a suicide, but now I wonder if she was a victim too."

Jean-Louis twirled his ale. "Perhaps someone suspected foul play and sent her away for her own protection."

"Who would—" The truth dawned on Henry. "Aelwyn lives?"

The Frenchman nodded. "At your estate in Ireland."

"The one you like to visit." The earl's face flushed with anger, but he kept his voice low. "Why did you not tell me? Gwyneth, Bri and I were devastated to lose her and Rychard at the same time."

"My instincts told me it would be safer for her. I've had men following you three daily since Rychard's death. The truth is, I've suspected Blackburn of some involvement since the beginning. I still have no proof. There's something wrong with him, but I cannot isolate it."

Henry sat back. "I need another ale."

Jean-Louis signaled the barkeep.

Boyd drank from his mug. "Blackburn was nearby when the runaway carriage was found."

Shocked, the earl was speechless.

"He said he'd seen the man run off in a certain direction. We fished him out of the river later that night, near where Blackburn indicated. As he is a respected man of commerce, we didn't question his word. I see the wheels, Frenchman. You think he eliminated the driver because he was a confederate and expendable."

"Exactly. Kill the killer to protect the procurer."

Henry glared at Jean-Louis, his delayed reaction to an earlier comment simmering to a boil. "You've had me followed ever since Rychard's death?"

"If I'm not with you, another is close."

"Tomorrow we go to Ireland."

"No. It's too dangerous. If we are correct about our suspicions, Blackburn may have people following you too."

Boyd nodded. "An ambush here is difficult enough to thwart. On a long journey, it would be nearly impossible."

"Damnation!" Henry pounded the table. "I found Aelwyn as a child, disguised as a boy, stowed away on a ship in the Mediterranean. Her parents had sold her into servitude, and she barely escaped her captors with her life. My father took her in as a ward. She is as a sister to me as much as a sister-in-law. You should have told me. Damn you, Jean-Louis."

The Frenchman shrugged. "You charged me with protection of your family. I do not apologize for my decisions."

Boyd stood to leave. "We'll talk more, Frenchman. I'll put men at your disposal."

Jean-Louis nodded. After Boyd had left, he swilled another gulp of ale. "There is another piece of the puzzle you should know."

The earl leaned forward and whispered. "Tread carefully. My patience is stretched beyond measure."

"Aelwyn was with child when Rychard died."

Henry's mouth dropped open and he leaned back in his chair.

"Ravenshire has a living male heir."

CHAPTER THIRTY-SEVEN

Saturday, March 30, 1811 – Lord Ravenshire's Townhouse
Bri

Over the previous two weeks, Bri and Edward had delved into the trading company documents. Their approaches were similarly detailed and analytical. When their conversations stayed within the bounds of their daily tasks, all went well. When their discussions strayed into Bri's plans for future investments, the tension between them intensified. They met most mornings over breakfast, before Edward went into the bank, to discuss the previous day's findings.

Edward waited for the server to remove their plates. "So far, nothing definitive. Weeks of research, and we have found no evidence of malfeasance. When the earl confronted Blackburn on one of the contracts, feigning a random check, Blackburn had a plausible explanation that in order to acquire specialized products, there was but a single source."

"Maybe we're wrong. We may have jumped to a false conclusion. Maybe someone is trying to make it look like Blackie is shady. Someone who wants to drive a wedge between my father and Blackie to harm the trading company." Bri looked off into the distance. "Wyndward Trading has carved out a niche of high-end products, luxury or rare items, rather than a large market. That is how we have avoided direct competition from the larger trading companies, which are not as agile as we, who do not give local representatives the authority to act. Our fleet is dispersed throughout the globe. We must be missing something. There is a mystery here that we must unravel."

Edward rose to his feet. "Let us move to the study and discuss this in more detail."

Bri stood and led him to the earl's study. She pulled out paper and dipped the quill in the India ink. "We should start at the beginning. Motivation. We have found no commercial competitor. That leaves us with personal motives."

"Does the earl have enemies?"

Tilting her head in thought, Bri shrugged. "None that I am aware of, but we should ask him. All trading companies are run by competitive men. Let's make a list of motives. Greed was our first thought, but we have found no evidence."

"Jealousy. But the earl gave Blackburn a great opportunity to rise in commerce."

"Perhaps the motive is jealousy of noble birth."

"Perhaps. Revenge is common, but again, the earl has been a source of advancement for Blackburn."

Bri stopped writing. "We're thinking of Blackburn only. We should view these motives in a wider context. Someone who thinks we'll believe Blackie is capable of murder."

"One minute he's Blackburn, the next Blackie. It annoys me that you refer to him in such a familiar way."

"I've known him all my life. I'm the one who started calling him Blackie because I couldn't pronounce his name."

"I don't like it."

"Ignore what I call him. Back to our analysis, all right? Basic human motives for murder are greed, jealousy, revenge—"

"To prevent truth from being known, keeping a secret."

"Most people have secrets."

"Politics and class conflict are possible, but unlikely. Blackburn has become a wealthy man, thanks to your father."

"Drunkenness or drugs are not applicable, to the best of my knowledge. Control is important to Blackie."

"Self-defense, survival, and protecting family are primal urges, but he feels no threat from us and has no family that we know of."

"We began thinking Blackie guilty of murder when I discovered the unusual contracts. Are we losing perspective? Are we trying to find reasons to fit our suspicion that Blackie killed Uncle Luc and Uncle Rychard and Aunt Aelwyn? And maybe my grandfather?"

"You may be correct. Are we permitting the conclusion to drive the analysis? Could my own jealousy of his pursuit of you cause me to think the worst of him? It's a possibility I must consider."

Bri smirked. "So you *are* jealous of him."

Edward stared at her. "You know I am."

She returned to her list. "We know little of Blackie's background. I know that he was born in Scotland and graduated from the University of Edinburgh. His mother died shortly after he was born and he never knew his father. As I recall, he was raised by his grandmother, who also died shortly before he came to work at the trading company."

"A convenient history if one wanted to hide something. If there is a secret, it's in his past."

"Jean-Louis has contacts with the Bow Street Runners."

Edward raised an eyebrow. "Jean-Louis seems to have contacts everywhere."

"He is an extraordinary and formidable man. Intrepid, Father calls him."

Edward leaned forward. "Could someone else in the trading company be using Blackburn as a shield? As the obvious beneficiary of the elimination of the Wyndwards?"

"A chilling thought. I do not intend to be eliminated."

"Nor do I intend to permit it."

Bri rang for Thompson. "Is Jean-Louis here?"

"He and the earl are talking in the stables, Lady Gabriella."

Bri pushed her chair back and stood. "Let's go join them."

Edward rose and followed her down the back stairs and through the garden to the stables. They overheard the earl and Jean-Louis talking about the horse auctions that afternoon. Chérie and Hector lay in watch nearby.

The earl's voice echoed in the high-ceilinged stables. "I agree. Do we have room for more horses?"

"More horses?" Bri walked in, followed by Edward.

The earl nodded. "More security means more horses, men and carriages."

Jean-Louis tilted his head toward the alley. "I checked down the street at the Dowager Turlington's stables. She keeps only a small carriage and two horses, with many empty stalls. After the death of her husband, she sold all but what she needed. Her stable master spoke with her and we can rent additional stalls and rooms for more men for an indefinite period."

"Is she in need of funds?"

"Apparently, from what the groom said, she's let go a lot of the staff."

Henry lowered his head and looked back at Jean-Louis. "Pay her more than the going rate. At her age, money worries should not trouble her sleep."

Bri squeezed her father's hand. *I hope I remember to think of others as he does.* Then she remembered her anger about his dalliance with the island woman. *Am I wrong to expect my father to act honorably at all times?*

Edward broached the subject. "Lady Gabriella and I were discussing motives for murder."

"A delightful breakfast conversation." Jean-Louis pulled his hat down further on his forehead. "There are as many motives as there are men." He looked at Bri. "Or women."

"Perhaps. But Mr. James and I realized we have been assuming Blackburn is the murderer without evidence. The files have produced nothing incriminating. We believe there must be a secret hidden in Blackburn's past."

The earl tilted his head. "I know little of his past, other than he came from Scotland...although I seem to remember connections to Ayr and Glasgow. I never heard that from Blackburn, but from someone else. Never mention either place to Blackburn."

Bri nodded. "We thought Jean-Louis and the Bow Street Runners might be able to find out."

The French former trapper rubbed his chin. "The Bow Street Runners will be of no use in Scotland. I have men at our Dunleigh estate in Perth. They can check the University of Edinburgh and work back from there. Not a bad idea." He looked at the earl. "Do you know Blackburn's date of birth?"

"It's in September...must have been 1771. This is the year he turns forty. Assuming he's telling me the truth about his age."

"We are no farther ahead than we were three weeks ago. We must remain on high alert."

***

Saturday, March 30, 1811 – *La Pâtisserie entre des fleurs*
Bri

Bri was relieved that she had arrived before the duchess. She wouldn't have to hear her grandmother admonish her that lateness was "unacceptable, unladylike and unjustified."

The duchess walked in and waved Bri over to select a delicacy from the glass-encased treats.

"I can't bring myself to say the name." Bri pointed to a flaky pastry.

"I'll give you a history lesson when we sit down."

"Let me guess. You will select the apple tart with *crème fraîche*."

"Predictability in some things is acceptable."

Bri and the duchess picked a table by the paned glass with a view of the flowering gardens.

"So it's not called a Napoleon?"

"It is, but that is a corruption of the name *gâteau napolitain*, after Naples. Originally, it was called *gateau de mille-feuilles*, cake of a thousand sheets."

The server brought tea and their pastries.

"So the name is Italian, not French?"

"No. Use that analytical mind of yours."

Bri nodded. "It is a French concoction, *gateau de mille-feuilles*, that was widely copied and became a favorite in Naples, where it became *gâteau napolitain*. That name has been corrupted to celebrate Napoleon in the minds of English-speakers."

"No one knows why it is called after that usurper. In Morocco, it is called 'milfa.' "

"I see. Various languages translate it to satisfy their own ears."

"As many of us hear what we want to hear."

"This is a lovely, peaceful setting."

"Not like the balls of the Marriage Season?"

Bri scoffed. "No comparison."

"I like that Mr. James. I approve."

"You don't have to approve. *I* have to approve. And my mind is not yet made up."

"It will be. How did Charlotte's Enrichment Day go?"

"The tables are increasing in number. Several women found employment, guaranteed for after their confinement."

"Charlotte is a talented administrator."

"Women should run the world."

"We do."

"We do not, Grandmother."

"The women of Lysistrata ended the Peloponnesian War."

"In case you've forgotten, that was millennia ago."

"Organized power works."

"Grandmother, you're sounding dangerously like a revolutionary."

"I won't be rioting in the streets, but money strategically placed around the *ton* can solve one problem at a time. That is all I can do."

"Like the foundling hospital?"

The duchess shrugged. "As they say, 'There but for the Grace of God go I.' We are rich by a mere accident of birth, not innate goodness."

CHAPTER THIRTY-EIGHT

Saturday, March 30, 1811 – Lord Ravenshire's Townhouse
Bri

Tonight Bri wore her hair down, which was unusual, but similar to a portrait she had seen of a 15th century Italian woman. Jane Anne arranged her curls, and set an aqua velvet ribbon around her forehead, tied in back, to complete the look.

Her dress, made of aqua linen with puffed sleeves and a low neckline, was trimmed with white lace. Her aunt would meet them at the Baxter Ball, with the count. She went downstairs to find her father in his study.

He looked up from his desk, took off his spectacles and stood. "You take my breath away, Bri. Your hair is stunning."

Bri couldn't help smiling. "At least I don't have to dance a long reel tonight. We will march around in cadence with the madrigals. Do you know what they call this ball?"

Henry shrugged.

"It's known as 'Lutes and Flutes.' The *ton* has a nickname for everything."

Her father stood, and they walked to the door.

Jean-Louis waited by the carriage, and opened the door. "Be careful what you drink tonight."

"Don't worry, I'm not going to follow Juliet's example."

As they rode in the carriage, Bri reached for her father's hand. "I think I am in love with Mr. James."

"I guessed as much."

"How can I know he loves me? Didn't you love my mother? When did it change?"

"We cared about each other, our families wanted us to marry, and we never thought about anyone else. It was expected. I wanted to test out my ideas first for the trading company and build something of my own. Selfish, people say. But you must follow your own path. Once I was established, after about three years, we married. You know the rest: we had a stillborn son, unnamed, within a year of our wedding. And then Nathaniel died after a short illness before he reached the age of two. We were both devastated, unable to communicate. I sailed away, ran away, in a sense, to Asia, got shipwrecked and—

"I've heard this all before."

Her father sighed. "When I got home, Jane had been under the care of a nurse for months, thinking me dead. Seeing me made her think she was imagining my presence. It took a lot of time to get her back to herself, but then the next couple of years were good. I took her with me on travels, and she seemed happy. When she was with child again, we felt she had healed and things would be as they should have been. Our hopes were so high." He looked down. "But then the delivery was fraught with problems. The elder Dr. Northcliffe struggled to keep your mother with us, but the birth was difficult and she died nearly at the moment you were born. Joy and grief ran through my heart at the same time."

"Maybe marriage is not for me." Bri sighed. "And what about Charlotte? You've been with her longer than you were married to my mother."

"She's very hurt. And I'm confused about Taita. I may be standing alone at the end."

"Your romantic life is not an encouraging example to emulate. Is anyone out there happy?"

"Marriage for you will be different. Your mother was a product of her time and yielded to others' expectations of her. I see that now, through you. You are strong. You will not succumb to pressure from without. You and Mr. James have a chance for something few achieve—a marriage of equals. I think he knows that too."

"He's asked me to marry him." Noticing her father's surprise, she added, "Don't be offended. He will ask your permission."

"What did you say?"

"I said I wanted to hear him say he loved me. He said that was pointless, and here we are at an impasse."

Her father frowned.

"Why the frown?"

"Charlotte demanded the same declaration, even before I knew of Taita's survival. Perhaps I should have complied and ignored Taita's visit. But I cannot."

"Men are so stubborn."

Henry laughed. "Young James would say the same of you."

***

Saturday, March 30, 1811 – The Baxter Ball
Edward

According to the invitation from Lady Maryann, the Baxter Ball, hosted at her mansion at Beekman Place, had a theme— *A Celebration of Romeo and Juliet.* It was conceived as a tribute to the upcoming season of the Shakespeare Festival as well as the Marriage Season.

Ancient madrigals echoed through the mansion, played on string and wind instruments by a small group of musicians. While it was not a costume ball for the guests, all the servants wore period garb, the servers wearing puffed doublets. No women servers were permitted, as they were not considered sufficiently "serious" to attend formal events.

When Bri appeared at the door, Edward's mouth dropped open. When she was sixteen, she'd worn her hair down, but it had been frizzy and wild. Tonight, soft auburn waves and curls framed her face, falling below her shoulders. *There is no contest. Lady Gabriella Wyndward is the most beautiful woman at the Baxter Ball.*

***

Henry

The earl kissed the gloved hand of Lady Maryann. She had been like a second mother to Henry when he arrived in London after leaving Merton College, Oxford.

Still youthful in her seventies, Lady Maryann had continued the long tradition of the Baxter Ball after the death of her husband, Sir John, a retired Lord Justice of Appeal. "You look elegant as ever, my dear Lady Maryann. The *Romeo and Juliet* theme is in keeping with the Marriage Season."

"It adds a bit of merriment to a process fraught with social jeopardy. Bri looks especially lovely tonight. She and the young Mr. James make an attractive couple. And there are rumors about you in the gossip rags, Henry." She brushed his arm with her fan in a playful manner. "Shame on you. I thought Charlotte would be heartbroken, but she seems to have found a new escort. One not to your liking, I'm sure."

"You would be correct. My life is at a crossroads. And events seem out of my control."

"Events are always out of our control, Henry. It's just that you've convinced yourself that you can will the outcome. You can't."

Henry bowed his head and smiled. "Beauty and wisdom."

"Wisdom is wasted on the willful. Don't frown. Dance!" Lady Maryann swept away to make an announcement, now that all the guests had arrived.

The madrigal singers stopped to allow the hostess to speak. "Good evening and welcome. As you may have noticed, there are no dance cards tonight. The numbers you were given on the cards as you arrived will be called by the dance master in random order. Women are even, men are odd." To twitters of laughter, she continued, "Circles of ten dancers each will be assembled."

An unusual feature of the Baxter Ball included chaperones and young people dancing together in the same circles. It was more of a soirée of the cognoscenti than a typical ball of eligible marriage prospects.

***

Edward

The musicians played a lilting tune, which made it easier to follow the steps. A dance master called out the movements—turn left, turn right, bow, twirl, stroll, or parade.

After the first few dances, Edward sought out Bri during a break in the musical interlude.

Anger rose in him when he glimpsed her talking with Blackburn, arm in arm, walking toward him. In fact, they almost bumped into him.

"Blackburn."

"James."

"You should watch where you stand."

"You should watch where you are going."

Bri took Edward's arm as well as Blackie's. "Let's all go get some punch."

"Just like old friends." The frost in Edward's tone was unmistakable.

Henry was standing near the punch, speaking with Gwyneth, Gio and the count. Bri approached them and introduced the count to Blackburn. Turning to her aunt, Bri asked, "I saw you in another circle. Did you like the steps?"

"It was more demanding than I expected, but I enjoyed it. The count followed the calls better than I and led me in the right movements."

"An early life in the military preceded my diplomatic work. I march on cue."

Blackburn looked around and appeared stunned by what he saw.

Henry noticed and followed his associate's gaze. Charlotte and The Nemesis were sipping Champagne.

"I thought the gossip rags made up their headlines. It's true?"

Henry nodded.

"And the island woman?"

Again, Henry nodded.

Blackburn remained silent.

"I have reaped what I have sown. Let that be a lesson to you all." Henry walked over to Charlotte and Drummond.

Gio shrugged. "Walking into fire...that's the earl we know and love."

***

Charlotte

"Henry, Bri looks beautiful tonight. I love her hair like that."

The earl looked toward his daughter. "She is amazing. She misses you."

"I'll go say hello later."

Henry was curt with The Nemesis, barely acknowledging his presence. "Drummond."

"Ravenshire. You know Nigel Norman, Member of Parliament, I presume?"

"Of course, Mr. Norman. Is Mrs. Norman here?"

"Yes, somewhat indisposed at the moment. How women relieve themselves in those dresses is beyond me. Our son is here somewhere."

Drummond grimaced. "I choose not to think about women relieving themselves, Norman. Kindly refrain from such a topic."

Norman shrugged. "Forgive me, O Master."

Henry smirked, nodded adieu to Charlotte, and left.

Norman walked away to find his wife.

Drummond lowered his voice. "Do you miss him? Am I but a pawn in your chess game?"

"Does it matter to you? You're annoying a man you despise. We're using each other to our own ends. Don't pretend you care about me. We both know better."

The political manipulator laughed. "Charlotte, my dear, if only women could enter politics. You would be a natural. If you were a man, I could make you prime minister."

"We've had queens, why not women prime ministers?"

"We cannot control accidents of birth that make queens. I can, however, control an election. The right seed planted in a susceptible mind yields fruit—and all minds are susceptible to persuasion—one simply has to understand their particular prejudices and play to them. A newspaper article passed along, rumors spreading through the *ton*, sensational accusations in the gossip rags. It's not difficult to mold public opinion."

"So you could make me prime minster?"

"Sadly, not yet. The world would not accept a woman prime minister. While women are not prohibited from voting, most men would never vote for a woman for such a post." He paused, "Not directly."

"What do you mean?"

"Simply musing, my dear. Suppose a woman were elected to a

lesser position in parliament, by some misguided local electorate, and all the other male leadership positions became vacant due to death or plague or war. Then, I could make *that* woman prime minister."

"Tottie, you are a dangerous man. I get the sense you might cause one or more of those disasters to reach your goal."

Drummond shrugged. "I am no more a dangerous man than you are a dangerous woman, Charlotte. As we speak, you know you are twisting a dagger in a man's heart."

"You have no heart."

"Of course not. I was speaking of the earl. Not that I care. The man is an affront to the *ton*. He was even more arrogant as a viscount than he is today."

"So he's matured in your eyes?"

"Perhaps he learned to control his baser instincts, to hide them from the *ton*."

"In other words, he's like you."

Drummond betrayed no hint of a smile. "No one is like me."

***

Gwyneth

A slightly florid middle-aged man with a paunch approached Gwyneth and the count.

"Sir Reggie, how nice to see you tonight. May I introduce—"

"Not necessary, Lady Gwyneth. The count and I were both posted to Sweden in the old days, before Napoleon took over most of Europe."

The count clicked his heels. "Sir Reggie."

"Ah, I'd forgotten the old heel-clicking greeting. It's good to see you again."

"How are things in the Foreign Office?"

"War puts a bit of a damper on diplomacy."

***

Bri

As the choice of partners depended on the circle the caller assigned people to, there was a carefree air about the Baxter Ball. Every eligible young person had been previously introduced, so there was no violation of the protocol of introductions. Bri relaxed and accepted what partner appeared.

The careful steps were more of a courtly march than a dance, until the occasional twirl was called. It wasn't until the end of the evening that she and Edward were in the same circle. He bowed and they joined hands with the other circle participants and followed the calls.

Bri let herself imagine life with Mr. James. *Perhaps I was wrong to avoid the Season for so long. But he is here now, so the time is right. Does Fate really control us? Or are we Fate? Is there an ethereal realm where different futures exist? Can we draw on our deepest desires and make them real? Did I always know I loved Mr. James, even as a child?"* Something about the regimented cadence of the madrigals soothed her mind.

As the dance ended, Edward took her gloved hand in his and kissed it. "This is a lovely moment, Lady Gabriella. I enjoyed the dance."

"Do you think Fate directs us, Mr. James?"

Edward pulled back and stared at her. "Where did that come from?"

"I was just thinking as we were dancing. I've never been a believer in Fate, but lately I'm wondering if Free Will is an illusion."

"I will not surrender to a pre-determined outcome. Our thoughts and actions must determine our futures or we are nothing. Our minds are a creative force."

"Hmm."

"Hmm? That is all you have to say?"

Bri shrugged. "What else can I say when you surprise me by sounding coherent?"

As the ball ended, Bri bowed to Edward, and went to join her father and bid Lady Maryann goodnight.

***

Sunday, March 31, 1811 – Pytchley Palace
The Duchess of Pytchley

Pytchley Palace was so massive that Bri once wandered for hours as a child to look at the endless rooms. Finally, the butler found her. She didn't think she was lost, just absorbed in the scope of the palace. The public décor evoked the grandeur of a museum, but the private rooms were comfortable and welcoming. The duchess enjoyed surprising people.

Hearing her granddaughter arrive, the duchess called out to her. "Bri, darling, come into the *Petite Bibliotheque*."

The small library, decorated with pale yellow walls and blue-and-white prints punctuated with fresh-cut white, yellow and blue flowers on mahogany tables, felt feminine and welcoming.

"Tell me all about the Baxter Ball. How is the eminently eligible Mr. James?"

"He surprised me by saying something I agreed with."

Their conversation was interrupted as the server brought tea. After it was poured, the duchess took a sip.

"Do you and Mr. James argue often?"

"Not often…well, we have spirited discussions. To be fair, he is persuadable."

"That's a point in his favor. Was Charlotte really escorted again by that despicable Drummond?"

"Yes. He has an air of deception and smugness about him."

"She is angry with Henry, but that man—" The duchess looked off in the distance. "That man has no honor. Someday, perhaps, I can tell you why I despise him." She waved her hand as if to dismiss the thought from her mind. "Charlotte can find a good match if Henry really wants to be with this mysterious island woman. But long-lost loves are generally best left lost."

"Why?"

"You are young, my dear. Life is more complex than you can understand at this point. You see life in black and white when it is shades of gray. People change over time. Memories fade. Reality trumps fantasy."

"I can't accept that Father loved that island woman when he was still married, and that he's abandoned Charlotte. Everything I thought I knew has been turned upside down."

"Didn't I just say that? Your mother had a delicate psyche, Bri. She didn't handle uncertainty well. I didn't realize how much she suffered. That is a burden I shall always carry. Henry thought he was stranded and he made the best of it. Life is for the living."

"But how can I ever trust a man when the man closest to me abandoned my mother and Charlotte?"

"Henry didn't abandon your mother. She knew she married an

adventurer. The young are foolhardy, but Henry survived. As for Charlotte, better for them both to be apart, reflect and confront the past. Do not burden Mr. James with the sins of your father." The Duchess leaned forward. "How does he accept your new role as Henry's man-of-affairs?"

"Grudgingly, I'd say. But he's coming around. Did Father tell you?"

"No. But don't worry. I approve. Still, you must strive to keep it secret. The *ton* is very provincial in its ways. Women control most of life behind the scenes. Someday we will be on equal footing with men."

"I never knew you felt that way."

"I had to wait until you were old enough to hear it. It's good that Mr. James accepts your role. He's passed an important test." She took another sip. "Have you tried the device yet?"

Bri blushed. "Not yet, but I've sent word to the suppliers and placed the order."

"There are ways to prevent being with child until you are ready. You need to be prepared. Don't look so shocked. I was young once. This whole marriage Season is run by women for women."

"What? This flesh market?"

"Bri, you have an indulgent father. Women know that money shields a woman from scrutiny. Many lead separate lives from their husbands. The right marriage can provide money, freedom and power. Nothing is as it appears on the surface."

***

Sunday, March 31, 1811 – Inverness, Scotland
Mirela

Lying in bed, Mirela fumed over a grocer who had ignored her earlier in the day. "No one notices Gypsies. They don't know we should being called Roma. We are being same to *gadjos*, the non-Roma. We are the travelers, nomads. We belonging to nowhere and to everywhere."

Catherine sighed. "Why are you telling me this now?"

"My men never returning three years ago and two years ago. It is because they being dead. My cards telling me dead. But the killer or killers hidden. It is true that they living dangerous lives. One cannot say how they died, only knowing they being dead. Now you ask me for more."

"They are dead because I ordered them dead. The dead are silent. I need more of your men to watch over Duff. You always say the cards do not lie, and the cards say Duff is in danger."

"True, but he always being in danger. Half the time you saying he weak, liking money over duty."

"You must help me. Fate extracts its price."

Mirela rolled over and surrendered. "Duff will having two men of my choosing."

CHAPTER THIRTY-NINE

Monday, April 1, 1811 – Lord Ravenshire's Townhouse
Bri

Bri focused on the investment plans for the businesses she planned to discuss with Edward the next day. Spotty was spunky, and wanted to play despite his splint, so she took him down to the garden for Nashmir to examine.

Nashmir squeezed areas of Spotty's leg, and the dog did not squeal in pain. "I don't want to take off the splint, because that is Dr. St. Cloud's decision, but I think you could take him in to get the doctor's opinion today."

"Have you noticed any problems between Spotty and Hector or Chérie?"

The Tibetan laughed. "They think Spotty is their baby with strange spots."

***

Tuesday, April 2, 1811 – Lord Ravenshire's Townhouse
Jean-Louis

When Bri walked into the foyer after her ride with her Uncle Oliver, she was unprepared for what awaited her.

Thompson announced a visitor. "Lady Gabriella, Mr. Blackburn has been waiting to see you."

Jean-Louis was in the hallway, having entered through the kitchen from the stables. He stationed himself outside the door where he could hear the conversation and peer in without being seen.

Blackburn held a bouquet of red roses, perhaps two dozen. He rose to offer them to Bri.

"It's early, Blackie. The roses are lovely. I did not know you planned to call on me."

Bri looked toward Thompson. "Please put these in a vase." She held out the roses for the butler.

"Would you like to join me for breakfast? I never eat before I ride."

"Yes, Lady G."

When Thompson returned with the roses, she asked him to set another place for breakfast. "Mr. Blackburn will be joining us." She turned to Blackburn. "I am expecting Mr. James this morning."

Blackburn narrowed his eyes.

"Don't act miffed. As our banker, Mr. James is familiarizing himself with the financial needs and operations of Ravenshire, which I run while Father travels. I was not expecting to see you until the Masquerade Ball next week. I hope we can dance together again."

That's it, Bri. Keep him on the hook until we can find out his motives. Jean-Louis was a man of patience as he listened for any hint of deception.

"Will not the eligible Mr. James be claiming you as a dance partner, also?"

"There are many lines on a dance card, Blackie. As I told you at Lady Elisabeth's ball, I am not ready to commit myself to any man. I believe that one should enter into courtship slowly. These balls and ways of the Marriage Season are unfamiliar to me."

Thompson appeared with plates of eggs, bacon and fresh baguettes. He poured the tea and exited unobtrusively.

"You are, of course, younger than I. Is there a chance for me in your heart?"

"Blackie, I've known you forever, as a family friend. I never thought of you as a suitor, and it's a bit unnerving. When I was a child, you taught me to play backgammon."

"And you beat me."

"You let me win."

"And now I find myself in love with you. Is that concept offensive?"

"Not at all, just unexpected."

"But you are not dismissing me?" Blackie bit into a piece of toast.

"No. I just need time. Please be patient."

"Are you in love with Edward James?" Looking at the empty place, he raised an eyebrow. "Is Mr. James always late?"

Jean-Louis observed a magenta blush appear on her cheeks. *Stay calm, Bri.*

"Mr. James is a business associate of my father, as are you. In fact, I find him rather arrogant at times. Yes, he is late. You, however, always conduct yourself as a gentleman."

"I am gratified to hear that, Lady G. May I escort you to the Masquerade Ball?"

"Blackie, you are persistent! I will accompany my father and Aunt Gwyneth, as is customary. Were you and I to attend the ball together would suggest that we are engaged, and as I have been trying to explain, I am not ready yet for such a commitment. Nonetheless, it is kind of you to offer to escort me. I do hope you will save a dance for me." The doorbell rang.

Within moments, Edward walked in, assessed the situation, and took a seat. "Early delivery for the earl, Mr. Blackburn?"

Bri brushed a tendril from her face. "No, Father is out riding with Hector. Blackie brought me these roses. Aren't they lovely?"

"All of these? A bit excessive, don't you think?"

Bri's face turned a deeper shade of pink. "No, *I* do not think so, Mr. James. Blackie knows that I love flowers. You've *never* brought me flowers."

Jean-Louis suppressed a laugh, catching Thompson's wary eye.

"An oversight that will be corrected." He stared at Blackburn. "Anything new at the trading company?"

"Feel free to set up a time to discuss business with me at the trading company, Mr. James, not at breakfast at the earl's home." Blackburn pushed his chair back. "Perhaps we can enjoy a more leisurely breakfast together another day, Lady G. I must attend to my responsibilities." He stood. "Good day to you, Mr. James."

Edward stood. "Good day to you, Mr. Blackburn. "

As the door closed behind him, Bri visibly relaxed her shoulders. "What a nightmare to come home to find him here."

The Frenchman walked into the dining room and sat down. "Blackburn is a very determined man." Jean-Louis rubbed his chin.

"We must all be on guard."

"Were you listening in the hallway?"

"Of course he was, Mr. James. Jean-Louis is everywhere. You may be interested to learn that, in addition to bringing me the two dozen red roses, Blackburn declared his love for me and wanted to escort me to the Masquerade Ball."

His lips forming a thin line, Edward bored in on Bri. "Exactly what did he say?"

"Only that he adored me and wanted to escort me to the Masquerade Ball. Of course, my grandmother would never permit that even if I wanted him to. I declined, saying it was not proper, but I promised to dance with him once. He seemed quite concerned about your interest in me, but I assured him that I found you arrogant. I don't think he completely believed me."

"Bri, stop acting coy."

"Father, I didn't hear you come up the steps."

"Let's go into my study while we discuss what we have learned. Jean-Louis, I want you to join us." Henry strode toward his study.

Bri signaled to Thompson. "Bring some toast and sausage for Mr. James."

When seated, Edward glanced at Jean-Louis. "Should we increase security? We suspect that Blackburn is a killer, but no proof. That doesn't mean we should ignore taking precautions. We might all be in danger if he becomes aware of our surveillance of him."

Jean-Louis shrugged. "Precautions have been taken."

"I haven't seen any unusual measures or people around."

"That is the point of security, Mr. James. It should be ever-present and invisible."

Henry slammed his hand on the desk. "We know little more than we did three weeks ago."

"Patience," cautioned Jean-Louis. "Let your prey think he is safe."

Bri stood. "I need to get out of my riding clothes before we talk, Mr. James. I'll be back down in about half an hour." Bri left the room.

***

Henry looked at Jean-Louis. "I'd like you and Dr. Northcliffe to go to Ravenshire and look around the area where Rychard died. Maybe you'll see something that others missed."

Edward leaned forward. "It's been almost four years. What could remain?"

The Frenchman shrugged. "Maybe nothing, maybe something. Dr. Northcliffe expressed concerns about Blackburn's behavior on the day Rychard died. We'll take a look, and Boyd is checking into any other activity around that time."

"On your way to the bank later, Young James, stop by the trading offices so that Jean-Louis can show you the birds in the dovecote. Our trade secret...a forgotten method of communication." Henry stood. "Let's tend to our tasks."

***

Wyndward Trading Dovecote
Edward

By pre-arrangement, Edward's carriage dropped him off at the back of the huge building that housed Wyndward Trading near the docks. The area was roped off with signs that read, *Under Construction: Danger!* Following the Frenchman's instructions, Edward found the door unlocked and climbed the four stories to the dovecote, a tower at the back of the building.

Stopping to catch his breath, the banker saw Jean-Louis talking to the birds. Three others, an old man, a middle-aged man and a boy were absorbed in caring for the flock.

A writing desk stood in the center, and each cage was marked with the caged birds' origin. "Is this how the earl's message to me about my father's illness was delivered?"

Jean-Louis nodded. "We have birds from all parts of the world. They are an integral part of our operations. Wherever they are born and raised until a certain age, they return. We can cover most of the world. When the trading company establishes a new outpost, we secure more birds as cargo for the return trip. We take them with us to breed in the new area. Only the top directors know of this project. It provides a competitive advantage."

"Lady Gabriella said that you learned this in the French army."

"Yes. For a time, I was assigned to the general in charge of communications. Homing pigeons have been used since the time of the Roman army. People forget. The French didn't. I didn't."

Jean-Louis explained the details and then they left. When they reached the ground floor, Edward asked about the men tending the birds. "You trust them?"

"Three generations are represented in that family. They are sworn to protect the birds."

"Blackburn knows?"

"Of course. He is the highest ranking man in the earl's operations. He's smart. And—perhaps—deadly."

CHAPTER FORTY

Wednesday, April 3, 1811 – Ravenshire and its Environs
Jean-Louis

After riding for five hours, Jean-Louis and Dr. Northcliffe reached Ravenshire after midnight. They were admitted by Young Thompson, the under-butler who was in charge when his father, Thompson, was in London with the earl.

Though it was late, the cook provided soup, bread, and meat. They arose at dawn, ate a quick breakfast and packed sandwiches for their return. Jean-Louis collected shovels from the stables and they set out to search the area where Blackburn and Dr. Northcliffe had found Rychard's body three years earlier.

As they rode to the stream that cut through the estate, the doctor pointed out that the direction of the tracks he had seen that rainy day was the same as the route they were taking.

He suggested that there might be a rock or hidden area where Blackburn could have waited until the opportunity to chase Rychard had presented itself. They scoured the terrain for clues as they rode for about two hours to the area by the stream where Richard's body had been found. Along the way they spotted several areas where one could wait in ambush, and agreed to check them for clues on the way back.

The clearing was about fifty feet by thirty feet, and they painstakingly used their shovels to dig through the first six inches of soil, carefully sorting through the debris for any link to Blackburn.

After several hours, they had found nothing of consequence, and stopped to eat some bread. A dog ran by them and began digging by one of the trees. A boy of about eight or nine came running into the clearing, calling to the dog to stop digging. When he saw the men, he looked frightened, and began to run away. Jean-Louis caught him, and said, "Don't be frightened. We will not hurt you."

"I will not give it back! I will not! I will not!" he cried.

"Give what back, boy? Has your dog discovered something in his digging? Whatever it is, we will pay you handsomely for it if it is what we seek," said Viscount Northcliffe.

"Well, it was filled with mud and I couldn't find the other one. It's a real leather bootie, maybe ancient." the boy confessed. "I tried to clean it, but I think the water made it worse. If it is wrecked, will you pay me anyway?"

"Let me see it."

Reaching into his pocket, the boy produced a leather bootie, sized to fit a large foot, with ties to fasten it. Northcliffe looked perplexed.

Jean-Louis looked off into the distance, as if trying to remember something from long ago. "When I was serving in the French army on a campaign in southern Spain, I saw booties like this on Gypsy men. The Spaniards said that the lack of soles made it easier for them to creep up behind unsuspecting targets. Gypsies, or Roma, were disdained. A fear born of unfamiliarity and old wives' tales, no doubt. The foreign often frightens the ignorant. But what would a Gypsy be doing near Ravenshire? And how can we be sure his presence would be related to Rychard's death? It proves nothing."

The boy opened his fist. A coin lay exposed, caked with mud.

Jean-Louis walked over to the stream and washed it off. It had the head of a king on one side and a pig with babies on the other. "This is a Gypsy coin, a brass coin sold to naïve seekers." *It has no value, but shows the Gypsy connection. What can it mean?*

Producing a gold coin from his pocket, the doctor asked, "Will this be adequate payment?"

"Is it real gold?" The boy's eyes were wide and unbelieving.

"Yes. 'Tis a one pound gold piece."

"One pound! I am rich! I am rich! Thank you, sir!" He ran off, his barking dog close at his heels.

The doctor laughed at the boy's exuberance. "At least someone is happy." He sighed and glanced at Jean-Louis. "We have found nothing of consequence."

"Unless there's a Gypsy connection elsewhere."

They mounted their horses and rode back toward the main road. Having spent the better part of the day searching, they returned to London in the late hours of the evening.

***

Thursday, April 4, 1811 – Lord Ravenshire's Townhouse
Henry

After they reached the earl's townhouse, Jean-Louis and Dr. Northcliffe arrived at the earl's townhouse, they left the stables, walked through the garden and up the back stairs. The earl was having dinner with Bri and Edward. Henry heard the footsteps and turned to see the two men. He told Thompson to set two more places. "You must be hungry."

They sat. The server poured two glasses of wine and refilled the others.

The earl leaned forward. "Did you find anything?"

Dr. Northcliffe shook his head. "Only a Gypsy bootie and a Gypsy coin. Nothing to implicate Blackburn."

Edward straightened up in his chair. "Hold on. The stable owner who leased the carriage and horses to the man who drove the runaway rig that killed the Comte de Merbeau told me that a Gypsy leased the carriage. And that the body of a dead Gypsy was pulled from the river the next day. How would Blackburn and Gypsies be connected?"

Henry cocked his head. "Something from my travels with Blackie comes to mind. We saw a Gypsy caravan camped around the outskirts of London one day on a trip to Wales. He made a comment that he didn't trust Gypsies. I asked how he knew of them. He just muttered, 'Damn fortune tellers, using tarot cards and crystal balls to fleece the unwary.' I remember that comment because I visited a Gypsy fortune teller a few times at Oxford." He directed his gaze at Edward. "With your father..."

Edward appeared stunned. "What? Father went to a fortune teller?"

"We all did. Parker, Beauchamp, AJ, Sir John...and Darlemont. Vincent, not Oliver. We went every spring when the Gypsy caravan came, but the last time, just before graduation, the Gypsy showed Darlemont the death card. The warning faded, but in one year's time, he was dead."

Bri nodded. "A bad heart. I've heard the story."

Her father looked down and Edward averted his eyes.

"You two act as if you are hiding something. What is it?"

The earl frowned. "I will tell you, but you must promise never to mention the truth to anyone, especially the duchess. "

"I promise." Bri leaned forward. "Tell me."

"Vincent was killed in a duel over a woman. I was his second—

"Father? You condoned such barbarity? You might have been killed too!"

"No, seconds make the arrangements. They don't step in to finish the job. I tried to stop the duel, but the other party refused to back down. Vincent faltered at the last moment and delayed his shot. The other did not."

"The killer should have been prosecuted."

"No, Bri. I just told you that we took great pains to hide the truth. There could be no prosecution without tarnishing Vincent's name and, by extension, the name of his father, the Duke of Pytchley."

Edward sat back. "Did the woman in question marry the shooter?"

"No. She married a Frenchman and lives in Paris. The shooter blames me to this day."

"Why?"

"Because I told her the truth about Vincent's hesitation. Both men pursued her, it's true, but it was Vincent she truly loved. The shooter hated Vincent for his title as much as for the earl's captivation of the young woman's heart. He hates me for knowing a secret that could bring him down."

"Do we know him?" Edward's face betrayed no emotion.

"He holds a position of considerable political influence."

"But Father, could his hatred of you extend to killing other members of our family? He has killed once. We know of no murders that Blackie has committed."

Jean-Louis, who had observed without speaking, weighed in. "All men can kill. Revenge propels men to do the unexpected. This dueler knows that gentlemen will keep his secrets. But my guess is that he would strive to accumulate his own store of secrets to use against all that know of his past. It is not inconceivable that he might want to eliminate you—if not by bullet, sword or knife, then by innuendo. Challenge by legal or political means also may loom. Whoever he is, he is a threat."

"I agree." Edward's tone was firm.

Bri's anger flared. "Do I hear you correctly? Are you suggesting we eliminate the dueler because his mere existence threatens you?"

Henry scoffed. "No. Of course not. It simply means we must be diligent."

"Who is it?"

"You do not need to know."

"Respectfully, Lord Ravenshire, if Bri is in danger, she should know who might present a risk."

Henry looked at Jean-Louis and then back to Edward. "Drummond."

Bri's eyes widened. "The man with Charlotte at Lady Elisabeth's and the Baxter Ball? Could she be in danger?"

"I don't think so. Drummond is nothing if not careful. To me, his actions were technically murder, but motivated by passion. Murder as tool of statecraft seems unlikely."

"Why? Power is a passion." Bri leaned forward. "Jean-Louis, you need to assign one of your men to protect Charlotte too. And follow that man. He could be the killer, not Blackie."

The earl nodded. "Very well."

Jean-Louis tapped his finger on the table. "It will be done. Now, back to the Gypsies." Jean-Louis looked up at the ceiling. "I have investigators looking into Blackburn's past in Scotland. Maybe there is a Gypsy connection. He could have used them as cut-outs."

"What's a cut-out?" Bri sat back and tilted her head.

"A person you hire to kill who cannot be traced back to you." Jean-Louis drained his wine glass. "An expendable body. Like the one found conveniently drowned the day after the comte was run over. Boyd is looking into any Gypsy bodies found in the days after Rychard's death. One is a coincidence. Two suggests a connection."

Edward nodded. "But we still have no proof. Only suspicion."

***

Friday, April 5, 1811 – Winters Foundling Hospital
Charlotte

Charlotte looked over the due dates of the women in confinement and compared them to the lists of couples who wanted to adopt. A thought stopped her in mid-task. *Should I adopt a child? If Henry and I never reconcile, would it be fair to a child to have only one parent?*

A knock on the partially open door interrupted her. She looked up. "Bri! Come in." she rose to embrace the girl to whom she'd acted as a mother and a friend.

"I don't want us to grow apart, no matter what happens between you and Father. And I believe in your work. I actually have a product that might be helpful to you, and I'd like you to meet with Dr. Northcliffe, who is thinking of opening a clinic to cater to the poor. He could use your expertise."

"Dr. Northcliffe?"

"He is the son of the doctor from Ravenshire. He recently returned from medical missionary work in the Cape Colony, where his wife succumbed to a tropical disease, leaving him with three children."

"How sad for them."

"I was lucky to have you and Aunt Gwyneth and Aunt Aelwyn. I hope we can help these girls feel safe."

"And the product?"

"Something to prevent becoming with child. It is inexpensive, easy to use, and can be washed and used over and over again."

"What? I've never heard of such a thing."

"It's a sea sponge soaked in vinegar. It's been used for millennia."

Charlotte leaned forward. "That would be wonderful for these women. Some have been raped or forced into relations with violent husbands. Other simply want to feel loved after a life of loneliness and pay a heavy price."

"Until recently, I hadn't thought of such things. It can be inserted before and left in afterwards, so if a woman does not want her partner to know she is using it, she has that option."

"This is a real step forward. I'm excited. There will always be unwanted children, but this can prevent an unwanted child from a life of pain. You are such a clever girl, Bri. A woman now. Have you used it yourself?"

Bri shook her head.

Charlotte smiled. "But you want to."

"Yes. Charlotte, how did you prevent—"

"Becoming with child? I can't bear children, according to doctors. Like many of these women, I was beaten by a stepfather and permanently injured."

"I'm so sorry."

"Don't be. I can help so many more children here than I could in one family."

"You are the only mother I've ever known, and—" Bri choked up. "I'll love you forever. Nothing can come between us."

***

Saturday, April 6, 1811 – An Abandoned Building in London
Dr. Northcliffe

"Lord Vaux, this building is crumbling before me. I need a safe structure for a hospital. Surely you understand that."

"Of course, Dr. Northcliffe. I've had an architect who specializes in structural integrity walk through this building and consult the original drawings on file with the city. It is sound. The façade is crumbling, but that can be repaired or replaced."

Bri had made the introduction and accompanied the two men to look at the possible location. "Is it safe to enter now to look around?"

"Yes, but we need to be mindful of debris."

After touring the building, the doctor became converted to Bri's vision. "This could work. This could work perfectly for the clinic I envision."

***

Tuesday, April 6, 1811 – The Firth Mansion
Bri

Bri and Lady Penelope put the finishing touches on the table for the dinner to follow the trousseau party for Clarissa. Ribbons, flowers, place cards and more were arranged.

Lady Penelope stood back and put her arm around Bri. "I love the colors! The yellow and royal blue are clever. It makes the mood happy, serene. Dr. St. Cloud is so charming. I went to his shop and adopted two small kittens. Father makes me keep them in my room, but they love to explore. Eventually they come back to my room and sink into the featherbed."

"And the baron? Are you still enamored with him?"

"Completely."

"Father ran into him at Tattersalls buying horses. Do you ride?"

"Not in London. I like to ride in the country."

"Why don't we ride in the park together? I could mention it to Father and he could invite the baron to ride with him and we would just 'accidentally' run into him. Then you would have chaperones and a chance to see each other in a different environment. We could go to *Chez Michel* for lunch."

"Could you?"

"Of course." Bri wrinkled her brow. "And if we do it before the next ball, maybe he would kiss you afterward, as he would feel more comfortable. He told Father he is quite taken with you."

Bri noticed that Lady Penelope appeared troubled. "What is wrong?"

"Nothing is wrong, but I've been wondering why a man of his age never married."

"I'll ask Father. They were at Merton College, Oxford, together. Maybe someone broke his heart and it took him a long time to get over it." *I hope she never hears the servants' gossip.*

The doorbell rang.

The butler showed Lady Patricia in with a large wrapped package. Lady Marianna and Lady Melanie arrived together.

Clarissa was late. Only Bri knew that the bride-to-be was rehearsing for *The Princess,* due to open in less than a week.

Keeping the conversation focused on light topics, Lady Penelope entertained the group until the doorbell rang.

The butler escorted Clarissa into the parlor.

"Please forgive me. I was unavoidably delayed."

Lady Patricia frowned. "You're wearing an inordinate amount of rouge, Lady Clarissa."

Bri pulled a handkerchief out of her pocket. "Perhaps you put it on in the carriage and your hand slipped."

Clarissa rubbed the rouge off her cheeks. "It's been a long day."

"Have a glass of sherry." Lady Penelope took Clarissa's arm and sat her down in front of a pile of gifts.

Bri held up her glass. "To the bride!"

The others echoed her words. "To the bride!"

Lady Melanie smiled. "Come on, open something."

Clarissa reached for a gift wrapped in pink paper and tied with a white ribbon. "I almost don't want to unwrap anything. They're all so pretty." She untied the ribbon and unwrapped the paper to find two white Witney blankets, made of the finest wool. Wrapped in a blue ribbon, Lady Marianna Mayfield's card lay on top. "Lady Marianna, these are wonderful. Everybody raves about Witney blankets. This is so thoughtful."

"I always sleep under them, and they keep me warm. Not that you'll need much warmth with Dr. St. Cloud nearby."

Clarissa's face reddened.

Bri tried to hand her another gift, but it was so heavy, she had to stand to lift it. "A heavy one."

She put it on the divan next to Clarissa.

Clarissa unwrapped the paper and gasped. "A picnic basket. What a wonderful idea. Thank you, Lady Melanie."

Lady Melanie beamed. "It's lovely for the park after a carriage ride."

The next gift was from Lady Penelope.

Clarissa unwrapped the gift. "What beautiful monogrammed linen napkins and tablecloth! Thank you so much, Lady Penelope."

The next one was lightweight. Opening it, Clarissa's eyes widened. She pulled out two lace-trimmed silk nightgowns, one in white and one in black. The labels featured a French name.

Lady Patricia took a sip of her sherry. "One for when you feel sweet and one for when you feel naughty."

Even Bri was shocked. "A bit scandalous, Lady Patricia." The shock didn't last long. "But where did you get them? They are exquisite."

"The French Boudoir, a little shop hidden away in the *ton*. I'll get you the same thing if Mr. James proposes."

Now it was Bri's turn to be embarrassed. "Mr. James is pursuing me, but I told him if he can't say he loves me, I will not entertain his proposal."

"What?" Lady Patricia put down her sherry. "You've been reading too much of Lord Byron's poetry. Don't be foolish."

Lady Melanie leaned forward. "Is it really foolish? Don't you want your husband to be in love with you?"

Lady Patricia rolled her eyes. "Most men have mistresses for love, and wives for producing heirs and pleasing Society. Don't confuse the two."

Clarissa reached for a large rectangular object. Tearing off the wrapping, there was an empty picture frame. "The card is from Bri, It says, 'A painting of Lady Clarissa by Gio.' "

"Ooohs" and "aaahs" came from the group. "He is the most famous artist in England."

Bri laughed. "He would correct you. He would say that he is the most famous artist in the world."

"Thank you, Lady Gabriella. I don't know what to say. It is an honor to have one's portrait done by Gio."

"And *very* expensive," sniffed Lady Patricia.

"He will paint you in any pose—your wedding dress, on your horse, in a costume—"

A knowing look passed between them.

Bri smiled. *A costume from the operetta.*

The butler rang a bell. "Dinner is served."

***

Sunday, April 7, 1811 – The Methodist Meeting House
Henry

Before dropping the earl off, Jean-Louis had asked, "Are you sure you want to enter?"

"I can't explain it, but yes."

The Frenchman drove to the meeting house, and waited outside with Chérie and Hector while Henry went inside for the service.

Henry wore a hat and turned up his collar, sat in the last pew, and tried to stay out of sight. The hymns moved him much more than the ones at St. George's. He needed some solitude in a different space, an interlude of peace. Henry was not a praying man, and not a true believer in salvation, original sin or the other dogma. But this church focused on good works as a path to salvation. That he could understand.

His mind wandered to good works. Bri had a sense of helping others, which gave him a sense of enormous pride. The day before, Bri had asked him to help fund Dr. Northcliffe's clinic and hospital for the poor. He agreed, and sought out Nashmir. He thought back to that conversation as the organ music soothed his soul.

***

"Nashmir, I've never told you that Wolcott left his fortune to you."

The Tibetan, a master of self-control, tilted his head. "Indeed?"

"It's been gathering interest at James & Co. If you had never arrived, he instructed me to donate it to the poor for medical care. It occurs to me that Dr. Northcliffe's clinic is what Wolcott envisioned, and it is a place where you could expand your role in developing potions to cure people. I believe the time has come to release those funds to your control. I wondered how you would feel about allocating some of those funds to helping sponsor Dr. Northcliffe's hospital. It is not required. I can fund it all, if necessary. However, I wanted to offer you the option of contributing in many ways to this project. It is long past time your life became more of what you determine."

"I chose to be here and I am happy. Yes, I would like to be part of that outreach to help the poor. And to provide whatever expertise in herbal healing that is requested. But it may be that Dr. Northcliffe is skeptical of my healing arts."

"No, I can assure you he is not. After several years in the Cape Colony, he is well aware of the efficacy of native healers."

"Then by all means, let us work together to build something for the betterment of all."

Henry put his arm around Nashmir. "I treasure the day I met you. You saved Wolcott's life as well as my own. Now, together, we can save more."

"I am honored." Nashmir bowed in respect to the earl.

***

The organ music ended, bringing Henry back to the present. He slipped out of the meeting house to rejoin Jean-Louis and the dogs.

CHAPTER FORTY-ONE

Wednesday, April 8, 1811 – Glasgow, Scotland
Arthur

Arthur, an estate agent in Glasgow, immediately spotted the two out-of-place men. He'd heard of the Bow Street Runners in London, but these specimens didn't look institutional enough to meet that standard. *Rougher.* Each scanned the surrounding area in opposite directions. *Surveillance. Why are they waiting outside my office?*

An accomplished liar, Arthur's skills had much improved since his first encounter with Galda, currently known as Catherine, on a coach from London to Glasgow. Nearly forty years earlier, Arthur had fled a life in London after his specialties of embezzlement and forgery were about to be uncovered. The unlucky clerk to whom he'd laid a path of incriminating evidence had been thrown into Newgate Prison. Arthur shuddered every time he thought about it, but it had been a long time since that regret had crossed his mind. Quivers gripped him involuntarily as he approached the unsmiling men.

"Just out seeing a client, gentlemen. Let me unlock the door." He turned the key, opened the door, and gestured for them to enter. "What kind of property are you looking for?"

"Not property. Information." The man handed Arthur a wad of currency. "You were mentioned in a constable's report. Do you remember the death of a child in Glasgow around forty years ago? The birth was recorded in the church records in Ayr, and a notation was recorded regarding the boy's death about a month later, in Glasgow. The retired midwife and the vicar remembered a Glasgow estate agent as a friend of the grandmother. The mother died shortly after childbirth. They told us that the grandmother sought medical help in Glasgow, but the child did not survive. The constable's files in Ayr referred to you as a witness who confirmed the death of the child in a letter to the vicar, because the physician could not be located. The Ayr locals said they heard that the grandmother died shortly afterward."

"Yes. I remember. Tragic. Apoplexy. Probably the shock of losing her daughter and grandchild. I saw to it that they both received a Christian burial in a small church graveyard here in Glasgow."

"We found the gravestones."

These are determined men. "Then why are you here? That's all I know." He handed the money back to the men. "I can't be paid for telling you the sad truth about that sad time."

The lead man held his hand up. "Consider it compensation for the burial."

Arthur shrugged and pocketed the money. "Why ask now after forty years have passed?"

"Just tying up loose ends." The talker said something in French to the other man, but Arthur didn't completely understand. His associate's answer was guttural and equally unintelligible. "It's part of our training to be Bow Street Runners. Old cases, new approaches."

"Frenchmen as Bow Street Runners? In Glasgow?"

"We're everywhere." He tipped his hat. "Good day, sir."

Arthur could feel drips of sweat on his face and neck. "Good day to you as well." After they left, he fell into his chair. *I can't go to Catherine right now. They might follow me. I'll wait.* A legitimate estate agent, now slightly over sixty, Arthur only had one client who required his illicit services: Catherine, the woman once known as Galda. *I won't be free until she is dead.*

Forgers labored in secret. Meeting with the men unnerved him, just as Galda had unnerved him so many years earlier. He'd forgotten how to lie with ease. *I forgot to get their names. Why were they here? What do they know?*

***

Voutain

The older man, Voutain, directed their actions. The self-described Bow Street Runners disappeared around the corner. "Is he stupid enough to leave now?"

"Probably not. But he's a bad liar."

Colvert laughed. "French Bow Street Runners…that was a good idea, Voutain. He knew it was a lie, and now he's panicking. Forty years on, he thought he was safe."

"My guess is, with what we learned in Edinburgh, we've found the link. But it's just a hunch. J-L wants proof."

Colvert shrugged. "We've come this far. If we watch him, he'll post a letter, take a coach. He's nervous enough to make a mistake. It won't be long."

***

Colvert

Several times during the day, Arthur came to the window in the front of his office and looked around the street.

The fool. We are not visible. Later, Colvert followed Arthur home. Again, he took up vigil where he could not be seen.

Around midnight, Voutain joined him.

"What did you find out?"

"Nothing. The grandmother and babe must not have stayed in Glasgow long…and it was forty years ago. This man is our link." Voutain nodded toward Arthur's house.

"He'll warn her. He's a forger, not adept at direct deception." Colvert nudged Voutain. "Right on target. It's two a.m. and he's saddled up."

"Get the horses. I'll keep him in sight."

***

Arthur

Arthur planned to ride about four or five hours to Edinburgh, and then catch a morning coach to Inverness, which would take about a full day with changes of horses at way stations every eight hours.

349

With any luck, I'll be there by tea time. Not that they'll offer me any hospitality. I'm the bearer of bad news.

***

April 9, 1811 – Inverness, Scotland
Colvert

The two Frenchmen followed the mail coach and traded horses when the teams were changed at way stations. When the coach arrived in Inverness, they got fresh horses, and stayed out of view when Arthur disembarked and hailed a Hackney.

The Hackney pulled up in front of an antiques store.

"You watch the front." Voutain inclined his head toward the alley. "I'll cover the back entrance. If the estate agent leaves, give me a signal and follow him. I'll follow whoever is inside. We'll meet at the pub across from the coach station."

Colvert nodded, dismounted and tied up his horse at a small stable around the corner. An urchin caught his eye. "Boy." He pulled a coin from his pocket. "I'll give you this now and two more if you'll do something for me."

The boy nodded. Colvert knelt down. "Go into that antiques store and ask if they've seen your dog. There's a slightly bent white-haired man in there. I want to know who he talks to and if you can overhear anything. It's a game, boy. Don't let on that you're being paid."

"I get it, guv'nor." The smudge-faced boy walked across the street into the store.

Colvert waited. And waited. *What is he doing in there?*

The boy finally came out, tearful, taking a handkerchief from an elderly woman, who patted him on the head and sent the boy on his way. The urchin ambled down the street, calling out, "Rover," as he went. *Dog's name. Clever boy.*

The woman watched the boy walk away, and then scanned the area before going back inside the store, giving Colvert a clear look at her face. *Piercing turquoise eyes. Elegant gray hair. Age could be right for the undead grandmother.*

The boy came sauntering up to him.

"You should be an actor." Colvert pulled the boy into the alley.

Beaming, the urchin smirked. "I heard what they were saying and

350

listened until they saw me, so I cried about my dog. She comforted me."

"Don't be coy. What did they say?"

"He said, 'Someone's following me, asking questions about you and him. They said they're Bow Street Runners, but I don't believe it. They're French.'

"When he said that, her face turned hard." The boy shuddered. "Hatred shot out of her eyes. Then she said, 'French? Say no more. That damn trapper sent them.'

"The man said, 'You have to leave. They'll find you.'

"She said, 'If they find me before we leave, it will be your fault. They probably followed you. I need you to prepare some papers.' Then she noticed me. 'You there...what do you want?'

"And you know the rest."

"Good work." He reached into his pocket and tossed him two more coins. "Find an acting troupe and make an honest lad of yourself."

"Right, guv'nor." He disappeared.

Someone pulled down the shades on the store windows and moved the sign from the "Open" side to "Closed."

Arthur didn't come out until three hours later and hailed a Hackney. Colvert followed him to the coach station.

He left his horse next to the pub, and went in to wait for Voutain. *She must be Blackburn's grandmother. She knows who J-L is.*

***

Catherine

After locking the door at the rear entrance of the shop, Catherine mounted the steps to her rooms above. Inside, she found Mirela had packed a travel bag for each of them.

"The cards telling me time to leaving."

Catherine sat at the table. "The earl's French trapper found Arthur. We're in the final chapter. If Duff won't act, I will. We leave for London tonight. Papers are prepared. Are you ready?"

"Always."

The chicken was charred, but provided needed energy. The two women ate their last meal in silence.

Rising to her feet, Catherine looked around. "I enjoyed the time we spent here. But Fate has set our path. I have been happy here, with you."

"As have I."

"You knew Arthur was coming."

"The cards do not lie."

Catherine picked up the two travel bags and walked to the door.

Mirela went to the closet and removed a bag. She unlatched it and spread bones and skulls in their bed.

Having thought herself immune to shock, Catherine was caught short. Her face registered horror. "What—"

"They must believing we are dead."

"Who—"

"Do not being asking."

"Fate extracts its price."

As she walked to the door, Mirela knocked the burning candle from its holder, and watched it roll toward the curtains. "It won't be long."

They left the door unlocked.

***

Voutain

Hiding in the shadows, Voutain watched the two elderly women come down the back stairs and walk through the alley toward the street. He remounted his horse. As he waited until they'd entered the Hackney, something told him to turn toward the upper rooms. *Flames.* He raised an eyebrow. *Leaving no trace.* He turned back and followed the carriage to the coach station.

He waited until he saw them board the midnight coach to London, waited until it left, then walked into the coach station. He ran to the ticket window, hoping his guess as to destination was correct. "My grandmother just left. I meant to say goodbye! What time will the coach reach London?"

The clerk shrugged. "With stops, changes of horses and no problems, our schedule allows four days, give or take half a day."

"Thanks. Maybe I can catch the coach."

Voutain went to the pub, found Colvert and sat down. They ordered a meal, and Colvert updated him. Before they left Inverness, they rode by the antiques store. A fire was raging. They turned and began their long ride back to London.

The two watchers sold their horses at the next coach stop and bought tickets to London, a few hours behind the one their surveillance targets were riding in. When they were within a day of London, they'd lease new horses and ride them hard to arrive before the coach.

CHAPTER FORTY-TWO

Thursday, April 11, 1811 – The London Coach Station
Voutain

Their prey did not exit the coach. *"Merde."* Voutain spit in fury.
"They got off somewhere on the way. Let's question the driver."

"What if he won't tell us anything?"

Shaking his head, Voutain said, "Colvert, what does Jean-Louis always say?"

"There are ways."

***

Thursday, April 11, 1811 – Lady Gwyneth's Townhouse
Gwyneth

Gwyneth was relieved that her dinner party a few days before the Masquerade Ball was proceeding without incident. *Bri is on her best behavior.* By the time the main course appeared, no contentious arguments or challenges had been issued by her niece. Viscount Armstrong seemed comfortable and no incidences of prolonged stuttering had interrupted his comments. She caught him stealing glances at the equally shy Lady Melanie.

It amused the hostess to imagine who was besotted with whom. Clearly the baron and Lady Penelope were entranced by each other, despite the age difference. *Davinia and I might find ourselves in competition for romance, or, at the least, age-appropriate conversation, with Count von Dusterberg and Dr. Northcliffe.* Edward and Bri were attracted to each other, without question. *He's proposed to her twice already.*

Of Vaux, Hanforth and Banfield, she wasn't sure which of the remaining selection of Lady Clementine, Lady Patricia or Lady Marianna would appeal to which gentleman.

And Gio was holding court with naughty tales of secrets of the aristocracy. He restricted himself to clarifying details swirling around vaguely known rumors and naming only those recently departed, so as not to impact his potential future portrait commissions, although, in his late sixties, he frequently said, "Every day I wake up is a surprise."

Lady Clementine, a tall mannish woman, interrupted the unnaturally handsome and dashing Viscount Hanforth as he was expounding on East Africa. "You make it sound like a nature preserve where you can shoot animals with impunity. Have you ever considered being their protector instead of their predator?"

Bri's impertinence is spreading to her acquaintances.

Hanforth sat back in apparent shock.

Is it the concept that shocks him or the challenge from a woman?

"As a matter of fact, I have."

Now it was Lady Clementine's turn to express surprise. "I'd like to hear your thoughts."

"There is an abundance of magnificent animals on the continent of Africa. It is their home, their territory. Once it was in balance. Now, as the population of men increases, resources are consumed faster than they can be replaced. Game is not used for food, but for sport. Mankind is like a swarm of ants. Industrious but destructive. I have been one of them. On my last trip, I came to see things differently after talking to a tribal chief. I may establish a Conservancy to protect the way of life of the native people as well as to preserve the breathtaking wilds the animals prowl.

"There is no doubt that herds need to be periodically culled. Controlled and licensed hunters could be permitted. Something as beautiful and eternal as the savannah, the Serengeti and the Ngorongoro Crater should be preserved. It is as yet 'undiscovered' by white men, protected by the tribes of Maasai who live there. I imagine someday a hunter will stumble upon this Eden and claim to have 'discovered' it. How can one discover something that has always existed? The march of civilization does not always signal progress. Often it brings destruction."

Lady Clementine leaned forward. "I completely agree. When I was in Africa, our camp under stars that are so often obscured by our weather here, I never felt so close to God. Despite our hubris, we are small. As you said, we are like ants swarming over our planet, devouring our gift. We should preserve it, not denude it."

Count von Dusterberg cleared his throat. "As you know, Nephew, I have spent a considerable amount of time in South Africa in the Cape Colony. Not all native tribes are the 'noble savages' Rousseau romanticized. Some are as brutal and deadly as any rabid, starving animal. You must not let your utopian view of a perfect environment blind you to reality. You might be battling forces on all sides."

"Perhaps. But I have wandered the world, seeking a purpose. I think I've found it. People call me a rich dilettante, and I did nothing to dissuade them of their perception. I intend to make Africa my home and work toward my 'utopian' dream, as you call it."

Banfield appeared sheepish. "My interest in musical composition seems self-indulgent compared to your dream, Hanforth."

"Don't belittle your talents, Banfield." Edward leaned forward. "Your music can move people to tears or to action. That is a power in and of itself."

Bri looked first at Hanforth, then at Banfield. "You two should collaborate on a musical composition that celebrates Africa, evoking its majesty, power and breadth."

Banfield's mouth dropped open. He looked at Hanforth.

Hanforth grinned. "What a great idea!"

Vaux winked at Bri. "She is always one step ahead of everyone else."

Gio raised his glass. "To Lady Gabriella!"

The group echoed, "Here! Here!"

Lady Patricia inclined her head toward Hanforth. "So your idea is that safaris should be only for culling the herds?"

"When I traveled to Africa with my late husband, Luc, I sketched animals rather than shot them. There are many ways to appreciate wildlife. I believe people would come to the Conservancy to see game roaming free in their natural habitat."

"I assume there is a fee for a game hunt," said Bri. "Alternatively, a system linking safaris, coaches and lodges to cater to tourists as well as hunters would provide income to help support your efforts."

Edward nodded. "We could help you develop your long term plan."

Lady Marianna laughed. "Have we been present at the birth of an idea? How novel!"

Dr. Northcliffe turned his wine glass in his hand. "I've just come from Africa. Make no mistake: the continent presents huge logistical challenges, existence is at a subsistence level, and disease is rampant. Folk cures are given more value than medicine. If you take a small area and establish a test conservancy project, others might follow your lead. However, it is Africans who must transform Africa. We will always be outsiders."

"Well, that's a bucket of cold water," said Lady Patricia. "One minute I'm imagining a dashing safari guide leading me on a night trek under the stars, and the next I'm imagining irate tribesmen marauding my camp. Which is it?"

The count shrugged. "It may be both, at different times in different places."

"Africa is all of what you describe and more. It is a large, unformed mass of humanity, wildlife and abundance. Such venues bring those with both good motives and bad. It is an artist's paradise, a politician's blank canvas, and a poet's inspiration." Gio raised his glass. "I toast myself for my brilliant insight."

Everyone at the table laughed and raised their glasses. "To Gio!"

Davinia leaned toward Gwyneth. "This is an interesting group. I can see I've been trapped in the country too long, caught up in arguments between the butler and the staff. Ever since I came to London to shepherd Beau through the Season, my intellectual stimulation quotient has exploded. I feel alive again."

With attention focused on him, Gio held court. "I'm going to start a new game. This is 1811. In five words or less, what change do you want to see in the world in 50 years? Lady Gwyneth, as hostess, you may begin."

Gwyneth raised an eyebrow. "I'd like to fly around"—

Gio held up his hand: "Begin again. Five words or less."

"Flying coaches."

"Like flying carpets? Fantasy is a pleasant distraction." Gio looked to the next guest. "Count?"

"A Europe free of Napoleon."

"A man who follows instructions. Excellent. Next?"

Vaux sat back and smirked. "Are you going to comment on every suggestion?"

"Probably. Go!"

"An end to bourgeois bias."

Gio frowned. "What does that mean?"

"It's your game." Vaux shrugged. "Figure it out."

Lady Patricia sniffed. "This banter will take all night."

"Do you have somewhere else to go?" Gio paused. "If not, five words."

"Better light to read by."

The dwarf nodded. "Lord Armstrong?"

"Green fields and rich harvests."

"For all of us or just for you?" Gio shook his head. "Never mind, don't answer. Lady Clementine?"

"The Hanforth East Africa Conservancy."

"Apropos. Lady Melanie?"

The shy woman swallowed. "Equal inheritance rights for women."

"A rabble rouser in prim disguise. Interesting. Banfield?"

"The late, great composer, Banfield."

Gio raised an eyebrow, but made no retort. "Davinia?"

"How about world peace?"

"How about it? Original and heartfelt, I'm sure. Lord Beauchamp?"

Turning to Lady Penelope, seated beside him, he said, "Penelope, Baroness Beauchamp."

Lady Penelope blushed a magenta hue.

Gio climbed up on his chair. "Is that a proposal?"

The baron stood, and then knelt. "It is. Lady Penelope, will you marry me?"

Rising to her feet, Lady Penelope nodded and whispered, "Yes."

"No one is surprised. Baron Beauchamp, you may kiss the bride-to-be." Gio raised his glass. "To love! The Marriage Season has triumphed!"

The baron rose to meet her kiss.

Glasses clinked. "To love!"

Bowing his head, Gio continued his demand. "Your turn, Lady Penelope."

Lady Penelope smiled. "Baron Beauchamp's 101st Birthday

Party."

"Optimism is always welcome. Dr. Northcliffe?"

"Pure air and clean water."

"All would agree. Lady Marianna?"

"Women admitted to British universities."

"Maybe you should move to Italy. Hanforth?"

"I echo Lady Clementine: The Hanforth East African Conservancy."

"Is another proposal in the offing? Don't be embarrassed. I'm incorrigible. Lady Gabriella?"

Bri straightened her back. "Full equality for women."

Gio rubbed his hands together. "We have the makings of a revolution. Mr. James?"

Edward raised an eyebrow and shrugged. "The triumph of scientific thought."

"Triumph over what?"

"Superstition."

Bri glared at Edward.

Gio tilted his head toward Edward. "The world changes slowly."

The banker leaned forward. "We should strive toward noble goals, should we not? I must admit, Lady Gabriella has moved me to reconsider my own prejudices on gender. I agree with her that it is foolish to dismiss half the population. It's a waste of economic resources. Will fifty years be long enough to change the world that much? I don't know."

The clock chimed midnight.

"Lady Gwyneth, I can't remember the last time I lost track of time at a dinner party. You are a marvelous hostess." Gio raised his glass. "To Lady Gwyneth!"

Shaking her head, the comtesse said, "You've dominated the conversation for the last hour. No wonder you think it's a delightful evening."

"Your smile softens the rebuke." The dwarf gave her a quick nod of the head.

"To Lady Gwyneth!" The group sipped their final toast and rose to leave.

***

Bri pulled Edward aside as the others said their goodbyes. "If you don't agree with me on the position of women in the world, I'll never marry you."

"I won't always agree with you. But your arguments on women's rights made me think. I am not fully persuaded, but I'm not as rigid as I was when we renewed our acquaintance." He put his arm on her back to steer her to the foyer to depart, whispering in her ear, "And you've turned down my proposal twice already. I may not ask again."

Shooting him an icy glance, she stood by her aunt and bid Edward goodnight.

CHAPTER FORTY-THREE

Saturday, April 13, 1811 – Lord Ravenshire's Townhouse
Bri

J ane Anne laid out Bri's gown for the Masquerade Ball that night. "I wish I could attend the ball and watch from the sidelines. I imagine it will be glorious…the costumes, the elegant masks, the music. Oh, what a wonderful life you lead, Lady Gabriella!"

Bri laughed. "Even I'm caught up in something I thought would be a bore. I'm excited too." Part of her assignment that evening would be to occupy Blackie. She had no interest in stimulating his imagination beyond its natural inclinations.

Her bath had been drawn. Bri went into her large bathroom to enjoy a few relaxed moments before the demanding evening ahead of her. Sinking into the warmth topped by bubbles, she closed her eyes and thought of Edward.

Her role in the evening's plan was distracting Blackie during the period that her father, Jean-Louis and Edward would be searching the suspected killer's house. No other evidence had been conclusive, so they had decided it must be hidden in Blackie's home. Boyd would accompany them only as an observer—no evidence would be removed, but a search warrant would be issued if they found anything, due to Boyd and Aldrich's cooperation. Worried for the safety of those she loved while simultaneously trying to divert suspicion about their absence might require her to act as if she were interested in Blackie romantically. Her nerves stood on edge. She consoled herself that all would most likely be over after tonight. But then it hit her. *What if they find no proof? What if Blackie is innocent?*

Her thoughts were interrupted by Jane Anne. "Milady, you had best start to dress. Mr. James is arriving at half-past seven o'clock."

Acquiescing, Bri emerged from the tub, donned her robe and walked to her vanity table.

Jane Anne began to work on her hair.

"Did you manage to make my friends look fetching for the ball this evening?"

"I hope so. Lady Penelope asked another friend to join her so I could work on both of them at the same time, and they insisted on paying me. She's so excited to be engaged to the baron. You were right to scold me and dismiss the ugly gossip. And thank you for letting me know a reasonable amount to charge. After I arranged Lady Clarissa's hair, she asked me to fix her hair for her wedding. I told her that you would have to approve."

"Of course! It will be a lovely day. It's so romantic to be certain of love immediately upon meeting someone." *I detested Edward initially but now I find myself in love with him. He is mysterious, compelling and utterly confounding.* Bri sighed. *Will Edward and I ever marry?*

She reluctantly admitted to herself that she had become a different person than she had been just a few short months ago, when she had reluctantly agreed to attend this Season to fulfill her familial duty. Planning to remain free and independent, Bri had considered marriage as a limiting trap willingly entered into by most women. Having reconciled herself to the prospect of trying to amuse herself at the balls and dinner parties, she had been drawn into the romantic intrigue despite her expectations.

As Jane Anne put the finishing touches on her hair, with cascades of red curls flowing down her back, Bri tilted her head.

"There, we are done. Does it please you?"

"Very much." *I hope Mr. James likes it.*

The fuchsia silk gown from Mlle. Bellerobe's shop lay on Bri's bed. It had a quilted silk empire bodice with a petite ruffle around the neckline, at the edges of the puffed sleeves, and down the front, set into the diagonal seaming of the bias-cut skirt. Jane Anne carefully pulled the dress over Bri's head, taking care to avoid disturbing her hair. Bri placed the matching dancing slippers into a carrying bag to avoid damage to the slippers by walking in the wet streets. Even from the carriage to the ball, shoes could be ruined.

For jewelry, Bri wore her mother's pearl brooch at the empire center where the panels descended. She slid on her double pearl ring and affixed her matching pear-shaped pearl earrings. Bri held the fuchsia velvet choker in place, centering its single dangling pear-shaped pearl in the center of her neck while Jane Anne tied the delicate silk tassels in the back.

Assessing her appearance in the full length mirror, Bri almost didn't recognize herself. The deep color would be a bit scandalous in a Season dominated by pastels, but confidence in her appearance would make it easier to surmount the evening's challenges. She picked up her contrasting feathered mask painted primarily in shades of blue and green, but with a few fuchsia splashes, topped off with peacock feathers, and held it up to see the entire effect. She wouldn't put it on until she exited the carriage for the Masquerade Ball.

Bri descended the stairs and found her father in his study, deep in thought. She cleared her throat to get his attention.

Startled, the earl looked up and said nothing for a moment. Tears misted in the corners of his eyes. "You are a vision, Bri. I have never seen you look so glorious. I wish your mother could see you tonight. You will triumph." He rose and embraced her.

Bri sighed. "The triumph will be in distracting Blackie while you search his home."

The earl's expression morphed into one of grim determination. "It should take little more than an hour. No one will miss us."

"It is dangerous, Father. We still have no real proof. All Blackie's actions can be explained away as merely circumstantial. Dr. Northcliffe's suspicions are unproven. Why must you and Mr. James take such a reckless chance?"

"Suspicion is like a cancer. We must kill it or it will destroy us. We need clear evidence. The irony, of course, is that I have given Blackie credibility by investing him with a high ranking social and political position in the *ton*. In a sense, I am fighting a deadly dragon of my own creation. Men often feel compelled to record their exploits, setting down their plans in detail. I imagine Blackie, who is quite a judicious writer of memoranda that chronicle his brilliant business decisions, has also described his personal exploits and actions in a diary. That is what we seek."

"But what of his servants?"

"Blackie once told me that he employed only day servants, resenting any intrusion upon his privacy in the evenings. He takes his dinner at his club each night, reviewing outstanding business items and determining strategy. As he is a man of discipline and habit, I am assuming that his philosophy on servants still applies. In any case, Bri, Young James and I are each quite capable of handling half a dozen men."

"Ha! You exaggerate, but do not try to placate me with false bravado. I shall be on edge until you both return."

Bri heard the front door open and squeezed her father's hand. She contained her excitement under a veneer of control as they walked out to greet Edward.

When he saw Edward, Henry pulled a corsair's mask from inside his waistcoat. The blood red oblong scarf had eyeholes cut out of it. The earl wrapped it around his head and tied it in back. "I ripped this off a pirate's face during one of my more eventful skirmishes. I think I'll make a rakish impression on the *ton*. Many call me a pirate behind my back anyway."

Bri and Edward laughed.

Turning to Bri, Edward stared. "Bri, you look magnificent." He appeared unaware that he had addressed her by her nickname instead of the more formal form of address that Society dictated except among those who were engaged. He offered her a stem of baby orchids in shades of fuchsia and violet. "I thought you might be able to wear these in your hair."

Thompson rang for Jane Anne.

The maid wove the stem of orchids around the chignon in Bri's hair.

Henry pulled Edward close to him and whispered in his ear. "Call her Lady Gabriella or Blackie will be on alert."

Edward nodded. "I will not repeat that slip of the tongue."

"It's time to go."

In the carriage, Bri's worry was evident. "I've tried to dissuade you both from this rash course. You men are so stubborn and foolhardy. I shall be relieved when you return to the ball. I have a double masquerade to pull off with Blackie."

"Fear not, Lady Gabriella. I am a formidable opponent under any and all circumstances."

"You do not have to play the hero for me, *Mr.* James."

Henry put up his hands. "Stop it, you two. We have arrived."

***

Saturday, April 13, 1811 – The Masquerade Ball at Pytchley Palace

Bri

As the earl's carriage approached the Duke of Pytchley's palace, Bri reflected on how many things had happened in so short a time. Perhaps the Marriage Season was distorting her normal senses, and she should slow things down a bit. But tonight was too important. She couldn't think about slowing down until her assignment with Blackie was completed. Hoping against hope that her father and Edward would find the needed evidence and escape unseen, Bri steeled herself for the evening ahead of her.

Noticing her silence, Henry squeezed her hand. "Are you ready?"

"Yes. You two must be careful. I must endure the uncertainty of your search and fend off Blackie's advances at the same time."

Stirring uncomfortably, the earl leaned back. "A dance is not an embrace, Bri. Tonight's trial will soon be over. You will be in a crowded room and quite safe, after all. Let us focus on the last dance of the evening. By then, with any luck, we shall have returned with proof and our charade with Blackie can end."

"We've found no evidence yet." Bri looked out the carriage window. "The torches from the duke's entryway are just ahead. It looks enchanting." Henry, Edward and Bri affixed their masks in the carriage and then stepped out into the wide outdoor foyer in front of the Pytchley Palace.

Built fifty years earlier, in a grand style, each room in the palace was decorated in a different color under the direction of the duchess, Bri's indomitable grandmother. Guessing who was behind the masks as guests milled about outside on the rare clear spring evening, they slowly moved toward the door, where the earl handed their invitations to the butler. While unnecessary to identify themselves, since they were part of the extended Pytchley family, they followed protocol.

Bri followed the crowd down the hallway into the ballroom. She had assumed a masked ball was a silly conceit, that she would easily recognize her friends. It was disconcerting however, to see so many strangers. The masks made her a bit uneasy.

Her father's corsair's mask set him apart. Edward wore a black hood with eye holes—an executioner's cap. It gave her chills. "A bit too literal, Mr. James?"

Edward ignored Bri's comment.

There were perhaps half a dozen other women in the room with the same general size and appearance of her aunt. While Bri's red hair was distinctive, she was not the only red-haired guest, and for a fleeting moment she hoped that Blackie would mistake someone else for her until she heard his voice from behind. "Lady G., I presume?"

Turning around, she smiled. "You have found me, Blackie. I was just thinking how much more difficult it is to identify people this evening than I had supposed. You, for instance, have a similar build as a number of other men here tonight. Your green dragon's head mask is distinctive—I like it. Since men of the *ton* generally dress in a certain style without the variation in gowns and color that women do, were it not for your voice, I might have mistaken you for someone else."

"Well, then, we have beaten the game. May I see your dance card?"

"They did not pass them out in the receiving line. Odd."

"The hostess is your grandmother. Why not ask her?"

"Why not?" *Grandmother will slice him with a look and burn him with a word.*

They made their way to the duchess. "Grandmother, you look amazing tonight as Cleopatra. That black wig is stunning."

"Bri, my darling. Daring choice of color for your gown. I approve. This wig was fashioned based on a papyrus your father brought back from Egypt years ago." She turned to the man in the dragon mask. "And Mr. Blackburn, I presume."

"Your Grace, I wasn't aware you knew my name. How did you recognize me behind my mask?"

"I know many things other people are not aware of, Mr. Blackburn. I've been told that you're a clever and enterprising merchant."

Blackie bowed, acknowledging the compliment. "Your Grace, I am honored to meet you. We were wondering if dance cards will be distributed."

Hitting Blackburn with her fan, the duchess scoffed. "Of course not! The ladies must recognize each gentleman by his mask and remember the order of the dances. It should prove thoroughly confusing after a few dances. I was bored with the usual protocol."

"Then I will immediately claim all dances, Lady Gabriella."

He is wise enough to dispense with familiarity in the presence of my grandmother. If he called me Lady G., she would have reprimanded him in a way he would never have forgotten.

"That is inappropriate, Mr. Blackburn, and you know it." The duchess gave him a look that would terrify most men. "Only one dance per gentleman is permitted unless your engagement has been announced." The duchess dismissed them with a wave of her fan and greeted more of her guests.

Blackburn shrugged in surrender.

The musicians in the small orchestra were taking their places for the first dance. People swirled around them, caught up in social chatter.

Bri smiled at Blackie. "How about the third dance and dinner? That is the longest time we can spend together. I trust that meets with your approval."

Blackburn tilted his head and squinted. "What about Mr. James?"

"Mr. James has annoyed me of late. I have made no promises to him." She did not have to feign her annoyance with Edward.

Henry and Lady Gwyneth approached her as Blackburn was leaving, and they compared masks.

"Lord R., you look quite the blackguard tonight."

"Many think me a pirate already, Blackie. Why not play to my enemies?"

Blackburn laughed, bowed to the comtesse and kissed her gloved hand before moving away into the crowd.

But the word 'enemies' reminded Bri of the evening's purpose and the grin vanished from her face.

The earl whispered in her ear, "Smile. Play your part."

Recovering quickly, Bri laughed again, a little too shrilly, and tried to cover it with a convenient cough.

At that moment, the orchestra played a few notes to gain attention, and the duchess stood to face the assembled guests. "Welcome to my Masquerade Ball. As some of you know, no dance cards will be provided tonight."

A soft din of murmurings conveyed the crowd's surprise.

"You must remember your selected dance partners by their masks or costumes. Masks may not be removed until the orchestra plays its final note tonight. And one more *caveat,* men: You are not permitted to identify yourself to your dance partner unless she recognizes you first." She gestured with a flourish of her gloved hand. "Conductor, you may begin."

Edward appeared behind Bri and whispered, "First dance?"

Bri smiled, turned and laughed. Loudly enough for others to hear, she announced, "I recognize you, Mr. Edward James. Do you recognize me?"

"Lady Gabriella Wyndward, no doubt. The red hair, the green eyes and the tart tongue could belong to no other. May I introduce you to my friend, Judge Aldrich?"

Aldrich wore a standard black mask, but looked athletically fit, nearly as tall as Edward. *His gaze is direct and analytical, the eyes of a skeptic.*

"A pleasure to meet you, Judge."

Scandalous to some, the first dance was a waltz, to Bri's delight. Edward expertly guided Bri around the ballroom. One long wall was mirrored floor to ceiling. Across the broad ballroom floor, the facing wall was covered in a pale green silk jacquard fabric, as was the corner of the narrower end of the room with the interior doors where the orchestra sat. At the opposite end were a series of double French doors, which opened onto the garden, framed by the same fabric as adorned the walls. The floor was a deep green marble, set diagonally with pure white set in a pattern that formed a huge 'X'. *All in all, this is a spectacular room. Grandmother is a visionary in her own right.*

Nervous about her performance later in the evening, Bri was silent during most of the dance. Near the end, however, she couldn't contain her curiosity another moment. "When are you going to leave?"

"Shortly after the second dance begins. We will walk into the garden and disappear through the back gate. Jean-Louis has arranged for us to exit and re-enter that way. This room is crowded enough that we should not be missed. Aldrich is aware of our task. Go to him if there is a problem with Blackburn. If all goes well, we should be back within an hour or two."

"Please be careful. I will keep Blackie busy, but seeing you again will be a great relief."

"Save the last dance for me," whispered Edward as the music stopped. Bowing low, he moved invisibly through the crowd.

"Lady Gabriella, I would recognize you anywhere."

Looking at the tall man with flowing blond locks standing in front of her garbed in full African safari gear, with some kind of wooden African tribal mask, Gabriella realized it could only be one person. "Viscount Hanforth?"

"Correct. Are you free for the second dance?"

"Yes, I'd be delighted."

As the notes for the second dance filled the room, Hanforth extended his hand to claim Bri as his partner for the Quadrille. Bri found it nearly impossible to speak during this dance, as the steps were so carefully choreographed. She went through her assigned paces, smiling at Hanforth, beginning to play her part for the evening.

CHAPTER FORTY-FOUR

Saturday, April 13, 1811 – The Masquerade Ball at Pytchley Palace
Edward

E dward moved through the dancers, grateful that the French doors were open, allowing guests to walk outside. Though it was cool in the evening, it was tolerable for most people. Edward and Henry left their cloaks behind deliberately, to avoid any questions or attract attention.

Standing on the terrace for a few moments next to Aldrich, overlooking the garden, Edward started down the steps in what he hoped would be considered an evening's walk between dances. Not everyone had mastered the demanding steps of the Quadrille, so his walk would not look suspicious. He disappeared into the darkness, behind the hedge outlining the garden, and made his way to the back gate.

Aldrich stayed back, to watch over Lady Gabriella.

***

Gwyneth

Shortly after Edward left, Henry, Gwyneth and Count von Dusterberg went outside for some air. Gwyneth's mask was of delicate light and dark blue feathers, complementing her light blue gown, while the count had a most unusual medieval armored mask from his collection of armaments. After a few moments, Henry indicated that he was going for a walk, and said to the count, "Keep an eye on my sister until I return." He went down the steps to the garden.

Noticing Gwyneth's concerned look, the count gently took her arm. "Are you going to tell me what's going on? It sounded to me as if he plans to be gone longer than it would take to walk around the garden."

"Henry does not want to attract any attention, and he has sworn me to secrecy. If he does not return within two hours, however, I have his permission to break that vow of secrecy and ask you to help me find him."

"Then it is dangerous. Tell me now." The count's Prussian tone unnerved her.

Gwyneth shook her head. "I cannot. Please allow me to maintain my part of the bargain. I will tell you everything when it is over, but no one else must know."

***

Count von Dusterberg

Irritated at the rebuff, the count deferred to her request, as he was left with no choice. "Very well. Let us watch Clarissa and Lady Gabriella as they perform their paces in the Quadrille." The count assumed an air of military alertness.

As they watched the dancers, the count noticed Blackburn, Henry's trusted right hand in the trading business, dancing with a masked woman. Obviously, Henry did not trust him or he would have taken him along on his "walk." The Count decided he would keep a close eye on Blackburn.

***

Edward

At the back gate to the Pytchley Palace garden, Henry exited and Jean-Louis replaced the lock, pocketed the key, and handed the earl the horse's reins. Boyd and Edward were already mounted. Henry and Jean-Louis leapt into their saddles and the four headed into the night toward Blackburn's townhouse.

After about fifteen minutes, they arrived at Blackburn's street. Jean-Louis led them into the alley. He expertly picked the lock on the rear gate, and the other three entered slowly. Reaching the back door, Jean-Louis again magically opened it. In the dark, Henry led the way to the library based on his memory of the house. He reached the door without incident. Inside, Henry and Jean-Louis pulled the drapes. Once satisfied that no one could see a light, they closed the door and lit a candle.

As their eyes got used to the low light, they noticed that the room was in perfect order. "We must take care to replace everything. With this man, orderliness is an obsession," said Henry. "Edward, check the books on the left, Jean-Louis those on the right. Do not remove anything, but look for something that might be a journal instead of a book. If you identify something, we will all watch as it is removed so that it can be replaced without leaving any traces. Luckily, the man must have this room dusted daily, so it should not be too difficult, but we do not want to take any chances. Boyd and I will check the desk."

Each set about his assigned tasks. Henry opened the upper left drawer, painstakingly reviewed its contents and felt for any papers hidden behind the drawer or in any false compartments.

Boyd watched to help remember the order of things.

Henry repeated his detailed search process for each drawer. By the time he reached the lower right drawer, nearly forty minutes had passed, and neither Edward nor Jean-Louis had found anything resembling a journal.

Opening the last drawer, the earl felt all the edges. The bottom section moved slightly. Getting down on his knees, he carefully inspected the contents of the drawer. It was full of different types of ink and sealing wax. With Boyd's assistance, Henry set each item in the same order on the top of the desk as they had been in the drawer. "I may have found it."

Seconds later, he had removed the false bottom and exposed a worn black leather diary with initials stamped in gold leaf— DB. "DB—Duff Blackburn. This must be it."

The others came over as Henry removed the diary and opened it. Entries were made neatly, recording Blackie's life since the age of nine.

An entry in another hand recorded the gift.

September 15, 1780—

To my grandson, Duff.
Record your life.
Learn. Remember. Act.

As years were clearly noted, Henry paged to the year of Rychard's
death, 1807.

May 10,1807—

My brother Rychard breathes no more.
I bear the guilt of fratricide.
Tonight marks another murder.
Revenge is a pleasing sensation.

Henry flipped the pages to 1809, when Luc died.

February 2, 1809—

Luc's unerring schedule hastened his death.
Almost easy enough for a child to execute.
I eliminated the driver.
He squealed in terror.

I liked the finality of his final guttural exhale
before I threw him in the river.

There's something empowering in
vengeance.
I'm beginning to see how my grandmother
thinks.
Another death mars not my conscience.

February 10, 1809—

Henry, Gwyneth, Bri are my priorities now.

Bri as my bride would secure my patrimony
when she bears me a son.
That is the best path to vengeance and
triumph.

Grandmother has arrived.
Tempus Fugit.

"That's it, said Edward. "The proof is written in his own hand."
"It seems so." Jean-Louis frowned. "Boyd?"
Henry stared at the Frenchman. "You doubt his guilt?"
Boyd shook his head. "Jean-Louis is cautious. There seems to be
only one way to interpret these words. It should be enough for a
search warrant. We must replace it, though. I was never here, and
neither were you. We must do this to act in accordance with the law
from now on."
The earl's eyes narrowed.
"What?" Jean-Louis knew how to read the earl's intentions.
"The death of my father in 1806." He went back to that year and
stopped when he found the page he hoped would be there.

November 20, 1806—

Neyl Wyndward, my father, the man who must be
punished for killing my mother—I spent time
alone with him today for the first time.

We'd been introduced at parties or receptions
over the years, but he'd never given me more than
a perfunctory acknowledgment.

Today, he offered me a sherry and we talked for
nearly an hour. He complimented me on my work
and said how much Henry valued me.

An errand for my brother, Henry, took me
to Ravenshire. Even if I had been born a
legitimate child of the earl, as the youngest
son I have inherited nothing of this

magnificent estate unless my older brothers had died.

My mother lived here for a short time. My father took advantage of a young girl, ruined her but would not marry her. She was not of his social class. He thought her beneath him and his life of inherited privilege.

His wife was dead. The children needed a mother. From what Grandmother said, they loved my mother and she loved them.

What cruelty drove my father to destroy her life and mine? The path of vengeance is filled with venom. It poisons me.

Yet, the man I met today did not seem an ogre, but rather a logical, thoughtful, respectful man. Lonely. Reserved. A man devoted to books, with a massive library. Today, after fifteen years of working for Wyndward Trading, I finally got to know the man who has lived in my imagination all my life.

I wish my path were different, but I will fulfill my destiny as it now lies before me.

Henry read another entry few weeks later.

December 8, 1806—

My father is dead. By natural causes, says Henry, who has traveled to Ravenshire for the burial. Bri is inconsolable.

Grandmother smiled when I informed her. No surprise registered in her face.

I must gird my courage to move as destiny demands. I cannot delay in following my plan.

Justice must be done.

"Damn him to hell!" said Henry, visibly enraged. "I would like to kill him myself at this moment."

"Understandable, Lord Ravenshire." Edward's voice remained calm. "But we need to let Boyd handle this. If we remove the diary, Blackburn will know we are on to him, and we cannot risk Lady Gabriella's safety. I do not mean to be harsh, but we must think of the living. We cannot undo the past."

"Early tomorrow morning," Boyd said, "a judge will grant a writ of search and we can then seize the diary and arrest Blackburn. We must be patient."

"You are right, of course," said Henry, closing the diary. "Reading this entire diary will be painful but enlightening."

He set the diary in the drawer, replaced the false drawer bottom and replicated the order of the items he had removed earlier, and closed it. They examined the area for any disruption and replaced the chair as they had found it.

Boyd blew out the candle, and then Jean-Louis opened the draperies. They left through the back door, re-locking it as they did the rear gate. Remounting their horses in silence, the men rode back to the ball, except for Boyd, who rode to the headquarters of the Bow Street Runners to prepare the paperwork for Aldrich to meet the requirements of the law. The next day, Blackburn would be arrested.

It had been arranged that Aldrich would state that the earl knew that Blackburn maintained a diary to avoid incriminating any of them in breaking and entering. They could not remove the diary without compromising the evidence.

CHAPTER FORTY-FIVE

Saturday, April 13, 1811 – The Masquerade Ball at Pytchley Palace
Bri

Bri summoned what she hoped was a convincing smile when Blackie approached her for the third dance.

"A reel, no doubt, to generate an appetite for supper. Perhaps after the dance, you will be sufficiently exhausted to accept my proposal of marriage."

"Now, Blackie, we have previously discussed my preference for taking things slowly. This is but the third major ball of the Season. I am not yet accustomed to the ways of the *ton*, let alone ready for courtship. Please understand that I need time to sort out all these new experiences."

"I know you are attracted to me, Lady G. I can tell by the way you look shyly away from me when we speak. I can tell by the way you look at me when you think I'm not aware of your observation. I can tell by the way you pretend not to want more than a mere kiss on the cheek."

Bri leaned back on her heels. "Blackie! You are embarrassing me."

"And I will keep embarrassing you until you agree to marry me. It's undeniable. You are so beautiful when you are embarrassed—those blushing pink cheeks attract many men."

"Irritating me is not the way to win my heart. You've known me forever. Surely that lesson has not escaped you. Your goal cannot be achieved by force of will."

"Are you saying I cannot force you to be mine?" Blackie's tone was mocking.

The music started and they took their positions. *I must remain in control and not argue too much. But if I don't argue at all, he'll know something is wrong.* Bri stopped to analyze her thoughts. *Am I really so disagreeable?*

After the dance, Blackie put his hand on Bri's back to guide her to the supper area. To keep her mind from worrying about Edward and her father, Bri turned the topic to commerce and trading. "The papers say that Napoleon's blockade is only sporadically effective. Have we lost many ships?"

"We?"

"I am the heir to Wyndward Trading. A woman can never be an earl, but Father built the trading company from his mother's bequest to him upon her death. So 'we' is appropriate. Someday I may be your superior, Blackie. How would you feel about that?"

It was the first time Bri had ever seen such a lewd, wicked smile. Her reaction was involuntary. She flinched but recovered quickly. "Don't leer at me."

"You can take a superior position to me at any time you like, Lady G."

What does that mean?

They took their seats at one of the many tables that filled an adjacent ballroom.

"Another massive ballroom?" Blackburn looked around. "Amazing."

"My grandmother loves to entertain."

"She's as feisty as you are, Lady G. You take after her."

"So she says. Blackie, tell me about your time in Brazil. I haven't been back since our trip when I was so young. Is it still wild and undeveloped? Trekking to the interior must have been daunting."

Visibly animated about the riches of Brazil, Blackie told story after story of the vast rain forest. How he had survived a bout with a tropical disease, cured by a medicine man with a bone through his nose—a Brazilian who fed him foul potions and danced around him waving torches. How the words of exotic parrots mimicking the sounds of other birds and nearby people had spooked him. How he had learned strange languages consisting of clicks and guttural utterances. How he had encountered naked tribespeople living in what travelers marveled as idyllic "innocent" circumstances until the inhabitants blew poison darts into the guides' necks to halt the usurpers encroaching on their territory. As Blackie spoke, he painted images of floods, man-eating fish, and undiscovered waterfalls that spilled pristine waters into valleys below.

Bri found herself enthralled by his animated storytelling.

In Brazil, it seemed, beauty and danger greeted an adventurer at every turn. Time seemed suspended—Bri forgot that Blackie might be a thief and a murderer. Fascinated, she was caught up in the detail, peppering Blackie with questions. She forgot that the search of his home was occurring at the same time. She couldn't get enough of Blackie's tales of Brazil. An idea popped into her head. "You should write a book, Blackie. *Blackburn's Tales of Brazil.* The *ton* would clamor for it."

"Perhaps in my retirement, Lady G. But my old gray head may not remember it all."

"Write it down, Blackie." Bri laughed.

"What is so amusing?"

"My tutor gave me a diary to record my thoughts. That was one of his frequent phrases, 'Write it down.' "

"I'd like to read it someday."

"It wouldn't take long. I think you'd be bored."

"Why? I'd like to have more insight into your thoughts."

"Blank pages tell no tales."

Blackburn pulled back and looked at her. "Nothing?"

Bri shook her head and popped a bite of potatoes into her mouth.

Sitting back, Blackburn said, "I can understand writing in code, to keep people from discerning the truth, but not to write down anything at all? You'll forget your life."

"I have an excellent memory, Blackie. It is unlikely that I shall forget anything important."

"We all forget at one time or another."

"Speak for yourself. I don't forget."

"Part of your charm, Lady G., is your utter and complete self-confidence. Shy women hold no appeal for me. I like your direct nature. We could be a good team. We could go to Brazil. Conquer a new world together. A new challenge every day would energize you."

Bri actually considered it for a moment until she returned to reality. "Maybe. Just maybe, Blackie. After the Season, maybe."

"That's better than 'no' or 'never.' "

"You see, Blackie, courting is paying attention to a woman's preferences. If your true desire is to court me, then persuasion, not force, is in order."

"Then persuasion it will be, my lovely Lady G. May I persuade you to let me call on you next week?"

"Ah, I fear I cannot, Blackie, as my friend Lady Clarissa von Dusterberg is getting married next week to Dr. St. Cloud, and I shall be helping her with the preparations."

"Then what better environment than a wedding to show me the preferences of a woman, Lady G? May I escort you to Lady Clarissa's wedding?"

Feeling cornered, Bri stammered a bit, "Well, ah, Blackie, another gentleman is escorting me to that event."

Stiffening, Blackburn spat out, "James."

It sounds like a curse.

***

Edward

More than an hour had passed when Edward walked back up the stairs to the terrace and caught a glimpse of Blackburn and Gabriella having an animated conversation. It infuriated him, but he drew on his Asian lessons in self-control to regain his composure. Taking a flute of champagne from a passing waiter, he melded into the crowd, as if he had never been absent.

***

Jean-Louis

The French trapper watched Henry walk up the back stairs moments after Edward. After the earl disappeared onto the verandah, Jean-Louis locked the back gate, mounted his horse, and led the other two horses back to Lord Ravenshire's stables. He hailed a Hackney to take him back to the ball to resume his guard post with Chérie near Lord Ravenshire's carriage.

***

Blackburn

Without waiting for Bri's answer, Blackburn scanned the room for his rival, finding James engrossed in conversation with the earl on the terrace. Inclining his head toward Bri, he said, "Making certain your father knows of his interest, I am sure. Lord R. trusts no one more than I, not even the pretentious Mr. James."

***

Bri

Realizing that their conversation was getting beyond her control, and a bit concerned that the next dance was promised to one of Edward's friends, Bri tried to catch her father's eye to come over to rescue her.

To her relief, Henry walked toward her, handing his plate to a passing server. He put his arm around Bri's shoulders. "Good evening, Blackie. Did you and my daughter enjoy supper?" The earl tried to gauge the situation from the look in Bri's eyes.

"Yes, Lord R., it was delicious. We had a long discussion about Brazil. I suggested that Bri visit Brazil with me sometime."

Bri bristled. "That would be inappropriate, Blackie."

"Not if we were to marry, Lady G."

"Again, Blackie, I am not ready for such a commitment."

Keeping silent, Henry raised an eyebrow at Blackburn.

"Forgive me, Lady G., my passion exceeds my manners. I simply cannot hide my love for you. I pray you will someday return that love. And now, as the orchestra is returning, I shall take my leave of you. Thank you for a delightful supper conversation."

"Lord R." He nodded to the earl and left.

***

Blackburn

Could I kill her? Am I capable of it? She is dear to me, but stands in my way. I love the trading company. I could find another to do it, and kill him. Footpads are willing to do anything for money. But could I give that order?

***

Bri

Edward waited until Blackburn had left, and then walked across the terrace with a purposeful gait toward Bri. "Did you enjoy the evening, Lady Gabriella?"

Bri whispered. "Ask me later. Were you successful?"

"Yes. We have proof."

Even though she'd hoped for proof, a deep sadness struck Bri. "Then it's true. He killed Uncle Rychard and Uncle Luc. What about Aunt Aelwyn?"

Gwyneth and the count arrived to hear Bri's reaction. Gwyneth's face drained of color.

Henry nudged her. "Not here. We must play our roles." He put his arm around his sister's shoulders and said in a low voice, "It is as we suspected. Boyd is seeing to the legalities." Addressing the count, he added, "I will explain all when we are alone. For now, discretion."

Nodding their agreement, Gwyneth and the count sipped their champagne.

"The garden is quite interesting, designed by a Frenchman, I believe." Edward spoke for nearby ears. "Not a complete maze, but enough twists to make for an interesting walk."

"Quite so, Young James. The air in here can get stifling. Nothing like a walk in the cool English night air to revive one's spirits."

The fourth dance was announced, and Bri partnered with Vaux, as arranged earlier. She had demurred for the fifth dance, pretending that she had a partner already. This dance was a variation of the previous reel, with more twirling and spinning. Edward's friend danced with flair. When they met in the center of the line to whirl around, he had only moments to speak. "You seem distant tonight. Not your usual spirited self."

Bri had a ready answer in case anyone noticed her distraction this evening. "My grandmother watches all that I do and gives me what she calls, 'helpful suggestions.' I feel as though I am one step away from falling, failing in her eyes."

"I don't believe for a minute that you cannot stand up to your grandmother. Dancing is freedom. Dance!"

Smiling, Bri's tension dissipated and she gave herself over to the moment.

CHAPTER FORTY-SIX

Saturday, April 13, 1811 – The Masquerade Ball at Pytchley Palace
Henry

As Henry watched Bri and Vaux, he noticed Charlotte and The Nemesis were in the same line. They danced and twirled almost under his nose. The muscles in his cheeks flexed with anger and jealousy.

Gwyneth touched her brother's arm. "Are you all right?"

"In a word? No." Shaking off his mood, Henry whispered in her ear, "Not until tomorrow morning when Blackie will be arrested."

"I wish I could kill him myself."

"Do not ever mention that wish to anyone, Gwyneth. Our family has suffered enough death. The authorities will handle this matter. Revenge is an empty passion. Do not let hatred destroy you as it has destroyed Blackie."

"He doesn't look destroyed to me. He looks confident and successful."

Edward shook his head. "He is cornered, Lady Gwyneth. He will strike out. We must be vigilant."

Bri and Vaux came to join them, breathless from the reel. "I need time to calm down before the next dance."

Edward flagged a waiter with punch. Everyone in the group took a glass.

Friends came around to pay their respects. Viscount Armstrong, who would have the next dance, wore a simple midnight blue mask.

After that, Bri would dance with Banfield, whose mask was painted as the keys of a pianoforte, in keeping with his musical skills.

Banfield whispered to Bri, "You and James are lucky. I haven't met anyone."

Vaux overheard. "Maybe next year, Banfield."

"Dear God, no." Banfield shook his head. "To go through this torture again?"

Charlotte and Drummond walked toward them.

Henry raised an eyebrow and fixed his gaze on Charlotte. "I see you are with Machiavelli's reincarnation. Are you supposed to be a subject of a da Vinci painting?"

"I am in the costume of Lucrezia Borgia."

The earl peered at her necklace. "Is that a vial of poison hanging from the braided cord? Shall I summon a taster for the balance of the evening?"

"No need to get melodramatic, Ravenshire."

"Naught but a bit of humor, Drummond." Drummond's smugness inflamed Henry's ire, but he checked himself.

"Humor about death, Ravenshire? Not what I'd expect of you. You appear to have no costume, but the privateer's mask is apt. Are you no one?"

Charlotte sipped her Champagne. "Tottie, stop it."

"Tottie? Your old university nickname. I've not forgotten Tottie's indiscretions."

"Nor I yours, Young Viscount."

"Is that what they called you, Henry?"

"Or His Excellency," added Drummond. "To Ravenshire, everything he liked evoked a comment of, 'Excellent.' "

The music began again and Bri took Viscount Armstrong's arm.

Time passed quickly, and after her dance with Banfield, Bri headed to a bench on the terrace. The cool night air revived her. Vaux followed her out of the ballroom with another glass of punch.

Vaux raised the punch glass and said, "To the last dance."

"I'm exhausted. I deliberately didn't agree to a last dance."

Edward walked over. "I heard that." He leaned over and whispered in Bri's ear, "I want the last dance with you."

Bri resisted. "Two dances with the same partner is tantamount to an engagement."

"Would that be so terrible?"

"So many things are swirling through my head, I don't know what to think about anything."

The duchess swept by and immediately deduced that another dance was in the offing. "I thought we had an understanding, Mr. James."

Edward nodded. "So we did, Your Grace. I've twice asked your granddaughter to marry me."

"If you know Bri well enough to ask her to marry you, you should know that forcing her to dance with you is a poor choice."

The duchess vanished into the crowd as quickly as she had appeared.

As the orchestra began to tune its instruments for the next dance, the voice of the duchess rose over the crowd. "For our last dance, another waltz, I am taking it upon myself to suspend the normal protocols of the *ton*. Ladies, you may choose your partner for the last dance. If you choose a man you danced with earlier, it will not be considered an intention to become engaged. It is merely a dance. This change in protocol applies to *my* Masquerade Ball only."

Mouths dropped open and normally shy women moved quickly to claim their partners. Lady Melanie picked Vaux, Lady Patricia chose Banfield, and Lady Clementine claimed Hanforth.

Bri looked at Mr. James. "Shall we?"

"I thought you'd never ask." Edward led her onto the ballroom floor and swept her up in his arms for the waltz. "An executioner's mask is somewhat off-putting, Mr. James. You look a bit sinister. Should I fear you?"

"Never." There was a tenderness in Edward's voice Bri hadn't heard before. "I will be grateful for the end of this ball, so that I will never have to see you in Blackburn's arms again."

"He is getting more and more bold in his assertions of love for me."

Feeling Edward's muscles tense, she was alerted to his anger as he said in a controlled tone of voice, "What do you mean?"

"Well, he cannot stop asking if he can court me, declaring his passion for me. He even tried to invite himself to Clarissa's wedding and asked me to go to Brazil with him."

Edward's voice was icy. "By this time tomorrow, he will be in jail."

"Will he be kept in jail?"

"Doubt not. My friend, Judge Aldrich, has assured me that Blackburn will be in jail until trial, and our evidence is incontrovertible. If we did not have to wait for a writ, then Blackburn would be arrested here, in full view of Society. That would be my preference, to embarrass him thoroughly, to ruin him publicly."

"I can feel your muscles tense up when I mention Blackburn, even though you have masterful control of your voice."

"I did not realize you could feel my tension. Apparently, I am not as 'masterful' as I thought."

"No, Mr. James. You cannot fool Lady Gabriella Wyndward. I am now an expert on you and can predict your every move."

Edward winced as he recalled he had said something similar to her. "Is that so, Lady Gabriella Wyndward? Well, maybe Mr. Edward James can find a surprise or two for you."

The music began and Edward whisked Bri around the ballroom.

***

Blackburn

One pair of eyes did not miss Lady G.'s selection of a dance partner. Anger, humiliation and possessiveness rose within him as he evaluated his situation. *Lady G. is clearly more interested in James than she is in me.* He had to be careful because his position at the trading company could be affected if Bri complained about his advances to Lord R.

His plan for years had been to marry Lady G. to secure an heir of his own to the Wyndward fortune. How much longer would he have to wait? She had to agree to marry him willingly. *Removing James as a rival by killing him is too dangerous. My aggressiveness is making Lady G. nervous, any fool could sense that. I must change my approach. Perhaps if I rescue Lady G. from an overly amorous James, I would be perceived by Lord R. to have saved her honor. Then she might marry me to save her self-respect in public. If I lose this opportunity, both Lady G. and Lord R. will have to die.*

A new plan began to form in Blackburn's mind. He would stroll outside for some air, and be waiting when James took her outside for another kiss. Seeing James kiss Lady G., he would pull her away. Lord R. would be grateful, James would be humiliated and Lady G. would have no choice but to reject the banker's advances as forced.

If she admitted to having permitted those advances, she would be ruined in Society. *An excellent plan.* He took a glass of champagne from a passing server and silently toasted himself.

When Edward and Bri began to dance, Blackburn went over his plan and convinced himself that it was flawless. Fury rose as he watched the couple dancing in each other's arms, in sync with the other's movements.

The first time the couple swept past the French doors, Blackburn suggested to Henry that they take some night air on the terrace, and they began walking toward the doors.

The next time they swept past, Henry and Blackburn paused to watch them. Blackburn said, "An attractive couple. I guess the best man won, and I must recognize when I am defeated."

"You've spent so much time in the office, Blackie, that you've missed out on the social benefits of your position. There are some other very attractive young heiresses here that I'm certain would find you quite a catch."

"Lord R., being an heiress is not a requirement for my affections. You have been so generous in my compensation that I need not look to any woman to enhance my financial position. Rather, I crave the warmth and closeness of a lifetime companion. If truth be told, sir, your daughter has always been like a goddess to me, so it is with great regret that I release her to the courtship of Mr. James."

Henry nodded.

On the third time past the French doors, Edward noticed Blackburn. *Damn! He saw me.* Blackburn guided Henry to a position around the corner, out of view. He hoped that Edward would think they had walked back into the ballroom and take a chance on another surreptitious kiss. Blackburn engaged Lord R. in small talk about Society and the *ton.*

But the young couple did not appear when expected and Blackburn began to doubt his plan until the whooshing sound of a lady's skirts as she waltzed directed his attention to his right. There they were, Edward embracing Lady G. with a passionate kiss.

"Hold there!" Blackburn approached them, speaking loudly. "How dare you take advantage of Lady Gabriella!"

***

Henry

Henry knew that despite Blackburn's obvious move, Edward would take the only course open to a gentleman and propose to Bri. Then he remembered that Edward had, in fact, proposed and that Bri had turned him down. *She must say yes now or be ruined in society.* He followed Blackburn over to the couple.

Startled, Bri and Edward pulled away from each other to find themselves surrounded by a shocked group of onlookers. Blackburn stepped forward. "I accuse Edward James of forcing his attentions upon Lady Gabriella. This is shocking behavior for a gentleman. I challenge you to a duel to defend the honor of Lady Gabriella."

The crowd gasped, as duels were outlawed. Still, everyone knew that hotheaded young gentlemen occasionally turned up wounded from such challenges. No one had been killed in recent years, but there was always that risk.

Bri was incensed. "My honor does not need to be defended in any silly duel."

Ignoring her outburst, Edward coolly assessed Blackburn. "Lady Gabriella has just agreed to my proposal of marriage. No duel is in order, as her honor is intact."

"What?" Gabriella's mouth dropped in disbelief. "What did you say, Mr. James?"

Henry joined the fray, saying, "My daughter is going to marry Mr. James, so there is no challenge to be met. We can set aside the notion of a duel and get on with the ball."

Bri embraced her father and whispered in his ear, "I have agreed to marry no man."

Henry whispered back through clenched teeth, "Be quiet and trust me on this."

Bri remained silent.

Audibly, Henry said, "The date is not yet certain."

The duchess swooped through the doors. "A wonderful evening for my granddaughter's engagement."

Henry pulled Blackburn aside. "There is no issue, here, Blackie. But I thank you for taking what you considered to be appropriate action to defend my daughter's honor."

The crowd dispersed, leaving Blackburn and Edward staring at each other with smoldering hatred.

"I repeat, James, I challenge you to a duel for the honor of the hand of Lady Gabriella."

"I accept your challenge, Blackburn. Pistols at dawn by the stables in the old city park."

"Done," said Blackburn and turned on his heel.

***

Edward

Henry stepped toward Edward. "This is a dangerous move. The constable will not be able to arrest Blackburn before dawn, and you risk imprisonment yourself should he die from your bullet. You are engaging in outlawed behavior. It is understandable but reckless." After the briefest of pauses, Henry added, "I shall be your second."

"Thank you, sir."

"Do I have any say in this matter?" Bri stomped her foot in frustration. "Your behavior is outrageous! How dare you men take my life into your hands and throw yours away at the same time? The constable will arrest the man tomorrow morning, but you have decided to kill him yourself to enact revenge? Is this not the very course you abandoned in favor of the legal one?"

"This is between men, Bri." Henry's jaw was set with determination.

"Oh, stop acting like schoolboys! We are talking about life and death now, and you have both lost your senses. I simply will not tolerate it!"

"You have no choice," said Edward. "It is decided. Now we must rejoin the ball so that the *ton* may congratulate us."

Bri fumed. "Do not expect a wedding date to be set at any time in the foreseeable future. I shall never marry such an arrogant, foolish man."

"I believe I understand your position." Edward took her arm. "Let us present ourselves to Society."

Resisting at first, Bri relented and entered the ballroom to polite applause in recognition of their engagement.

CHAPTER FORTY-SEVEN

Saturday, April 13, 1811 – Blackburn's Townhouse
Blackburn

L eaving the ball, Blackburn impatiently demanded that the
stablemen bring his horse. He paced until it was brought to
him. After mounting, he galloped directly to the stables
behind his home and instructed his grandmother's recently arrived
Gypsy henchmen to stay on alert. He stormed through the back
entrance to his house and headed into his study.

"Years of planning destroyed," he muttered. Thinking through his
options, he consoled himself with the pleasure he would gain from
killing James. An excellent shot, he expected to take James by
surprise, and then make his escape on a ship sailing later that
morning to North Africa. He made it his business to know the daily
sailing times in case he needed to leave on a moment's notice,
whether for his job or his survival. From his landing in North Africa,
he would make his way to Alexandria, where the main bank that held
his secret funds was located. He went to his safe and took all the cash
in various currencies, as well as several letters of credit issued by a
Swiss bank that would be accepted at any major bank in the world.
He had small fortunes stashed on all continents. In his experience,
trust could be short-lived in foreign jurisdictions, even at banks.

His weathered leather traveling bag, packed at all times for a
getaway, held passports in several identities and nationalities. He had
acquired them for a pittance during his legitimate business trips

abroad. *There is a black market for anything.*

His riding boots were specially designed to hide knives in each, and he had a small pistol he camouflaged in his waistcoat, which also held pockets where he secreted his cash and letter of credit. As he looked around his study and the house he had inhabited but never embraced, it struck him how little he would miss it. Vengeance thwarted left him feeling empty. *The game is afoot. I will not accept defeat.*

The diary that contained his innermost life would be his companion as he reinvented himself in a new mold in a new land, or lands. He would get word to his grandmother. When he opened the drawer where the diary was hidden, his senses went on immediate alert. The ink bottles had been moved. He had instructed his day butler never to touch the contents of his desk. *Could I have disobeyed?*

Blackburn recalled that today had been the day butler's holiday, and he had written the most recent entry in his diary the night before. He distinctly remembered rotating the ink bottles, as was his habit. The blue ink was in front of the green ink. According to a pattern set years before, the bottle of blue ink had been placed in back of the bottle of green ink and not in front of it.

At dinner, he had not seen James or Henry. *Bri lied to me. She knew they planned to search my house. She danced with me and supped with me to distract me.*

Warily, he picked up the diary. *It has been opened.* His obsession for secrecy had not been foolish. A black thread around the strap that held the diary closed was meticulously woven around it each time he closed the diary. That thread was missing. Blackburn knelt on the Oriental rug, whose design concealed the thread, but he moved his hands over the surface, felt it and lifted it up. The expression on his face froze. *So you know.*

Blackburn, methodical as ever, evaluated his options. He could go immediately to the docks and catch the midnight ship to South America. But that would mean abandoning the revenge that had fueled his life. His grandmother would brook no such abandonment. She would act if he did not. His task was clear.

First, he wrote a set of instructions for his butler about mailing letters, informing him that he had engaged an estate agent in Scotland to sell his home, and that he would provide letters of reference to all employees as well as a year's wages. He then wrote a series of letters. One to his grandmother explained his need for a quick departure and requested patience for many months until he would be able to contact her from his new location. Another letter went to Arthur, his grandmother's confederate, instructing him to come to London to sell Blackburn's house and give the proceeds to his grandmother. Both letters were sent to Arthur's attention. Last, letters to each of his small staff expressed appreciation for their service, and contained one year's wages in cash as well as a letter of reference for each. He melted sealing wax, trickled it on each letter, and pressed his seal, carved with the crest he designed for himself, into the hot drippings.

James must pay for foiling my plan. Bri should be mine. Furious, fuming and frustrated, the answer came to him in a flash. *I will advance the timing of the duel. I will follow them and confront James tonight. He will not have a weapon. Perhaps I should take Bri by force, maybe take her with me. Perhaps I should let James live to know that he could not protect his lady. But I must beware that damned Frenchman. He is a force to be reckoned with.*

Resolved that he had found the key to punish James, Blackburn placed the diary in his bag, signaled to Midnight to jump into it, and strode out of the study without looking back. He locked the door, even though there was nothing left to hide or protect, mounted his horse, and headed into the night. *I have one more task to complete in the event of my death.*

CHAPTER FORTY-EIGHT

Saturday, April 13, 1811 – The Masquerade Ball at Pytchley Palace
Bri

Edward and Bri strolled through the room, aware that they were the subject of everyone's conversation. Feeling trapped by the *ton* and its arcane ways, Bri was torn between wanting to marry Mr. James, but having vowed that she would only marry for love, she saw no way out. Mr. James would be forced to marry her to save her honor. Of course, he had proposed before tonight, which was of some comfort, but now she would always feel it was Society that had caused their marriage, not love.

For a moment, she considered the possibility that they could delay the marriage long enough that tonight's embarrassing scene would be forgotten. Even as this idea crossed her mind, she knew it to be no more than a futile hope. *Tonight's confrontation will be etched in the minds of the* ton *for a long time. Gossip has a long life.*

***

Edward

Edward likewise said nothing, His mind was focused on the upcoming duel. He was an excellent shot, but he assumed that Bri was right about Blackburn. He would no doubt cheat. What were the implications for a gentleman under those circumstances? The old model of walking ten paces, then turning, would not fit against an opponent like Blackburn. Edward decided to insist they take their positions facing each other, then being handed their pistols by their seconds. It would be unusual, but the only real protection against an early move by Blackburn. Then it hit him: Blackburn didn't have a second. Since no negotiations were needed, which was the usual job of a second, it didn't matter. The time and the place had been decided.

As the applause surrounding the announcement of their engagement ended, Edward stared into Bri's eyes. "No matter what you think now, I am marrying you because I want to, not because I must save your honor. I proposed in the past, and I ask you again, "Will you marry me?""

Bri's expression showed her frustration. "Can you understand how insignificant I feel? As if the world is making my decisions and I have been reduced to the status of a child? Let us end our talk of marriage until I have had more time to reflect. But I understand my duty, and I shall make no more outbursts that might embarrass you, Aunt Gwyneth or Father."

"Your outbursts are an annoyance, not an embarrassment. I am not concerned about your outbursts. I am concerned about your willingness to marry me."

"So my feelings annoy you? Do not push me any more tonight, Mr. James. I am exhausted and confused. The ball is over now. Oh, God help us, here comes my grandmother."

The duchess whisked her fan in front of her face. "An unclever way to announce your engagement. And that Mr. Blackburn left in a huff. Rejected suitors can be dangerous."

"It's all happened rather quickly, Grandmother. We aren't setting a date yet."

"No rush." She swooshed away to bid her guests farewell.

"Please take me home, Mr. James. Now that we are engaged, we can ride together in your carriage."

"Very well. I'll tell your father of our plan."

Edward found the earl, whispered something to him, and gathered their cloaks.

There was a lengthy wait for carriages, augmenting the tension between them.

***

Blackburn

In a nearby alley, Blackburn and two of his grandmother's Gypsy henchmen, sworn to obey Blackburn's commands, waited in the shadows.

After Bri and Edward climbed into Edward's carriage, Blackburn signaled to his driver to follow them.

This is going to be easier than I thought.

***

Edward

In the carriage, Edward took Bri's hand. "There will be no duel. It is simply a ruse to be certain of Blackburn's whereabouts tomorrow so that we can have him arrested. Your father and Aldrich have talked and Aldrich is sending word to Boyd and the Bow Street Runners." Putting his arm around her, he softened his voice, "This is already over, darling. Perhaps his arrest will deflect attention from our engagement announcement and any scandal will blow over as he is exposed as a criminal."

Bri's hopes rose. "Do you think that is really possible? The idea of being forced into a marriage without love saddens me. I love you, Mr. James, but knowing that you do not love me would make the marriage a sham and break my heart."

"Must you be so melodramatic? I care for you very deeply and you mean more to me than anyone I have ever known. Is that not enough?" He pulled her close to him and kissed her. "Since we are engaged, can you call me Edward instead of Mr. James? The formality is off-putting."

"Edward."

"Imagining you dancing with Blackburn nearly drove me mad. I wanted to draw a pistol against him. Is that not wild enough for you? I would kill for no one else." He intensified his embrace and kissed her again, deeply.

***

Bri

Bri gasped as Edward's tongue forced her lips apart and explored her mouth. She found it hard to breathe and felt her heart beat so fast she feared she might faint. They became so entwined that they did not notice the slight bump that bounced the carriage, but then they were thrown to the floor as the carriage came to an abrupt stop.

The door flew open and Blackburn laughed at their dishevelment, awkward positions and shocked faces. "James, no duel is necessary. I have decided to take Lady G. away with me tonight to Brazil." He pulled the gun from his waistcoat. "Do not move or I shall be forced to kill you both. Lady G., get out of the carriage."

Looking at Edward then back at Blackie and his gun, Bri slid toward the door as instructed.

Edward never flinched while he kept his gaze trained on Blackburn. "So you know."

"Of course I know, you inept fool. Did you think you could read my diary undetected? You think you have discovered the truth but you know nothing of deceit. The only question now is how I will exact my final revenge." He glared at Bri. "I will not make you suffer, Lady G. You will not die. Not like your Uncle Rychard, nor your Uncle Luc." Glancing back at Edward, he added, "But she will be lost to you, James. I shall take her away, tonight. I want you to live to know this, to imagine her in my arms."

Bri's face was frozen in terror. "Come out now, Lady G., so I can make you a real woman. You'll beg me for more." He pulled her roughly out of the carriage.

Edward reached under the seat of his carriage and pulled out a pistol.

Bri's eyes widened. *I didn't know Edward kept a gun in his carriage.*

The men stood with guns cocked, staring at each other.

Blackburn taunted him. "You might hit Bri. Are you such a good shot, James, that you can hit me without killing your love?"

Taking advantage of his focus on Edward, Bri slipped out of Blackburn's grip long enough for Edward to fire a shot, but Blackburn ducked and the shot missed.

Edward lunged toward Blackburn, who fired, hitting the banker in the shoulder. He fell to the ground, writhing in pain.

"Edward!"

"He's only wounded. If I wanted to kill him, he would have been dead when I opened the door." Blackburn kicked Edward's pistol under his carriage and waved his gun at the driver. "Move and you're dead."

The driver nodded and put up his hands.

The shooter pulled Bri to her feet and dragged her toward his horse. He secured the pistol in his breeches, lifted her up, then mounted, spurred the horse and took off.

To avoid being thrown, Bri had no choice but to let Blackie's arms envelop her. Bracing herself as they rode, Bri sat immobile with fear. Many times she had asked her father how he had escaped dangerous situations. "I played for time, distracted my captors with talk, and eventually the prospect of ransom persuaded them to release me," she remembered him telling her. *Blackie doesn't want ransom, but I can distract him. But if I don't know where he's taking me, how will Edward and Father find me?*

CHAPTER FORTY-NINE

Early Sunday, April 14, 1811 – Interior of Lord Ravenshire's Carriage
Henry

Wrapping up the story of Blackburn for Count von Dusterberg as they made their way through the streets to the earl's townhouse, Henry added, "And that is what we learned tonight." Pulling up to the front door, Lady Gwyneth, the count and the earl exited the carriage. Henry looked up and was surprised to see the footman, in the driver's perch.

"Where is Jean-Louis?"

"He followed Lady Gabriella and Mr. James on horseback. He was worried Blackburn might be lurking to ambush them."

Henry's face clouded. "I didn't think of that." Walking up the steps to his townhouse, he turned and called to the footman, "Where did he get a horse?"

The footman shrugged. "He borrowed one."

The earl led Gwyneth and the count to the parlor and poured three glasses of sherry. Just as they raised their glasses to their lips, Thompson called out, "Lord Ravenshire! Hurry!"

The butler rang for Nashmir.

Putting down his glasses, Henry rushed to the door to see Edward staggering up the stairs with the help of his driver, bleeding from the shoulder.

Thompson and Henry reached for Edward as he sank into unconsciousness.

***

The Streets of London
Bri

As Blackburn's horse carried them through the moonless night, Bri knew that she had to think quickly and clearly. Her initial fear and shock had dissipated somewhat but she steeled herself against the lingering sense of foreboding that threatened to engulf her. *Edward is not dead. Surely his driver will take him to Father. If I can keep my wits about me, I will survive.*

They were moving too fast, hooves clomping over cobblestone streets, to permit conversation. It was just as well, as Bri needed time to formulate a plan to deal with her precarious situation. The ride seemed to take hours when in fact she knew it lasted but minutes. Soon she began to suspect that they were heading toward the offices of the trading company. It made sense. Blackburn had access at any hour, and if he planned to leave the country and claim the money she was certain he had hidden in various foreign banks, he could easily board a departing ship from the adjacent docks and disappear forever.

They turned into the alley next to the Wyndward Trading building.

His two henchmen stayed out of sight, following Blackburn and his captive at a distance to remain unseen.

***

Wyndward Trading Offices
Blackburn

Blackburn dismounted. "Come, Bri, this is our rendezvous. No more 'Lady G.'—you are mine now." He pulled her off his horse.

Two swarthy men on horseback approached. He looked to one and said, "Watch for any unwelcome visitors." He motioned to the other to follow him.

Forcing one of Bri's arms behind her back, Blackburn pushed her toward the rear entry, which he unlocked without a problem, and shoved her into the dark stairwell.

"Up." Bri stumbled several times, trying to slow down her

progress as much as possible.

Her abductor relentlessly pushed her on.

When they reached the top, he unlocked the door to his floor. He motioned to his henchman to stay. "Guard this entrance."

He pushed her toward his office, forced her into a chair, and then closed the door. "We will have our moment together, Bri. If you had just gone along with my plan, our son would have been the heir to the Wyndward Trading and Ravenshire fortunes. Mr. James, that preening, foppish banker, ruined everything."

Bri found her voice and tried to disarm him with warmth. "Blackie, I've always liked you and looked up to you, ever since I was a child. Did you always hate me?"

"I do not hate you, Bri. You are the one who first called me Blackie, and made me feel part of your family." He scoffed. "Your family. I hate what your family represents. Money. Power. Landed nobility. From my earliest memories as a child, I hated your grandfather, the 10th Earl of Ravenshire."

"How could you know anything about him when you were a child? Hate is such a strong word. Why did you hate my grandfather?"

Blackburn smirked. "It is not unusual for a son to hate his father, Bri. Such hatred is the stuff of history."

"Your father?" *Could it be true?* "If that is true, then Uncle Rychard was your brother. And you killed him! He was kind, he never hurt you."

"You think you know the truth. You never will. Your grandmother, Lady Rebecca, died before you were born. Did you know that your grandfather took his pleasure with an innocent young girl employed in his household? My mother cared for Rychard, your aunt and Henry after the death of their mother." Blackburn's tone became increasingly angry. "He forced himself upon my mother repeatedly, and afterward tossed her aside, threw her out into the street with a few coins. Sadly, she loved him. A foolish girl whose mistake killed her."

"What? She died?"

"Yes. She died shortly after I was born. I was raised by my grandmother. She vowed to wreak vengeance upon the 10th Earl of Ravenshire and all his descendants, and I was to be the weapon." Blackburn slammed his hand down on his desk in rage. After a few moments of silence, he regained control. "Mr. James thwarted my initial plan for revenge, planned for so long. You were the key to avoid any more bloodshed. I am wealthy now and have many resources throughout the world. I shall leave with the knowledge that I have achieved a small measure of vengeance by taking you with me. Anyone who tries to stop me will die." Blackburn's tone conveyed a calm determination. "Who knows when I will return to claim the rest of my inheritance?"

"But your name. Would not my grandfather or Father have recognized it?" Bri stalled for time. *Will Father guess he took me here?*

"You foolish girl. Blackburn is a name I chose. My true name is of no import. Your grandfather could have married my mother and made me legitimate, but he did not. I doubt you know my middle name. Do you?"

Bri shook her head.

"The name I chose for myself is Duff MacNeill Blackburn. Duff means 'dark.' MacNeill means 'son of Neyl. I avoided the unusual spelling of your grandfather's name." He scoffed. "You Wyndwards and your 'y's. I am the unwanted son, the dark son."

Momentarily speechless, Bri gathered her wits. "Was there not a record of your birth? You told me you grew up in Scotland."

"You try my patience, Bri. My death was recorded shortly after my birth. Such recordings are easy to acquire with the right payment to the right official or cleric. I had thought you cleverer than you reveal yourself to be. New identities shielded my grandmother and me, even from the reach of the powerful 10th Earl. I'm certain he wanted me dead along with my mother."

"She died following childbirth. That was not his doing."

"It *was* his doing. She was too young to survive a difficult birth."

"My mother died in childbirth. It was not my father's fault."

"Really? Ask your uncle, Lord Darlemont. He believes Lady Jane died of neglect and melancholy."

"How do you know that?"

"I make it my business to know about your family…my family."

"How did you acquire new identities?"

"Enough of your questions." He got up and circled her. "I know your mind, Bri. I've seen it in operation all your life. You're trying to distract me."

"We're waiting for a ship's departure, correct? We must not be noticed. Crowds must be milling about. We might as well pass the time in conversation, Blackie. I'm curious, as you know. You've worked with my father for over twenty years. Why now?"

"Securing a position at Wyndward Trading was essential to my plan. I am a patient man, more so than my grandmother. She dispatched your grandfather with poison."

Bri gasped. "We thought it apoplexy."

Blackburn laughed. "Of course you did, that was the plan." He sat down again. "I found myself quite suited to the work at the trading company. In fact, I rather like Henry. Your father, my older brother. That is why he still lives. I needed him and his protection to propel me to my current position."

"But why kill Uncle Rychard and Uncle Luc?"

"You think you know the truth, but you are gullible. You cried over your grandfather's death. A man with no respect for women. Rychard and Luc were killed to eliminate the possibility of a male heir. As you developed into a young woman, I rather fancied you as a bed partner, although as a half-niece, it's a forbidden love. I am confident that you will breed well." He warmed to his tale.

Bri encouraged him with her attention, knowing that each moment's delay increased her chances of escape or survival. Blackburn was an enigma, a terrifying enigma. *A hurt child, cheated of his mother's love, his birthright. An understandable hatred nursed by a bitter grandmother.* "But why did you not appeal to my father's sense of fairness?"

Blackburn scorned her query. "*My* father had naught but disdain for the law. Blood revenge was the only course available. There was no way to prove my mother's claim that he had been her only lover."

"But you are intelligent, successful. By all appearances, you have built an enviable life for yourself in Society and gained respect throughout the world. Grandfather rarely left the estates. You have become so much more than he. You should be proud of your accomplishments, not bitter at your losses."

"Do not lecture me." Blackburn's rage flushed his face. "I will not tolerate that from a Wyndward!"

"But you are a Wyndward yourself." Bri leaned forward. "Don't you see that you have destroyed yourself by killing the others? And that by taking me by force, you are no better than he?"

"You don't know what you are talking about. I am not destroyed, but your family will be. When you are no longer virginal, do you think your noble Mr. James will want you? No, my darling niece. He will walk away from you and not tarnish his family with your shame. Perhaps we might even create our child and heir tonight. That would be rich. The captain on the ship can perform our marriage ceremony. Our union will be legal, not by force."

As he stood and moved around the desk toward her, Gabriella tried to deflect his attention. "Marriage without my consent is marriage by force. Don't you see that you would be committing the same crime as my grandfather? Why kill Uncle Luc?"

"Are you not paying attention? To avoid another potential male heir. He was not a bad sort. Now, Bri, any more questions for me?" He leaned against the desk in front of her and crossed his arms. His eyes widened as the door flew open.

Jean-Louis held a pistol in his hand. "Release her."

Blackburn's gun was on the desk.

"Move and I'll shoot you."

"Where—"

"*Your* men?" Jean-Louis scoffed. "Indisposed."

A swarthy man staggered in behind Jean-Louis, and knocked him to the floor.

Taking advantage of the moment, Blackburn reached for his pistol, grabbed Bri and forced her out of the room, leaving Jean-Louis and the guard alone. Over his shoulder, Blackburn called, "You should have killed him, Frenchman. I thought you knew how to deal with predators. Maybe you're not the greatest trapper of all time."

Stop it!" Bri cried out. "Stop it, Uncle Duff!" *Maybe I can shock him for a moment so that I can escape.*

Instead, he pulled her closer to him. "Shut up, niece. I will teach all the Wyndwards a lesson through you." He forced her into the hallway.

A shot rang out in the office behind them, followed quickly by another. The silence terrified Bri more than Blackburn. *Jean-Louis...*

CHAPTER FIFTY

Sunday, April 14, 1811 – Lord Ravenshire's Townhouse
Henry

Thompson and Henry carried Edward to the kitchen and laid him on the worktable that doubled as the servants' dining table. Nashmir arrived from the garden, instructing Henry to boil water and sterilize a knife while he examined Edward's wound.

Obeying without regard to his position, Henry did as Nashmir ordered. In matters such as this, Henry recognized that whoever knew the most should assume command. Henry watched Nashmir probe Edward's wound.

"It is deep, but not fatal. No blood vessels were hit, and the bullet is lodged in the muscle. I can feel it, and should be able to remove it when the water is boiling and the knife is sterile."

"About another minute."

"In the second drawer on your left are some smelling salts. We must revive him as I need to gauge his strength while I am dislodging the bullet."

Henry opened the drawer, retrieved the smelling salts and handed them to Nashmir.

Holding the acrid salts under Edward's nose revived him. He sputtered, blinked his eyes and winced with pain until he was fully conscious.

Nashmir kept him from moving. "Mr. James, I am going to remove the bullet—"

"No, no," Edward interrupted. "We must save Bri. Blackburn has her. He has threatened to—," then Edward could not speak, having become faint. Nashmir held the smelling salts under his nose, bringing him once again to full sensibility. Edward continued, "He has threatened to harm her, to rape her to shame the Wyndward family and me. I fear for her safety. We have no time to spare. We must find her now!"

Henry's jaw set with determination. "How did this happen?"

"After he left the ball, he went home and detected that we had found the diary. He came back, lay in wait, and followed Bri and me when we left the Masquerade Ball."

The count frowned. "Where would he have taken her? Did he give you any indication?"

Edward shook his head.

Henry squinted as he considered the options. "If he intends to leave the country, as I suspect, he will go to the docks, to catch the next ship."

"He was dressed in traveling clothes." Edward coughed and grimaced in pain.

"He might try the trading company offices to wait out of sight," mused Henry. "He could get in and at this time of night there would be no activity. We should head in that direction and fan out until we find them. If Jean-Louis followed him, we are one step ahead of Blackburn already. Thompson, prepare three horses." Looking at the count, Henry asked. "I hope you will accompany us?"

"I would have been insulted if you had not asked. And anticipating your next question, I am always armed."

As Edward rose to leave, Nashmir pushed him back into his chair and looked at Henry. "Give me the knife."

Henry wrapped a towel around the hilt and took the knife from the boiling water. He handed it to Nashmir.

The Tibetan glanced at Edward. "Be still and this will be over soon." Expertly, Nashmir cut into the shoulder. Edward winced in pain. Nashmir extracted the bullet, and used a towel to stop the bleeding. He rubbed an unguent on the wound, then ripped another towel into strips and wrapped it around the wound in makeshift binding. He offered Edward a swig of whiskey. "I know you intend to ride to find Lady Gabriella. This may dull the pain. Lord Ravenshire, please take some smelling salts, in case Mr. James loses consciousness again." Looking back to Edward, he added, "You are in no condition to ride, but I know I cannot stop you."

Edward, the count, and Henry walked to the stables and rode to the trading company, faster on horses than any carriage could transport them. They rode grim-faced and single-minded in purpose.

Arriving, they noticed a candle flickering on the top floor. "His own office. The blackguard," muttered Henry. They dismounted. Reaching into his saddlebag, he pulled out two pistols and a knife. "Edward, which suits your pleasure?"

"A pistol. I can shoot nearly as well with my left hand."

"Count?"

"I have a knife, my preferred weapon."

Henry took the other pistol and the knife. "I suspect Jean-Louis is nearby. He is always armed." Peering around the alley that led to the rear entrance, he spotted Blackburn's horse and two more. A body lay on the ground. "Approach carefully. It may be a ruse."

The count bent down to check the man's pulse, knife at-the-ready. He quickly determined that the prone man was dead.

"There was probably another man who went inside. Be on guard. Remain silent until I give you a signal."

They followed the earl's lead and silently made their way up the stairs, running into Blackburn and Bri on the second floor landing.

Blackburn whirled around, grabbing Bri by the throat and holding her in front of him as a shield, his knife pointed at his brother. "Do not come any closer or I will break her neck."

The sight of Bri's dishevelment, her dress ripped across the top and sleeves, the skirt askew, her hair tousled, enraged Henry. "Damn you, Blackie. I trusted you. All these years, I trusted you with my life, my company, my family."

Holding firm to Bri, Blackburn simmered. "We will leave here undeterred. Back down the stairs slowly."

"No. Let Bri go, Blackie, and we will spare your life."

"You spare my life, dear brother? I think not."

"Yes, brother. I know you are the bastard son our father sired."

Blackburn appeared stunned. "You knew of me? And you did nothing?"

"I knew our nanny disappeared one night. We loved her. You should know that, why I care to tell you, I don't know. On his deathbed, our father told me of a bastard son. Sir John's father had found out and then lost track of the child, declared dead in court records. Father made me swear to make things right by my unknown brother if he lived. The will contained a provision of lands and an annuity for that son should he ever be identified, and the money has been earning interest at James & Co. since his 'death.' So you see, Blackie, had you been honest from the beginning, you would have been accepted and even richer than you are now. Instead you killed our brother, Rychard—our brother-in-law, Luc—and how many others?"

Blackburn laughed. "You think you have all the answers. You are wrong about everything. I didn't kill our father, but he didn't die of apoplexy. Poison is the handiwork of my grandmother. In fact, I rather liked him after I met him. An impatient woman, she acted without telling me." Blackburn paused. "So he acknowledged me at the end. That is some comfort. I always liked you Henry. That is why you are still alive."

While Blackburn spoke, Henry didn't shift his focus, but saw Jean-Louis in the blur of his peripheral vision, bleeding, creeping soundlessly down the stairs from the third floor as a mountain lion stalking its prey.

Momentarily distracted by Henry's revelation, Blackburn relaxed his grip on Bri's neck.

Bri managed to slip out of Blackburn's grasp. She dropped to the step and tried to slide down the stairs, but Blackburn grabbed her by the hair. She screamed.

Seeing his opportunity, Edward shot the knife out of Blackburn's right hand. Blackburn bent over in pain, but pulled another knife from his boot with his left hand and lunged at Edward, who fell backward into the earl and they both tumbled to the bottom of the ground floor landing, knocked unconscious. Again, Bri screamed. "Father! Edward!"

***

Blackburn

The count threw his knife in a split second, embedding it in Blackburn's left shoulder, opposite his injured hand, causing Blackburn to drop his knife.

With Edward and Henry sprawled unconscious at the bottom of the steps, Blackburn tried to pull the Count's knife out of his shoulder with his wounded right hand, but could not maneuver his fingers adequately. Using his left hand he was able to remove it. It fell to the floor and he bent over as if to pick it up, but instead pulled a gun from its hidden position in his breeches and rose with the gun and pointed it at Bri.

The count stood disarmed.

Blackburn stared at the count. "Move out of the way. You have no weapon."

"But *I* do." The voice of Jean-Louis came from behind Blackburn.

The count raised an eyebrow. "We are at an impasse, Mr. Blackburn."

"Get out of my way, you Prussian dog."

Blackburn was losing blood and he began to sway. He sat down, still holding his gun, whirled around and shot Jean-Louis in the gut, causing him to drop his gun.

Bri paled in horror. "Jean-Louis! Are you all right?"

The Frenchman fell to the side of the steps, holding his hand over his bleeding abdomen.

"No, dear niece, your Frenchman is mere moments from death." Blackburn struggled to his feet and kicked the count.

The count fell backwards toward the others, his cry stifled when he hit his head on the banister.

Blackburn scrambled down the stairs, pulling Bri behind him, pain searing through his arm, but he maintained his grip. He yanked her over the pile of unconscious, perhaps dead, bodies at the base of the stairs and out into the cool night. A soft rain fell. He wrenched Bri's arm as he pushed her toward the docks. Scanning the ships docked along the wharf, Blackburn reckoned it was past three o'clock in the morning. The next ship to sail would be to North Africa, at dawn.

He looked at Bri, whose scraggly appearance would be noticed at once if anyone saw them, not to mention his own bleeding. The black shirt he had donned for his escape hid the stains when viewed from a distance, but from close scrutiny the bleeding was evident. *We must move fast to avoid detection.*

Making their way to the docked ship, Blackburn bribed a deck hand to let them aboard. He found an empty storeroom and pushed Gabriella down on sacks of flour. "I may die from these wounds your impotent would-be protectors inflicted on me. But you will be ravaged by the crew when they find you. He kept the gun pointed at her. "Be honest, Bri. Don't you want to travel with your uncle?"

"You may have killed my father, Edward, the count and Jean-Louis. You are evil, bereft of honor."

"You speak to me of honor? A Wyndward speaking of honor?" He started to laugh, and the eerie sound of it echoed in the small enclosure.

***

Bri

Blackburn's manic behavior gave Bri a boost of energy. She felt beside the flour sacks for a weapon of some sort and felt something that she guessed to be a section of pipe. She calculated that if she were able to strike Blackburn hard enough, she could push the door open and escape. Her youth and lack of injury gave her more than an even chance to outrun Blackburn, especially if she ran screaming to attract attention.

Blackburn was tending to his wounds.

Bri knew she must act now or endure the unspeakable. Firmly holding the pipe, she brought it down rapidly toward Blackburn's head, surprising and enraging him. The next blow she delivered to his wounded left shoulder, and he doubled up in pain. It was enough movement for her to slip off the sacks, and stand. She hit him again and leaned against the door lever, opening it with the force of her body. She stumbled, then quickly recovered and began to run along the deck, screaming, "Help! Please, someone help me!"

She heard shouting by the gangway and thought she recognized her name. Just as she reached the railing to exit the ship, a shot rang out, a bullet whizzed by her head, missing by a fraction of an inch. She turned to see Blackie staggering with the gun in his left hand. Ducking below the railing, which had canvas laced on each side, she raced down the gangplank into Edward's arms. Henry called to Blackburn to give himself up to Boyd, who had arrived upon being notified by Nashmir of the group's suspicions.

"Never!" Blackburn disappeared into the caverns of the ship.

Henry turned to Edward. "Take Bri to safety."

Boyd and Henry ran into the ship to find Blackburn.

Turning to Edward, Bri's fear shone in her eyes. "Jean-Louis?"

"He's alive. The count is tending to him."

They headed in that direction.

Bri looked back at the ship. "How will they ever find him?"

"They will." Edward's eyes rolled up into his head as he lost consciousness and fell to the ground.

∗∗∗

Boyd

Boyd and Henry raced directly to the bridge. The officer on duty informed them that only a few crew members would be on board until about an hour before sailing. He showed Boyd and Henry a diagram of the ship and suggested there were innumerable places Blackburn could hide.

Boyd told the officer, "I have the authority to prevent this ship from leaving the port. We need this man, dead or alive."

"You can't do that! We have two cargo holds with many sections, not to mention the crew decks, kitchen, store rooms. Any delay in sailing will be financially disastrous. We'll miss the tide."

"Then help us find this man."

The officer rang the alert bell. The few men on board scrambled to find out what was wrong. "A fugitive is on board, bleeding from a hand and shoulder. He has a gun. Tell us where he is and we will apprehend him. Do not approach him." The officer explained their mission.

A crewman volunteered, "I saw a man bring a young woman on board earlier."

"You should have told me. We do not permit women on board. You will be disciplined. The woman was in danger from that man, but she is now safe," said the officer. "Beware the man we seek—a cornered, wounded animal is dangerous. Call for help. Do not try to capture him yourself."

The crewmen were divided between Boyd and Henry. The earl gave Boyd Edward's gun and each took a section of the ship, directing the crewmen where to search.

After an hour, they still had not turned up any evidence of

Blackburn, and by pre-arrangement, met back on the bridge. As they reviewed the ship's diagram to see where they might have missed something, they heard a shot. Looking toward the docks, the count was waving wildly, pointing to the back gangplank. Henry and the others ran outside on deck to see a black-garbed figure running down the back gangplank, and they headed for the front gangplank to exit dockside, racing down to chase the black figure.

For a wounded man, Blackburn moved well. He pulled a man off his horse, mounted and rode away, black bag in tow. He disappeared before they could make chase.

With little more than an hour before dawn, the passage of time had increased traffic in the area. Boyd convened the group. "He may return. Leaving by ship is still his best option. He is wounded. Adrenaline may fuel his actions, but time is on our side. Edward, your wound is bleeding again. Go back to the constable's carriage where one of my men is with Lady Gabriella. The rest of you take positions along the dock, with one of my runners with each of you, to prevent his boarding any of these ships."

***

Blackburn

Blackburn had gotten off the stolen horse almost immediately after he disappeared into the crowd. He circled back around to position himself behind a building where he could see his horse. Bri had one Bow Street Runner guarding her. He spotted another one nearby.

He laughed. *These people are so predictable.* Bri was looking at the ship. The second runner was out of her line of sight. Blackburn stole up behind the runner, pulled out a knife, and hit the runner with the hilt, knocking him out. He dragged the body around the corner into an alley and changed clothes with him, being careful to keep his bloody shirt and pants. He left the way he'd come. *Bri never heard a thing.*

Now dressed as a Bow Street Runner, he pulled the hat down, waved to Boyd, and strode up the gangplank. *People see what they expect to see. They looked at the hat, not the black travel bag. I'm escaping right under their noses.*

Blackburn thought it best to hide out in the ship the Bow Street

Runners had just searched, figuring that they would not suspect he would return to the same place. He saw he was right when he got to the deck of the ship. From his high vantage point, he spotted them moving toward ships farther down the docks. Walking slowly with his bag, he moved into the shadows of the ship, ducking into the same storage closet where he'd held Bri. Deck hands, cargo handlers and officers were beginning to arrive. While their presence made it more difficult to spot Blackburn, they also increased Blackburn's risk of arousing suspicion among the ship's personnel.

A drunken crewman wandered into the storage closet and mumbled, "Who the hell are you?"

CHAPTER FIFTY-ONE

Sunday, April 14, 1811 – The London Docks
Bri

A black-clothed body fell overboard, hitting the water in full view of onlookers, including Bri, Edward, Boyd and Henry. The body was bashed against the dock and began to sink. While the constable tried to rope in the body, it was outside their reach.

"We will have to wait for the tide," said Boyd, "but I believe that we have seen the end of Mr. Blackburn."

At Boyd's direction, Bri and Edward rode in a Hackney, accompanied by a Bow Street Runner. Henry and the count mounted their horses. Jean-Louis was lifted into the constable's carriage with Boyd. A Bow Street Runner rode the Frenchman's horse, borrowed from Pytchley Palace, and took the reins of Blackburn's and the other two horses that belonged to the dead men. They agreed to meet at the earl's townhouse.

Inside the Hackney, Edward put his arm around Bri and pulled her to him. "Are you all right?"

"Shaken, but safe. How can we be certain Blackie is dead?"

"Boyd's men will find the body." Edward's hand had been bandaged, but blood was seeping through. "It is the most obvious conclusion."

"That is why I doubt it. Blackie is a planner, a plotter, a patient man. He waited to kill, stalking us for years. His actions are rarely spontaneous."

"You're imagining the worst. The man is dead. You'll see."

When they arrived at the earl's townhouse, Jean-Louis was carried inside. Edward limped behind them. The count and Henry were bruised from their falls, but nothing serious. They stood outside to speak with Boyd. The Bow Street Runners saw to the settling of the horses, and commandeered them to service. "We can always use more horses for the runners, courtesy of Mr. Blackburn."

One of his runners approached and handed Boyd a message. Boyd crumpled it and his jaw set in anger.

"What is it?"

"One of my men was found dead, naked in an alley. That's how Blackburn got by us." He shook his head. "The man with the hat was Blackburn. I thought it was one of my men."

"Then who fell?"

"It could be Blackburn. The body will wash up. Then we'll know." Henry turned to the count. "The sun is up. You have a wedding in a few days."

The count laughed. "Yes. I need sleep."

"That knife throw was impressive."

Shrugging off the compliment, the count demurred. "Standard army training. Good morning, Lord Ravenshire." He stopped and turned, adding, "Happy Easter."

"Easter? I completely forgot in the terror of last night." Henry walked inside to find how Nashmir was treating the wounded.

Bri was begging the Frenchman to lie still.

"Nonsense," argued Jean-Louis. "I have been in far worse shape before. Nashmir will repair this minor wound quickly. I trust him more than any Society doctor." Looking at Bri, he asked, "How is Mr. James?"

Edward was sitting while Nashmir stitched his shoulder. Bri hovered over him.

Henry tilted his head. "A masterful job, Nashmir." Standing by Jean-Louis, he sighed. "Just how many lives do you have, old friend?"

"So far? More than a cat."

Edward looked glum as he looked at Bri. "I could not protect you from that man. I failed you."

Bri disagreed. "Edward, Blackie was driven by a vengeance that made him dangerous and unpredictable. Luckily he was so wound up in boasting of his murderous exploits that his abduction of me failed."

"Edward, I want you to spend the night here so that Nashmir can check on you and Jean-Louis."

"That is not necessary, Lord Ravenshire."

"It is not necessary, Edward, but it is my wish." Henry's tone signaled that he would tolerate no more discussion.

While Nashmir tended to Jean-Louis, Henry filled a pot to boil more water and dropped two clean towels in the water. "I know my role in these matters."

Bri went to review the provisions in the large guest room. It had two beds, the best venue in which to place the two wounded men. She went upstairs, and satisfied herself that all was in order. Returning, she indicated that the guest room was ready for them.

"Perhaps you should sleep a bit." Henry appeared concerned.

"I am not a delicate flower."

"True. But you were in the grip of a madman. Perhaps one of Nashmir's teas will help you sleep."

"Not for me, but for Edward and Jean-Louis, most definitely."

She kissed Edward, and then walked over to kiss Jean-Louis on the forehead.

"You were both very brave. Thank you for coming after me."

When Nashmir finished repairing the Frenchman's wounds, Henry and Thompson helped Edward and Jean-Louis up the stairs.

He had pre-mixed the tea for them, and the cook brought it up on a tray.

Bri saw to their settling in the guest room, and then left. She climbed the stairs to her rooms, and greeted Jane Anne, who was waiting for her.

"Milady, were you terrified?"

"At moments. I'm exhausted." With Jane Anne's help, she discarded her ripped and ruined dress, hoping that Mlle. Bellerobe might be able to duplicate it for another occasion.

She splashed water on her face, climbed into her bed, and immediately fell into a deep sleep.

CHAPTER FIFTY-TWO

Monday, April 15, 1811 – Lord Ravenshire's Townhouse
Bri

When Bri awoke, it was dark. She stretched and felt Spotty's tongue on her cheek. "How did you jump up on the bed? The splint is off. You're frisky as ever!" Smiling with her eyes still closed, she wrestled with her new friend and then opened her eyes, realizing this was the most relaxed she had been since the whirlwind of her discovery of Blackie's deception. Slowly she rose from the bed, pulled open the drapes and looked out on the moonlit garden.

Jane Anne knocked on the door, and Gabriella called out to her to enter. "Come in, Jane Anne."

"You slept all day. Are you hungry?"

Calmly, Gabriella walked over and put her arm around Jane Anne's shoulder, saying, "First, I am quite unharmed. Second, I was too busy trying to figure out how to keep Blackie talking to be terrified for very long. And he really did not intend to kill me. He wanted to abduct me to punish our family for my grandfather's rejection of his mother. The truth is, Blackburn was an illegitimate son of my grandfather. All this time, he hated our family for my grandfather's sin. Hate and revenge destroyed him."

Jane Anne was stunned. "Is he really dead?"

"The constable has assured us that when the body is recovered from the water, it will be Blackie."

"But you are not sure. I can hear it in your voice."

"It seemed too simple. To fall to his death? I'll believe it when Boyd, of the Bow Street Runners, confirms the body is Blackie's. I am looking forward to a soothing bath tonight, but first I must eat something. Where are Mr. James and Jean-Louis?"

"They are downstairs. Dinner is almost ready."

Bri splashed water on her face and sponged herself off. She selected a dress and Jane Anne helped her pull it on. Her hair had been loose last night, so the maid gathered it up on top of her head. "We can wash it tonight."

Going downstairs for supper, Bri felt relieved and wondered if it was because Blackie was truly dead. *Could I have a sixth sense about it?*

Bri stopped in mid-step when she saw her father, Edward and Jean-Louis. The bruises of the night before stared back at her. Her father's head had a purplish bump on his temple, a gash near his ear, and he was using a cane to support his weight. Edward's shoulder clearly bothered him, impeding the use of his right arm. She remembered him refusing any painkillers from Nashmir the night before. *Why suffer in pain? I don't expect him to be a hero.* In addition to a black eye and other red swollen areas on his face, Jean-Louis looked ashen. *He must have lost a lot of blood.*

"I'll be right back." Bri quickly went down the steps to the greenhouse. "Nashmir?"

The Tibetan was tending his herbs. "Yes, Lady Gabriella?"

"They look terrible! Is there something you're not telling me?"

"Your father fell and injured his head and his leg. Nothing is serious. Edward's wound will heal with time. Jean-Louis was the most seriously hurt."

"He looks like he lost a lot of blood."

"He did, but I gave him something that will help it regenerate. The body is capable of healing itself. He needs to restrict his activities."

"Unlikely."

"At night, I'm giving him a special healing tea to sleep. Sleep is a special time of healing. You, however, seem to have escaped physically unscathed. But you must not bury your memories of last night. There can be mental wounds as well."

"I don't know what you're talking about. I'm perfectly fine. I slept all day."

"You were kidnapped and might have been taken from us forever. We might not have been able to find you. Blackburn might have done unspeakable things to you. For you to dismiss this is not how most people would react."

"I'm fine, Nashmir. If I can't sleep or have frightening dreams, I will come to you. Last night, I felt that if I could keep Blackie talking, the delay would give Father and Edward time to find me. Truly, I was much more afraid for them than I ever was for myself."

"Sometimes the mind builds walls to protect itself. Months from now, that fear may surface when time has passed. Be aware of that possibility. It may surface as irritation or a short temper to push the discomfort out of your mind."

Bri gave him a half-smile. "Some might say I'm always like that."

Nashmir shook his head. "You have strong opinions, and become impatient when confronted by injustice. You're not intentionally rude or cruel. That is the change in behavior to watch for."

"Come with me to tell them to rest. They think they're invincible."

"As you wish."

They walked back upstairs and Nashmir stood with Thompson on the side of the dining room where they had moved to wait for her to return.

"Tell them."

"Lady Gabriella requested that I remind you that you must ease back into your normal activities slowly."

Bri took a seat.

The men grumbled.

"There is plenty to keep us busy now that Blackie is gone. There is a great deal of work to be done and having you overdo things and make yourselves sicker will make things worse. We need to do one of those hundred year plans Blackie and Mr. James attribute to the leaders of the Far East. We all know the world is changing. Our strength is working together."

Jean-Louis smiled a crooked line.

"And one more thing. No more secrets. Secrets give others power over us."

"*Foutre*! Just when I think you've learned a lesson, you reveal your innate idealism." The Frenchman scoffed. "As long as people exist, they will keep secrets."

***

Jane Anne

Jane Anne watched Bri with Spotty, petting him and examining his leg carefully, and went to run the bath. "Ready."

"Please let Spotty go downstairs on his own. He's ready."

Bri sank into the tub, covered herself with bubbles and sighed with deep relief.

Jane Anne untangled Bri's hair and poured water over it, then used a special shampoo she had created from fruits, herbs and special creams. It smelled like a fresh morning, and Bri luxuriated in its lather as Jane Anne expertly massaged her head. As the shampoo was rinsed out, Jane Anne gently placed Bri's tresses in a smaller towel, anchoring it closed with a pin. She then left Bri to relax, and gathered up her soiled and ruined gown and shoes, intending to see if there were any possible repairs that could be made.

Certain that Bri would stay in the tub awhile longer, Jane Anne went to the sitting room. She hoped to surprise Bri when she came out of the bath.

On a dress form she'd found in the attic, Jane Anne arranged a magnificent silk taffeta wedding dress, draping the veil over the shoulders. It had been Bri's mother's dress, and Henry had ordered it brought from Ravenshire and cleaned and refurbished in case Bri wished to wear it to marry Mr. James. Everyone had known she was in love before she would admit it, and Jane Anne smiled as she thought of Bri's protests to the contrary. As a final touch, she placed on the floor delicate white silk slippers ordered from Mlle. Bellerobe by Aunt Gwyneth, and hung a diamond pendant from the earl over the dress form.

Only Jane Anne knew that Mr. James and Henry had discussed the possibility of a double wedding with Clarissa and Dr. St. Cloud before the Masquerade Ball, and she was only too aware of her mistress's dislike of others trying to plan her life. Their hope was that when she saw the dress she would appreciate the gesture as offering her an option that was hers to accept or reject.

Jane Anne took a deep breath and hoped that she would not be the subject of Bri's wrath when she saw the dress. Going into the bathroom, Jane Anne held the thick peach-colored cotton robe that

Bri loved as she stepped out of the bath. "Thank you. I feel so much better now."

"Wonderful, milady," said Jane Anne, bracing herself as Bri went back into her bedroom. Not hearing an outburst, Jane Anne shyly stepped into the bedroom and saw Bri staring at the dress.

Looking at Jane Anne with a raised eyebrow, she silently demanded an explanation. "Your father had your mother's wedding dress brought out from Ravenshire in case you might have some use for it."

"And just what use would that be?"

"In case you decided to marry on an impulse, he wanted you to have the option of wearing your mother's dress."

"So you were in on the conspiracy?" Bri's voice didn't sound threatening.

"Yes, I agreed to clean and refresh the fabric so that you would approve. I also had it altered slightly to fit your slim figure."

Silently, Bri walked over to the dress and examined it closely. She had seen it once as a child, and Gio's painting of her mother in it at Ravenshire had always comforted her, but seeing it as an adult, aware of all the implications, was quite an experience. It was more than a beautiful dress. It was a rite of passage to womanhood. "The slippers?"

"From your Aunt Gwyneth. And the pendant from your father."

"Well, well, well," Bri said in a non-committal tone.

Jane Anne did not know what to make of it.

Bri put on her bedroom slippers and went out the door and started down the stairs.

***

Bri

Bri stopped in the second floor guest room where Jean-Louis and Edward had retired after supper. Jean-Louis was up and limping, testing his strength. Nashmir was applying a fresh poultice to Edward's wound.

"Nearly finished with him, Lady Gabriella," explained Nashmir. "As soon as I am certain no infection remains inside the wound, I will stitch it up again. The temporary stitches from last night were ripped out during the altercation. Mr. James will be as good as new."

"Better, I hope."

"What? No sympathy, woman? After I saved your life?"

"I rather think I saved my own life, Mr. James. Your assistance, however, did not go unnoticed."

"Oh, thank you, Lady Self-Sufficient Wyndward. Men are superfluous in most situations. I believe that sums up your philosophy."

Looking at each other in an amused way, Nashmir and Jean-Louis left the room, closing the door. Bri went to the door and locked it, leaving her alone with Edward. Uncertain of her intention, Edward tried to sit up, but winced in pain.

Unsympathetically, Bri said, "Sometimes your behavior is so obnoxious that it is a wonder no one has taken a shot at you before, Mr. James. I believe we had some unfinished business before the late Mr. Blackburn interrupted us. She slowly walked over to him and sat on the bed next to him, then leaned down to kiss him, shocking him by placing her tongue in his mouth. His eyes opened wide and he tried to push her away with his good arm, but she was as strong as he with only one arm and had the decided advantage. She pushed against him even more intensely, and said, "In this particular instance, Mr. James, you are not superfluous."

"Bri," he whispered passionately between kisses. "I thought I had lost you when he shot me, then when we saw the candlelight in his office, my heart soared that you were close by. When he got the better of us, and dragged you out of the office, I was gripped by a fear unlike anything I have ever known. When you screamed on the boat, I feared the worst. I realized then that I loved you and I would kill anyone who ever harmed you."

"Edward! Look at me and say it again, out loud."

"Lady Gabriella Wyndward, I love you. Will you marry me?"

"Yes, Mr. James...yes, yes, yes!" Bri sank down on top of him. Her robe fell open, partially exposing a breast, and Edward kissed it gently, feeling Bri breathe more deeply. She immediately closed it and pulled away from him. "Not until we're married, you rogue."

He moved his good arm slightly to prop himself up in the bed. "Yes, Lady Gabriella. I intend to make you an expert on certain mysteries of love very soon."

"This is a bit of a shock, Mr. James. I do not know what to say. I must confess I had never really thought much beyond kissing."

"Surely you cannot be so ignorant."

"Young ladies are not taught in detail about biological functions, Mr. James. Awkward though it may seem, you will have to be my tutor, *after* we are married."

"Bri, marry me now. I do not want to wait another day."

"No, Mr. James. There is plenty of time. No rush. Now you must sleep."

"A parting kiss, and I will obey your commands."

"Ah, but your wish is my command, master." Bri kissed him on the forehead. She unlocked the door to return to her rooms and sleep again.

CHAPTER FIFTY-THREE

Wednesday, April 17, 1811 – Sir John's Townhouse
Bri

Edward's parents had insisted on seeing him after they found out he had been wounded in Bri's rescue from her kidnapper. Bri chose a gown from Mlle. Bellerobe that was suitable for a ball or a dinner party. *We're engaged. Edward loves me.*

Jane Anne fixed her hair and helped her on with her dress.

"Have a wonderful evening, milady."

"It won't be a long night. Mr. James needs rest." Edward's wound was healing, according to Nashmir.

She went downstairs and found her father in his study. "Do you have any advice for me about dinner tonight?"

"Why do you need advice? You've known Edward's parents forever."

"But now Edward and I are engaged. Things might be different. He nearly died saving me. They might resent me."

"Nonsense. Just be yourself, Bri. Watch for signs of Sir John's stomach pain. Nashmir's potent herbal remedies have rarely failed, but I want to know if more needs to be done for my old friend."

Edward came downstairs with his arm in a sling fashioned by Nashmir.

"My fiancé, wounded in defense of my honor. My knight in shining armor."

"I don't feel in a shining mood."

"We'll make it an early night."

The earl, Bri and Edward went to the waiting carriage.

Edward winced as he tried to get comfortable.

"Bri, try to remember Edward's parents aren't used to your barbs. Hold your tongue."

"Shall I be a mouse? Is that what my new fiancé expects?"

"Not at all. I believe I have met my match."

"Must everyone be defined in terms of you? Your 'match?' Do not flatter yourself so."

The earl whispered, "Hush."

Edward offered her his uninjured arm and they strolled through the heavy wrought iron gates that reached up twelve feet, ending in an intricate scroll pattern that reflected the rays of the sun.

The butler, Reed, stood at the door. "Good evening, Mr. James, Lord Ravenshire, Lady Gabriella."

"Good evening, Reed."

Reed took Bri's coat. "Sir John and Lady James, as well as Mr. and Mrs. Sterling, are waiting in the library."

Much like Aunt Gwyneth's Music Room, the library featured floor-to-ceiling bookcases. In place of the two pianos were two overstuffed sofas facing each other over a low table.

Rising at their entrance, Sir John said, "It is a pleasure to see you again, Lady Gabriella."

"Please call me Bri, Sir John. And Lady James, your collection of paintings is stunning."

"Ah, you have the eye of a connoisseur, my dear. I must admit to a love of art. Although it can get to be a rather expensive hobby. That is a spectacular dress, Bri. Who designed it?"

"Mlle. Bellerobe."

Lady James raised an eyebrow. "Well, despite her rather risqué reputation, she has an excellent eye for draping and detail. Perhaps I shall visit her salon myself."

"Annabelle, it's been too long." Bri embraced her childhood playmate. "And Mr. Sterling, we must all get together more often now that Edward and I are engaged."

Reed appeared with six Champagne flutes and a cup of tea.

Sir John popped the Champagne, and poured it for the others. He held up his teacup to make a toast: "To health and long life!"

"To health and long life," echoed the guests, raising their flutes.

"Which you both almost lost." Lady James leaned forward. "We were terrified when we heard what happened to Bri."

"Father, Edward, the count and Jean-Louis rescued me."

"Ravenshire, you're looking a bit worse for wear."

"A few bumps and gashes. Edward was wounded but seems to be on the mend. Jean-Louis was shot and lost a lot of blood. He nearly died, but protested as always that he knows when he will die and it won't be any time soon. As if anyone could know that!" The earl shook his head in disbelief. "The count disabled Blackie with an expert knife throw, but Blackie still got the better of us in our first confrontation. At least he is dead now. Let us speak of him no more." The earl turned to Annabelle. "Your ankle is bandaged. What happened?"

"We could not attend the Masquerade Ball because I sprained my ankle tripping over toys."

"If she can't dance all night, my wife is easily bored. Annabelle is permissive, believing creativity in children is more important than organization and storage of their toys. I lose many arguments."

"Do not pretend, Eli, that winning was ever a possibility with my daughter." Sir John laughed.

"I'm caught. I surrender."

Reed announced, "Dinner is served."

They rose and crossed the hall to the dining room. The first course was a creamy pumpkin soup, an unusual delicacy as pumpkins had only recently been introduced to the *ton*. The main course was pheasant stuffed with breadcrumbs and walnuts, rice and spinach. "Bite gingerly, Lady Gabriella," cautioned Lady James. "There may be some shot left in the birds."

"Jean-Louis can hit a pheasant with a bow and arrow. He tried to teach me, but I always missed on purpose." Seeing Edward's smirk, she spoke before he could. "I know it's inconsistent, because I eat what others have killed. I used to perfect my bow shots on high tree branches until Nashmir told me I was harming the consciousness and integrity of trees. So I abandoned the sport." Taking a bite, Bri chewed as instructed, and discreetly used her fork to remove the stray pieces of shot. "The stuffing has an enticing mix of flavors, Lady James."

Lady James smiled. "I thought it might be a light delicacy that wouldn't sit too heavily in your stomachs after all the recent excitement."

"Sir John, you are having only soup and rice?"

"Instructions from your father's man, Nashmir. It has done wonders for me so far, and I am loathe to tamper with success. There will be many other nights to taste my cook's delights once I am fully recovered."

Bri changed the subject. "Mr. James, I mean Edward, is quite an accomplished dancer. I must admit I was surprised at his skill. Did you insist on his taking lessons in his youth?"

Sir John laughed "He fought us tooth and nail, but Miss Courtney's Cotillion was *de rigueur* in the James family, as she had been my mother's roommate in Lausanne. And as everyone learned sooner or later, there was no denying my mother's wishes."

"That is an understatement, dear." Lady James spoke in a tone of wry humor that elicited laughs from the group.

Eli took a sip of Champagne. "Tell me more of this Jean-Louis. He is somewhat of a legend, I understand."

Henry nodded. "He can ride and shoot an arrow like one of Genghis Khan's riders. As a fur trapper in North America, he spent time with native tribes and learned their ways. He has skills I could never master. I once saw him shoot a poison dart through a tube in his mouth – he blew on it and it felled a marauding cannibal chasing us in Java. The rest of the tribe set on him, giving us time to escape."

Bri laughed. "That is an invention of fancy."

"Is it?" The earl raised an eyebrow.

"Do not believe all you hear about Jean-Louis." Bri leaned forward. "But he has ways that are mysterious. Underestimate him at your peril. Many have."

Dessert entranced Bri. A light, fluffy, chocolate soufflé, with a sauce made with an orange-flavored liqueur on the side was placed in front of her. She took a small taste and sat back. "This is wonderful. It's like eating clouds of chocolate sprinkled with cinnamon."

"Remind me to have some when I can eat again as a special reward," sighed Sir John, resigning himself to the bland milk pudding in front of him. "Still, I am grateful to Nashmir. The man is a treasure, Ravenshire. This is the first meal I've enjoyed in months. The pain in my stomach is gone, and I am delighted."

Henry smiled. "Nashmir mentioned to me that he would like to check to be certain that your symptoms were gone. Assuming that you are well, he will then prepare a less potent herbal tea formula that will maintain your health. He said that the ingredients can be easily grown in small herb pots in a sunny window, and he will write out full instructions on growing the herbs from the seeds he has cultivated as well as the recipe for the herbal tea mixture."

"In that case, I shall visit him tomorrow morning," said Sir John. "An interesting man."

"I have seen Nashmir bring people from the brink of death back to life. You're looking at one of them. He has that mysterious Eastern calmness and deep spiritual awareness of nature. A natural healer is rare."

"I will go with you tomorrow, darling," said Lady James. Her eyes misted as she covered his hand with hers. "I want to thank the man who returned you to health."

Edward cleared his throat. "Speaking of returning to health, I am exhausted. I haven't done much but rest since I was wounded, and Nashmir has told me that I must pace myself."

Sir John rose from the table. "Then, by all means, let's make it an early evening."

"Take care of yourself, darling." Lady James embraced her son.

Edward stood and felt dizzy, falling back into his chair.

Bri brought out the smelling salts, and he coughed and blinked his eyes at the acrid odor. Eli and the butler helped him to the carriage, as Sir John and Henry had their own ailments to consider.

Reaching home, Thompson and Nashmir helped Edward upstairs. Nashmir examined his wound. "The stitches have held. You weren't ready for a dinner party, Mr. James. You must rest or you will never recover. We will bring meals to you. Perhaps you may come downstairs for dinner tomorrow evening. Perhaps."

CHAPTER FIFTY-FOUR

Thursday, April 18, 1811 – Dumfries, Scotland
Mirela

Aneira, the new incarnation of Catherine, stood at the window of an inn. After the fire, they had traveled to Dumfries to plan their next move. "I grow weary of waiting. Decades have passed. My vengeance is only half accomplished."

Mirela beckoned her friend to sit across from her. She reached down into her carpet bag and pulled out her crystal ball. She placed her hands on it and chanted the words she had been taught so many years ago.

Catherine peered, staring at the faceted orb. After a few minutes, she looked away. "I see nothing."

"Concentrate."

She tried, but to no avail. "The time for waiting is over. We need to send more watchers."

"My other watchers vanishing. The cards saying they are dead."

"Then they were unlucky or incompetent. We need eyes on the ground who will not fail."

"Let us sleeping on it. Come."

The gypsy led her friend to their bed and wrapped her arms around the woman whose lust for vengeance and hatred of men she had shared since their first meeting so long ago, and began to kiss her neck, inhaling her scent, and pulling her closer, entwined in an embrace.

CHAPTER FIFTY-FIVE

Friday, April 19, 1811 – St. George's Church
Bri

In keeping with church requirements, the banns for the marriage of Clarissa Hanforth von Dusterberg and Nicholas St. Cloud were first read on March 24th and had been repeated the following two Sundays.

On the wedding day, at nine o'clock in the morning, the bridesmaids wore pale pink and carried pink tulips, Clarissa's favorite flower. Bri served as maid of honor, with Lady Patricia, Lady Penelope, Lady Melanie, Lady Clementine and Lady Marianna as attendants.

Jean-Louis served as best man, with James, Hanforth, Lord Lt. Thornton, Vaux and Banfield as groomsmen.

Clarissa's gown by Mlle. Bellerobe was of ivory silk, with puffed sleeves, empire bodice, and a train.

Standing next to her as Clarissa and Dr. St. Cloud said their vows, Bri was totally focused on holding the flowers for Clarissa while she said her vows, and keeping in mind how the processional should flow. She was so lost in her thoughts that she barely heard a word of the ceremony. When the word "love" was used, she stole a glance at Mr. James, who was also looking at her. He winked and she smiled, and then returned her gaze to Clarissa. She focused on the final words—

> I give you this ring as a symbol of my vow, and with all that I am, and all that I have, I honor you, in the Name of the Father, and of the Son, and of the Holy Spirit.

Dr. St. Cloud put the ring on Clarissa's finger.

The vicar joined the right hands of Clarissa and Dr. St. Cloud and said,

> Now that Clarissa and Nicholas have given themselves to each other by solemn vows, with the joining of hands and the giving and receiving of a ring, I pronounce that they are husband and wife, in the Name of the Father, and of the Son, and of the Holy Spirit.

> Those whom God has joined together let no one put asunder.

The newly married couple kissed, and then turned to walk down the aisle out of the church, accompanied by triumphant organ music, followed by Bri and Jean-Louis, and the other bridesmaids and groomsmen in order of their positions.

The guests threw flower petals in front of the couple as they walked by.

Carriages outside ferried the wedding party and guests to the Hanforth Mansion for the reception.

***

The Hanforth Mansion
Edward

When the guests arrived, servers immediately appeared and began to move through the crowd with champagne, and tables with hors d'oeuvres were uncovered while the dinner was being prepared.

We could have been married today, but better that the day belong to Clarissa and Dr. St. Cloud alone. The harrowing night with Blackburn still haunted Edward. *I almost lost Bri.* Returning to their normal lives, the rites of passage of the *ton,* and the world in general, seemed irrelevant when contrasted to the stark realities of life and death that they had just faced.

As the butler rang the bell announcing the main meal was served, the guests retreated from the garden and took their places in the grand dining room.

The table at the front of the room was configured for the wedding party. Bri sat with Edward. Female and male wedding attendants alternated seating placement. Jean-Louis sat on Clarissa's right next to Lady Clementine.

Bri leaned forward and whispered to Clarissa, "Are you going to be the star on opening night?"

"It would appear so, as the original actress is quite ill and no one else is prepared for the role. I have used your suggested subterfuge of a wig to convince Father that I can perform until the designated actress recovers. I have chosen a stage name that I think you'll appreciate—Violetta Vinci."

Bri laughed. "I like it."

Edward and the veterinarian looked at each other, shaking their heads in amused disbelief. Edward said, "I guess that is the lure of the stage—becoming someone else."

"Perhaps you should try it, Mr. James." Bri picked up her flute of Champagne and sipped. "What would your stage name be?"

Brushing her request aside with a wave of his hand, Edward said, "I have come around to your way of thinking in terms of financing the theatre as a legitimate enterprise. Do not push me any farther, Lady Gabriella. Bri." *I can't get used to calling her by such a familiar term. Why does she still call me Mr. James?*

"Oh, you have no idea what is in store for you, Edward James."

Looking at the doctor for support, Edward shrugged. "No man ever does." Taking Bri's hand and raising it to his lips, he added, "But I am going to enjoy finding out."

"With the arrival of the Sultan tomorrow and the opening of *The Princess* on Monday there is no time for a proper honeymoon. The doctor and I have been discussing an extended trip to Africa with my cousin as a guide after our obligations to the play are completed. Would you like to accompany us?"

"Before we are married?" Bri glanced at Edward. "Maybe with a chaperone. We are looking for a townhouse where Edward will live until we are married."

"It's time I got out of the club."

"Finding the right home, decorating it and hiring the staff will be time consuming. Along with my work on the estate, I cannot envision taking the time to travel for a number of months, so the timing may coincide with the end of the operetta's run. Shall we break some more rules and take our honeymoon before the marriage?"

"It seems that we have entered the modern age, St. Cloud. The obligations of your wife and my fiancée are dictating our honeymoon plans. Perhaps we should occupy ourselves by picking out the wallpaper."

Clarissa shook her head. "That is a frightening thought."

"If we need furniture moved, then we will request your decorating assistance." Bri sipped her Champagne. "Otherwise, occupy yourselves elsewhere."

***

Friday, April 19, 1811 – Dumfries, Scotland
Mirela

The elderly Gypsy looked over the vegetables at the market, took the newest offerings, selected the ripest fruit and bought a freshly butchered chicken for dinner. Carrying her shopping bag, she trudged along the rainy streets until she reached the stairs to the apartments over the antique store where she and Catherine lived. Sighing at the prospect of pain from her arthritic knees on the steps, she hoisted herself up each one, opened the door and hobbled to the kitchen table. After she put the food away, and affixed the chicken on a spit, which she would turn every twenty minutes, she sat down, exhausted.

A nagging internal voice, one she never ignored, told her to pull out the cards. Absent-mindedly, she dealt them into a pattern on the table and stared at it. Disturbed, she gathered up the cards, shuffled them, and spread the array again. *The same result.* She looked out the window. *More change. No rest for us. Will he failing? Will my Catherine losing her battle?*

CHAPTER FIFTY-SIX

Friday, April 19, 1811 – Lord Ravenshire's Townhouse
Bri

After the wedding, Edward returned to the guest room in the earl's townhouse so that Nashmir could supervise his recovery from the bullet wound and fall.

Jean-Louis moved back to his room adjacent to the stables.

Edward was still awake when the door opened and Bri came in. She locked the door and tiptoed over to him. She was carrying a small bowl filled with liquid.

"What is that?"

"A sponge soaked in vinegar to avoid pregnancy."

Edward stared at her. "You shouldn't speak of such things."

"Really, Mr. James, we are not yet married and it would not do to produce a bastard. This is an ingenious device used for millennia. Biblical, almost. Ancient Jews used this method. They say Casanova used a lemon cut in half to cover the cervix."

"The what?"

"Do you know nothing of human anatomy, Mr. James? Just because you can't see it doesn't mean it's not there."

"You are making this scientific rather than spontaneous."

"Would you like a spontaneous baby?"

"No."

"Very well, then. I have practiced the technique. Watch. You dip the sponge in vinegar and insert it." She handed the bowl to him.

Edward blanched. He lifted the sponge from the bowl and saw a string attached to it. "What is this string?"

"It's to pull out the sponge after we're done."

The banker looked as though he might cough up his dinner.

"Really, Mr. James, if you are going to put yourself inside of me, why does this implement shock you?

"I just didn't expect to talk about such things."

"You just thought you'd have your way with me? And never consider the consequences?"

Bri was met with silence. "Ah ha! I'm right. And you think women are flighty? Incapable of analytical thought? It seems to me that not taking into consideration the consequences of one's words, actions, investments, and decisions in general is foolish. Don't you agree?"

"I surrender."

"I don't want you to surrender. I want you to think. If men could get with child, the world would be a different place. Women bear all the consequences."

"Are you talking yourself out of this?"

"Perhaps." She stared at him.

"How did you learn about all of this…" he waved his hand.

"Aunt Gwyneth and my grandmother."

Edward recoiled in shock. "You discuss such things with them?"

"Are you completely dense? Of course. Where else would I learn these things? Once I did the research, I convinced father to import these sea sponges. Women wrap them in silk and attach the string. Distribution is discreet, in ladies shops, hairdressers, and I'm thinking about brothels. We could expand that way."

"What? Are you mad?"

"Not in the slightest. Are you squeamish or prudish? The oldest profession is vast and needs these products. Are you entirely uneducated?"

"When do we put it in?"

"Before we get started." Bri handed the bowl to Edward.

Using his left hand, he lifted it out and squeezed out excess liquid.

"There's lemon juice in there too."

Bri straddled Edward and he awkwardly pushed the sponge up as far as he could. "I thought you intended to wait until we were married. Are you certain you want to do this now?"

"Completely."

He kissed her cheeks, her neck and lips. They spent most of the evening exploring each other's bodies and initiating each other into the ecstasies of love.

Long after midnight, they fell asleep, wrapped in each other, two parts of a puzzle that finally fit together.

CHAPTER FIFTY-SEVEN

Friday, April 19, 1811 – Lord Ravenshire's Townhouse
Henry

Alone in his study after Clarissa's wedding celebration, Henry found himself torn between Charlotte and Taita. *Could Davinia be right that Charlotte is the woman for me? Would the Sultan free Taita? Would Taita stay? Will I really be able to make her part of my London life?*

Against all odds, she was alive. *Is it my fault? Could I have saved her?*

The Sultan, by all accounts, was a man of sensibility and sophistication, but a ruler without the restraints of a parliament or council to temper his ways.

Taita, a princess who once presided over a gentle civilization, had spent more than twenty years as a slave, a prisoner in a gilded cage in a foreign land. *Will she still love me or has too much time passed? How will I feel?*

Despite the count's assertions to the contrary, Henry could not help but wonder if Taita loved the Sultan. He had read of the bonds formed by master and slave, torturer and victim and examined in his own mind the decisions she must have faced. *To be alive is to have a chance.* That is how he survived his days on the island, where he thought he would never return to his family.

A sliver of Taita's island remained. The islanders had chosen Bando, a mystical man, as their new chief. Who could say how that idyllic civilization had changed over these many years? Surely other trading ships had passed, and some off-islanders had chosen to stay. Outside influences could broaden as well as destroy. *How arrogant we are, imposing our will on other cultures.*

Taita had known him as a man in his prime. Henry was still a commanding presence, but, like all men, he feared that his sexual attraction and potency would be tested and found wanting. *Age molds the body to its dictates, but the mind is ever the same.* Desire did not wane, but the body did not always rise to the occasion.

And Charlotte had done nothing to deserve to be ignored. Guilt washed over him. *I must know about my feelings for Taita, or my life with Charlotte would always be one of wondering what might have been.* He told himself he had waited to marry Charlotte because Bri needed his full attention, and his father had warned Henry of the cruelty and duplicity of stepmothers. *Perhaps Father was wrong and should have married Brigid.* We all loved her. And the Wyndwards had enough money to overcome petty gossip. *And perhaps I should have married Charlotte long ago. But Taita always lingered in the back of my mind.* Having endured twenty-five years without Taita, he found himself unbearably impatient knowing that within the span of three days he would see her again.

Nashmir knocked on the study door and asked if Henry wanted anything more before he retired, and Henry released him of any further obligations that evening. "Not tonight. You provided incomparable service lately. I can never repay you."

"No repayment is necessary."

Henry snuffed out the candle in his study and climbed the stairs to his bedchamber on the second floor. He sat by the window, staring into the night, reliving his moments with Taita on the island and wondering if life as perfect as those months could ever be recaptured.

And if by hurting Charlotte he had lost his only real chance at love. He thought of her words. *Am I only thinking of myself? Are all adventurers selfish?*

As the night cleared to reveal a moon surrounded by stars, he knew that she had spoken the truth.

***

Saturday, April 20, 1811 – Lord Ravenshire's Townhouse
Bri

Lying in the pre-dawn darkness, Bri peered closely at Edward's shoulder. It's healing. *There is no redness or odor of infection.* She gently pressed around the wound to see if Edward felt any pain.

He stirred slightly and said, "Nurse, I think you are feeling the wrong part of my body."

"Edward, you rogue!" Bri brushed her lips lightly across his. "Where would you like to live, darling?"

Edward groaned. "Must we decide that now?"

"Yes. If there is a particular section of town you like, we can look there. Otherwise, I shall engage an estate agent Monday, and I shall look at what is available. Do you want to accompany me or not?"

"Since you have already told me that you are making all the decisions, would I not be superfluous?"

"Probably, but I thought it only polite to ask, darling."

"If you intend to look at houses in the *ton* Monday, I shall attend to my business at the bank. There is still the matter of securing signatures on all the matters relating to financing the operetta. That can be accomplished Monday if I get an early start." Edward closed his eyes. "But I need sleep. Monday evening we meet the Sultan and Taita. I hope for the earl's sake that he is not disappointed."

"Do you think too much time has passed to rekindle romance?"

"There is no telling what influences may affect a person over more than twenty years in a foreign land, especially when made to live as a slave, no matter how highly regarded. A slave is a slave, and your father may be disappointed. She may blame him for her fate. One can never predict these things."

"By *these things*, do you mean a woman's behavior?"

"Not at all. The impact of all the forces that changed Taita's life cannot be measured, that is all I am saying. All my comments are not necessarily derivative of a disdain for women, Bri. I am not an ogre, and methinks you doth protesteth overmuch."

"That was a pathetic attempt to quote Will Shakespeare. I will see that our children receive a better education than you. Shocking, really. We do have a few hours to sleep." She stretched her arms and yawned. "But I should go to my own bed before the house stirs."

Bri rose from the bed, put on her robe, and started to move

toward the door.

"Don't forget your implement."

"Good point. That would be difficult to explain." Bri took the sponge and bowl with her.

"Wait! Aren't you going to kiss me goodnight?"

"Haven't you been kissed enough tonight, Mr. James? Time to sleep."

CHAPTER FIFTY-EIGHT

Sunday, April 21, 1811 – Lord Ravenshire's Townhouse
Bri

Bri awoke, stretched her arms over her head on her pillow, and thought about last night and the night before with Edward. She had tiptoed back to her room after their stolen interludes. Thinking about the events of the last few days, she realized how vital Nashmir's healing efforts had been. A germ of an idea took root.

After she dressed, she sat at her desk and jotted down her ideas for investments in Nashmir's potions, Ali's saddle and tack designs, and the final points for the sponge imports to be discussed with Edward before making final arrangements with Mlle. Sabine.

She sat back and thought about where all of her ideas might lead. Ravenshire needed more than her sporadic oversight. A manager or agent they could trust. Someone who understood agriculture, livestock, forestry, relations with wool mills, as well as the operation of the actual household, gardens, stables.

I cannot do everything. Father pays little attention to estate matters. When I spend more time in London, the estate will languish. She gave herself a new project—to transform the management of the estates into areas of responsibility with accountable directors. The complexities in a changing economic environment of the new century would require experts, and take a few years to fully implement. *If I have children, how can I balance all of these responsibilities?* She shook her head and smiled as she recognized what her grandmother already knew. *I am not ready for children. That sponge is essential.*

***

Sunday, April 21, 1881 – Lady Gwyneth's Townhouse
Bri

Dr. Northcliffe walked across the street to meet Bri and Gwyneth for a visit to the Winters Foundling Hospital. Today was Enrichment Day, the third Sunday of the month, and the doctor was intrigued with the hospital and its location near where he planned to build his clinic and hospital.

Guy pulled the comtesse's carriage to the front of her townhouse.

Gwyneth and the doctor climbed into the carriage.

When they arrived at the foundling hospital, Bri was pleased to see another table. She sought out Charlotte. "Who is that?" She pointed to the new face.

"Believe it or not, Mr. Krench is a solicitor who will help women understand their legal rights, meager though they be."

"Come, Charlotte, I want you to meet Dr. Northcliffe."

After the introductions, Charlotte took the doctor on a tour of the hospital while Gwyneth and Bri went over to sit at Bri's table to interview women for positions at Ravenshire.

Bri touched her aunt's arm and said, "The last time I was here, Blackie was here briefly and spoke to that woman. She runs some kind of a school. Maybe she doesn't know Blackie is dead."

***

Gwyneth

Gwyneth walked over to the table marked "Seminary for Women's Work," and introduced herself. The woman sitting there stood and said, "I am Miss Englewood."

"Miss Englewood, my niece, Lady Gabriella," Gwyneth pointed to Bri, "thought she saw Mr. Blackburn here last month. Is that correct?"

Miss Englewood appeared flustered and didn't answer.

"I inquire only because I wasn't sure that you knew of his

441

unfortunate accident."

Henry had kept Blackie's death out of the papers until he could develop a plausible explanation for Blackie's death or disappearance. Perhaps, Henry had mused to Gwyneth, he could say Blackie sailed off and met with a storm or pirates or died of some disease. Miraculously, word of the events following the Masquerade Ball had not been discovered by the gossip rags.

The seminary representative blanched. "Accident?"

Gwyneth went around to the other side of the table and asked the woman to sit down. There was an extra chair, which Gwyneth took. "I've know Mr. Blackburn for over twenty years. I'm sorry to tell you that he died in an accident last week. This is not yet widely known, so please do not repeat it."

A tear rolled down Miss Englewood's cheek. "Mr. Blackburn funded our school over the last five years."

"I can provide funds."

"But you don't know me."

"If Lady Winters has approved you to be here, that is enough of a recommendation."

"Thank you, but Mr. Blackburn set up a trust to fund the school in perpetuity."

Gwyneth sat back. "That was very generous of him."

"He was an orphan, you know, and he saw how women of poverty were treated unfairly. He said that his mother was the victim of poor treatment."

"So you have the funding you need?"

"Yes. We train women to be seamstresses, to work in shops, to become nurses, nannies or governesses." She sighed. "But I relied so much on Mr. Blackburn's advice. How shall I ever replace it?"

Gwyneth smiled. "I know a banker and a woman who has a flair for commerce who can help you. Do you have a board of trustees?"

Miss Englewood shook her head. "But I have a banker who can help. A Mr. Eli Sterling. Do you know him?"

"Yes. He is a friend of my family. We will all help you, Miss Englewood."

A woman heavy with child walked up and shyly inquired as to training to be a nurse. "I've watched the women here and I would like to learn more about the jobs."

Gwyneth watched and listened as Miss Englewood kindly and

expertly discussed the offerings of the school. *This is why I doubted Blackie's guilt. A generous spirit who never bragged of his generosity. No man is all evil. But he recorded his murders in his diary. There is no doubt.*

***

Monday, April 22, 1811 – Office of Greenwich Estate Agents
Bri

Jean-Louis was still unable to climb up to the driver's seat in the carriage as a result of his leg injury, so he instructed the stable assistant, Paul, to drive Bri to the office of Greenwich Estate Agents.

Mr. Greenwich stood to greet her as she entered.

Bri explained her preference, a townhouse on a suitable street, with a park nearby and garden in back. The estate agent looked through his files and identified three that would meet her requirements.

"One is on Eaton Square, a large flat perfect for a newly married couple, with a shared garden. Another is on Berkeley Crescent. The owner is moving to America, and is under some financial distress. The last is in Knightsbridge. That owner recently died and the children do not like London. For all properties, you have the option to take possession with all the furniture and servants, should you so desire."

"As you know," Greenwich continued, "most of the land in the *ton* is owned by trusts under original land grants from monarchs granted during various periods in history. You can expect a 50- or 99-year lease. It is rare that one can buy fee simple land, but the Knightsbridge property I described falls into that category."

"Fine," said Gabriella. "I would like to see these today. My carriage is outside."

"Very well, Lady Gabriella." Greenwich turned to his assistant. "Miss Jones, would you please see to the office and any clients while I am out?"

"Of course, sir."

Bri asked, "Is Miss Jones an estate agent?"

"Oh, no," Greenwich said. "She just makes the appointments, sees the properties first, deals with the clients and paperwork."

"What do you do?"

"I beg your pardon?"

"What is your role?"

"I take clients to view properties."

"To the properties selected and previously toured by Miss Jones? With the clients interviewed by Miss Jones? And sell properties for which the paperwork has been prepared by Miss Jones?"

"Well, yes."

"Then, I should like Miss Jones to accompany us. If someone needs to remain at the office, then that can be you."

Miss Jones didn't waste the opportunity. She stood, took the files out of the hands of the stunned Greenwich, and said over her shoulder, "We'll be back in a few hours." After she climbed into Bri's carriage, Miss Jones laughed. "I'll probably lose my position when I return, but I'm tired of doing all the work while he gets the glory."

"How long have you worked here?"

"Twenty years."

"And you never married?"

"The job is demanding. Men don't like women who enjoy working."

"I've noticed. Tell me, Miss Jones, why is your boss so young?"

"His father owned the license, and as the son, Greenwich inherited it about a year ago when his father died."

"Did his father also expect you to do most of the work? Show clients homes and then turn everything over to you?"

"Yes. And, well….let's just say that he wanted more from me than I was willing to give, but I resisted. It was a battle every day when he and I were both in the office together."

"Do you think you could run an estate office?"

"I already do."

"Could you prepare a list of costs to set up an estate agent's office?"

"I pay the bills, too, so I can do that."

"How long would it take to generate profit?"

"One to two years, I should think."

"Assuming Greenwich doesn't relieve you of your job, prepare a proposal for me for a three-year plan, the amount of money for leasing and office furniture, paperwork, licenses, your living expenses, etc., and come to my home in a week. If he dismisses you, come tomorrow morning."

Stunned, Miss Jones asked, "Why?"

"Because I want to support women in commerce, and I have the money and will to make it happen."

"There is the matter of a license. It might not be granted to a woman."

"Let me take care of that with my solicitors and bankers. As a friend of mine often says, 'There are ways.' "

Miss Jones looked out the window. "Here we are at the Knightsbridge townhouse." The white-washed stone building had black shutters and a massive black door. Miss Jones rang the bell. The door opened to reveal a corpulent butler. He had the red, swollen nose of a whiskey lover.

In fact, Bri smelled whiskey on his breath, and it was not yet ten o'clock in the morning. She decided that this butler would be relieved of his duties immediately, should Edward purchase this house. Often the staff remained with a house when possession changed, subject to approval of the new inhabitant.

The house itself was in need of repair. There was some water damage on the plaster around the windows. When Bri pointed it out, the butler said he forgot to close the windows during a bad storm. *What else might he forget to do?* The public rooms were shabby and the private rooms were musty and covered with a layer of dust, unused except the largest bedroom, which emitted odors of an unsanitary nature. *Even if Greenwich hadn't mentioned it, I would have known that someone died here.* They completed their tour of the house.

Once again in the carriage, Bri and Miss Jones compared their impressions of the house. "Repairs are clearly in order. How soon would Mr. James want to take possession?"

"While the physical space approximates our needs," Bri said, "the state of disrepair suggests it would not be habitable for months. Mr. James can continue to reside at his club, so timing is not critical. One of my fiancé's friends likes to renovate homes. Maybe there's a commercial opportunity for these homes beyond my initial intention of finding a place for us to live. Most people want to walk into a home that is ready to live in, not one that requires months of repair."

"I have some tradesmen I use in similar situations to prepare a house for new owners."

Bri inclined her head as she thought. "A crew. I can see possibilities here."

The next property was located on Eaton Square. It was a flat, one floor in a multi-unit building. While beautifully decorated and would have suited a couple quite well, Bri wanted a home where they could add children and build a cohesive environment instead of moving again and again. "This will not work."

Finally, the house on Berkeley Crescent near Aunt Gwyneth was familiar to Gabriella. As they went up the steps, she could hear children laughing, and took that as a good omen. The butler opened the door. Bri recognized him. "Larsen! Do you remember me?"

"And how could one forget Lady Gabriella Wyndward? You have become a beautiful young woman." Brit turned to Miss Jones and explained, "Larsen is from Ravenshire. He was butler to the elder Dr. Northcliffe, who cared for the townspeople and my family." Turning back to Larsen, she added, "I didn't know the younger Dr. Northcliffe lived across from Aunt Gwyneth. We've been so absorbed in the Marriage Season, we've not been very neighborly."

"Dr. Northcliffe's lease is short term. He wasn't sure he would stay in London or return to Ravenshire."

Miss Jones nodded. "The lease has three months to run."

"Is Dr. Northcliffe in?"

"No, ma'am, but I expect him within the hour."

"We have come to look at taking over the house when Dr. Northcliffe's lease expires. May we trouble you to show us around?"

"No trouble at all." Larsen bowed. "The foyer is slate from the north country. On the left we have the library," and as he opened the door, Bri gasped, for it was almost an exact match to the Music Room of Aunt Gwyneth's home that she had always loved.

"Do you know who the architect of this house was? This room is so similar to one in my Aunt Gwyneth's house."

Miss Jones shook her head. "I don't know the name, although I believe that all the homes on this Crescent were designed and built by the same man."

Larsen continued the tour. "The parlor is here," he said, opening the door to the room across from the library. It was the same as her aunt's parlor but without the built-in bookshelves that distinguished her home. Like the other room, it had a fireplace on the outer wall.

Following Larsen past the staircase, Gabriella saw the large kitchen, pantry, and a dining room that looked out over a lovely garden. A small suite of servants' rooms was located off the kitchen, where the cook and server lived. In the kitchen, these two were busy with one of the children, making cookies. "A treat for the wee ones," said the rosy-cheeked plump woman with a Scots accent. *She must be the cook.* The server was petite, and resembled the cook. "I am Flora, and this is my daughter, Heather," said the cook.

A girl of about six years who was helping wield the cookie cutters looked up.

"And who are you?"

"Julie." she said in a shy voice.

"It's nice to meet you Julie. Your grandfather and father took care of my family for many years."

The child smiled and went back to her cookie cutters.

As they entered the dining room, Bri saw the two older girls playing outside in the garden when she looked through the bay window. One was white and one was African. *He must have adopted an orphaned child.*

Bri had never considered the responsibility of raising children. *How many children will we have? When?* She didn't hear Larsen until he cleared his throat and repeated his words.

"The men's quarters are downstairs, milady, and the women's quarters in the attic. There is room for additional staff, should you so desire."

Upstairs, on the second floor, there were four large bedrooms, each with a bath. There was a central sitting area that was open at the back of the hallway overlooking the garden. "I have never seen an arrangement such as this," said Bri. "I like it very much. The open feeling is quite refreshing."

On the third floor was a master bedroom opening to a sitting room overlooking the garden. At the other end was a large room that was unfurnished. A nursery, thought Bri, again struck by the realities of marriage and its implications.

"Thank you, Larsen. This is a lovely home and I will speak to my fiancé about it. Is there a time when we might both view it together?"

"I am on duty always, even on Sunday, milady."

"I imagine you will be moving with Dr. Northcliffe. Were you in the Cape Colony with him?"

"Yes, Lady Gabriella."

"Thank you again, Larsen." Bri and Miss Jones descended the staircase and stood outside the house. "It appears to be in good repair."

The townhouses in the Crescent were all painted white, differing only in the color of their shutters. Aunt Gwyneth's were dark blue, and the ones on this house were black. *I would paint the door red.* Bri assessed there was little work to be done beyond new paint and maintenance that would be revealed on a more detailed inspection.

"Overall, this is an outstanding possibility, Miss Jones. "How much does the owner want?"

The estate agent checked her notes and quoted a figure that Bri knew was reasonable for this section of the *ton*. "The butler will go with the current lessee, but the other servants are willing to stay."

"How long a lease will they offer?"

"Fifty years."

Bri nodded. "That's possible. Could we do a sub-lease during that period?"

"Yes, but whoever signs the full lease would remain the responsible financial party."

"That is satisfactory."

"I will speak to my fiancé about it tonight and call you tomorrow. I am impressed with the staff and they would suit me quite well," said Gabriella. "Shall I drop you back at your office?"

"No, thank you, as I have an appointment on the next street anyway. I'll take a Hackney back to the office later and see if I still have a job. I'll call on you next Monday or tomorrow, depending on what happens."

Bri extended her hand. "I have enjoyed this time with you, Miss Jones."

As it was past noon, Bri decided to see if Aunt Gwyneth was free for lunch just as Dr. Northcliffe arrived home. She explained her tour of his home. "I was going to walk across the street to see if Aunt Gwyneth is free for lunch. Would you like to join me?"

He agreed amiably, but offered to serve them both lunch with his daughters.

"That sounds delightful! I just met one and watched the other two play. You are a very lucky man, Doctor."

As the two walked, he said, "Yes, I am, but my daughters need a mother and I fear I am considered too old by the young ladies of the *ton* as husband material. Taking over as mother to three young ones is a daunting task. Perhaps my search will be futile."

"I hope not."

Nambotha smiled. "Lady Gabriella, what a surprise!"

"Nambotha, this is Dr. Northcliffe. Is Aunt Gwyneth home?"

Before he could answer, she appeared, "Of course I am, Bri. And Dr. Northcliffe, welcome."

"Madame la Comtesse, I have invited your niece to lunch with my daughters and me at my home. Will you join us?"

"I'd be delighted. It is sunny so I do not need a cloak to cross the street." Gwyneth walked outside. "And none of this 'Comtesse de Merbeau,' Percy. We have known each other since we were children and do not have to observe the formalities of Society in private."

"Thanks. Wynnie. I did not want to presume informality."

Bri looked at the doctor. "Have you heard about Blackie? We believe he fell to his death."

"Yes, Wynnie told me yesterday at the founding hospital. Is it certain?"

"Not yet. The constable is waiting for the body to surface in the river."

"One can only imagine the hatred that would drive a man to do what he did." The doctor shook his head.

Gwyneth sighed. "Fraud and murder…multiple murders. All for a revenge that never had to be." The comtesse pulled on the doctor's arm to stop him to talk before they entered his house. "As an old friend, you should know the truth. Blackie was the illegitimate son of my father and the nanny, Brigid. That was his motivation—revenge."

Bri looked at the doctor. "While money was provided for him in my grandfather's will, I am not so sure that an inheritance would have been enough. By the time Grandfather died, Blackie was in his mid-thirties, fueled by a hatred that could not be quelled with mere money. It was recognition of his birth, and perhaps the love of a father, which he craved far more than money. Even though I saw him fall to his death from that ship and I feel in my bones that he is no longer a threat, talking about him makes me uneasy. It's not as if I were summoning the devil, but I liked him all these years. I considered him a friend. As a child, he taught me backgammon. I traveled with him and Father. We were like a family, which makes his betrayal so much more bitter."

"Then let us speak of him no more," said the doctor.

Larsen opened the door and welcomed them in.

"Larsen! I didn't know you were here, right across the street."

The butler bowed. "Lady Gwyneth, you are as lovely as I remember."

"Tell Flora that we will have two extra guests for lunch. We will take tea in the parlor until she is ready."

"Very well, sir," said the butler.

In the parlor, Bri admired the paintings. The doctor said that the owner had amassed quite an impressive collection, but was now preparing to move to America permanently since the death a year earlier of his wife. "These possessions remind him too much of her."

Larsen appeared with the tea, poured it discreetly, and then left.

Gwyneth and Percy reminisced about their childhoods and Bri wondered if Aunt Gwyneth were more suited to Percy than to Count von Dusterberg, whom she had assumed Aunt Gwyneth would like because he was the only man of the right age of whom Bri approved. *Why have I not thought of the doctor? Probably because he might want to return to Ravenshire and Aunt Gwyneth loved the pace of the ton. Well, maybe the doctor will not know what hit him. I didn't expect to fall in love with Edward.* The Northcliffe farm had run without the doctor while he was in Africa. The girls would get a better education in London. *Why am I thinking this when we are simply having lunch? Am I becoming one of those annoying women who is always seeking to make matches?*

By the end of the lunch, Bri thought her initial impression might have merit. Julie and Rachel were charming, and Kaya, the African girl, spoke barely accented English. *Will she be accepted? The* ton *can be brutal.*

"I must stop by the theatre to see Clarissa before tonight's performance," said Bri. "You should bring the girls. I'll see if I can get four more tickets."

Dr. Northcliffe seemed at a loss for words.

Gwyneth explained. "An operetta called *The Princess* opens tonight. It's an old faerie tale set to music, and the girls would enjoy it. If not tonight, we can go together another evening."

Aunt Gwyneth just invited Dr. Northcliffe to the theatre.

Gwyneth rose to kiss Bri goodbye and escort her to the door, adding that she would stay awhile to talk more with the doctor.

Bri said her goodbyes and her carriage headed to the theatre.

Upon entering, she found Clarissa in the middle of a rehearsal for the key song, *Taita's Song*, as Bri thought of it. *I mustn't be against Taita, but my heart rests with Charlotte. It is Father's life, but I am affected too.*

Clarissa's high, lilting voice filled the theatre. She remembered Edward's completion of the legal requirements for the financing, and felt a sense of shared accomplishment for helping the operetta have a successful run.

When Clarissa finished the song, Herr Kramer shouted, "Brava!" and Bri echoed it.

"Brava! Brava Violetta Vinci!" They all laughed, and Bri approached the stage. "Edward has all the negotiations committed to paper—signed, sealed, and delivered. You can stay in this theatre for as long a run as the public will permit."

Herr Kramer bowed and Bri saw a tear in his eye. "Thank you."

Looking at Clarissa, Bri said, "No matter what happens in life, you will always be known as the incomparable Miss Violetta Vinci who sang the role of The Princess."

"I hadn't considered that. I am not used to the name Mrs. St. Cloud, but I see your point. I will always be Miss Vinci."

"Always?" asked Herr Kramer. "Do you intend to perform beyond the illness of this one actress? Or continue in another operetta? I do not think that is what your father has in mind."

"Her father never controlled her life, nor do I," said The Wizard. "Her choices are her own and I am certain that Miss Vinci will have a long and successful career on the stage, should she choose to seek it."

Embracing him, Clarissa said, "That is one of the many reasons I love you, Nicholas. You are strong enough to let me pursue my own dreams."

Would Edward say the same thing?

"Wizards are full of words of wisdom, my dear. I can always make you vanish — poof!— should you disobey me."

"Well, I shall leave you to your rehearsal." Bri stood to leave. "What time does the Sultan arrive today?"

"As we speak, Father is waiting at the docks. He and his entourage should arrive at our home by four o'clock. The performance begins early tonight, at six o'clock, and then the reception and dinner at our home will begin at nine. How is your father?"

"Nervous and lost in thought. So many years have passed, he is not certain what to expect."

Clarissa nodded. "Who could?"

CHAPTER FIFTY-NINE

Monday, April 22, 1811 – The Sultan's Ship at The London Docks
Count von Dusterberg

The count arrived at the Sultan's ship shortly after receiving his message. Boarding the ship, Xerxes, the Sultan's vizier, escorted the count to where the Sultan awaited him. They greeted each other with an embrace, and the count bowed and clicked his heels in Prussian style as he greeted each wife in turn, and then Taita. The count turned his gaze to the Sultan. "I've arranged a train of carriages for you, your other wife, the healer, bodyguards, servants and trunks."

The Sultan and his entourage followed the count, who directed Xerxes as to which carriages were designed to carry trunks and valises, and which were allocated to the wives, servants and others. The count's carriage held the Sultan, his chief wife, Anja, and her son, Szilard. Taita rode in a separate carriage with the Sultan's newest and youngest wife, Rana.

The bodyguards climbed onto the count's carriage—two in the traditional positions of footmen and one next to the driver. *Scimitars strapped crosswise across bare-chested well-muscled men will be quite a sight in the streets of London.*

Inside the carriage, the Sultan touched his host's arm. "I'm sorry I could not witness your daughter's marriage."

"It was a whirlwind romance, Your Royal Highness. Many factors affected the date. Her husband is a veterinarian, kind and dedicated.

452

He and Clarissa share a love of the theatre. As you may know, we are producing *The Princess* here. It opens tonight. I have arranged special seating for you and your party before a reception tonight."

"How delightful!"

"I want you to be aware that my daughter's husband and she will be performing under stage names."

The Sultan's brow wrinkled. "In public?"

The count sighed. "It is a passion for them. I believe the draw to perform will run its course with this operetta. In the end, they are in control of their own lives. Look at me—the misfortunes of war have driven me from my own country. No one knows what life will bring."

Anja, the Sultan's chief wife, said, "I look forward to this adventure tonight. The opening performance of an operetta, a new marriage and time for us to learn about life in London."

Perplexed by her comment, the count looked at the Sultan.

"I have decided to look for a home in London. My wives like the excitement of the city. I indulge them."

"Wonderful! I will look forward to having an old friend in London when you visit."

Szilard, the first son, appeared bored. "Is there any hunting nearby? I am not one to sit in a theatre or live a soft life."

Before the count could answer, the Sultan stared at his son with fury. "A guest is respectful. You hunt at home. You don't have to come back to London again. But while we are here, now, you will do as I say and remain silent if you cannot speak without sounding petulant."

Szilard's lips narrowed into a defiant line.

Szilard wants power now. The Sultan knows it. This boy is dangerous.

The chief wife, Anja, glared at her son.

The count moved to a lighter note. "You arrived on a rare sunny day. You are seeing London in an unusual light, although I must confess, I've developed a love of the fog, the mist, the ever-present rain of this city. It washes the soul and focuses the mind."

"Now, my friend, I hear the voice of a poet. You should write your memoirs. Many an interesting life is rendered boring by a pedantic hand. You could bring a wordmaster's touch to the life of a military man turned diplomat...a man who chose working toward shared goals through negotiation over the utter destruction and scars of war."

The count sighed. "We both know that many wars have been started over a misunderstanding or miscommunication."

The carriages arrived at the Count's home, where there seemed to be pandemonium as the trunks and visitors crowded into the foyer and were led to their respective guest rooms.

"Your Royal Highness, before you go to your rooms, may I speak to you in private?"

"Of course, my friend. Lead the way."

Once they were seated inside the count's private library, the count spoke. "I am not fully acquainted with all the customs and mores of your culture, so I want to apologize in advance if what I have to say might offend you in any way. I have a friend, Henry Wyndward, the Earl of Ravenshire. His daughter and mine are friends."

"Wyndward Trading ships my spices to England, although those transactions are handled by others in my government. But let me not distract you any longer. What is the topic that you fear may offend me?"

"When the earl began his venture into trading, a typhoon battered his ship and destroyed it. He and a few crewmembers clung to what remained of the ship and they drifted on the tides to a small island in the Pacific. It was uncharted and may remain so. He fell in love there with the daughter of the chief. A volcanic eruption and typhoon separated the lovers. He believed her dead. The woman's name was Taita."

The Sultan frowned. "And you believe this Taita and mine to be one and the same?"

"We are certain of it. The song that Taita sings in the evenings, accompanied by her lyre, was set to music by Herr Kramer, whom you will meet, after Clarissa sang it for him. When Lord Ravenshire heard the song, he was stunned. The man has been a major business power in the *ton* for thirty years, and this song moved him to tears. He has never forgotten Taita."

"No man could."

"At the risk of being indelicate, Sultan, would you give Taita her freedom if she wished to remain in England and recapture the love of so long ago? It would be her decision, of course. She would be free to reject Lord Ravenshire."

"Granting freedom to a slave is rare. I confess I am quite in love with her myself although my own code of honor has prevented me from forcing her to become my wife. You see, dear count, I am not a cold man. I want a woman to want me as much as I want her. Taita appreciated my kindness, but that is all. I could see in her eyes that she pined for another, yet accepted her fate. It seems, however, that fate is not yet finished with her."

"Then you will agree for them to meet?"

"Perhaps. I shall meet with your friend." The Sultan leaned forward. "The loss of Taita would be incalculable. Just this past summer, she healed one of my children from an unknown disease. That act in and of itself is more than enough to cause me to grant her freedom, but it is one of many that she has performed over the years. I will not stand in the way of her happiness. If she wants her freedom, I shall grant it. In my land, I need only say, 'I free you' three times and it will be done. So you see, my friend, you have not offended me. On the contrary, you have honored me. I may at last have found a way to show Taita that I truly love her, by letting her go."

CHAPTER SIXTY

Monday, April 22, 1811 - Lord Ravenshire's Townhouse
Edward

E dward and Bri came downstairs dressed for the theatre, joining Henry in the foyer where Thompson held Bri's cloak. Jean-Louis had improved over the last week, but was not yet strong enough to drive. He directed another one of his drivers to replace him in the driver's perch. "I am not so foolhardy as to put others at risk," he'd told the earl.

Edward escorted Bri down the stairs and into the carriage. Her father was already inside, along with Jean-Louis. The Frenchman was now accorded family status by the count and included in the invitation to the operetta and the reception.

Bri put her hand on her father's arm. "My feelings are jumbled, but whatever happens tonight, I love you."

Henry said, "And I love you more than you can ever know." He looked out the window and they sat in silence all the way to the count's mansion.

Edward knew Bri was still torn between her love for Charlotte and her desire to see her father happy. Disinclined toward displays of emotion, Edward maintained silence. *I can't imagine what it would be like to have lost Bri to Blackburn only to find her twenty-odd years later. I couldn't bear it to think of what she might have gone through under Blackburn's control.* He realized how foolish he had been to spurn Bri's request for words of love. Money could be inherited, squandered, stolen or earned, but one could always get it back. Power could be wrested from one's grasp at any moment, leaving one naked but for the remembered deeds of one's life. *But love? It might be offered but once.* He had almost lost her, lost her without having told her of his love. In truth, he had been afraid to commit himself, afraid to risk looking foolish. *Henry is a far braver man than I.* Facing the uncertainty that the earl faced tonight was more than Edward felt he could ever endure. *Carpe diem.* He leaned over and whispered in Bri's ear, "I love you."

She turned and kissed his cheek.

Edward knew that tonight would never be forgotten, by any of them. The theatre came into view. Edward realized, belatedly, that Henry would be forced to watch Taita for hours before he could actually speak with her.

CHAPTER SIXTY-ONE

April 22, 1811 – Theatre-Royal Haymarket
Bri

After they arrived at the theatre, Bri showed Edward where their seats were located. "Edward, we are seated in the upper right box facing the stage—Father, Aunt Gwyneth, your parents, Dr. Northcliffe and his three daughters. The count and the Sultan and his party will be in the upper left box facing the stage. I am going backstage to see if Clarissa needs any help."

Walking toward the stage, Bri moved aside the curtain, and knocked on Clarissa's dressing room door. "Violetta, it's Bri."

"Come in."

Clarissa wore the light blue costume of the princess. An attendant was anchoring her black wig with hairpins.

Bri beamed. "You look beautiful—just like a real princess!"

"I don't have time to be nervous."

The attendant fitted the tiara on her wig, and adjusted her makeup. Another knock came at the door.

The Wizard stood resplendent in his costume. "You look just like a princess!"

"Well, it is unanimous, Violetta!" Bri sighed. "It's time for me to get to the box. I'll see you at the reception."

Clarissa turned to Bri. "There would be no operetta at all if you and Edward had not been so enterprising, negotiating successfully with the theatre owner and the Shakespeare Festival. Now we can have a long run. Initial ticket sales have sold nearly every seat for the next month."

"Five minutes to curtain," said Nicholas. "Time to take our places."

Exiting the curtain toward the stairs to their box, excitement gripped Bri. *The theatre is full.* She joined her party, and they chatted for a few moments.

Bri glanced across the theatre at the count's box. She leaned toward Edward. "Which one do you think is Taita?"

"The one with the unusual headdress, like a tiara with feathers. She seems to be looking this way."

Bri looked at her father. His eyes were locked with Taita's. As the house lights went down, her face faded from view.

Herr Kramer took the conductor's podium in the orchestra pit. Edward took Bri's hand. "You were right. I suppose you'll never let me forget it."

"Oh, don't apologize now, darling. It's going to happen so many more times."

***

Edward

Edward smiled, loving her for her feisty nature. *She is the only woman I have ever met who can match me move for move.*

As the orchestra played the overture, Taita's theme was introduced. Edward's eyes grew accustomed to the darkness and he could see Taita. *Her race will attract twitters of disapproval.* It was rare for a mixed race couple to be seen in Society, although it occurred frequently in the foreign reaches of the British Empire. He nodded to Viscount Hanforth, who sat with the count's party. He knew that Banfield and Vaux were in the audience too.

The curtain went up, and Bri squeezed Edward's hand.

Violetta appeared and sang her first soliloquy. Her bright soprano tones rang true in the theatre, and the audience burst into spontaneous applause when she finished, and Edward felt Bri relax her hold on his hand. He knew then that the operetta was going to be a success, and heard Bri breathe a deep sigh of relief.

The actor playing Thomas the Bard had a magnificent tenor voice that captivated the crowd as he introduced Taita's song.

When the Wizard appeared, their duet was an instant hit as well. The doctor's rich bass tone and Clarissa's high lilting notes meshed perfectly. Bri noticed the audience swaying to the beat of the music. *A good sign.*

In the final scene, Clarissa sang Taita's theme. The monkey turned back into Thomas the Bard and they finished the song together. The audience rose, cheering "Bravo! Brava!" while applauding.

When the curtain came down, the audience demanded several curtain calls and an encore of Taita's song. Flowers were thrown at Clarissa, and she knelt, picked them up and bowed her thanks. Herr Kramer came to the stage and took his bow as the composer, and himself bowed to Taita in thanks for her melody. She, in turn, blew him a kiss. A tear ran down Henry's cheek. Edward heard him say to Gwyneth, "Taita will always live through that song."

Sir John nudged his son. "A triumph, Edward. We were fools to have initially passed on this operetta as an investment opportunity. I trust we have redeemed ourselves."

"Bri was right, I was wrong."

Lady James smiled. "And that lovely young lady will no doubt be a star of the stage after tonight. Violetta Vinci. Odd, I have not heard of her. And the Bard and Wizard, too, were charismatic."

Edward looked at his mother. "What would your reaction be if I told you that the princess was a young lady of Society singing under a stage name?"

Lady James thought a moment. "My reaction would be that she is a marvelously talented young lady, Society denizen or not. If your question has to do with her acceptance, I think that her beauty and undeniable talent mitigate any of that old prejudice against the theatre. After all, this is not a bawdy review, but a well-constructed operetta. I should be happy to introduce her to Society and the *ton*."

"Interesting." Edward glanced at Bri, but said nothing more.

As they waited for the crowd to depart, the groups in the two boxes waited for Clarissa, Nick and Herr Kramer to appear. When the theatre had cleared, the two boxes emptied and they exited the theatre to their waiting carriages.

The actor who played Thomas the Bard accompanied The Wizard and The Princess in a separate carriage. The other carriages filled up.

Edward saw Taita turn to look at Henry just before she stepped into the carriage. Sadness filled her eyes, evoking a sense of loss that tugged at Edward's heart. The earl's grim face echoed her isolation.

***

Monday, April 22, 1811 – The Hanforth Mansion
Henry

As soon as his carriage arrived, Henry sought out the count.

"Come with me." The count directed Henry to his library. "The Sultan will speak with you. I'll be right back."

Henry paced. *What will he say?*

***

Count von Dusterberg

The count sought out Taita and pulled her aside. "Did the Sultan speak to you about Henry?"

"No, but I saw him at the theatre. Is he here?"

"Yes. I am bringing the Sultan to meet with Henry in my library. Do you want to meet with Henry?"

In the softest of whispers, Taita answered. "Yes."

"Follow me to the parlor, where you can have privacy while you wait."

Seating Taita, the count left the room and closed the door. He was unnerved to see a scimitar-armed bodyguard stand in front of the doors.

Finding the Sultan, the count tapped him on the shoulder. "Your Royal Highness, the earl awaits you."

"Good. I like to make an entrance."

As he led the Sultan to the library, the count overheard the Sultan's vizier, Xerxes, corral the other wives who were gossiping that the handsome count would want Taita as his bride. Chattering away in their language added to the perception of the count that the Sultan's household was out of control.

***

Henry

The Sultan was clothed in western garb except for a purple turban. His beard was full and flecked with white.

Henry stood when the Sultan entered.

After their introduction, the count poured each a brandy.

The Sultan accepted the snifter. "Count, I should like to be alone with Lord Ravenshire."

The count bowed in acknowledgment and left the room.

Before the door closed, Henry glimpsed two bodyguards with scimitars outside. *I've traversed the planet, but have never seen such men or weapons.*

After the Count left, the Sultan held his glass high. "To Taita, the woman we both love."

Without dropping his gaze, Henry raised his glass and drank along with the Sultan.

"You are not surprised, I am sure, to know that I love Taita. She has been a wise counselor and a mystical healer. Just a few months ago she cured my little daughter Ayla of an unknown disease. She has been an invaluable aid to me in governing my people."

Taking another sip of brandy, the Sultan ran his tongue over the liquid that remained on his lips. "I never imbibe spirits in my country. I was educated here and picked up some bad habits, which I indulge only while visiting and only—"

He cocked his head toward the door. "In private. As I said, I love Taita. However, she does not love me. Oh, she likes me and I treat her well. And to be fair, I love other women." He shrugged. "My chief wife and my newest wife are here in London with me. But Taita is a spiritual being, a creature unlike any I have ever known. We have respect between us, Lord Ravenshire, nothing more. Never would I force myself on a woman. Too many come willingly.

"The count spoke with me this afternoon, about your shipwreck so long ago. I knew there was another man from the past who lingered in Taita's heart, and so now I meet him. I will surprise you, perhaps by telling you that I have decided to grant Taita her freedom. I would have done so at any time had she asked, but it pleases me to offer it to her as a gift. As to her feelings toward you, I profess no knowledge. But I will not stand in the way of her choice, whatever that may be. She deserves to be free to choose her own destiny. In the past, destiny was forced upon her. She will always have a home in my palace should she choose to return."

Henry felt as though punched in the gut. *Will she choose to return? To leave me?* "What is the next step, Your Royal Highness?"

Extending his hand in the western manner, the Sultan said, "I judge men quickly, Lord Ravenshire, and I judge you to be a man of integrity and honor. The Count would not call you his friend were it not so. I shall speak to Taita. Wait here."

"Your Royal Highness. I must confess I was horrified to learn that Taita had been taken into slavery, but it is my understanding that she occupies a position of high rank in your household. I am grateful for that. I could not bear to think that she suffered."

"Nor could I, Lord Ravenshire," said the Sultan. He bowed and left the room.

***

Taita

Taita dutifully stood as the French doors opened and the Sultan entered the parlor.

"Please be seated, Taita." He took a seat next to her. "As you know, I have been touched deeply many times over the years by your acts of healing. Miracles have occurred in my household under your spell. I care for you very deeply, my dear Taita, and I think I may have finally discovered a way to reward you for your many gifts."

"No reward is asked, Your Royal Highness."

"A man awaits you in the library. He has carried you in his heart for many years. His name is Henry Wyndward."

"I saw him at the theatre. I had hoped against hope that he had survived the volcano and typhoon. I thought I'd lost him forever." *Will he still love me?*

The Sultan stood. "In gratitude for your many acts of healing, your wise counsel and your gentle soul, I have decided to grant you your freedom. Should you decide to remain in England, you have my blessing. Should you prefer to return with me to Madagascar, you will want for nothing. You are the greatest treasure this Sultan ever found."

Taita rose to her feet. "Fate was an unfamiliar concept to me when I came to your palace. Fate has been kind to me. Although it was slavers who pulled me from the ocean, their intervention saved my life, and while I was sold to you as a slave, life as a slave in your palace has been in name only. You have always treated me with respect, as your trusted advisor. I will value knowing you for the rest of my life, no matter what happens."

"I free you, I free you, I free you," intoned the Sultan, fulfilling his promise. He extended his hand to her. "Come with me."

She took the Sultan's hand.

***

Henry

Henry stopped pacing when the door handle turned.

Taita stepped through the doorway and stood still. The candlelight from the hallway candle sconces illuminated her.

Henry whispered, "You look like an angel surrounded by an aura. I thought that you were lost to me forever. Providence has permitted me to see you once more."

"Fate? Providence? The ways of the universe? All that matters is that we stand here together. Alive."

"Please sit."

Taita walked over to a chair and sat down. "I used to dream of our time on the island. Life in the Sultan's palace was privileged. It was losing you, thinking you were dead, that tortured me. The slavers told me that my entire island had been destroyed. My people have vanished from the face of the earth."

"Don't you know? A sliver of the island remains, a crescent of land around the lagoon created by the volcano and a crescent of coral on the other. I am sorry to tell you that your father died in the cataclysm. Bando was elected chief. When a Dutch ship arrived, I left and returned to England, to the wife I told you about. She died in childbirth, but I have a daughter. You will meet her tonight, should you wish to."

A fleeting mask came over Taita's face. "A daughter. You have a family. I am glad."

They stood and awkwardly approached each other. Henry took her in his arms.

He touched her cheek. "Clarissa and Herr Kramer brought your song to life again."

"That song is a prayer. My prayer of love to the stars has been answered. Kiss me, Henry. Kiss me now."

Henry kissed Taita, but they could not restrain their emotions and both broke down in sobs of pain for the time lost to them.

When they regained their composure, Henry blotted her tears—and his—with his monogrammed handkerchief.

"May I keep it?"

"Always."

"I have known no man but you since our joining." Seeing his fear, she smiled. "But I did not expect that you would remain celibate if you lived. That was my choice. Long ago, we made many promises to each other. Much has happened in twenty-five years. We will be in London for one week. Let us renew our understanding of each other slowly."

Henry nodded. "Only one week after five-and-twenty years?" *What if she will not stay? Will I be able to let her go?* "They are waiting for us to come out for dinner."

They left the parlor just as the butler rang the dinner bell.

***

Bri

Henry introduced Taita to the guests.

Bri took an instant liking to the island woman, pangs of guilt stabbing at her. *What about Charlotte? Charlotte loves him too.*

Taita answered questions about life in the palace, about all the Sultan's wives and children and the region he ruled in Madagascar—a land of spices, beaches, forests, and mountains. The exotic tales fascinated them, and Bri tried to imagine being so restricted.

"But what if you wanted to leave?"

"There is no reason to leave. We have everything we need. Whatever I request is provided."

She speaks as if she still lives there, as though she intends to return. "But to be so trapped—"

"I don't see it that way, Lady Gabriella. We travel with the Sultan. I have seen many parts of the world. That never would have happened had I stayed on my island. I have not been mistreated."

Taita looked at Jean-Louis. "You have been silent, sir. Yet you stare at me."

"Forgive me, I didn't mean to stare. You remind me of someone I knew once, a healer like you."

Bri tried not to betray her surprise. *Jean-Louis has a secret lost love?*

As dessert was being served, the main players, Thomas the Bard, The Wizard and The Princess went to the center of the room. Herr Kramer took his place at the piano. They sang a reprise of Taita's song. When they were finished, the Wizard removed his hat, wig and beard and the Princess removed her wig and tiara. Only Sir John and Lady James of the small group did not know the truth until that moment. "Why, Count von Dusterberg," Lady James shook her head, "you sly fox, eliciting my prejudices without any indication of your daughter's *nom d'étage*. I stand by my assessment. She is a talented young woman and need not hide behind a stage name unless it suits her fancy. Although I must say that the name Violetta Vinci is quite memorable."

Everyone laughed in relief and hugged each other in celebration of their spectacular opening night.

Henry and Jean-Louis decided to take a Hackney. *Father will go to the docks to walk and think.*

Driven by the footman, Bri and Edward were alone in the earl's carriage on the way home. Edward turned to Bri. "You are my Princess."

"And you my monkey in a banker's disguise."

"You think you're so clever."

"I don't think it. I know it."

Edward pulled her to him in a passionate embrace.

CHAPTER SIXTY-TWO

Tuesday, April 23, 1811 – Lord Ravenshire's Townhouse
Bri

In keeping with her resolve to restore her life to as normal a routine as possible, Bri completed her early Tuesday morning ride with her Uncle Oliver.

When she climbed the back stairs from the stables, Edward was sitting at the table with Henry and Jean-Louis, waiting for her before eating breakfast. He kissed her on the cheek and then said what he'd warned her to expect when they were alone the night before.

"I thank you for your hospitality, Lord Ravenshire, but it's time for me to move back to my club. My recovery is complete, although my face still looks as though I've taken up boxing.

"Bri looked at some houses with my friend Vaux yesterday, and there's one in particular that may work for our needs, although it needs renovations."

"So you intend to move in alone and then marry?"

"Yes. Bri and I would not co-habit without marriage. That goes without saying."

"Any ideas on a date for the wedding?"

"Maybe in a few months or so. There is no hurry. And I'd like the house to be ready."

"Will you be Mrs. James or Lady James—"

"Jean-Louis, after all these years, are you still not familiar with how titles of address work here in this country?"

"Apparently not. Or, I just may want to give you a chance to express your opinion."

"It is not opinion that the daughter of an earl may keep the Lady designation and her first name if she marries a commoner. No offense meant, Edward. This is simply a statement of fact."

"No offense taken."

"Yet." Jean-Louis sat back in his chair with a look of amusement on his face.

"So I can remain Lady Gabriella. The convention is that I become Lady Gabriella James. I have not yet decided to change my name. While it is convention, I have recently learned that it is not the law. As I am partial to my independence, I may remain Lady Gabriella Wyndward, married to Mr. Edward James, rather than becoming Lady Gabriella James. Although," she mused, "I could be Lady Gabriella Wyndward-James, but never Mrs. Edward James. There is something so medieval about being addressed as the derivative of a man."

Edward glanced at Jean-Louis. "You knew this was coming."

The Frenchman shrugged.

Henry sat back in his chair. "The only land granted by the crown is Ravenshire Forest. All the rest was purchased. We can discuss the best way to transfer the land and other estates at a later date. You are the heir of Wyndward Trading and run the money side of it anyway. We can create trusts or other mechanisms to prevent Edward from gaining control of your assets. No offense meant, Edward."

"No offense taken, again. Edward Wyndward doesn't work. Two 'wards' in one name."

"Wyndward-James isn't bad. It's accepted." Henry shook his head. "You two work it out and the paperwork can follow."

Jean-Louis laughed. "Watching you two will never be boring."

***

Wednesday, April 24, 1811 – Interior of Bri's Carriage
Clarissa

Clarissa had told Bri that she wanted to see the foundling hospital, and they agreed to go together. When Bri's carriage arrived to pick up Clarissa, Taita walked out of the Hanforth Mansion with her and climbed into Bri's carriage.

"Bri, Taita expressed interest in seeing the hospital, so I invited her too."

Momentarily speechless, Bri recovered quickly. "Wonderful. You'll be impressed with what Charlotte, Baroness Glasspool, has created. Her late husband encouraged her endeavors."

The two younger women made small talk on the way. Before they exited the carriage, Bri put her hand on Taita's arm to restrain her for a moment. "Charlotte was my father's companion for the last fifteen years. She broke it off when she learned of your arrival and my father's uncertainty as to his feelings. I tell you this so that you will not be surprised. Charlotte does not know you are coming, and neither did I."

Taita looked at Clarissa.

Clarissa grimaced. "I thought if I were either of you, I would want to know the other. Perhaps I was wrong."

The island woman sighed. "Whatever happens between Henry and me will not be decided by one encounter, nor two, nor three. It may shock you to hear that I intend to return with the Sultan to Madagascar. Kindly let me tell Henry that myself when I see him tomorrow." She looked at both young women.

They each nodded.

"The Sultan is buying a palace here, and we will return next year. That will give us all time to think. Too much time has already passed to make any rash decisions. Now, I very much want to see this hospital."

They went in and Clarissa noticed Jean-Louis exchanging a look at Bri. She shrugged.

He shook his head and rubbed his dog's neck.

Charlotte was standing in the foyer when an aide came running to her. "Come quickly! The doctor needs you."

Turning to follow her aide, Charlotte didn't see her new guests.

They trailed behind her, concerned at the aide's distress. A baby's cry came from the room Charlotte had just entered.

Bri stuck her head inside. The doctor and aide were working furiously on the mother, who appeared delirious and sweating profusely. Taita saw what was happening and pushed Bri aside. "Doctor, I've seen this before. I think I can help."

The doctor looked up and said, "I don't know who you are and I don't care. What help can you give me?"

"It looks like maternal sepsis, blood poisoning."

"Agreed."

Taita walked over, placed one hand on the woman's chest and the other on her head, closed her eyes and hummed a low tone. Within two minutes, the woman had begun to breathe normally and the purplish-red color of her face returned to normal. Taita's hum turned into an unintelligible chant, and slowly softened until it stopped. Taita removed her hands.

The woman's chest rose and fell. She opened her eyes. "I had a dream. A dream that I left this earth and was pulled back. What does it mean?"

"It means you are here with us and here you will stay."

The doctor listened to her heart and the aide wiped her forehead with linen. He told the aide to stay with the patient.

Outside, he closed the door and turned to Taita. "What did you do? How did you do it?"

"The best way I can explain it is that I raised her resonance to mine, to one of health from one of sepsis. Touching helps the connection, although it is not essential. But the hands should be no more than one inch above the body."

"Teach me. Show me."

"Alas, it is not that easy. If you do not hold your resonance to its highest level, yours will lower to hers. You could become ill and collapse from the strain. You must practice for a long time, calming yourself, connecting with a higher power, and willing the sick person back to health. It does not always work. The individual must want to live."

Charlotte stared at the woman who had come between her and Henry. "Henry told me of your healing powers, how you saved him and what remained of his crew. Now I have seen it. You have an extraordinary gift. Thank you for saving this woman."

"Come, Charlotte, walk with me and show me this hospital." When Bri and Clarissa stepped forward to follow, Taita turned and held up her hand. "Just the two of us." Taita and Charlotte moved away, absorbed in deep and animated conversation.

Clarissa glanced at Bri. "Will your father be angry with me?"

"Probably. But he'll get over it. She's going back? Back with that slaving, polygamous Sultan? Why?"

"Maybe it's as simple as she says. A week is not long after five-

and-twenty years. They are different people now, with different ideas. Can you say what you would do if you and Edward were parted for such a long time? No one knows. It is for them to determine."

Bri frowned. "Poor Charlotte. We ambushed her."

"*I* did. It seemed like a good idea earlier today."

"But a woman is alive who most likely would have died, so it was a good idea." Bri touched her friend's arm. "Don't forget that. What we saw was a miracle."

***

Thursday, April 25, 1811 – Lord Ravenshire's Townhouse
Taita

The count's carriage stopped in front of the earl's townhouse.

Taita exited and walked up the steps.

Thompson opened the door before Taita could ring the bell. "Good day, Miss Taita. The earl is waiting for you in the parlor."

Henry stood when Taita came in.

Thompson brought tea and then left, closing the French doors behind him.

Taita embraced Henry and kissed him. She reached up and touched his face. "Henry, I am going back to Madagascar with the Sultan. We will be back next year. That will give us time to think."

"We've had decades to think!"

"Henry, I am not of your world. I will go to my home. I will think. Where I live now, there are people of many cultures and languages who depend on me. Here, I have no means of support, no respect for my race. I am looked at with suspicion.

"I am connected to the universe. I fear that if I move here permanently, amid the noise and the filth of the city, I may lose my connection, my resonance, my gift. You would not want that, would you?"

"I want you."

"I am not a commodity. We were together once. Let us remember those days. Always."

"No. I will not give up on us."

"Us was long ago. Us is no longer real."

"Then I will take you back to your island."

"I am no longer of the island. I am of Madagascar. Do not make demands, Henry, for I do not intend to trade one form of slavery for another."

"I would never treat you that way."

"We thought each other dead. This rendezvous is a shock for both of us. I cannot be forced to stay, Henry, no matter how much the memory of our time together means to me. I have made a new life, as have you. I met Charlotte."

"What? How?"

"I wanted to see the foundling hospital. Lady Clarissa made an error in judgment, but do not hold it against her. Charlotte was as surprised as I was. She is a lovely person. You have hurt her. Perhaps that can be undone. I am not hurt, but I am confused. But I will not stay." She stood to leave. "We will see each other next year. I will write when the timing is set."

Henry stood in silence.

"Be not sad. We found each other for a moment. We must hold that moment in our hearts."

***

Saturday, April 27, 1811 – Lord Ravenshire's Stables
Jean-Louis

A knock on his door awakened Jean-Louis. He rubbed his eyes and rose to open the door. It was Voutain, one of the two men he had sent to Scotland more than two weeks earlier. Jean-Louis took him to the small eating area in the back of the stable house, and set a pot of water over the fire for tea. "Hungry?"

"Absolutely."

Jean-Louis pulled bread baked the day before and a hunk of cheese and placed it on the table. "I trust you have information."

With his mouth full, Voutain nodded. He finished chewing and began the story. "We started in Ayr, checking birth records and found a baby boy born in September, with a note that the mother died shortly after his birth. Brigid Lowerth is the name on her gravestone. The babe was named Brian but never baptized. We found the old midwife who attended the birth and the elderly priest who kept the church records. They directed us to an estate agent in Glasgow, but first we located a grave in a small church in Glasgow that matched. I wrote it down—Here together lie Galda Lowerth, grandmother, born 3-20-1734, died 11-10-1771 and Brian Lowerth, born 9-15-1771, died 10-23-1771. Preceded in death by Brigid Lowerth, 9-22-1771."

"That's a lot for a gravestone. Maybe a little too complete? And Welsh names in Scotland. Go on."

"Before talking to the estate agent, we rode to Edinburgh, and bribed our way into the archived university files. We found Blackburn's records. Sparse. Something about a charity case referred by a parish priest. Bright, passed the entrance exam. No mention of family."

Voutain grimaced. "Few people are around from twenty years ago. No barkeep remembered him, but I found a groundskeeper for the university who remembered him. Seems that Blackburn worked part-time tending gardens. Had an affinity for it. One night the groundskeeper, MacBeth—he got a lot of jokes from students about that—"

"Understandable."

"Colvert didn't get the meaning."

Jean-Louis shrugged. "I don't pay him for his knowledge of literature."

"Anyway, back in the day, MacBeth found his assistant sitting on a bench staring at the harvest moon at twilight. The term hadn't begun yet, so the campus was deserted. Turned out it was Blackburn's birthday.

" 'I was born under a harvest moon,' Blackburn told him.

"The groundskeeper pulled a flagon of whiskey from his pocket and offered Blackburn a drink.

"The young student took it. Believe it or not, young Blackburn couldn't hold his liquor. After a couple of swigs, Blackburn started talking, which was unusual, according to MacBeth. Talked about his future, how he would be a powerful man one day. 'Like my father. The man spurned me at birth. He'll pay for it someday.' MacBeth said the venom in Blackburn's voice frightened him. Another thing MacBeth said might interest you."

"What?"

"Blackburn advised his boss to start up a groundskeeping business on the side, to provide for his retirement and how to do it. MacBeth followed Blackburn's advice, eventually bought a home and improved life for his own children. His sons graduated from the university. He kept his university job because he liked the students. Many of them worked for him over the years. You could say that Blackburn changed his life."

"Then why was he so free with information? Maybe he'll report back to Blackburn that somebody's looking for him."

"I promised him Blackburn would never learn of our conversation. All I have is a rough approximation of the month of his birth from the groundskeeper that matches the time period date on the gravestone and in the church. And he hated his father. Not much. Not definitive."

"Actually, in the time you've been gone, we've learned Blackburn knew all along that he was the 10th Earl's bastard. Brian Lowerth didn't die in 1771. Now I wonder…did the grandmother?"

"I wouldn't bet on it."

After listening to the rest of Voutain's story about Inverness, Jean-Louis sighed. "And?"

"The grandmother and the Gypsy got off at Langholm, Scotland, and we tracked them to an inn in Dumfries. Blas and Giles are watching them. We have a wool mill in Carlisle with a dovecote if something develops. It's about a day's ride from Dumfries."

"It's the middle of the night. Get some sleep."

Voutain shook his head. "We're at first light now."

"Sleep anyway." Jean-Louis closed the door to his room. "*Foutre! Foutre! Foutre!*" *The Gypsy connection is the grandmother. Blackburn may be dead, but she is a deadly risk.*

CHAPTER SIXTY-THREE

Sunday, April 28, 1811 – Dumfries, Scotland
Mirela

The Gypsy's friend rose to walk toward a mirror. "Arthur and I picked a name for my new identity papers—Aneira. Catherine, like Sorcha and Galda, is dead."

Mirela scoffed. "I needing no new papers. I being called only The Gypsy. There existing many Roma like me. Who can proving Roma or no? We having no documents. No one wanting us nowhere in 'civilization.'"

Catherine stood at the mirror, examining her appearance. "How should I change to become Aneira?"

"As Galda, you having hair of the mouse. As Sorcha, you showing color of blood. As Catherine you allowing graying of head. As Aneira, what coloring of hair pleasing you?"

"Black as Welsh coal. And another thing. I'm tired of eating a sparse diet to remain thin. My vocation in early life was a baker's assistant. For the time I have left to live, I will bake, and bake, and bake. Pastries, pies, cakes, breads, croissants, brioches, muffins. We're going to move to London, open a restaurant and cater to the *ton*. Maybe even a Wyndward or two will frequent our café."

"Poisoning them in your food sounding dangerous."

"I'm sure you can find a poison that works slowly. By the time they die, it will not be able to be traced to me. But if I kill them, why do I care whether or not I live? Fate extracts its price. My life's work will have been done. All Wyndwards must die."

***

Monday, April 29, 1811 – The London Docks
Taita

Taita stood on the deck and raised her hand in farewell to Henry, the man who had changed her life. *He doesn't understand. He must let me go. My life is not in London.*

***

Henry

With Jean-Louis at his side, Henry raised his hand as Taita did. "It's not over."

Jean-Louis nodded. "The Sultan bought a palace fallen into disrepair."

"What? Here?"

"Yes. It will take a great deal of renovation, but he said to spare no expense. He left the project with Mr. James to handle. Apparently, his friend Viscount Vaux has experience in such transformations. She will return."

"Charlotte expects an answer and all I can do is delay any decision."

Jean-Louis said nothing.

"You disagree?"

"I do not believe the baroness is waiting for an answer. I believe she has deduced the answer from your behavior. The gossip rags will keep this alive even after Taita has sailed away."

"So I've lost them both."

"For now."

***

Tuesday, April 30, 1811 – The London Docks
Constable Rampell

On a bone-chilling cold rainy dawn in London, two weary watchmen

476

were standing around a badly decomposed body that had washed up between some boulders not far from the docks.

Battered by the ravages of water, scavenger fish, and rocks, the face was unrecognizable.

Constable Rampell, a short, stubby constable elbowed his equally rotund partner. "Here he comes."

Soaked to the skin, his partner muttered, "About time. Bloody cold out here."

The third man on their team had left more than an hour ago to roust Boyd, who had placed the entire department on alert for just such a discovery.

Boyd, followed by the third man, walked over with an air of authority. He eyed the corpse. "A grim result. Checked the wounds, did you, Rampell?"

"Yes, sir. Bullet wound to the right hand and wrist, knife wound in the left shoulder and head injuries, but of course with the rocks it's hard to identify much else."

"Height?"

"About five feet, ten inches, I should say, sir."

"Matches." Boyd knelt down. "Any identification on him?"

"A passport, sir, identifying him as one Albert Louis Cortez, a Spaniard. Age 42. Brown eyes, brown hair."

"Probably a fake. Easier to get into Napoleon's territory. Looks a bit too neat. The man we're seeking had an obsession for detail. Any money on him?"

"A little. The passport was tied in a pouch around his waist that was ripped. It's amazing anything is still inside after the bashing he got on the rocks. Money might have been washed away."

Boyd rose to his feet. "Men, take this body to the morgue. I have eighty percent certainty that we have the body of Duff Blackburn."

"That's better than most bodies we fish out of this river. They lie in the morgue until they go to a pauper's grave."

***

Wednesday, May 1, 1811 – The London Morgue
Boyd

Boyd led Jean-Louis down the winding stairwell, in disrepair with peeling paint, until they reached the sub-basement of the morgue.

The Frenchman coughed. "The stench confirms we are in the bowels of the building."

Shrugging, Boyd handed Jean-Louis a handkerchief to fend off nausea. Once on the lowest landing, they walked toward the hallway toward a room at the end.

The morgue held rows of tables with bodies covered by white sheets.

Jean-Louis scanned the room. "Altars offering up the dead."

The investigator scoffed. "Some will be offered up. Most will be offered down to the devil himself, like Blackburn. Over here." Boyd led the Frenchman to table nine and checked the tag on the toe. "This is it."

The Bow Street Runner pulled off the sheet to reveal a face bashed beyond recognition by being submerged for two weeks of water and serving as food for scavenging fish and other river creatures, after a deadly fall from the large ship onto the rocky edge of the river bank.

"The right hand shattered by a bullet, agreed?"

The Frenchman nodded. "Agreed."

"Knife wound in the left shoulder."

"Agreed."

"Height the same. Clothing the same."

"Agreed, but damn it all, the eyes are gone."

"Fish eat them first, I've heard."

"You don't know that."

"I've heard. So far, no fish have corroborated the story."

Jean-Louis laughed. "Blackburn had unusual eyes. I was hoping they would still be attached."

"No such luck."

"It's probably him. He was grievously wounded. These clothes show bloodstains despite being submerged in water for two weeks. I agree with your assessment. Most likely, Blackburn is dead." Jean-Louis tipped his hat to the Bow Street Runner. "Until the next time."

Boyd winced. "In our line of work, there's always a next time."

***

Thursday, May 2, 1811 – Lady Gwyneth's Townhouse
Gio

Gio was the last to arrive for the celebration. When the butler opened the door, the dwarf looked up. "Nambotha, I want to paint your portrait before I die. I'll need scaffolding to reach the top of the canvas, but challenges are nothing new to me."

The butler bowed. "I would be honored, Lord Ostwold."

The dwarf dismissed the formality with a wave of his hand. "Gio in private, Gio in public. My eccentricities permit it."

Nambotha led Gio into the dining room.

Gio bowed.

Gwyneth scolded, "You are late."

"You know I like to make a memorable entrance. After all, what is the protocol to rejoice in the death of someone we all knew? His half-finished portrait sits in my studio." Gio took his seat and swirled the wine in his glass.

"Rejoice is not the proper word." Henry sighed. "Someone we trusted betrayed us. We rejoice in freedom from a stalking specter of death."

"Quite a darkly poetic turn of phrase, Father. I wish the diary had survived. For some reason, I want to understand the thinking of a man I had known since childhood. That he could be, at his core, so evil…it's frightening."

Edward shrugged. "He no doubt took the diary with him and what remains of it lies at the bottom of the river."

"I'm waiting." Gio took a sip of wine.

The earl raised an eyebrow. "Waiting for what?"

"For the comtesse and Bri to say three words."

Gwyneth shook her head. "Blackie's jaw."

Bri threw her head back.

The earl took a sip of wine. "I still don't understand."

"Gio saw a resemblance between you and Blackie in your jaw line."

"Bone structure is often similar even if the other features are different. Artists notice what others miss." Gio sat back, waiting.

"What are the three words you're expecting to hear?" Edward looked at Bri to explain.

Bri and Gwyneth looked at each other and echoed each other.

"You were right."

Gio raised his palms outward. "I'm always right."

"Now that it's all over, Father, I'd like to invite Edward to Ravenshire for the weekend. It would be a good time to show him all of the estate's operations."

"Edward, consider yourself invited. We'll all go. A change of scenery will do us all good. You're invited, too, Gio."

"Of course I am." *I know all their secrets.*

CHAPTER SIXTY-FOUR

Friday, May 3, 1811 – Ravenshire
Edward

Bri, the earl, the comtesse and Gio had left together to travel to Ravenshire because Edward had business to attend to at the bank. During the carriage ride, he reflected on how much his life had changed in only a few months.

Arriving at Ravenshire for the first time since he left for the Far East, Edward paid more attention to the estate's boundaries than he had as a younger man. Almost half of the land between London and Ravenshire formed the earl's holdings. As Edward's carriage passed by the rain-misted verdant fields and rolling hills, the lakes reflecting the gray skies, and the vast forests of oak, beech, sweet chestnut, willow and ash, he remembered Bri's description of the family's stewardship of Ravenshire's lands. The Wyndward ships were hewn of the estate's oak trees, its lamps burned with the oil made from crushing beech nuts, sweet chestnuts were sought-after holiday treats, the thinnest branches of willow trees were woven into fishing nets, and ash sculpted into strong tool handles. Local artisans carved furniture and decorative pieces, choosing their preferred species. International markets clamored for the skilled workmanship of Ravenshire's tradesmen.

Not many women would care about such particular details, but Bri was no ordinary woman. Edward's wry grin confirmed his understatement of her extraordinary nature.

Newly engaged, he marveled at the twists of life. While he traveled the Far East in search of adventure, he'd dreaded his return to London to assume the mantle of banker—an imagined life of duty devoid of choice or stimulation. *How wrong I was. I've learned more about life, myself and the world since I returned than I did in the six years I was gone.* He shifted his gaze back to the countryside. *But maybe I wouldn't have been able to handle the recent and tumultuous, unexpected shifts of fortune if I had not left to explore the world.* He sat back on the carriage bench, stunned. *Until this moment, I didn't realize the truth. I wasn't exploring the world. I was exploring myself, becoming myself.*

The crumbling remains of Ravenshire Castle dominated a hill a half-mile behind the massive house that was Ravenshire Manor. The scale of Bri's home had escaped his comprehension as a younger man. *How could I not have remembered that Ravenshire Manor rivals the size of Buckingham Palace?*

As if greeting royalty, the Wyndward-liveried servants were arrayed in semi-circles on each side of the manor's entrance. Bri, her father and aunt stood in the center of the assembly.

A Ravenshire footman opened the carriage door.

For the first time, Edward stepped into his new life.

***

Bri

Bri's excitement had been simmering for two days. *Now that we are engaged, we can be alone.* When Edward exited the carriage, she mock-curtseyed, and walked into his embrace. He kissed her on the cheek, aware of their audience.

The earl and the comtesse greeted him, and Bri took his arm as they walked into the house. "Rhodes will serve as your valet. Don your riding gear. I'll meet you here in twenty minutes. A late afternoon ride will invigorate you."

Gwyneth scoffed. "Bri, Edward's been in a carriage for five hours. I should think riding would be his last choice of activity."

Edward laughed. "I must adjust to being told what to do."

Bri's face fell.

"Don't look glum. I'm joking. I love to ride at twilight."

The earl put his hand on Edward's shoulder. "I hope you can jump. She'll put you through your paces."

"That will be nothing new." The foyer was framed by a curving set of twin staircases to the second level. Edward followed the valet up the right side, while Bri ascended the left.

After she dressed, Bri peeked around the corner and waited until she saw Edward start down the stairs. She ambled toward the steps. *He looks dashing in his riding gear.*

Once he was on the last step, she started down. As Edward turned to watch her descend, he smiled at first. The smile vanished as he leaned forward, consternation evident on his face. "What the devil are you wearing?"

"A riding habit."

"A *man's* riding habit."

"Indeed not. These were made for me by Mme. Mottier, to my specifications and measurements. I ordered several."

Edward pressed his lips together in a thin line.

"Don't look so petulant. I only wear this at Ravenshire when I ride astride."

"Astride? Astride! It simply isn't done."

"I'm going for a ride." Bri stomped out the door.

Shaking his head, seeming to contain his disapproval, Edward was at her heels. "Must you always make a scene?"

She turned her head and spoke over her shoulder, not altering her pace. "Always?"

"You never listen."

"Never?"

Edward sputtered. "What do you mean by your retorts?"

"I mean that words like 'always' and 'never' do not advance the art of conversation."

"Neither does stomping off in the middle of one."

Bri stopped and turned toward him. "I will not conform to outdated notions of what women should say, wear or do. You know that. We are in a private, protected preserve. If I cannot ride here in safety and comfort, then I cannot be happy."

"I want you to be happy. If we disagree, I would like to think that we could discuss our reasons, rationally and calmly."

"Then don't stand in my foyer and yell, 'Astride!' as if it were a declaration of war."

"I was caught off guard. Don't pretend you didn't intend to shock me."

She held his gaze, then took a deep breath. "Truce?"

"Truce. Next time I'll remember to hold my tongue and we'll speak in private."

"And I will try to remember to alert you in advance."

"So I *must* and you'll *try?*"

She smiled in a beguiling way. "That sounds about right." She raced off toward the stables, leaving him no choice but to catch up.

They rode over the hills, jumped streams and low fences, and, as the sun set in a lavender glow over the trees, Bri guided him to the last standing tower in the once-grand castle. She led him into the round keep and ran her hands along the stone walls.

"Once upon a time, as they say, Aunt Gwyneth played in here with her imaginary faerie friend, Petal, and found a cache of treasures behind a stone near the winding staircase. I'll ask her to tell the story again tonight at dinner." Bri took the broom and swept the dirt to reveal the mosaic-tiled floor beneath. She cleared off enough to show Edward the intricate detail.

"When was this done?"

"As best we can reconstruct, perhaps a thousand years ago. Before the Normans, we know that much. This might be the oldest tower, and the last one standing."

Edward knelt to look more closely, and Bri playfully knelt beside him, knocked him over, and sat astride him. "Am I to be ridden as a horse?"

"Really, Mr. James. It simply isn't done." She collapsed to his chest and kissed him until she pulled away to catch her breath. "Since you became well enough to move back to your club, I've missed this." She looked outside to gauge the light. "There's time, you know."

Edward adjusted his position. "Did you bring one of those confounded things?"

Bri reached into her boot and pulled out a pouch. "Of course."

"Let me put it in." Realizing what he'd just said, they both laughed. He eased her out of her breeches, she eased him out of his, and he expertly placed the sponge into position. The next kiss enveloped them in a haze of desire.

Bri had a fleeting thought. *I didn't know what I was missing until I met this extraordinary man.* Thoughts ceased as sensations thrilled her to her core.

EPILOGUE

The streets of Alexandria teemed with a cacophony of life, as usual. An Arab dressed in white robes and a dark blue head covering known as a *ghutra*, with a black *agal* holding it in place, surveyed the streets for familiar landmarks. Carrying a black traveling bag, he melted into the crowd and walked for a mile or so until he arrived at his destination, an Egyptian outlet of a Swiss bank. A clerk welcomed him when he entered. He retrieved a letter of credit from his robe and handed it to the clerk.

After a slight delay, he was ushered into the bank manager's office and greeted with excessive flattery. He produced a letter of detailed instructions on his business holdings in Egypt. "I shall require the utmost discretion and secrecy in the handling of my accounts."

"As you wish, sir."

"I shall require currency in the following amounts." He handed the bank manager a list.

After receiving the currency, he left the bank and walked the streets, taking alleys with the confidence of a familiar traveler. He came to a small inn which he had purchased years earlier and climbed to a room that always remained empty for his use, even if years passed between his visits. Splashing water on his face, he stared back at his reflection in the mirror. Brown eyes stared back at him. *The potion is working.*

He locked the door and lay down on a bed for the first time in months. Healing on shipboard for weeks, working as a crewman to regain strength, and sleeping on the deck under the stars had taught him a great deal. He had analyzed the actions required to achieve his overarching goal. He had refined his strategy and devised the tactics to implement it. His Arabic was now flawless and the sun had tanned his skin to a Mediterranean hue.

The Egyptian passport, acquired years earlier through a bribe to a government functionary, provided an official identity for the persona he had cultivated for years. Thwarted in London, his taste for revenge unsatisfied, he began to plot anew.

Secrets of Ravenshire: Romance and Revenge
Quick Reference for Main Characters

Character names are varied partly for proper address by others, and partly to avoid constant repetition. A "Lady" is a title designated by birth, not marriage. Lady Gabriella is of noble birth. Someone who is a lady by marriage, like Aelwyn, who married Henry's brother Rychard Wyndward, was known as Lady Rychard Wyndward, not as Lady Aelwyn, before she disappeared.

M., Mlle., and Mme. are abbreviations for French forms of address meaning Monsieur, Mademoiselle and Madame, respectively.

Gabriella is known as Bri to family and close friends, Lady Gabriella to others, and more formally as Lady Gabriella Wyndward. Servants occasionally call her "milady." She secretly acts as her father's "man-of-affairs."

Henry Wyndward is the 11th Earl of Ravenshire and Bri's father. Friends call him Ravenshire. He is formally addressed as Lord Ravenshire. Servants call him "milord." In the narrative, he is referred to variously as the earl, Lord Ravenshire or Henry. He founded Wyndward Trading as a young man.

Gwyneth Wyndward Craigfell de Merbeau is Henry's sister and Gabriella's aunt. She is Lady Gwyneth, or the Comtesse de Merbeau, and referred to by some as Madame la Comtesse or the comtesse or her childhood nickname, Wynnie. Servants occasionally call her "milady." Her first husband, Jamie Craigfell, died in a riding accident. Her second husband, Luc de Merbeau, died in a mysterious carriage mishap.

Rychard Wyndward, brother of Henry and Gwyneth, was found dead, thrown from a horse. The next day, his wife, Aelwyn, disappeared and was presumed dead.

Duff MacNeill **Blackburn** has worked for twenty years with Henry at Wyndward Trading as his right-hand man. Bri nicknamed him Blackie as a child.

Edward James is banker to the Ravenshire family, recently returned from years in the Far East. He is also called Mr. James, Young James, or the banker

Vanessa Craigfell, the Duchess of Pytchley, is Bri's grandmother, mother of Oliver as well as the late Lady Jane, Henry's wife and Bri's mother, and the late Vincent.

Oliver Craigfell is the sole surviving child of Vanessa and Bentley, the Duke and Duchess of Pytchley. His wife is Lady Abigail.

Charlotte Winters, Baroness Glasspool, is a widow. She has been Henry's paramour and partner for fifteen years, meeting him seven years after the death of Lady Jane. She is not of noble birth. As a widow, she may be addressed as Lady Winters, but most call her Baroness.

Jean-Louis Chevalier met Henry in Canada in 1790 and returned with him to England in 1792. He is called The Frenchman, the fur trapper, the former trapper, the tracker or the driver.

Nashmir met Henry in Tibet many years earlier, and is known as the Tibetan, the herbalist, and serves as Henry's valet.

Laurence (rarely used first name Philip) tutored Henry, Gwyneth, Rychard, Nate, Aelwyn and Bri.

Gio da Garfagnini is a dwarf and renowned artist who taught Gwyneth as a child and is a close family friend. Also called the dwarf, the artist, or Lord Ostwold, he is a confidant of many *grandes dames* in London Society, known as the *ton*.

BY NOËLLE DE BEAUFORT

Short Stories

"The Search for the Snow Tribe"
"The Flight of the Eagle Feather"
"The Promise of the White Buffalo"

A series of short stories centering on
Jean-Louis Chevalier in North America,
available for Kindle at www.amazon.com

Secrets of Ravenshire, an epic historical family saga
The Gabriella Trilogy

Secrets of Ravenshire: Romance and Revenge
Book One (1811)

Secrets of Ravenshire: Temptation and Treachery
Book Two (1811-1812)

Coming Soon
Secrets of Ravenshire: Venom and Valor
Book Three (1812-13)

Prequels and Sequels in process
Publication updates on www.noelledebeaufort.com

ABOUT THE AUTHOR

Noëlle de Beaufort weaves insights from her background in finance, her studies of French language, culture and literature, and her love of history, travel and art into novels exploring generations of the Wyndward family. The *Secrets of Ravenshire* series, an epic historical family saga with elements of romantic suspense, spans centuries. Occasionally, the author writes short stories about secondary characters in the series.

Under her birth name, the author holds a B.A. in French from Denison University, and an M.B.A. in Finance and International Business from NYU Stern. She currently lives in Nevada with two very demanding felines. One is an organic shredding machine, attacking any stray piece of paper that flies off the desk (or that she captures in a furtive move), while the other (when he isn't sleeping) drapes himself above her keyboard and bats her fingers with his paw as she writes.

www.noelledebeaufort.com